THE CLOCKWORK SKY

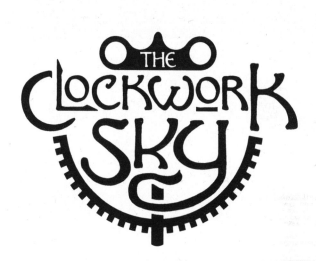

THE CLOCKWORK SKY

VOLUME TWO

Story and Art by
MADELEINE ROSCA

Lettered by
TOM ORZECHOWSKI

TOR®

A TOM DOHERTY ASSOCIATES BOOK
NEW YORK

This is a work of fiction. All of the characters, organizations, and events portrayed in this graphic novel are either products of the author's imagination or are used fictitiously.

THE CLOCKWORK SKY, VOLUME TWO

Lettered by Tom Orzechowski

A Tor Book
Published by Tom Doherty Associates, LLC
175 Fifth Avenue
New York, NY 10010

www.tor-forge.com

Tor® is a registered trademark of Tom Doherty Associates, LLC.

The Library of Congress Cataloging-in-Publication Data is available upon request.

ISBN 978-0-7653-2917-2

Tor books may be purchased for educational, business, or promotional use. For information on bulk purchases, please contact Macmillan Corporate and Premium Sales Department at 1-800-221-7945, extension 5442, or write specialmarkets@macmillan.com.

First Edition: August 2014

Printed in the United States of America

0 9 8 7 6 5 4 3 2 1

THE CLOCKWORK SKY

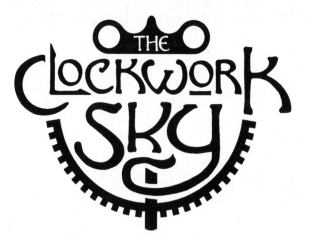

THIS...
THIS WASN'T
WHAT HE
PROMISED...!

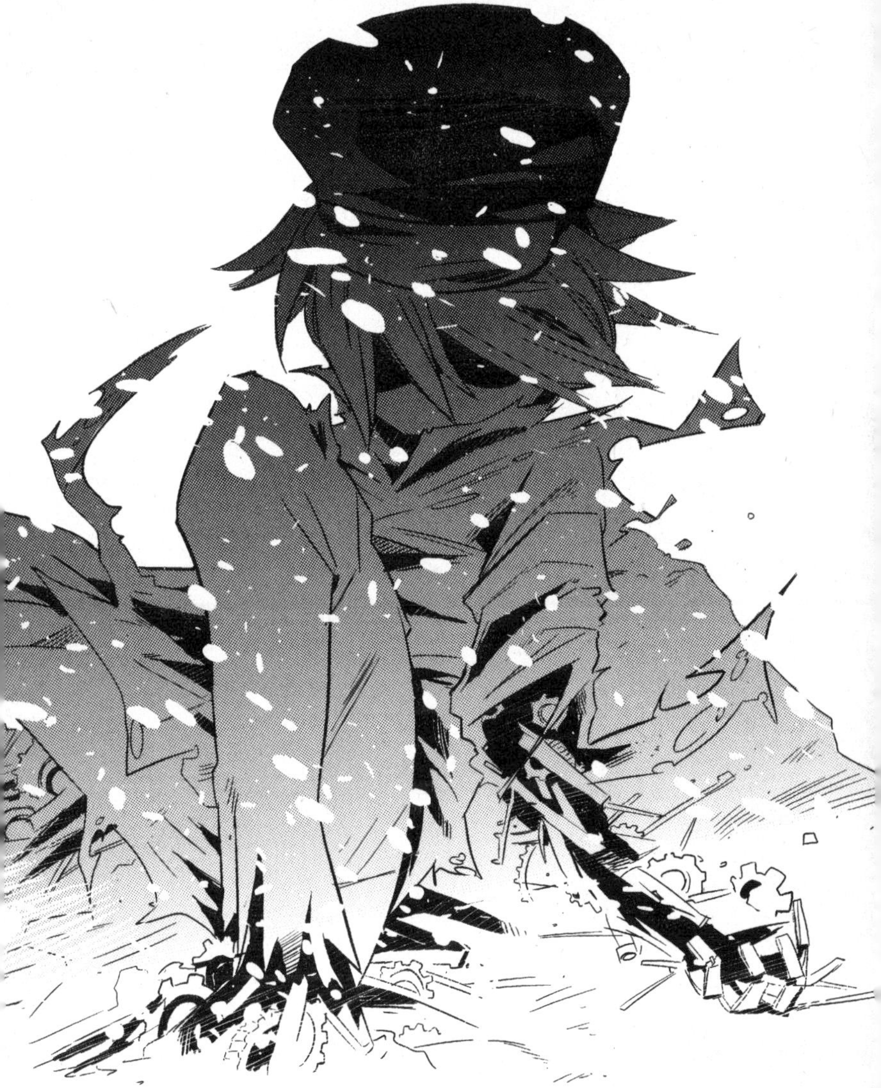

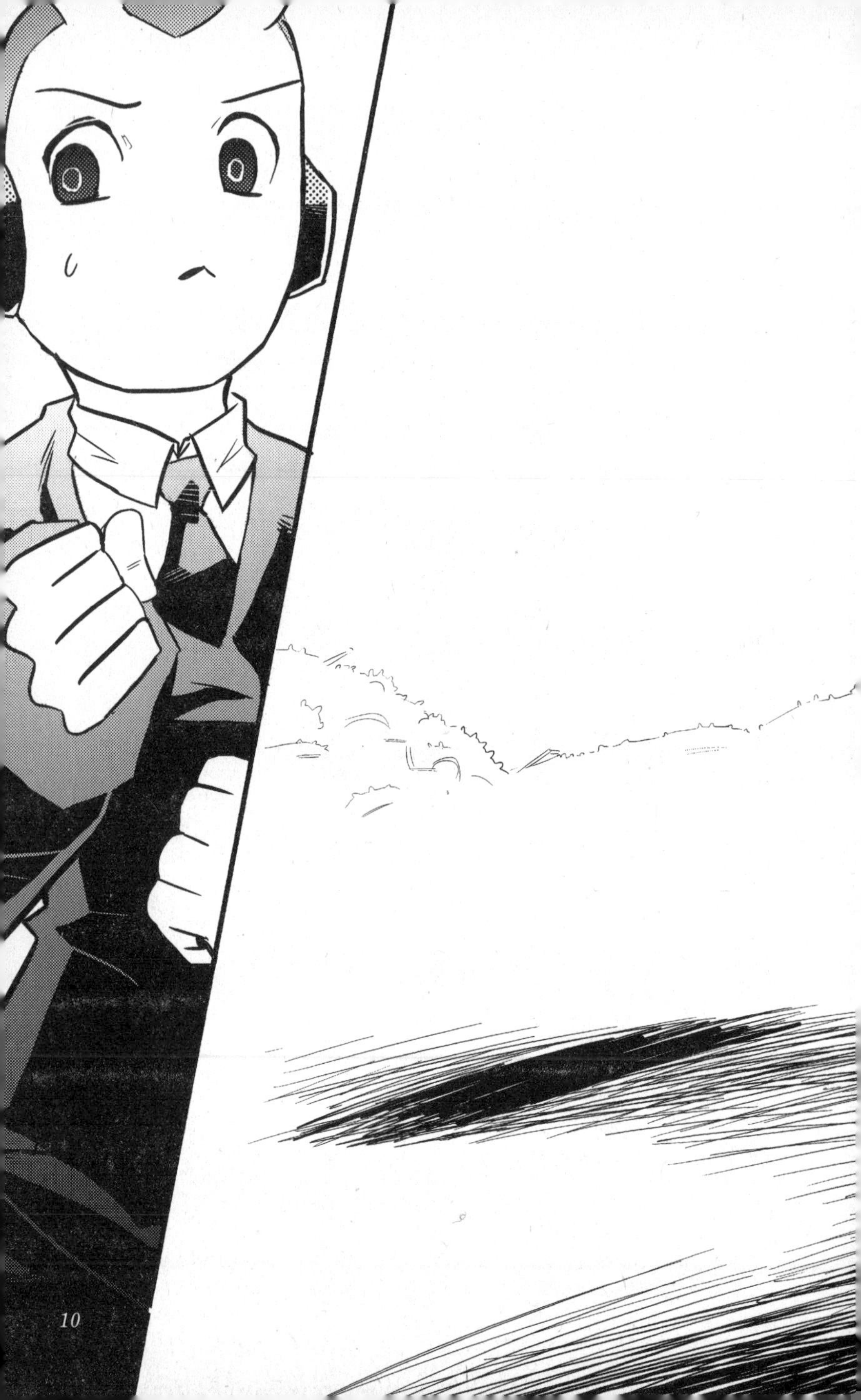

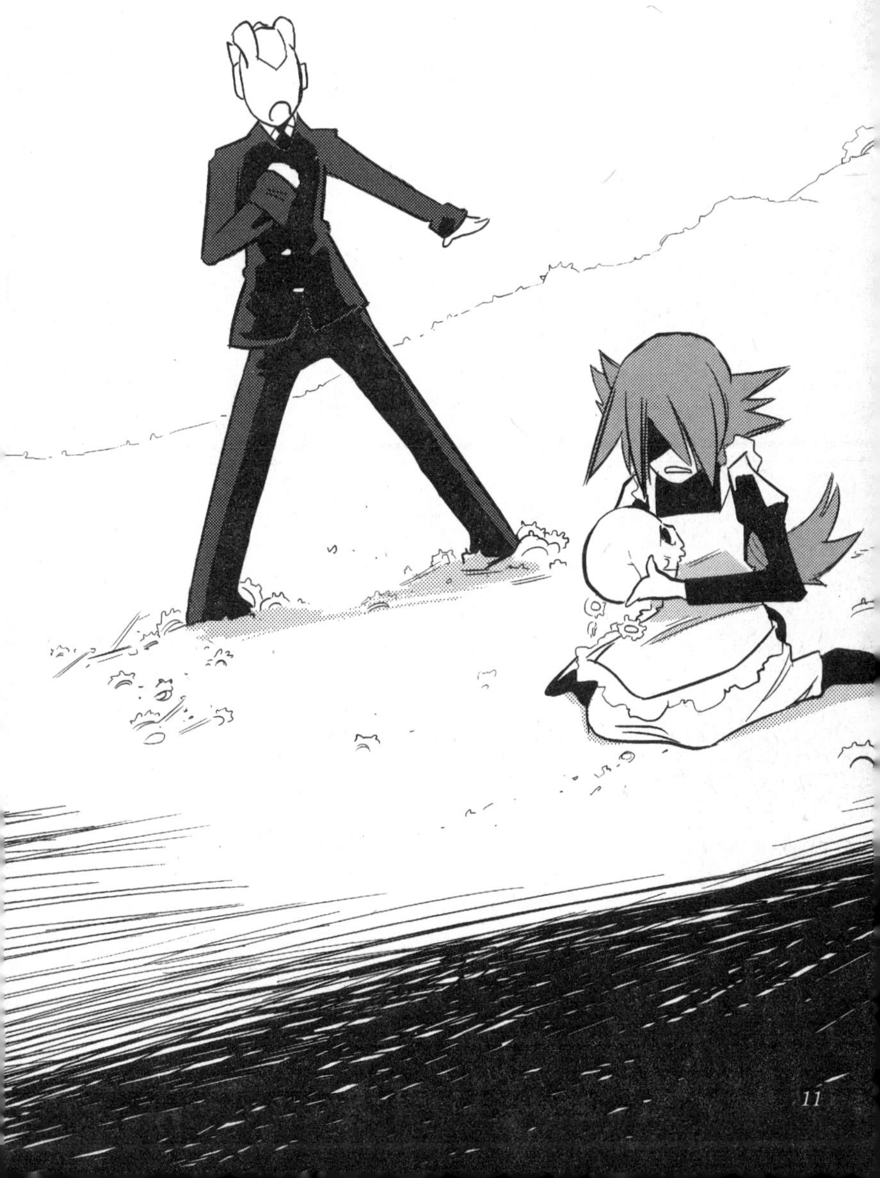

fwsshhh

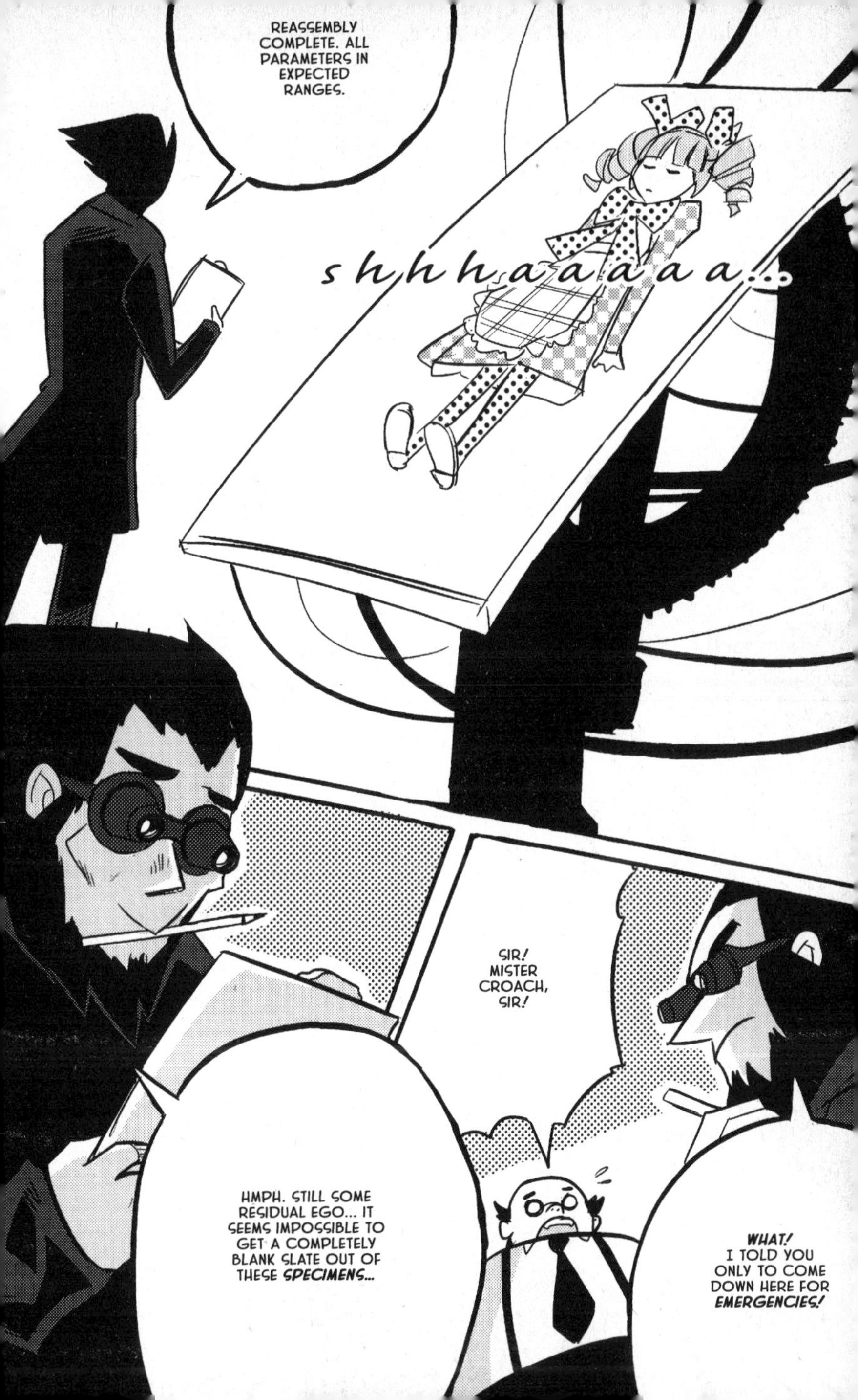
REASSEMBLY COMPLETE. ALL PARAMETERS IN EXPECTED RANGES.
s h h h a a a a a a...
SIR! MISTER CROACH, SIR!
HMPH. STILL SOME RESIDUAL EGO... IT SEEMS IMPOSSIBLE TO GET A COMPLETELY BLANK SLATE OUT OF THESE *SPECIMENS*...
WHAT! I TOLD YOU ONLY TO COME DOWN HERE FOR *EMERGENCIES!*

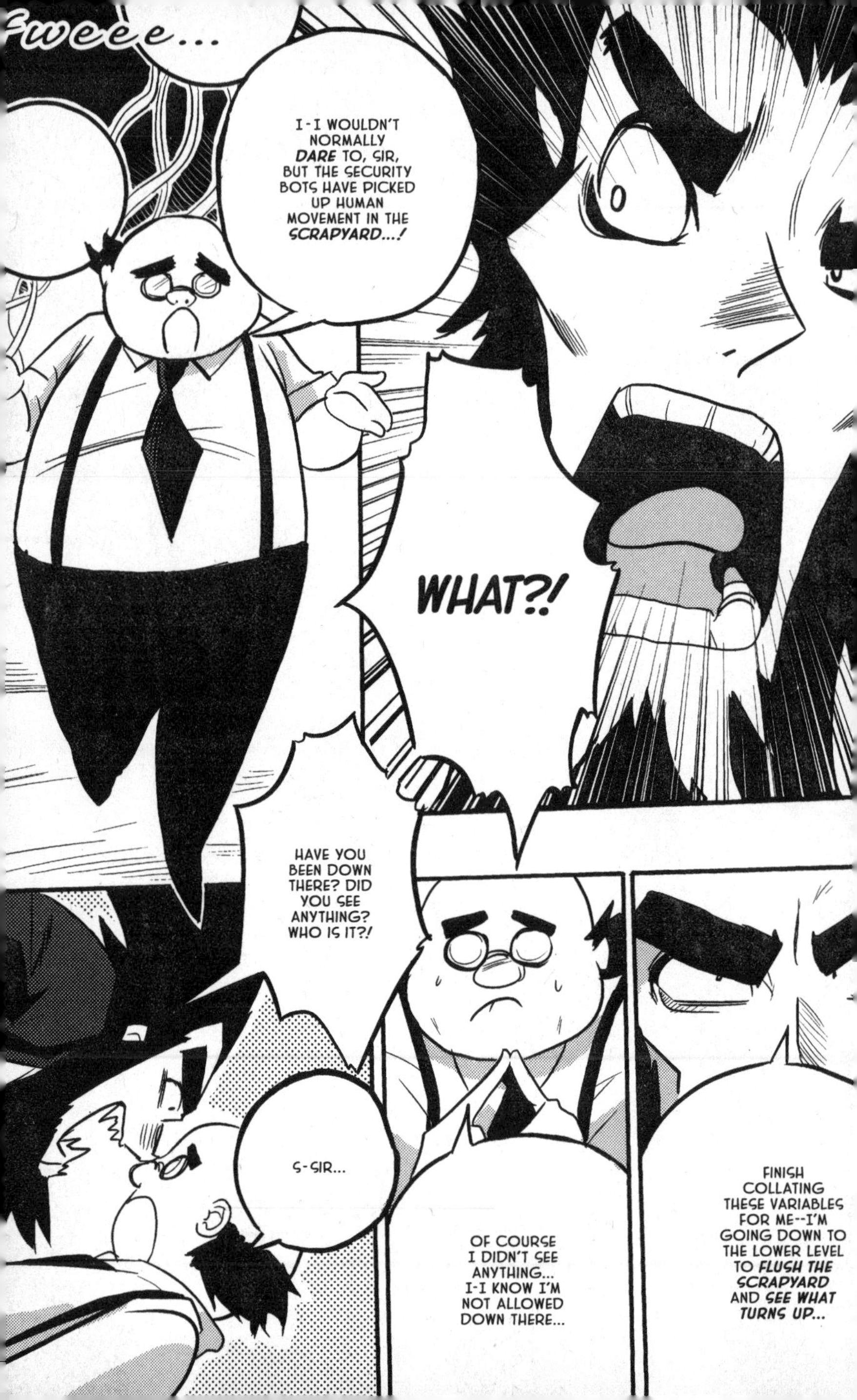

Fweeee...
I-I WOULDN'T NORMALLY DARE TO, SIR, BUT THE SECURITY BOTS HAVE PICKED UP HUMAN MOVEMENT IN THE SCRAPYARD...!
WHAT?!
HAVE YOU BEEN DOWN THERE? DID YOU SEE ANYTHING? WHO IS IT?!
S-SIR...
OF COURSE I DIDN'T SEE ANYTHING... I-I KNOW I'M NOT ALLOWED DOWN THERE...
FINISH COLLATING THESE VARIABLES FOR ME--I'M GOING DOWN TO THE LOWER LEVEL TO FLUSH THE SCRAPYARD AND SEE WHAT TURNS UP...

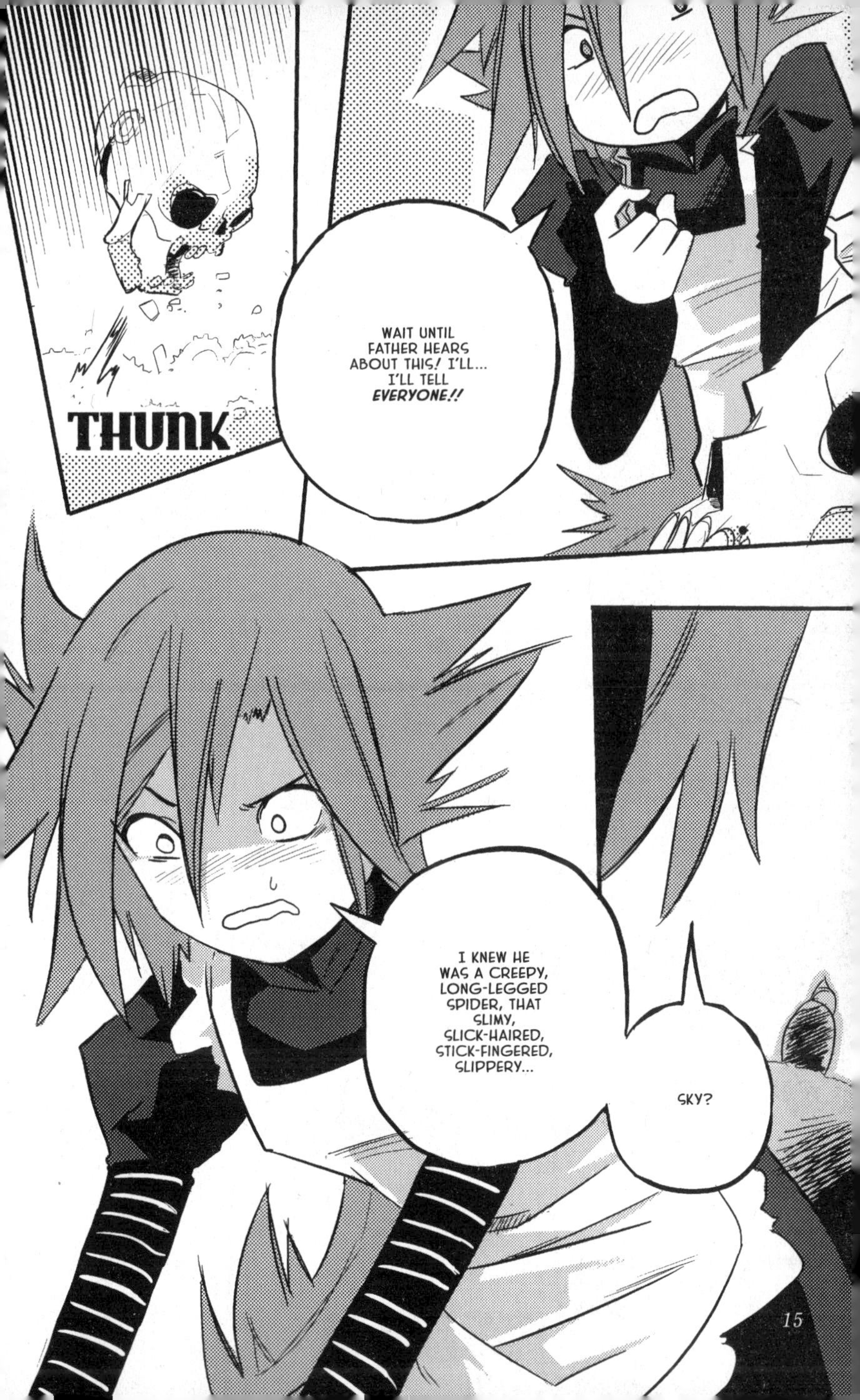
THUNK
WAIT UNTIL FATHER HEARS ABOUT THIS! I'LL... I'LL TELL *EVERYONE!!*
I KNEW HE WAS A CREEPY, LONG-LEGGED SPIDER, THAT SLIMY, SLICK-HAIRED, STICK-FINGERED, SLIPPERY...
SKY?

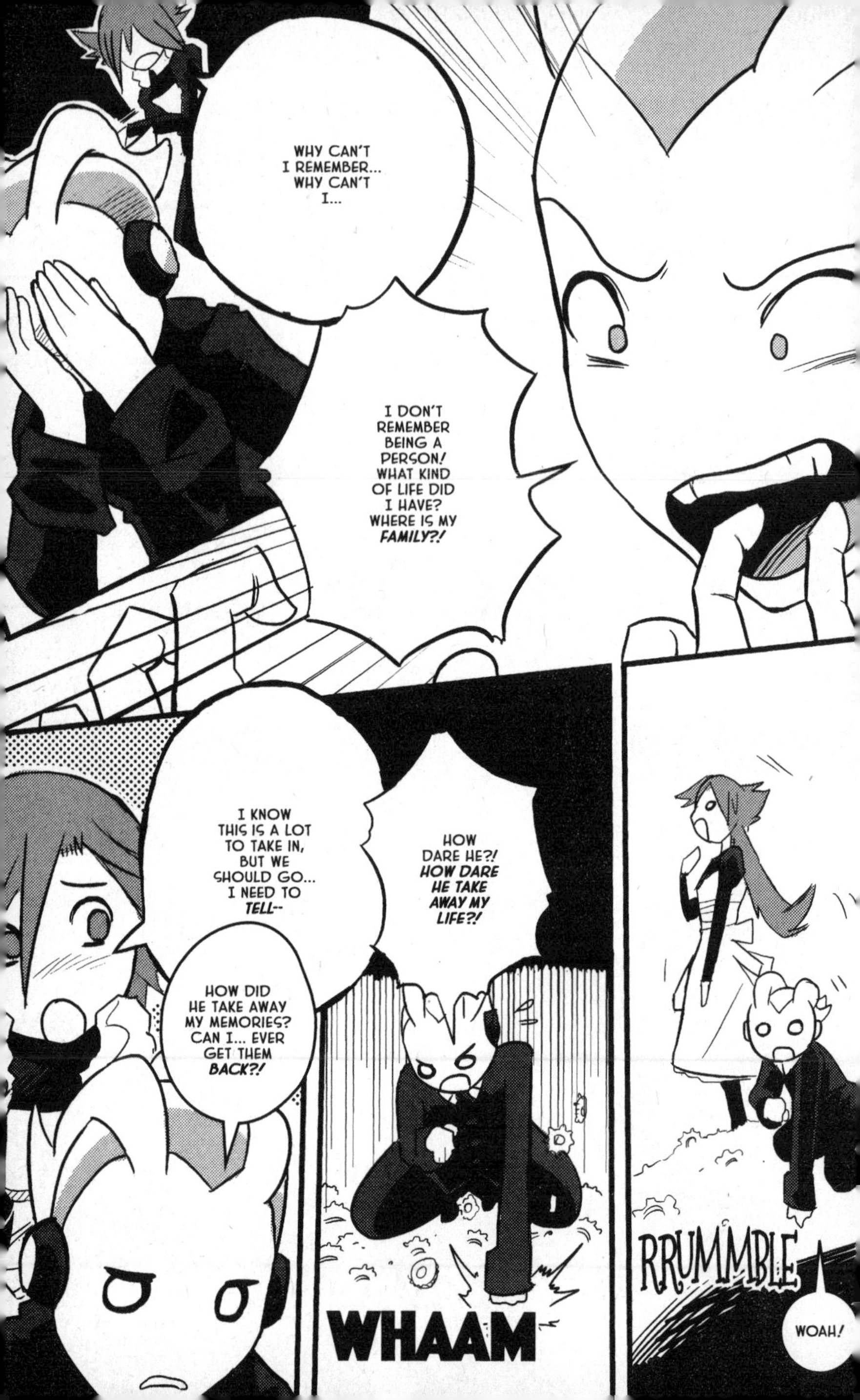
WHY CAN'T I REMEMBER... WHY CAN'T I...
I DON'T REMEMBER BEING A PERSON! WHAT KIND OF LIFE DID I HAVE? WHERE IS MY *FAMILY?!*
I KNOW THIS IS A LOT TO TAKE IN, BUT WE SHOULD GO... I NEED TO *TELL--*
HOW DID HE TAKE AWAY MY MEMORIES? CAN I... EVER GET THEM *BACK?!*
HOW DARE HE?! *HOW DARE HE TAKE AWAY MY LIFE?!*
WHAAM
RRUMMBLE
WOAH!

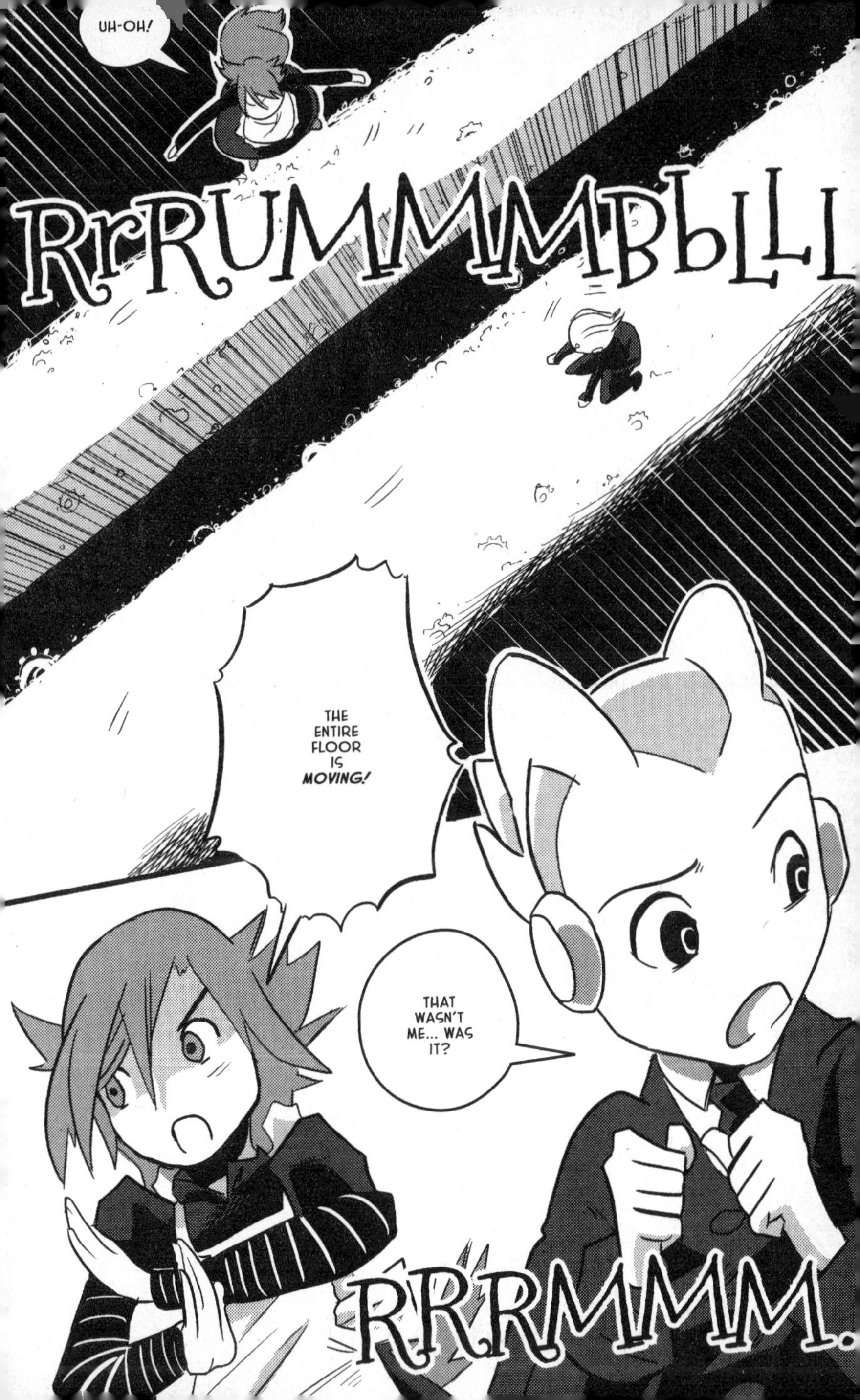
UH-OH!
RrRUMMMMBbLLL
THE ENTIRE FLOOR IS *MOVING!*
THAT WASN'T ME... WAS IT?
RRRMMM.

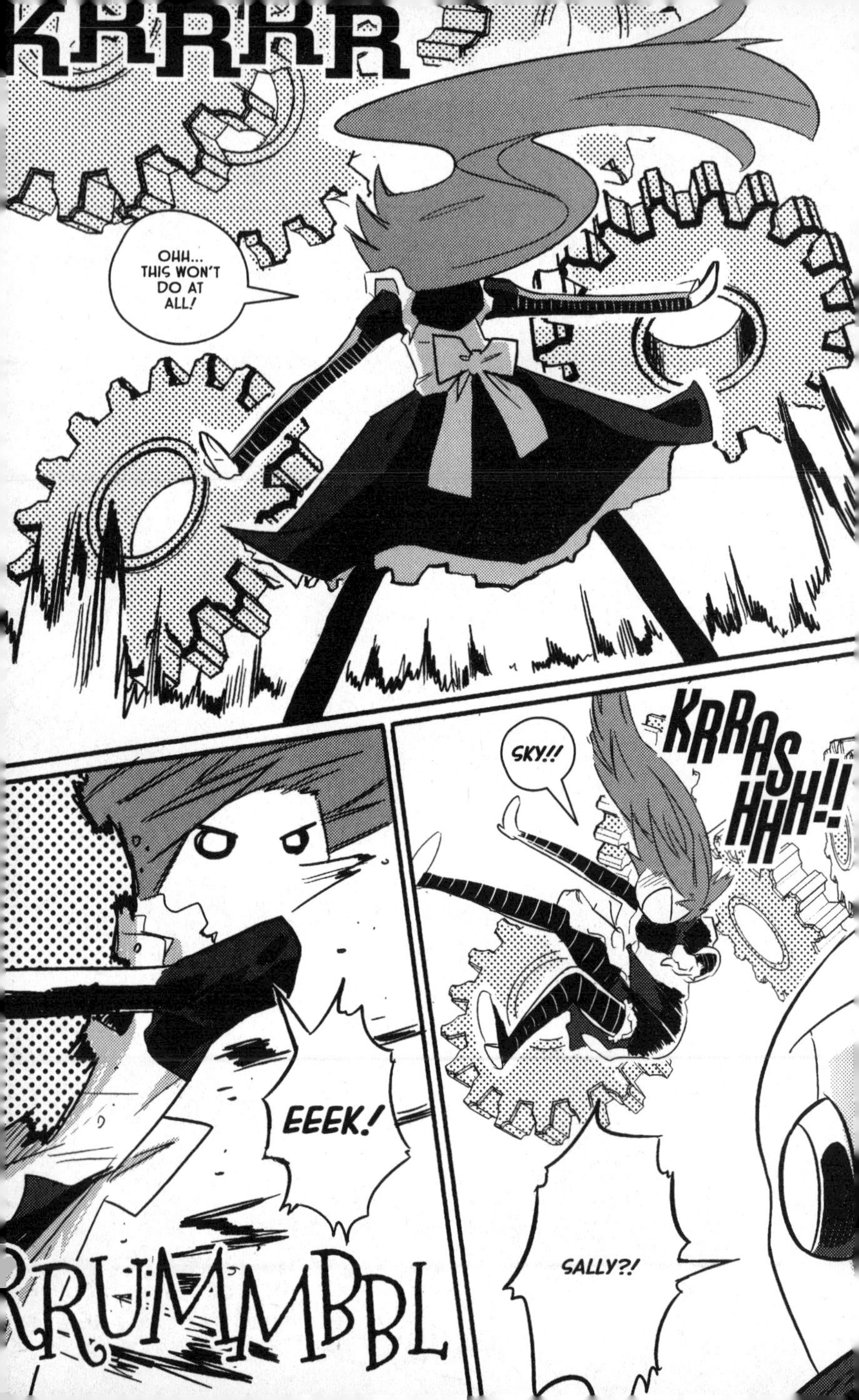
KRRRRR
OHH... THIS WON'T DO AT ALL!
EEEK!
RRUMMBBL
SKY!!
KRRASHHH!!
SALLY?!

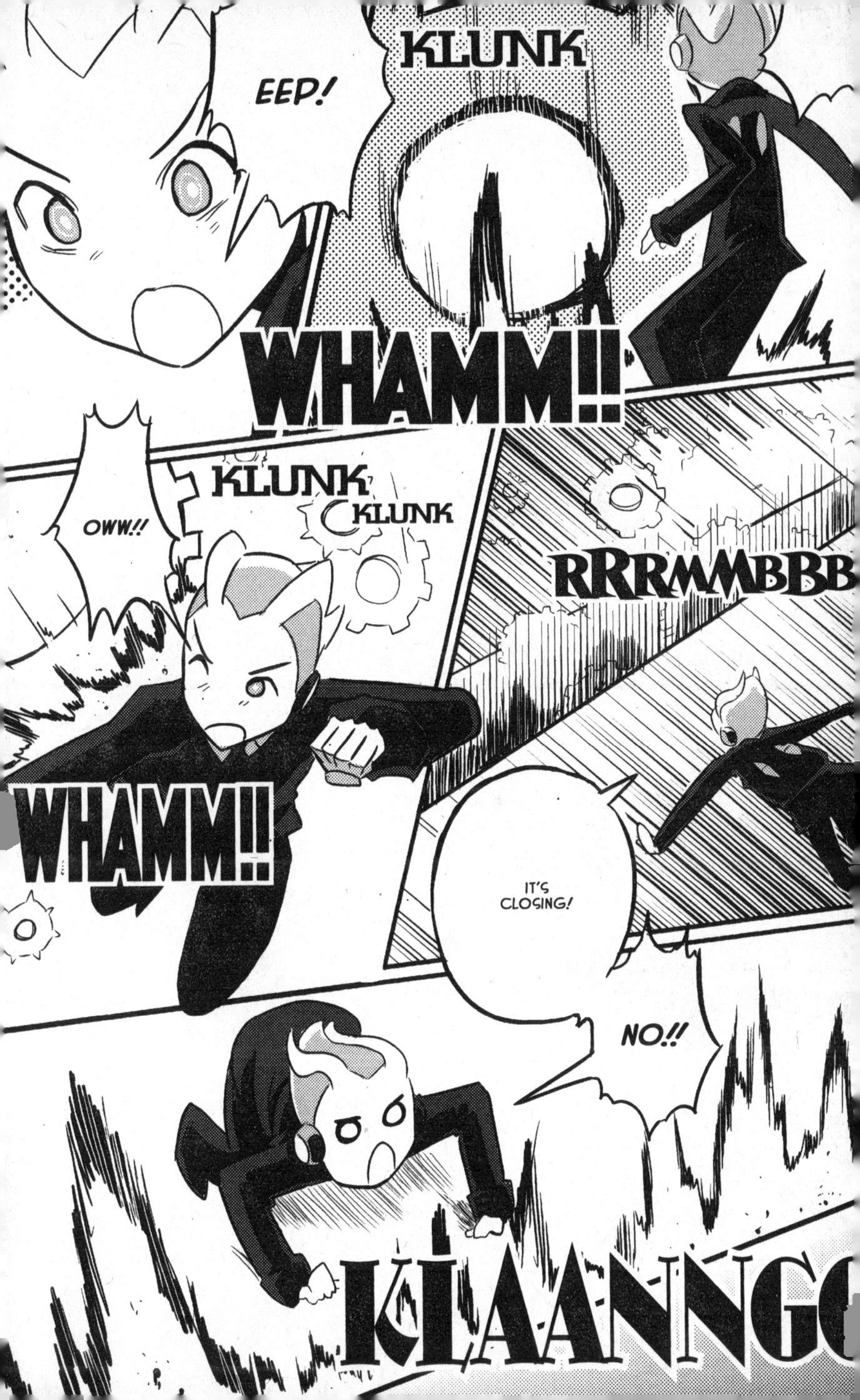
EEP!
KLUNK
WHAMM!!
OWW!!
KLUNK
KLUNK
WHAMM!!
RRRMMBBB
IT'S CLOSING!
NO!!
KLAANNG

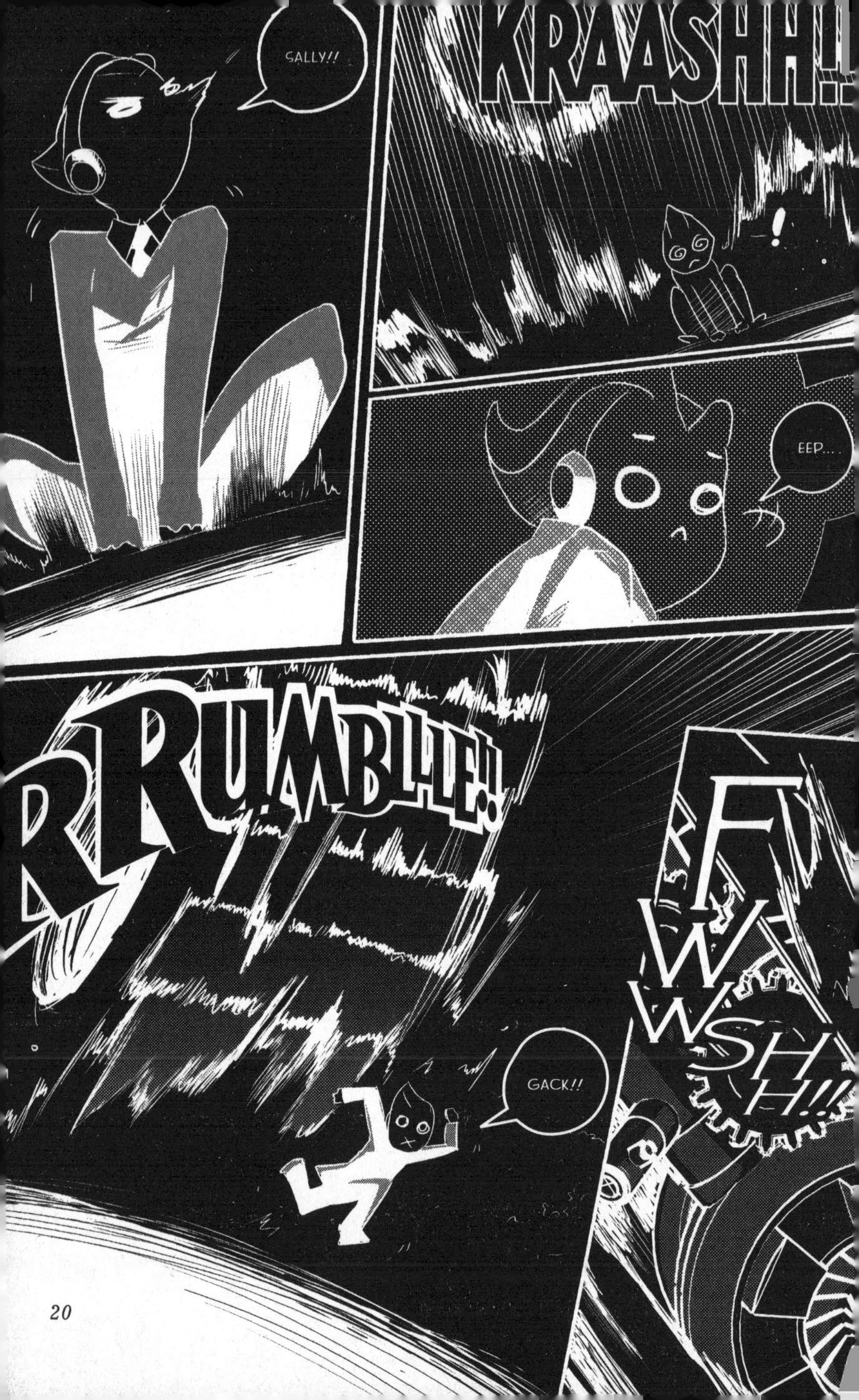
SALLY!!
KRAASHH!!
!
EEP...
RRUMBLLE!!
GACK!!
FWWWSHH!!

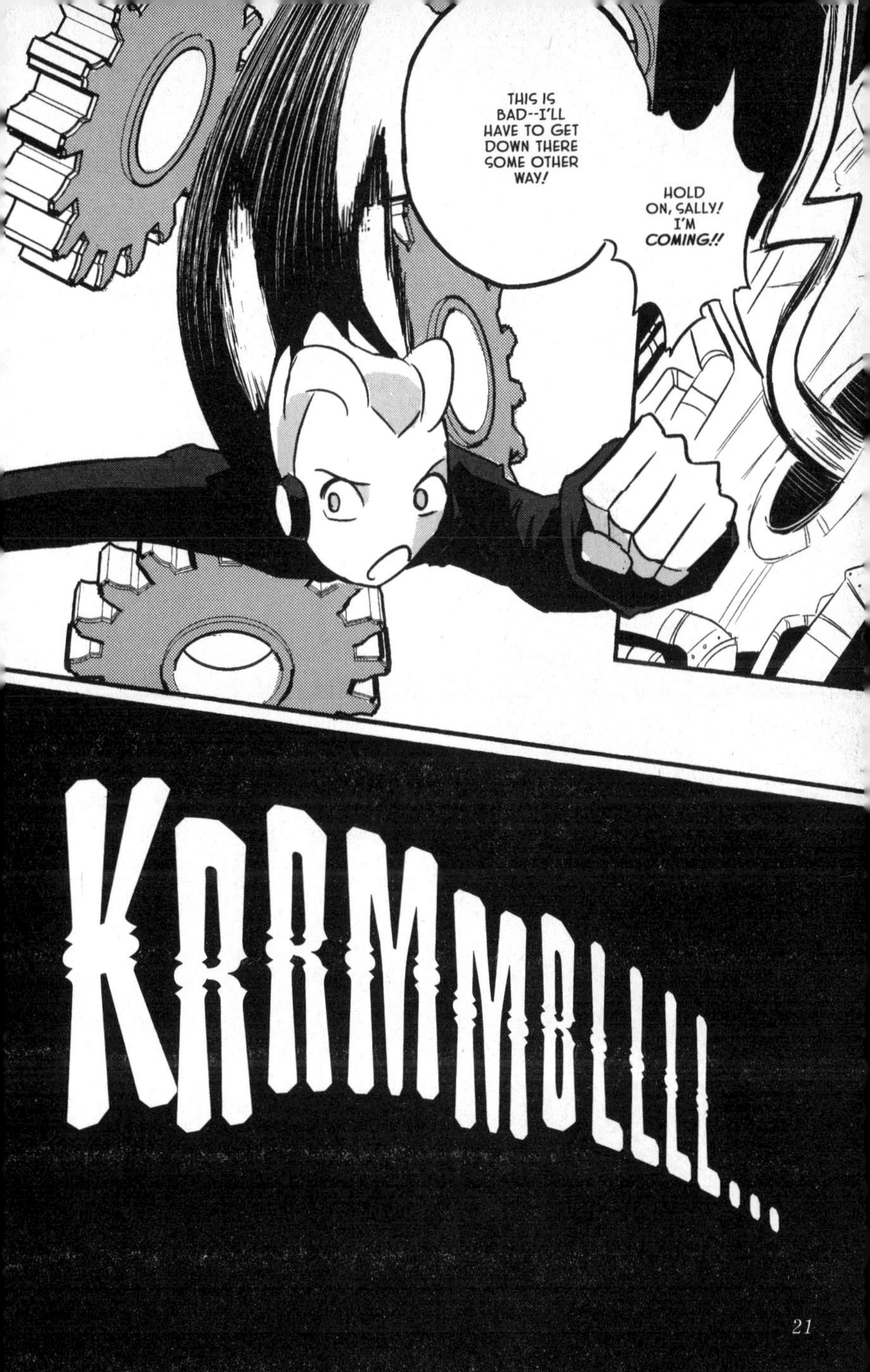
THIS IS BAD--I'LL HAVE TO GET DOWN THERE SOME OTHER WAY!
HOLD ON, SALLY! I'M *COMING!!*
KRRMMBLLL...

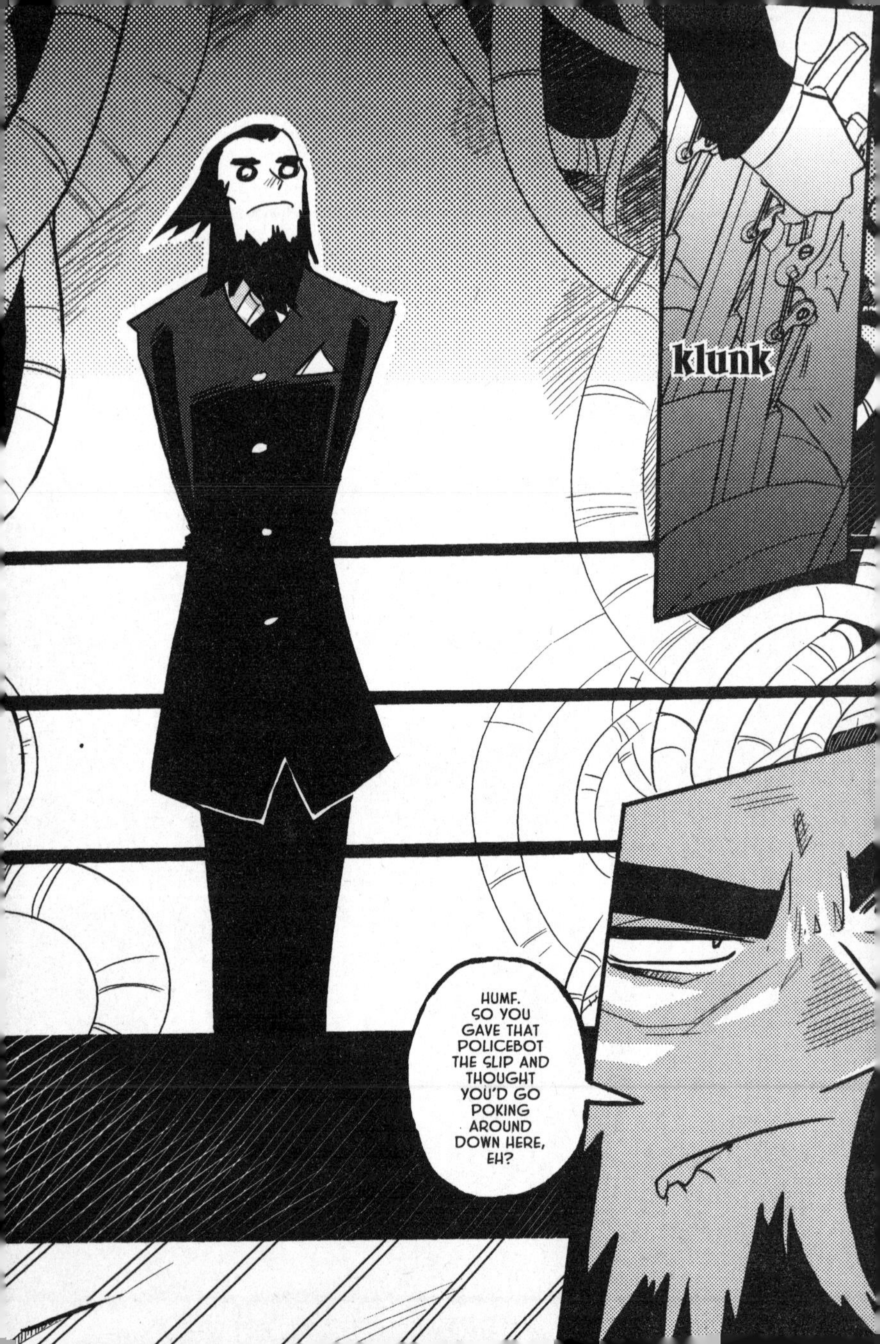
klunk
HUMF. SO YOU GAVE THAT POLICEBOT THE SLIP AND THOUGHT YOU'D GO POKING AROUND DOWN HERE, EH?

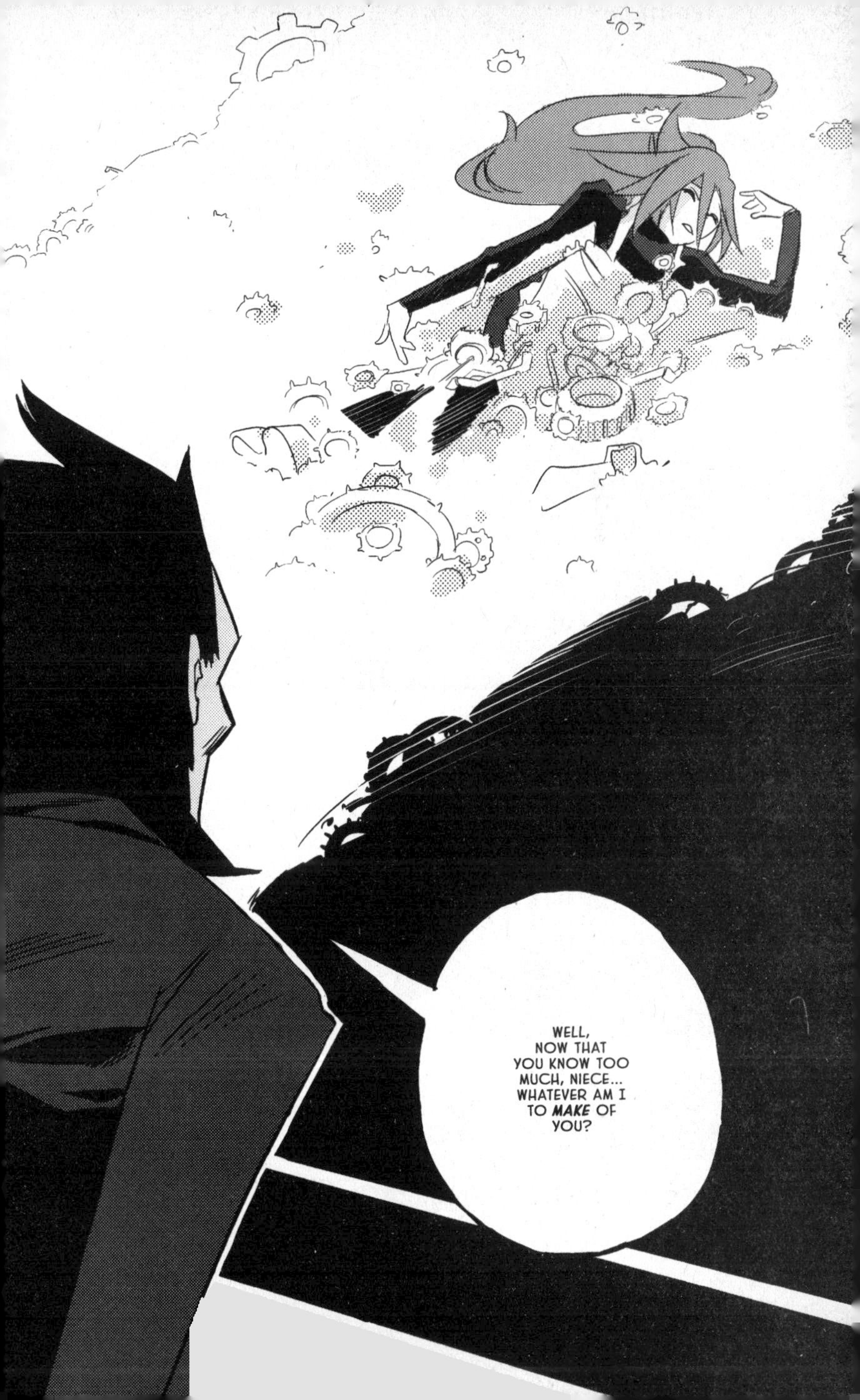
WELL, NOW THAT YOU KNOW TOO MUCH, NIECE... WHATEVER AM I TO *MAKE* OF YOU?

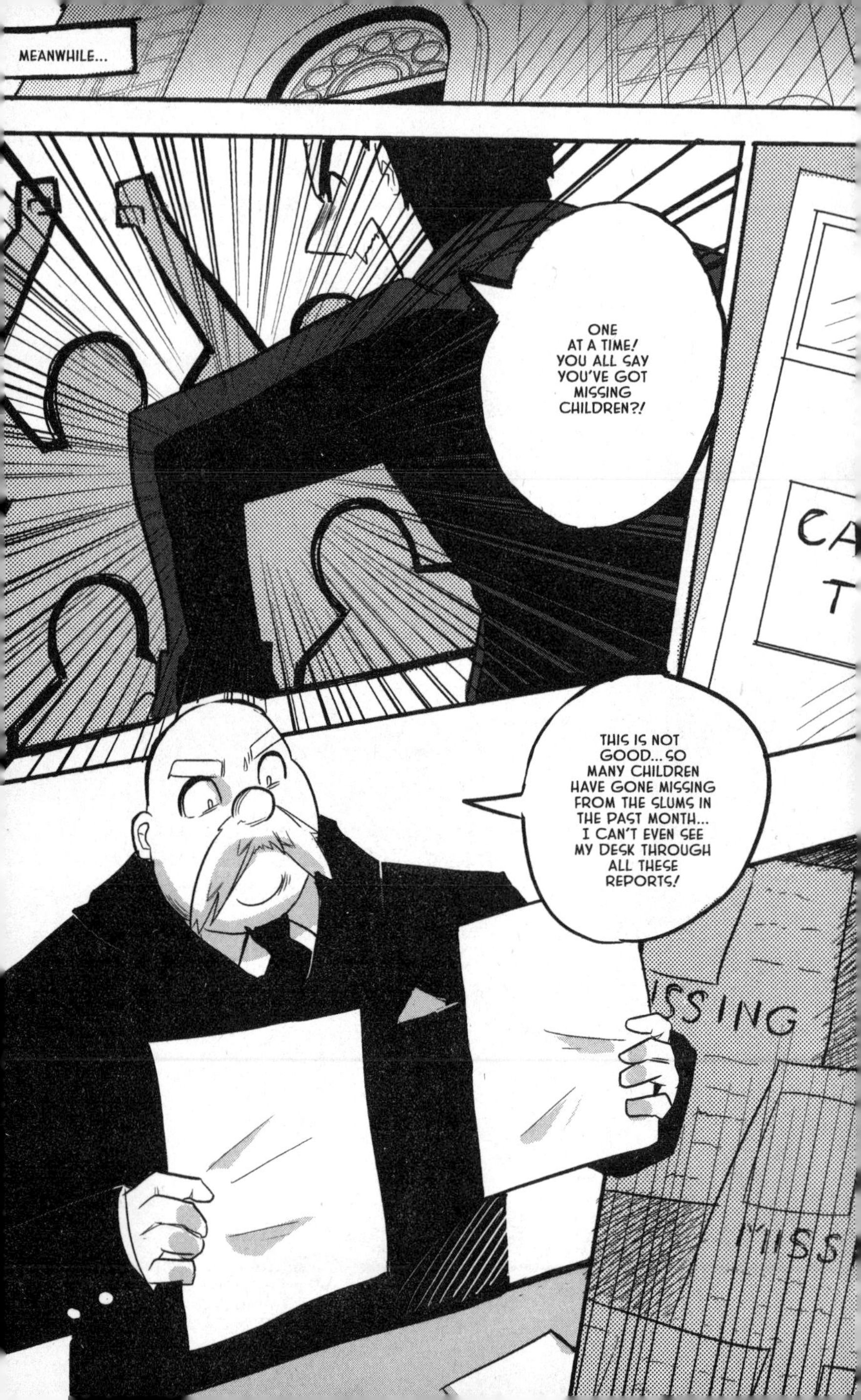
MEANWHILE...
ONE AT A TIME! YOU ALL SAY YOU'VE GOT MISSING CHILDREN?!
THIS IS NOT GOOD...SO MANY CHILDREN HAVE GONE MISSING FROM THE SLUMS IN THE PAST MONTH... I CAN'T EVEN SEE MY DESK THROUGH ALL THESE REPORTS!
ISSING

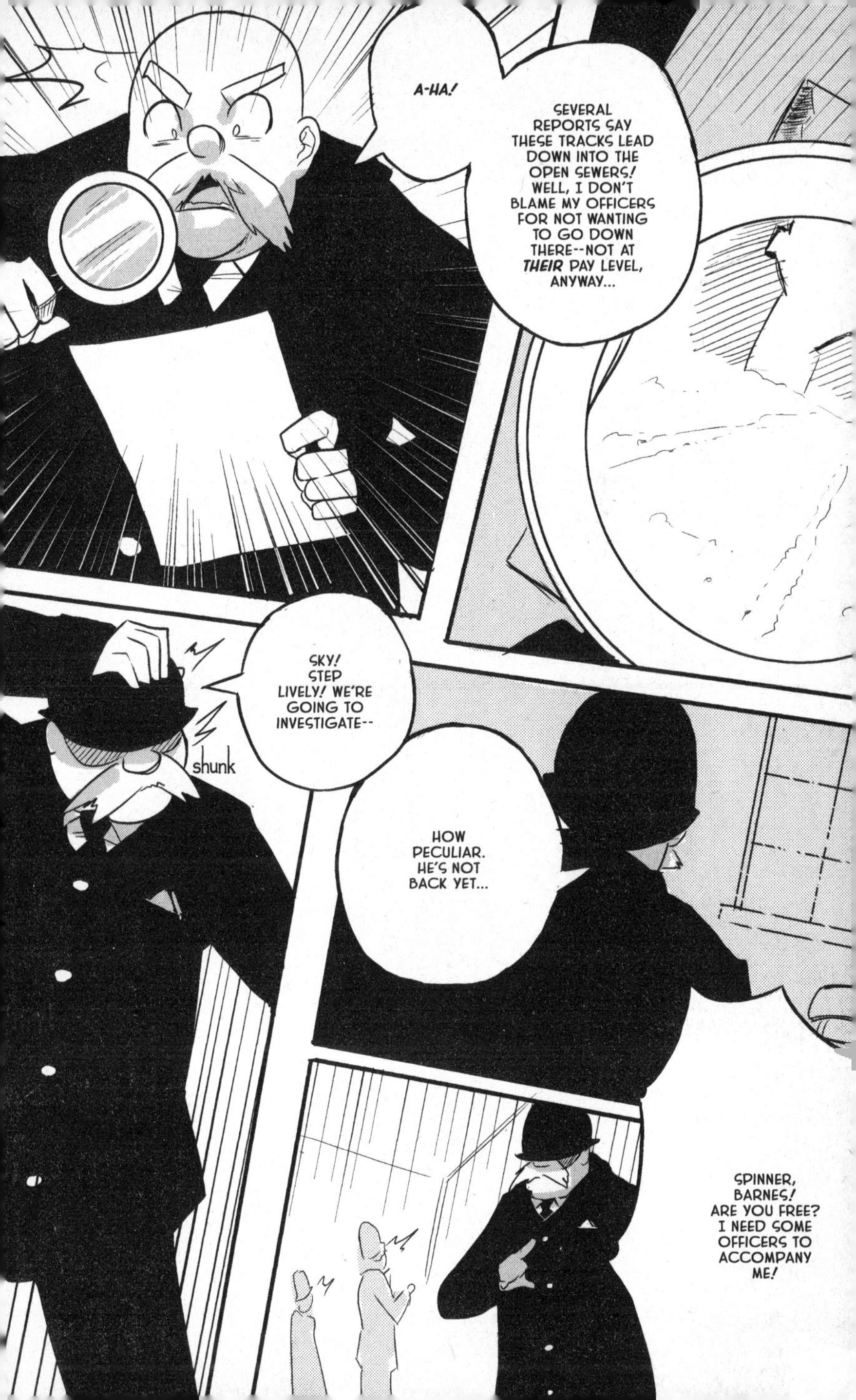
A-HA!
SEVERAL REPORTS SAY THESE TRACKS LEAD DOWN INTO THE OPEN SEWERS! WELL, I DON'T BLAME MY OFFICERS FOR NOT WANTING TO GO DOWN THERE--NOT AT THEIR PAY LEVEL, ANYWAY...
SKY! STEP LIVELY! WE'RE GOING TO INVESTIGATE--
shunk
HOW PECULIAR. HE'S NOT BACK YET...
SPINNER, BARNES! ARE YOU FREE? I NEED SOME OFFICERS TO ACCOMPANY ME!

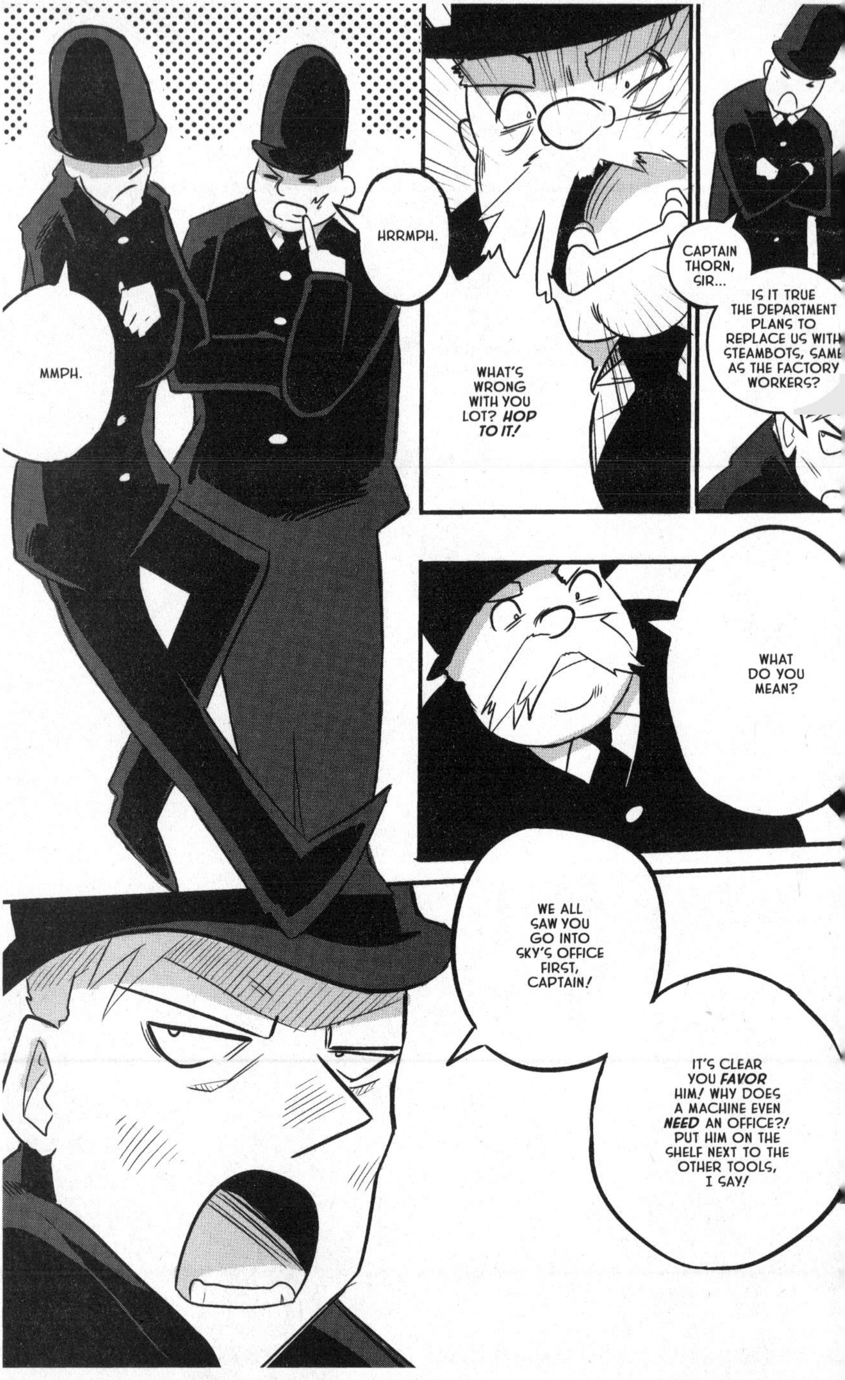
HRRMPH.
MMPH.
WHAT'S WRONG WITH YOU LOT? *HOP TO IT!*
CAPTAIN THORN, SIR...
IS IT TRUE THE DEPARTMENT PLANS TO REPLACE US WITH STEAMBOTS, SAME AS THE FACTORY WORKERS?
WHAT DO YOU MEAN?
WE ALL SAW YOU GO INTO SKY'S OFFICE FIRST, CAPTAIN!
IT'S CLEAR YOU *FAVOR* HIM! WHY DOES A MACHINE EVEN *NEED* AN OFFICE?! PUT HIM ON THE SHELF NEXT TO THE OTHER TOOLS, I SAY!

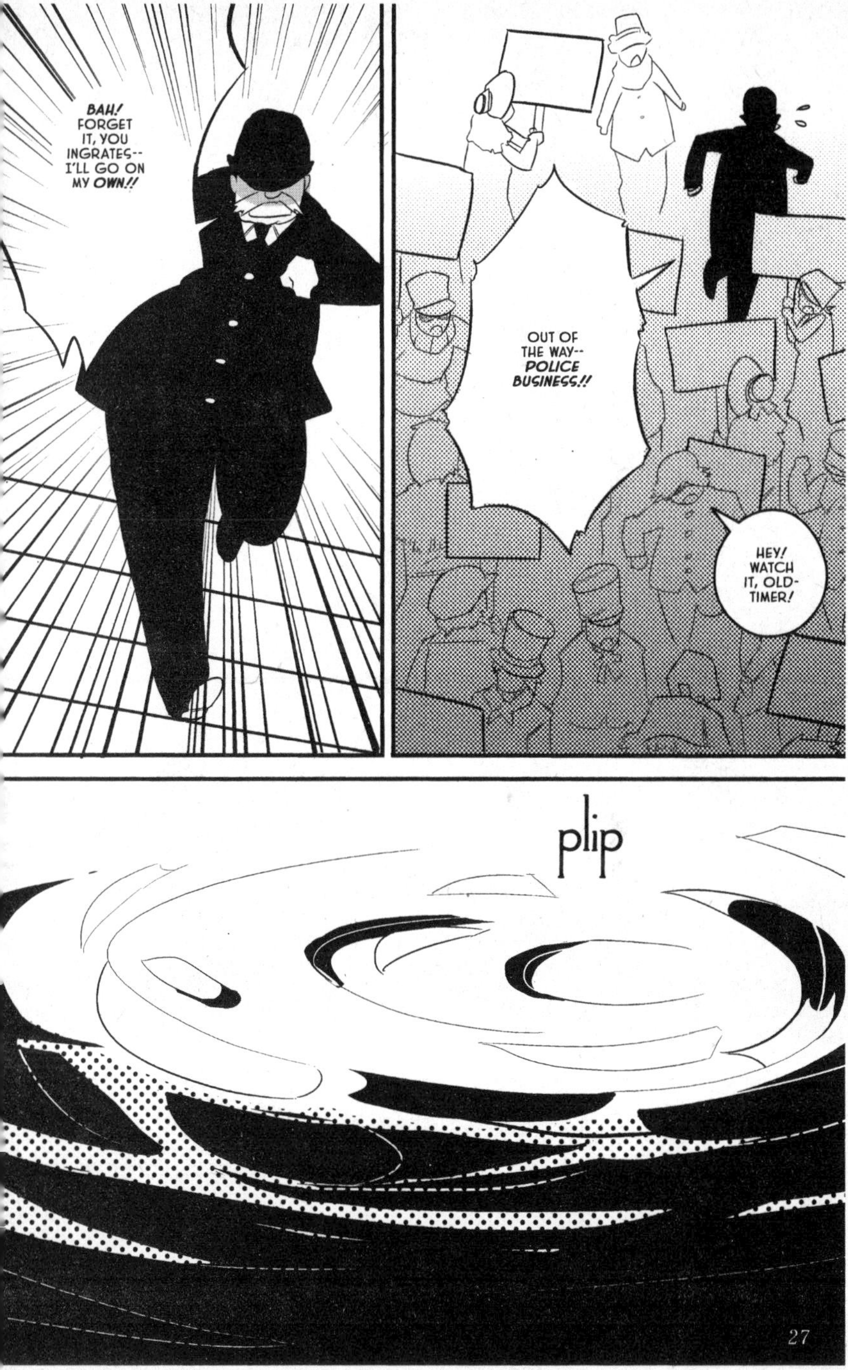
BAH! FORGET IT, YOU INGRATES-- I'LL GO ON MY OWN!!
OUT OF THE WAY-- POLICE BUSINESS!!
HEY! WATCH IT, OLD-TIMER!
plip

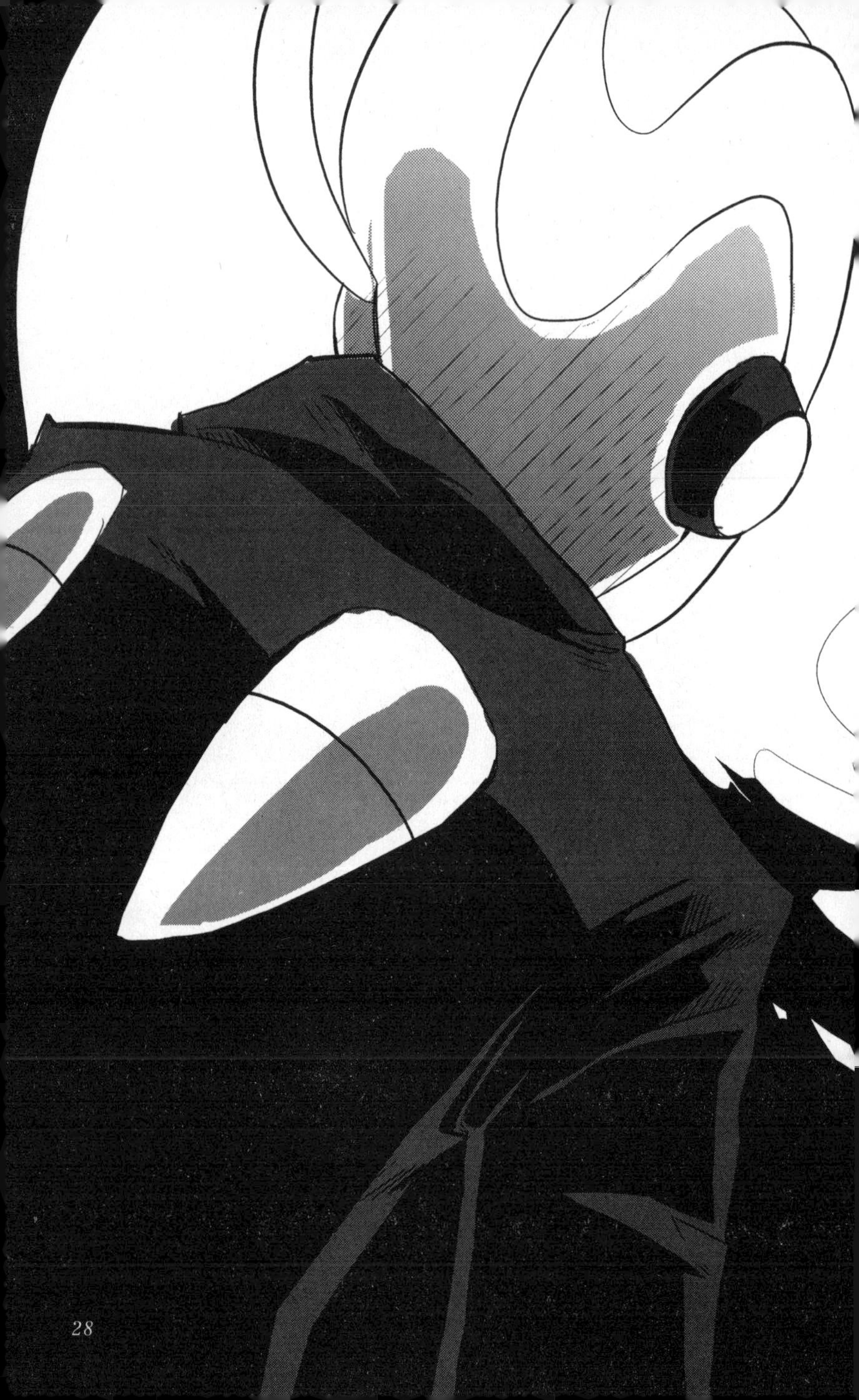

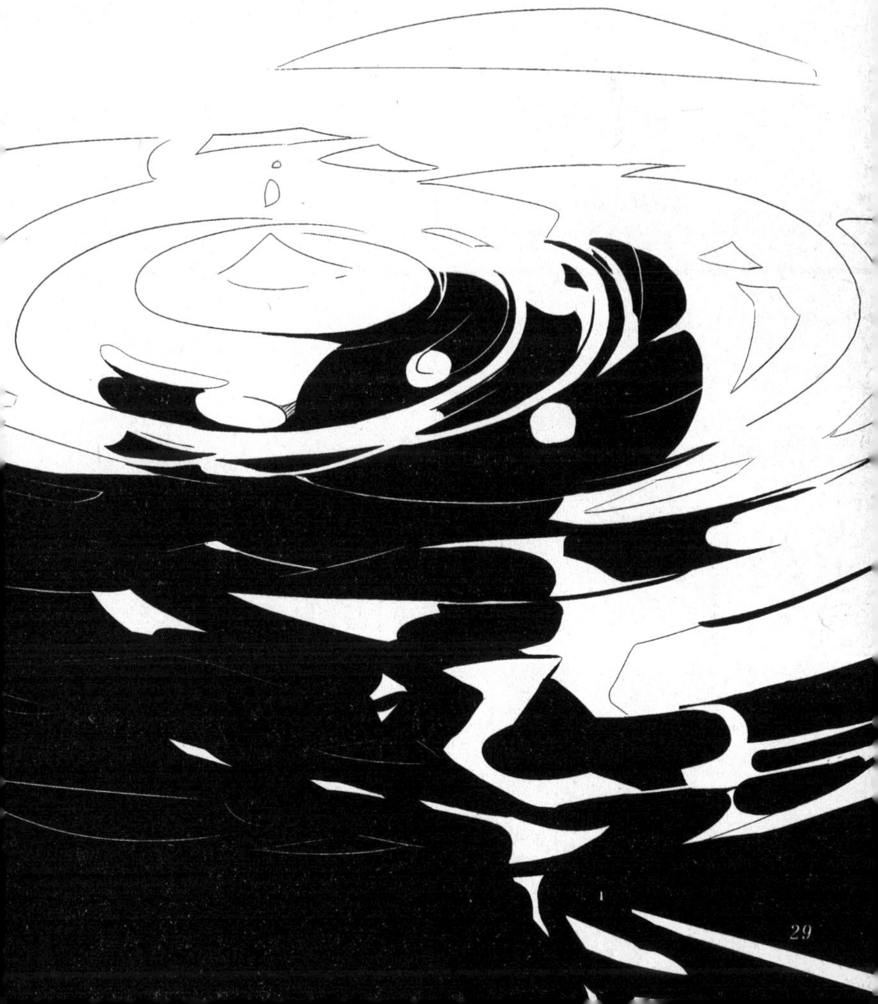

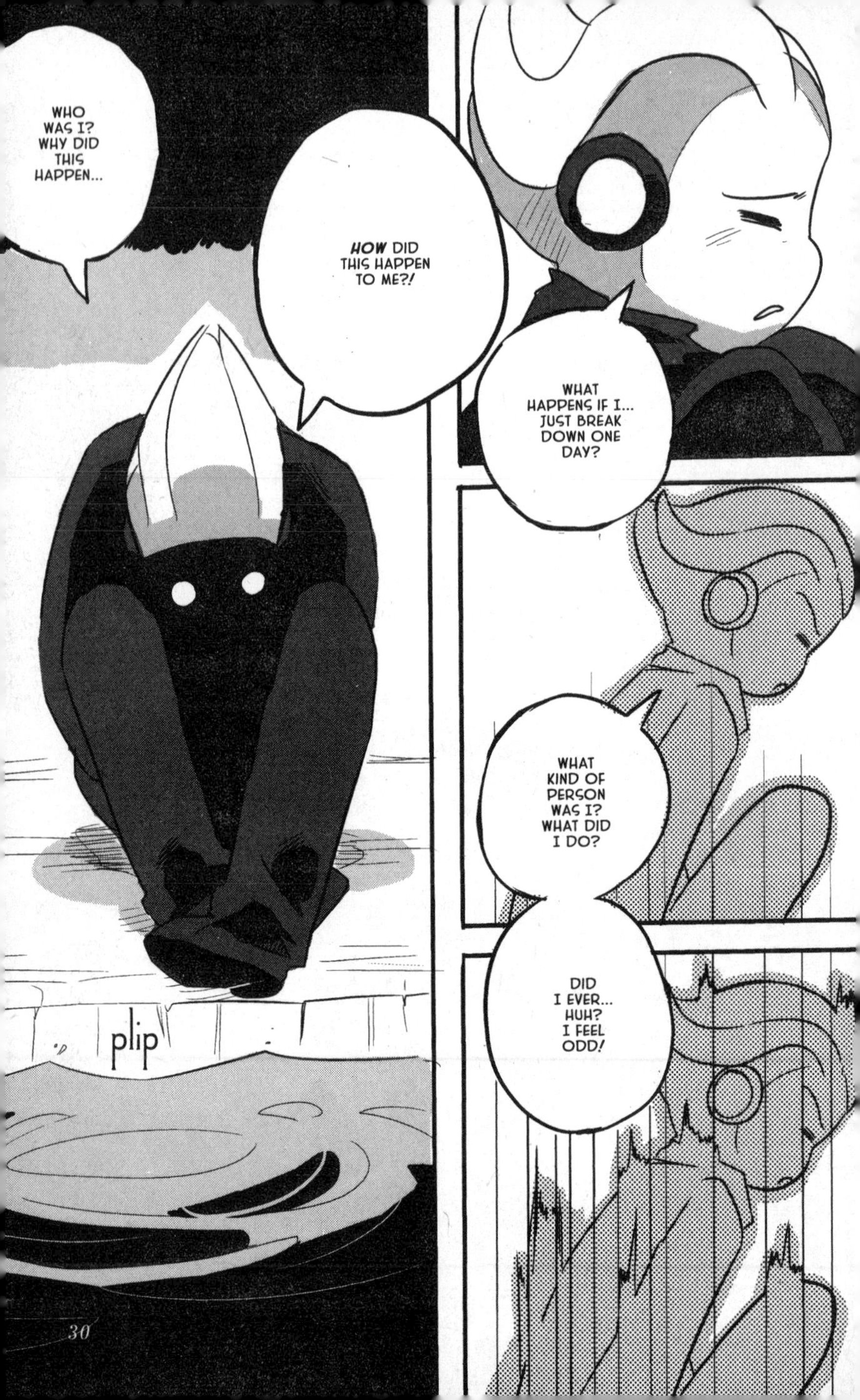
WHO WAS I? WHY DID THIS HAPPEN...
HOW DID THIS HAPPEN TO ME?!
plip
WHAT HAPPENS IF I... JUST BREAK DOWN ONE DAY?
WHAT KIND OF PERSON WAS I? WHAT DID I DO?
DID I EVER... HUH? I FEEL ODD!

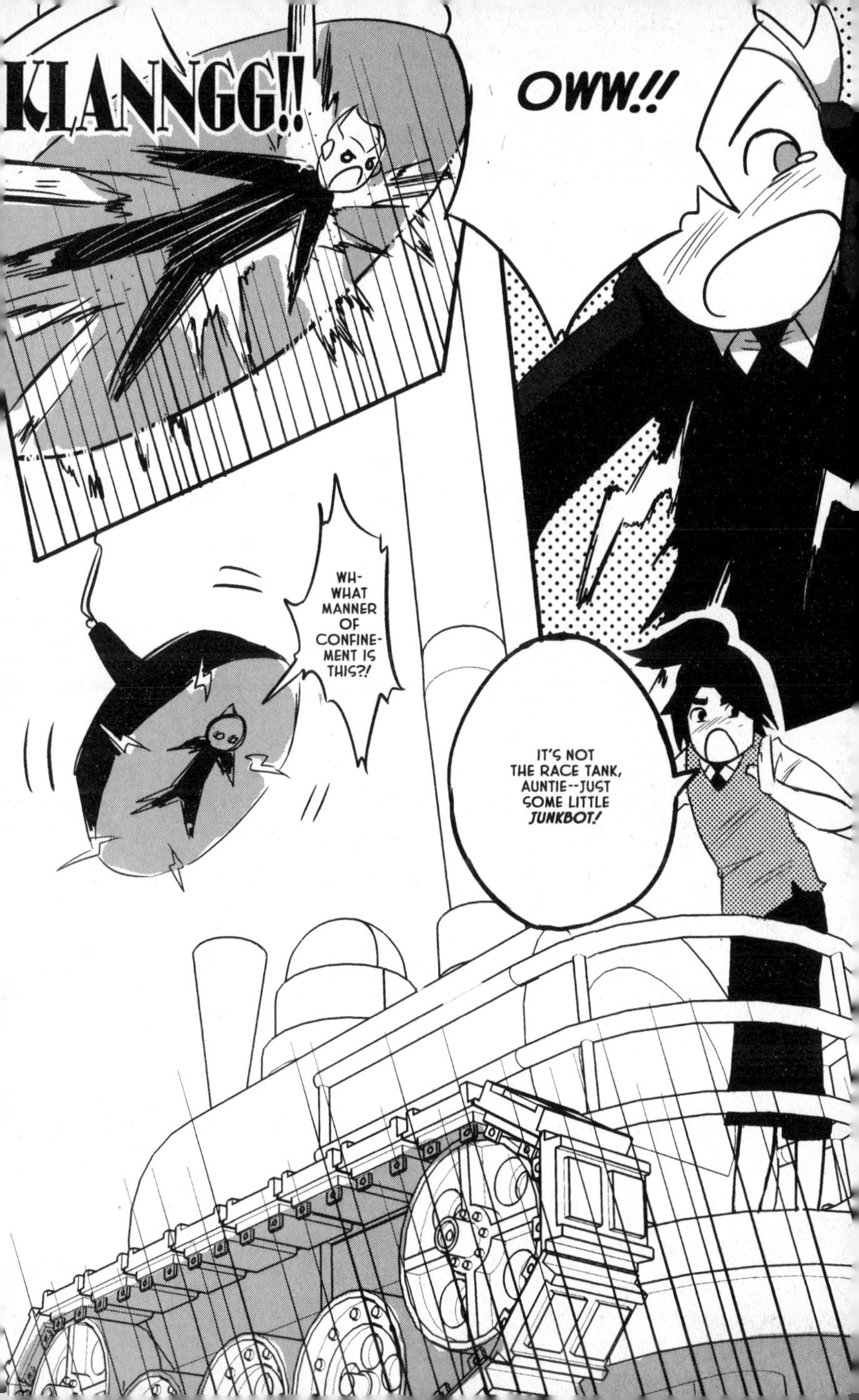
KLANNGG!!
OWW!!
WH-WHAT MANNER OF CONFINE-MENT IS THIS?!
IT'S NOT THE RACE TANK, AUNTIE--JUST SOME LITTLE *JUNKBOT!*

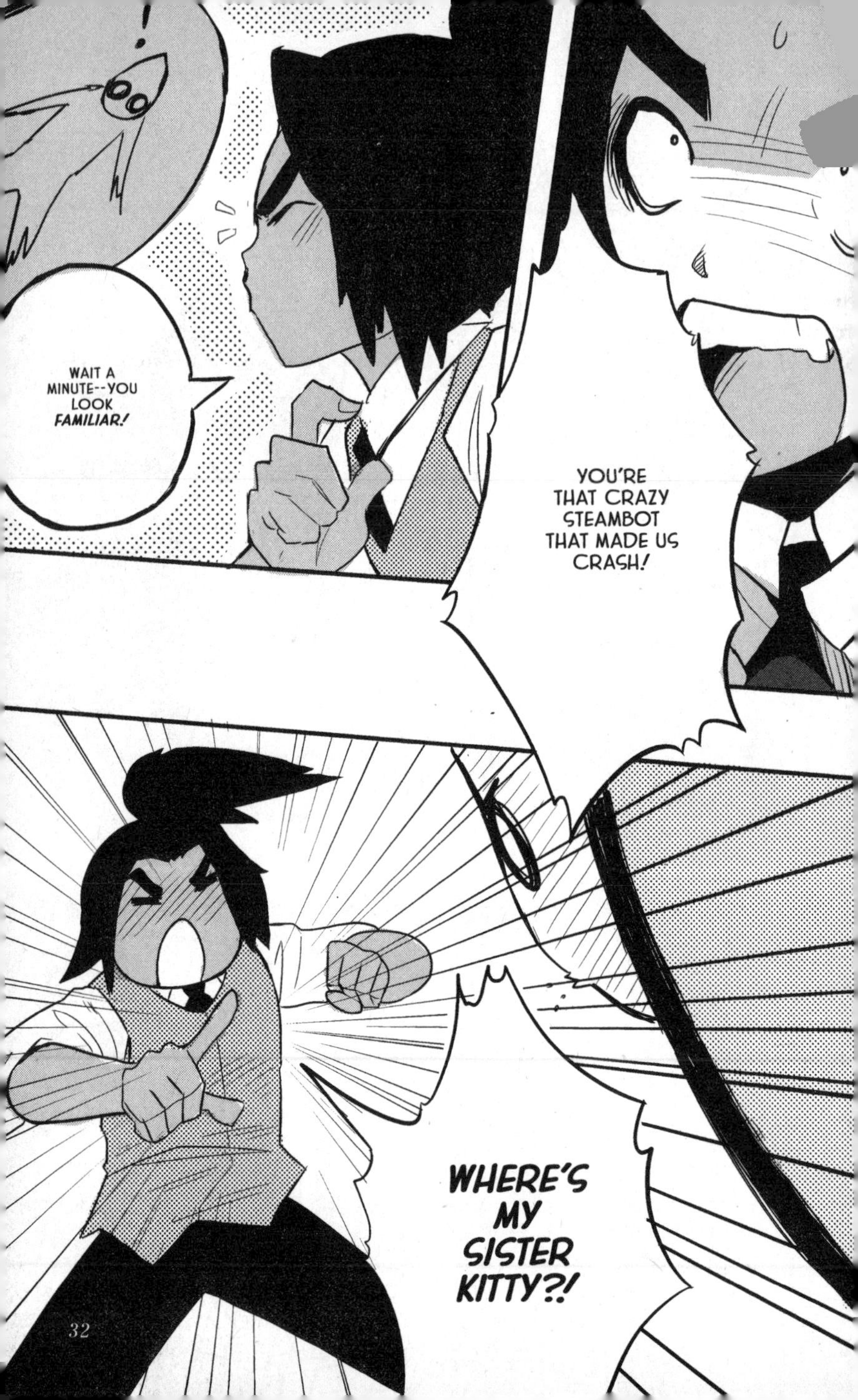
!
WAIT A MINUTE--YOU LOOK *FAMILIAR!*
YOU'RE THAT CRAZY STEAMBOT THAT MADE US CRASH!
WHERE'S MY SISTER KITTY?!

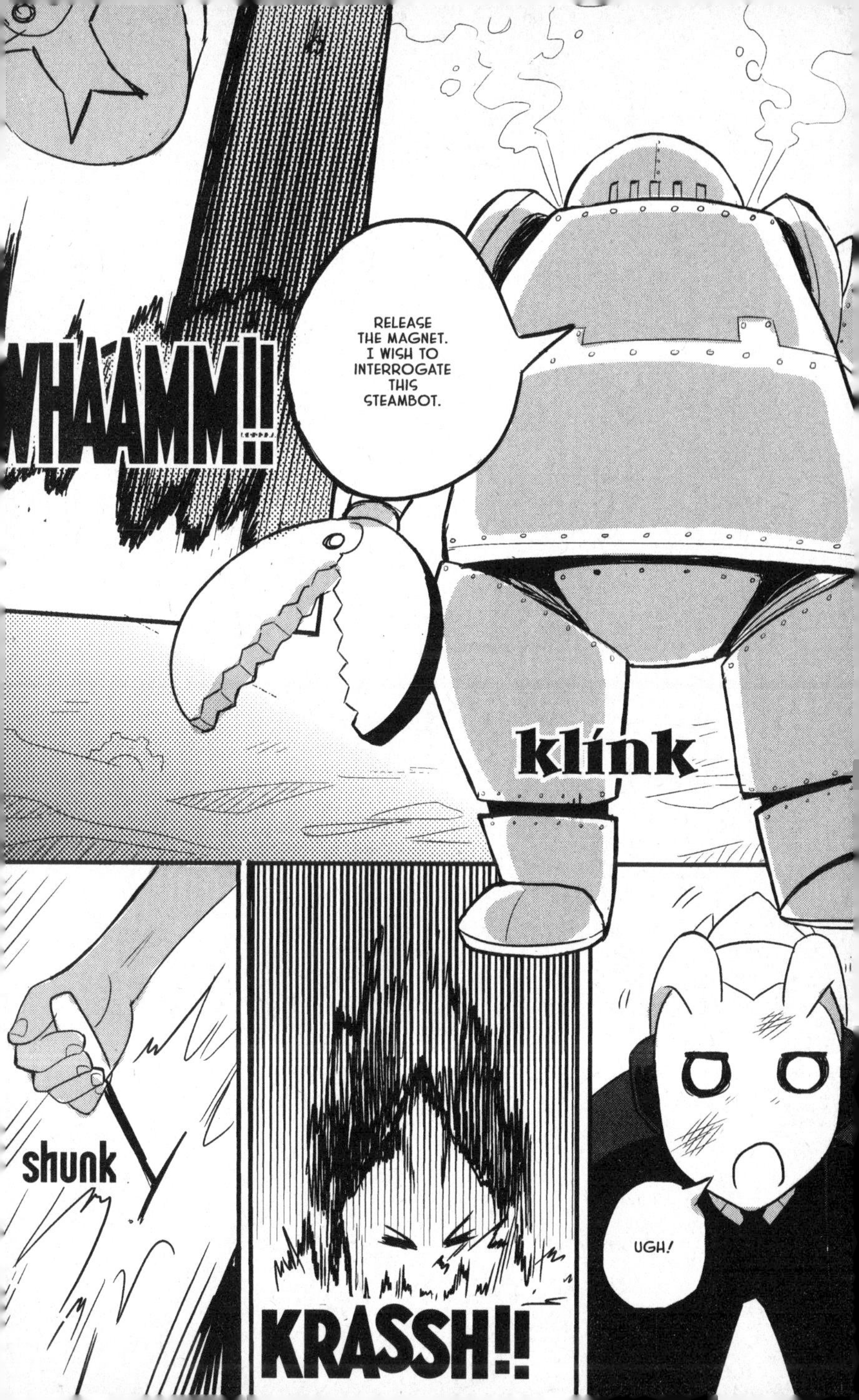
WHAAMM!!
RELEASE THE MAGNET. I WISH TO INTERROGATE THIS STEAMBOT.
klink
shunk
KRASSH!!
UGH!

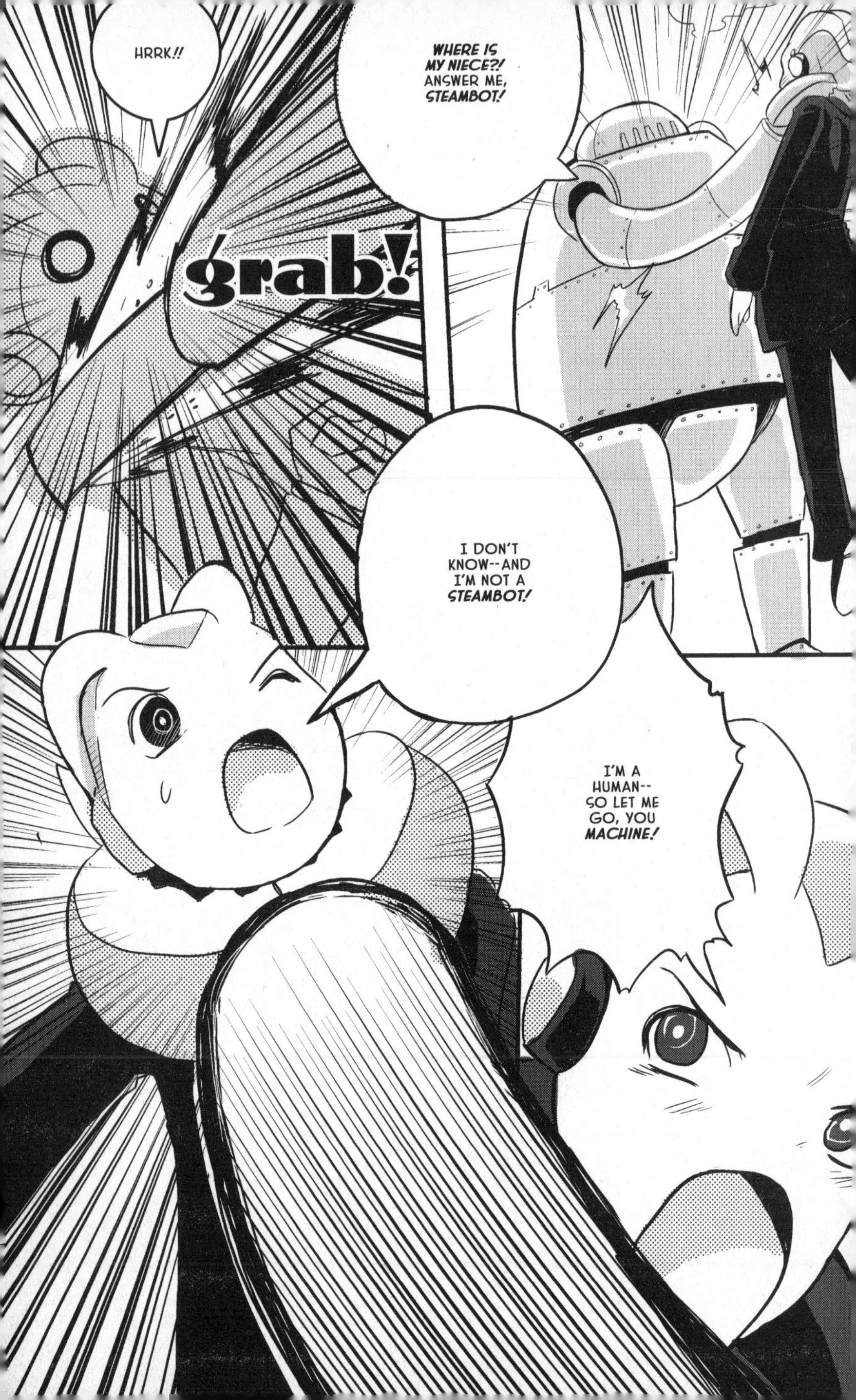
HRRK!!
grab!
WHERE IS MY NIECE?! ANSWER ME, STEAMBOT!
I DON'T KNOW--AND I'M NOT A STEAMBOT!
I'M A HUMAN--SO LET ME GO, YOU MACHINE!

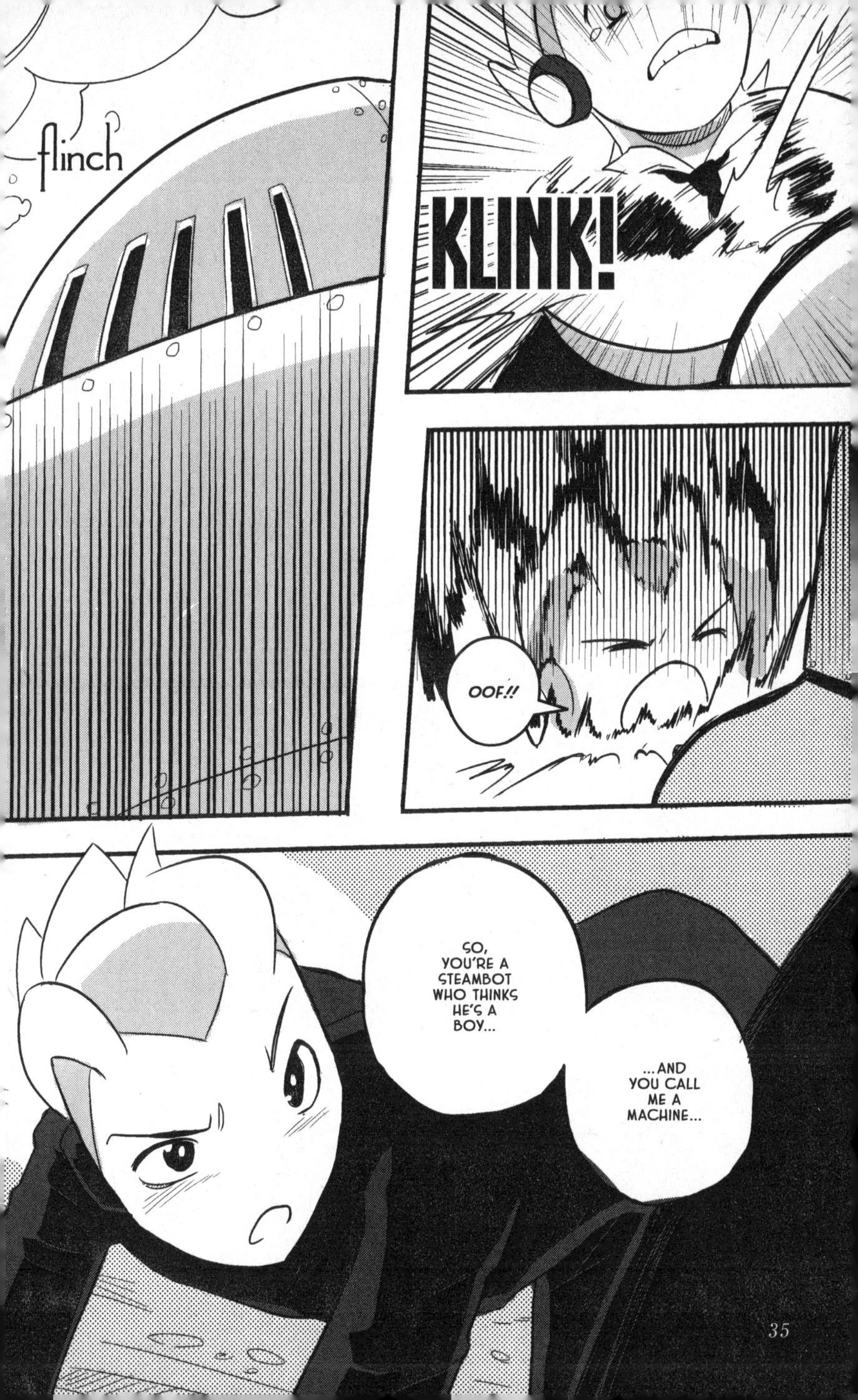
flinch
KLINK!
OOF!!
SO, YOU'RE A STEAMBOT WHO THINKS HE'S A BOY...
...AND YOU CALL ME A MACHINE...

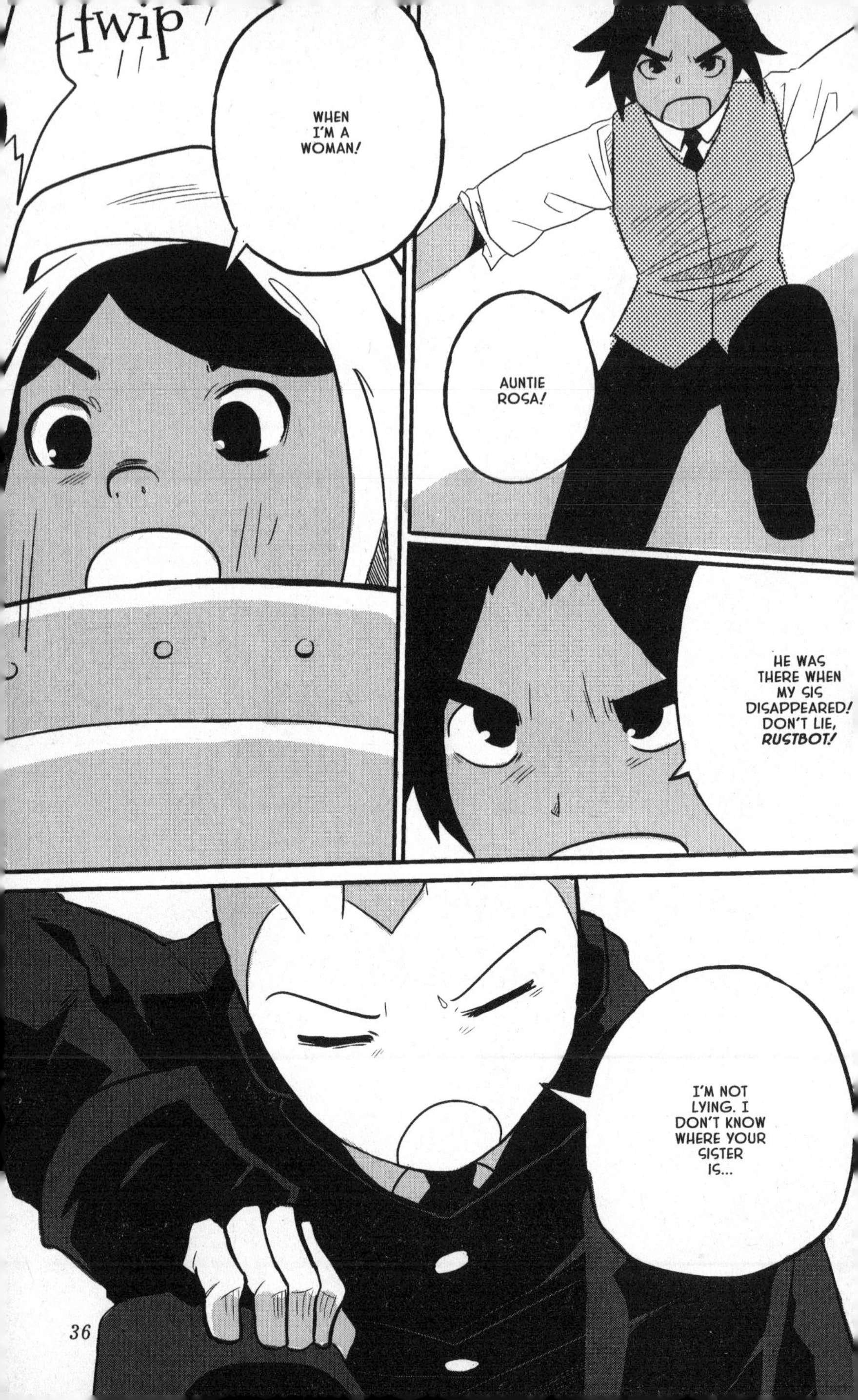
twip
WHEN I'M A WOMAN!
AUNTIE ROSA!
HE WAS THERE WHEN MY SIS DISAPPEARED! DON'T LIE, ***RUSTBOT!***
I'M NOT LYING. I DON'T KNOW WHERE YOUR SISTER IS...

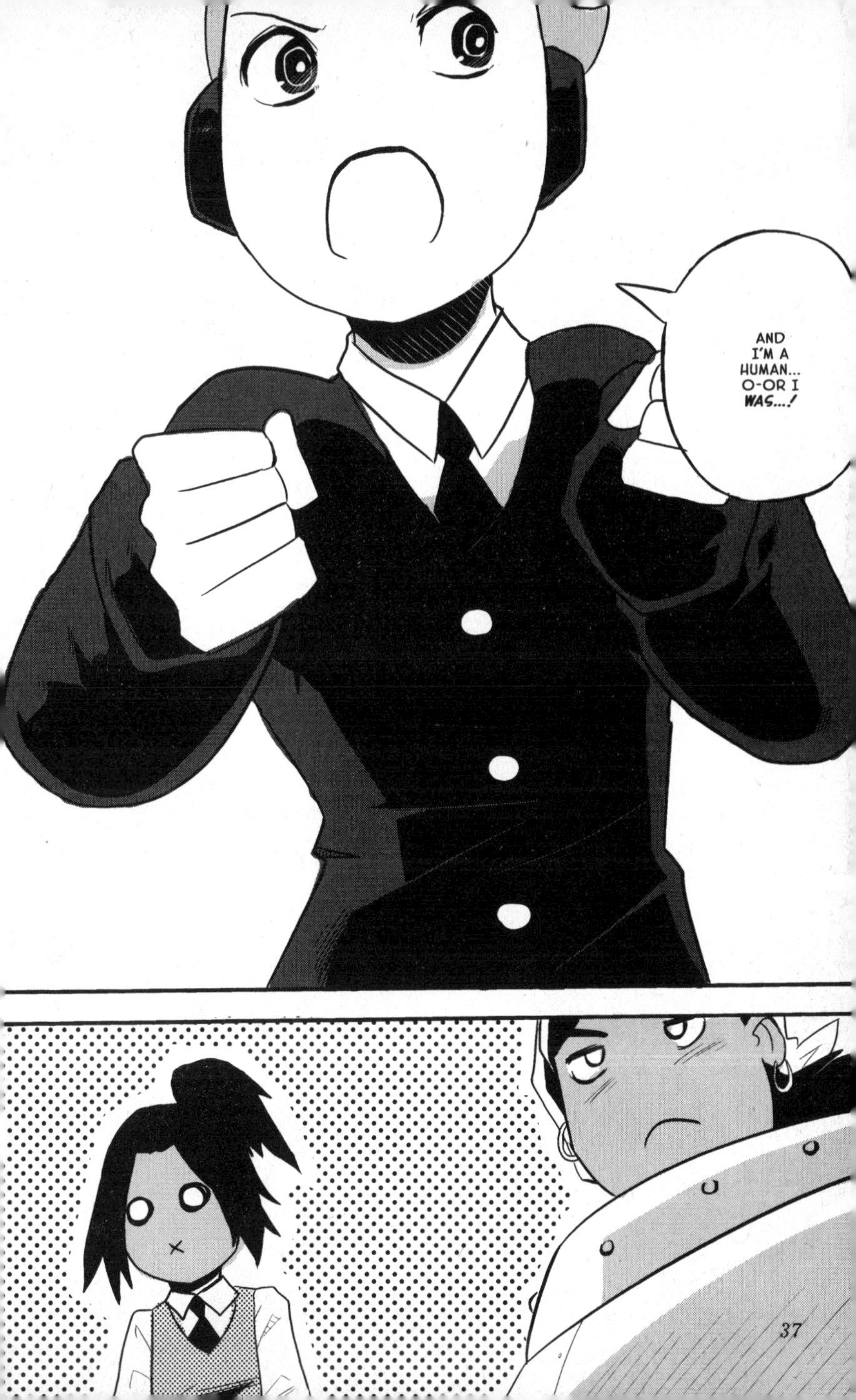
AND I'M A HUMAN... O-OR I *WAS*...!

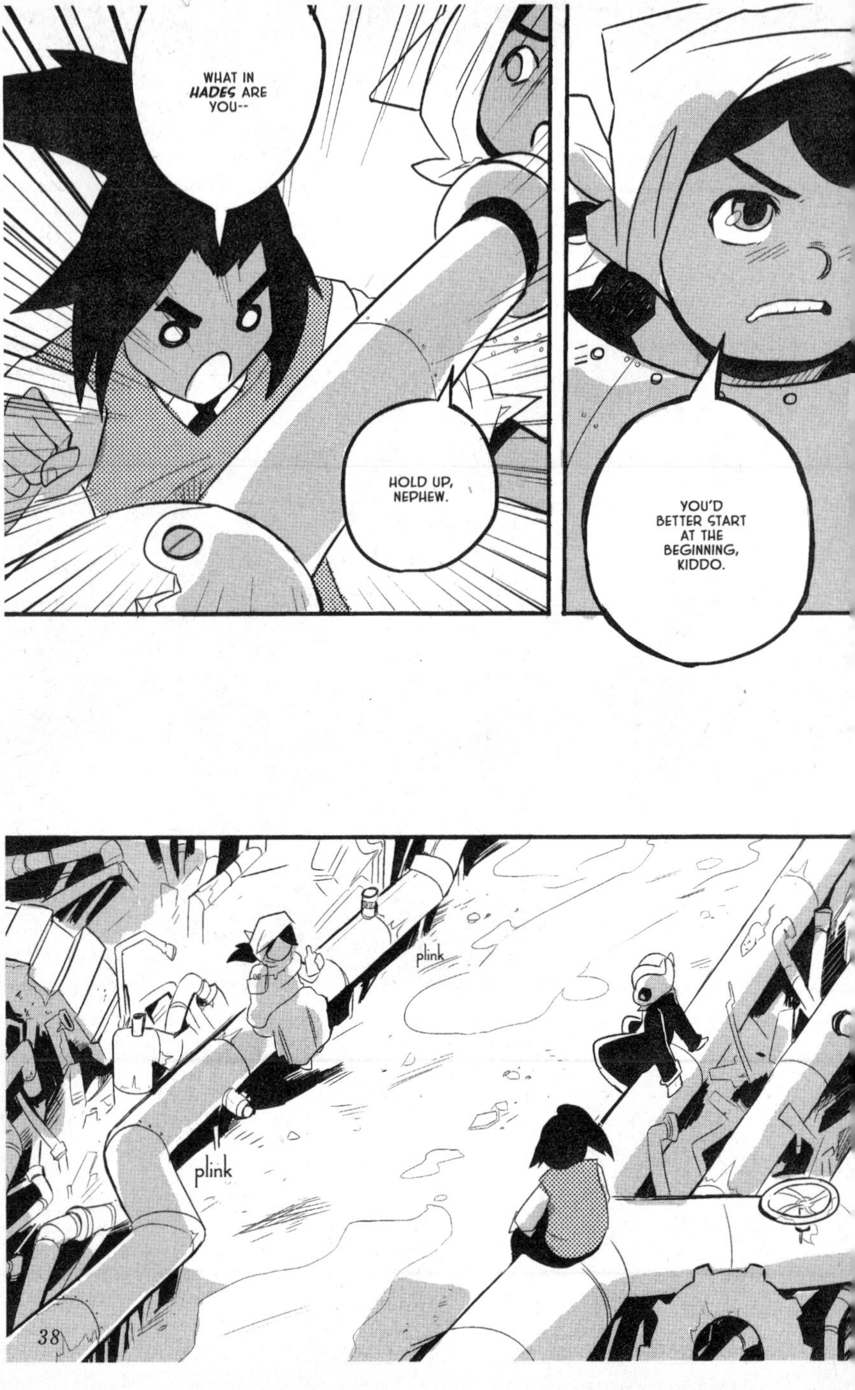
WHAT IN *HADES* ARE YOU--
HOLD UP, NEPHEW.
YOU'D BETTER START AT THE BEGINNING, KIDDO.
plink
plink

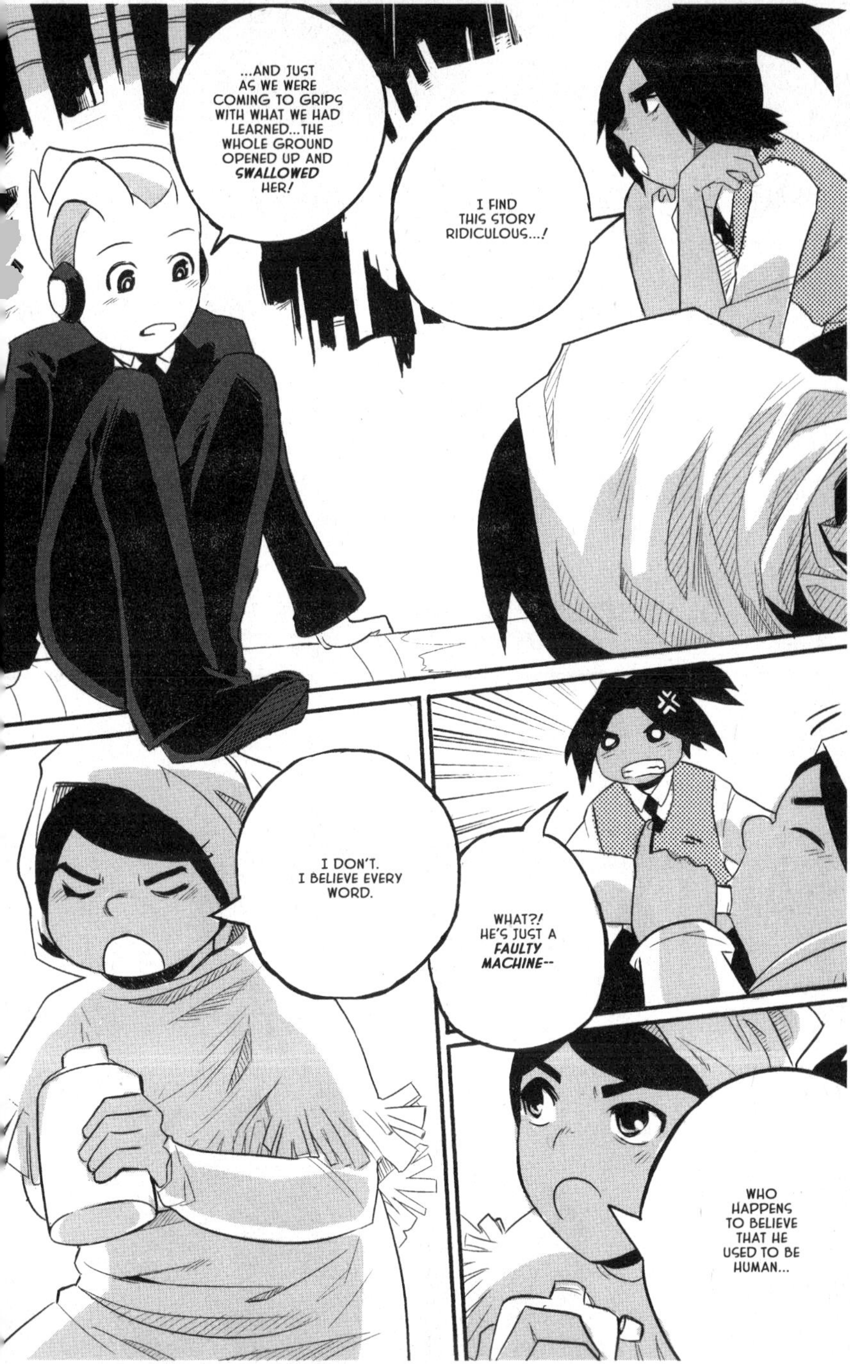
...AND JUST AS WE WERE COMING TO GRIPS WITH WHAT WE HAD LEARNED...THE WHOLE GROUND OPENED UP AND SWALLOWED HER!
I FIND THIS STORY RIDICULOUS...!
I DON'T. I BELIEVE EVERY WORD.
WHAT?! HE'S JUST A FAULTY MACHINE--
WHO HAPPENS TO BELIEVE THAT HE USED TO BE HUMAN...

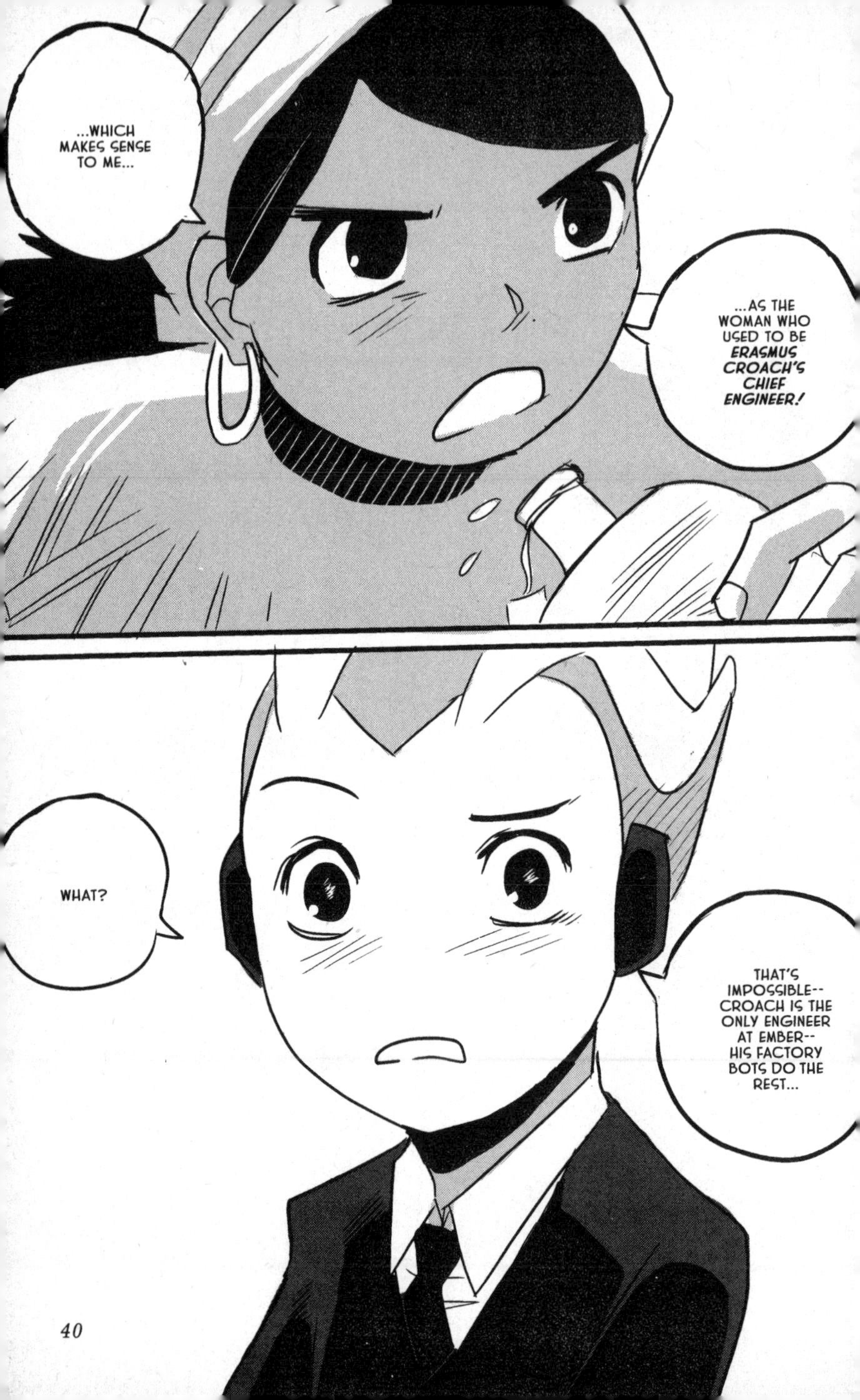
...WHICH MAKES SENSE TO ME...
...AS THE WOMAN WHO USED TO BE ***ERASMUS CROACH'S CHIEF ENGINEER!***
WHAT?
THAT'S IMPOSSIBLE-- CROACH IS THE ONLY ENGINEER AT EMBER-- HIS FACTORY BOTS DO THE REST...

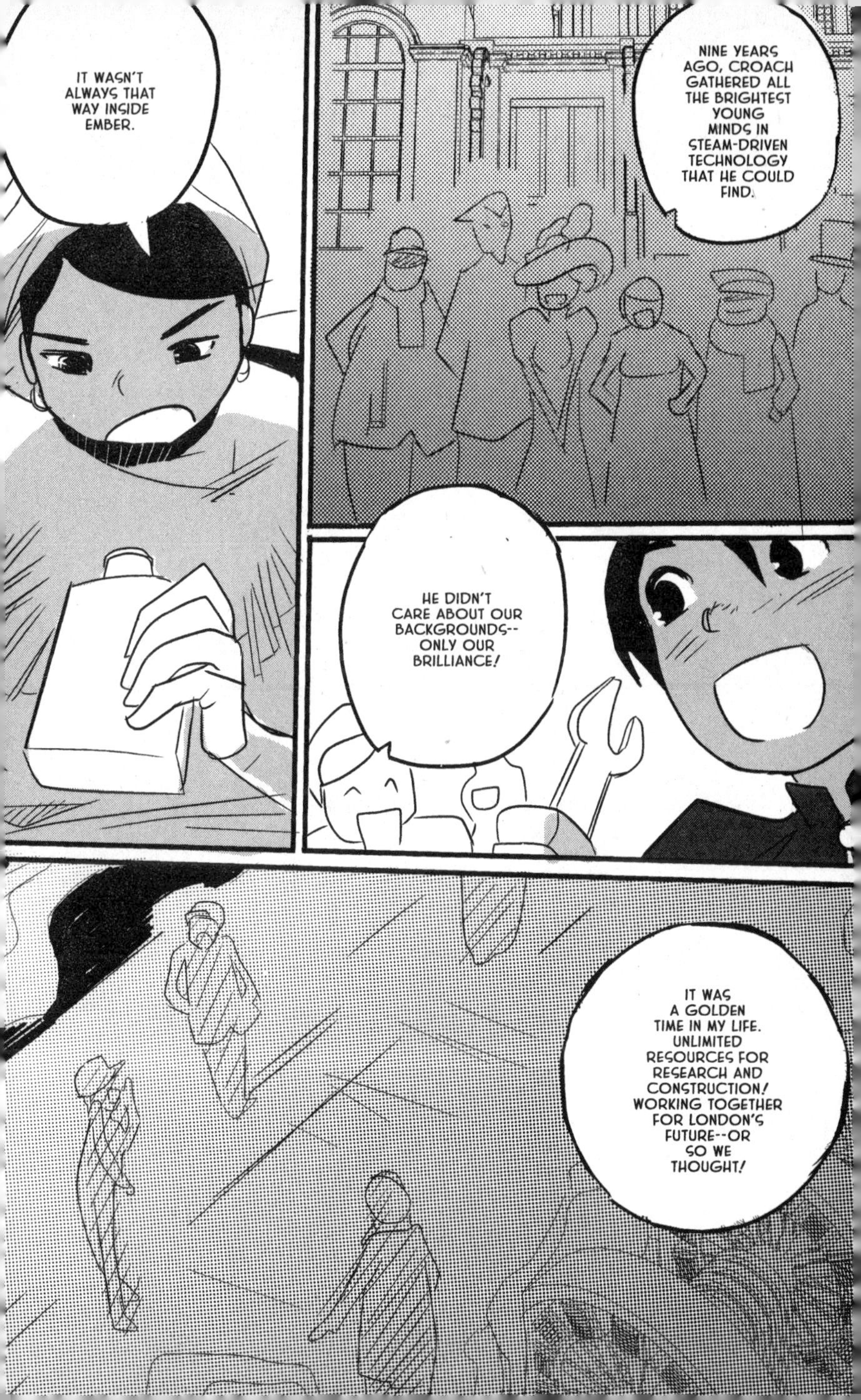
IT WASN'T ALWAYS THAT WAY INSIDE EMBER.
NINE YEARS AGO, CROACH GATHERED ALL THE BRIGHTEST YOUNG MINDS IN STEAM-DRIVEN TECHNOLOGY THAT HE COULD FIND.
HE DIDN'T CARE ABOUT OUR BACKGROUNDS--ONLY OUR BRILLIANCE!
IT WAS A GOLDEN TIME IN MY LIFE. UNLIMITED RESOURCES FOR RESEARCH AND CONSTRUCTION! WORKING TOGETHER FOR LONDON'S FUTURE--OR SO WE THOUGHT!

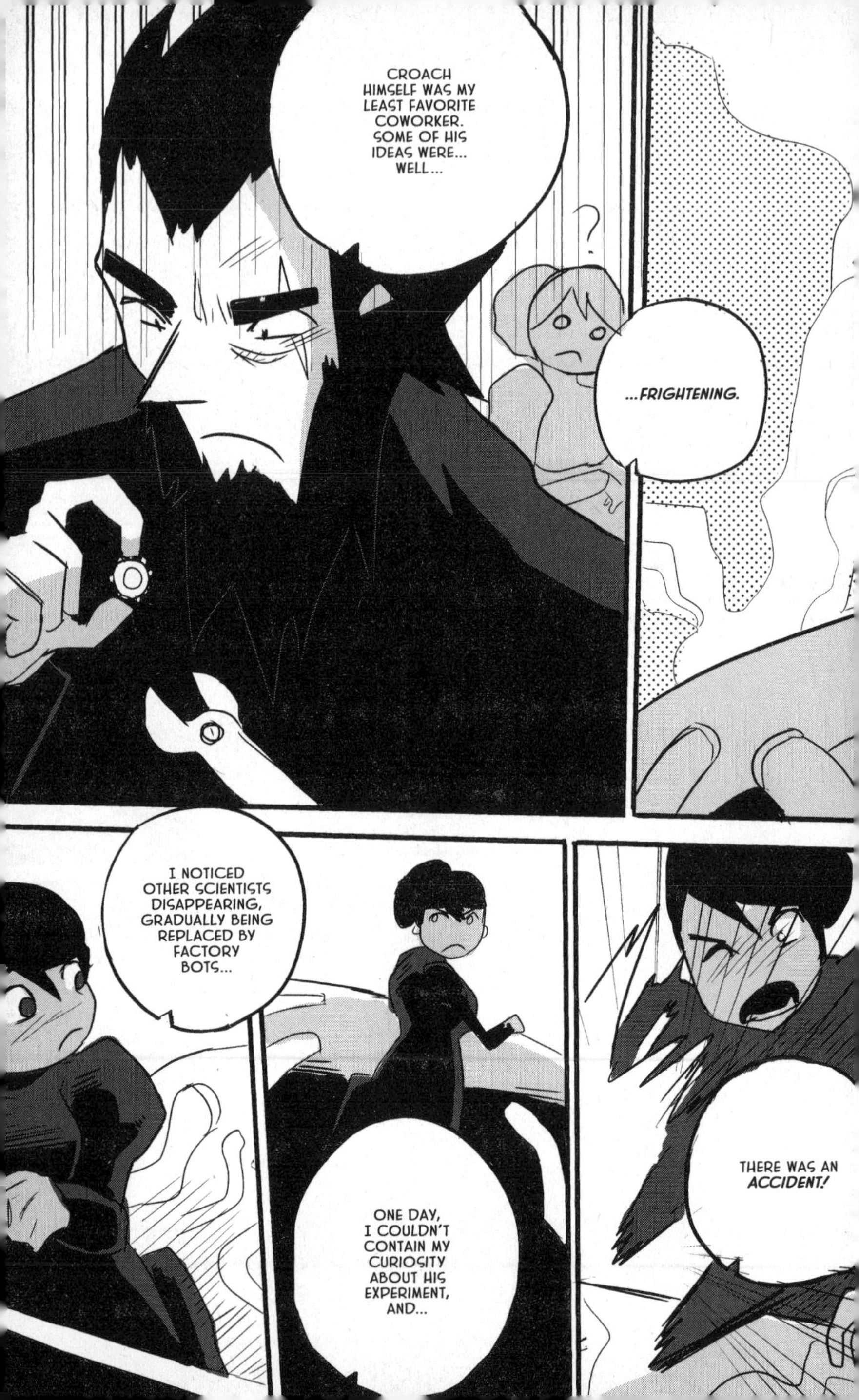
CROACH HIMSELF WAS MY LEAST FAVORITE COWORKER. SOME OF HIS IDEAS WERE... WELL...
?
...FRIGHTENING.
I NOTICED OTHER SCIENTISTS DISAPPEARING, GRADUALLY BEING REPLACED BY FACTORY BOTS...
ONE DAY, I COULDN'T CONTAIN MY CURIOSITY ABOUT HIS EXPERIMENT, AND...
THERE WAS AN *ACCIDENT!*

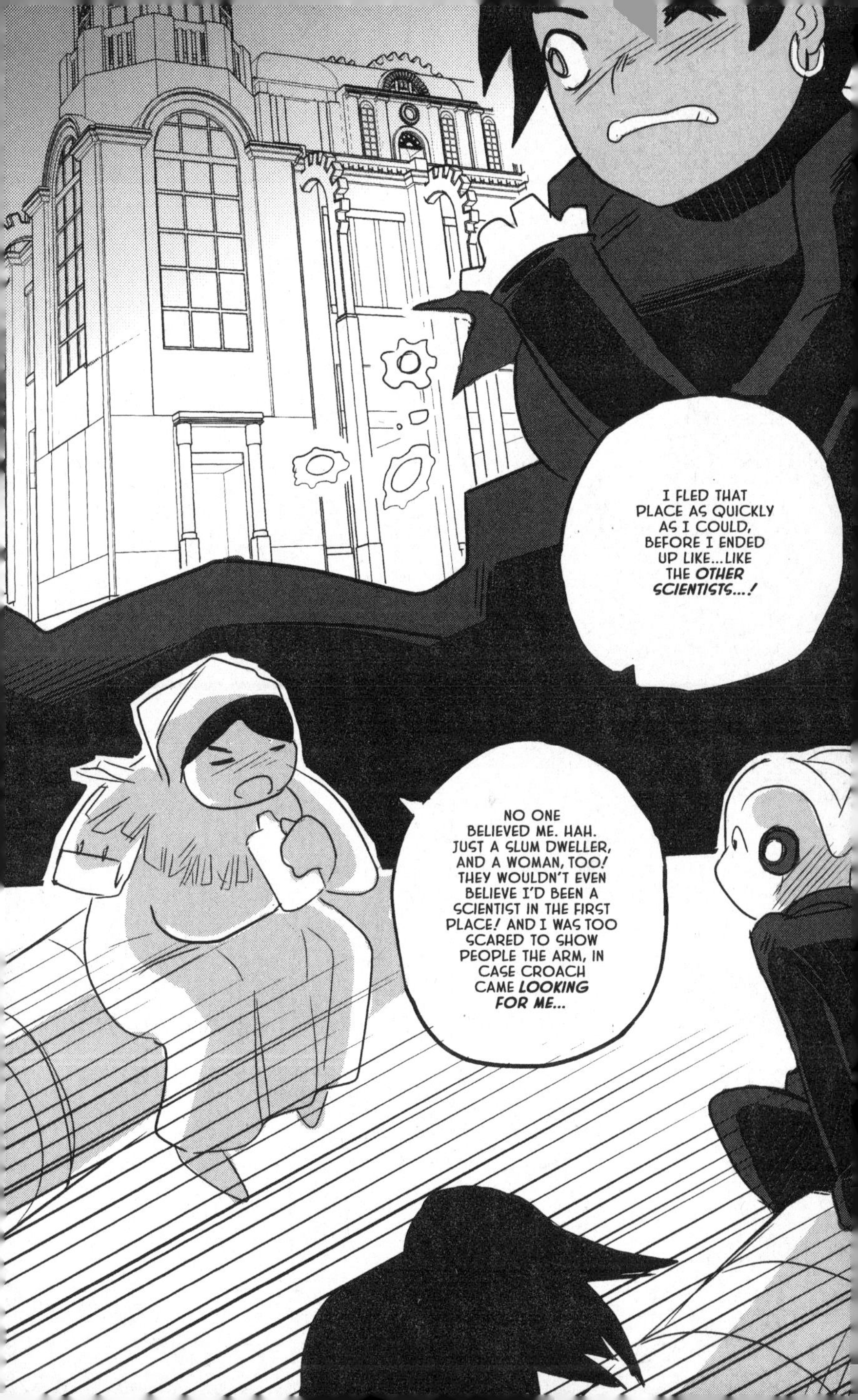
I FLED THAT PLACE AS QUICKLY AS I COULD, BEFORE I ENDED UP LIKE...LIKE THE *OTHER SCIENTISTS...!*
NO ONE BELIEVED ME. HAH. JUST A SLUM DWELLER, AND A WOMAN, TOO! THEY WOULDN'T EVEN BELIEVE I'D BEEN A SCIENTIST IN THE FIRST PLACE! AND I WAS TOO SCARED TO SHOW PEOPLE THE ARM, IN CASE CROACH CAME *LOOKING FOR ME...*

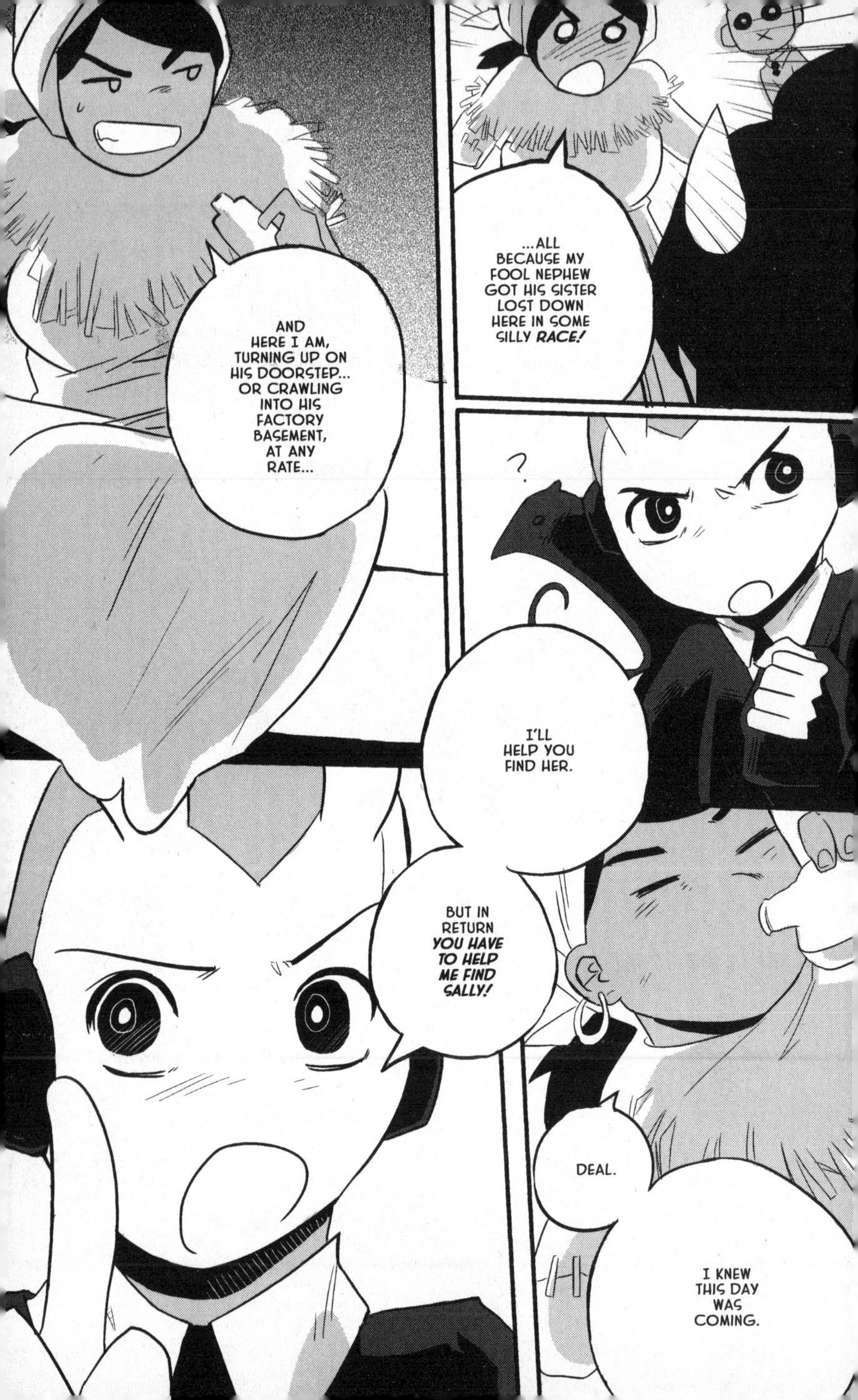
AND HERE I AM, TURNING UP ON HIS DOORSTEP... OR CRAWLING INTO HIS FACTORY BASEMENT, AT ANY RATE...
...ALL BECAUSE MY FOOL NEPHEW GOT HIS SISTER LOST DOWN HERE IN SOME SILLY *RACE!*
?
I'LL HELP YOU FIND HER.
BUT IN RETURN ***YOU HAVE TO HELP ME FIND SALLY!***
DEAL.
I KNEW THIS DAY WAS COMING.

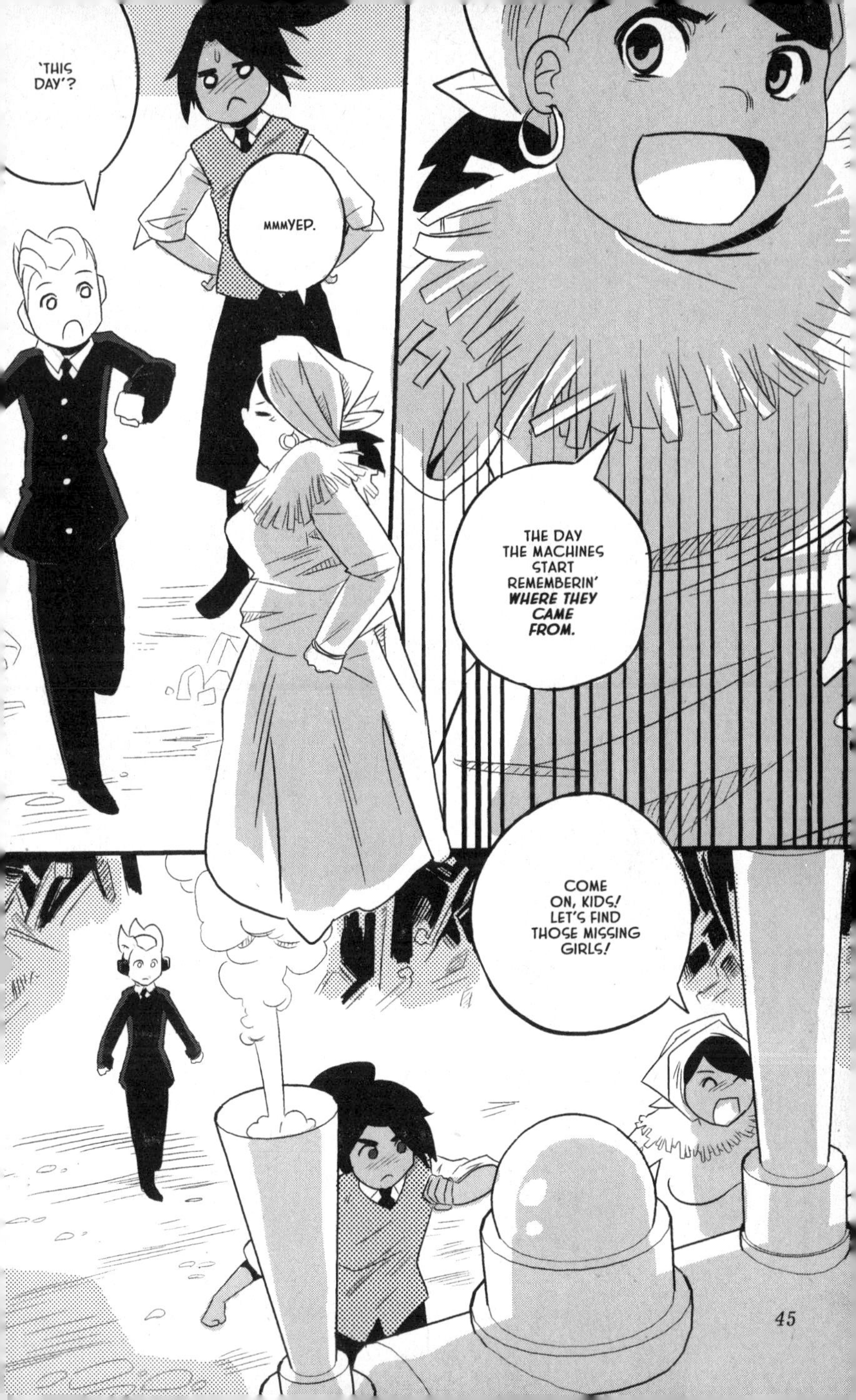
'THIS DAY'?
MMMYEP.
THE DAY THE MACHINES START REMEMBERIN' ***WHERE THEY CAME FROM.***
COME ON, KIDS! LET'S FIND THOSE MISSING GIRLS!

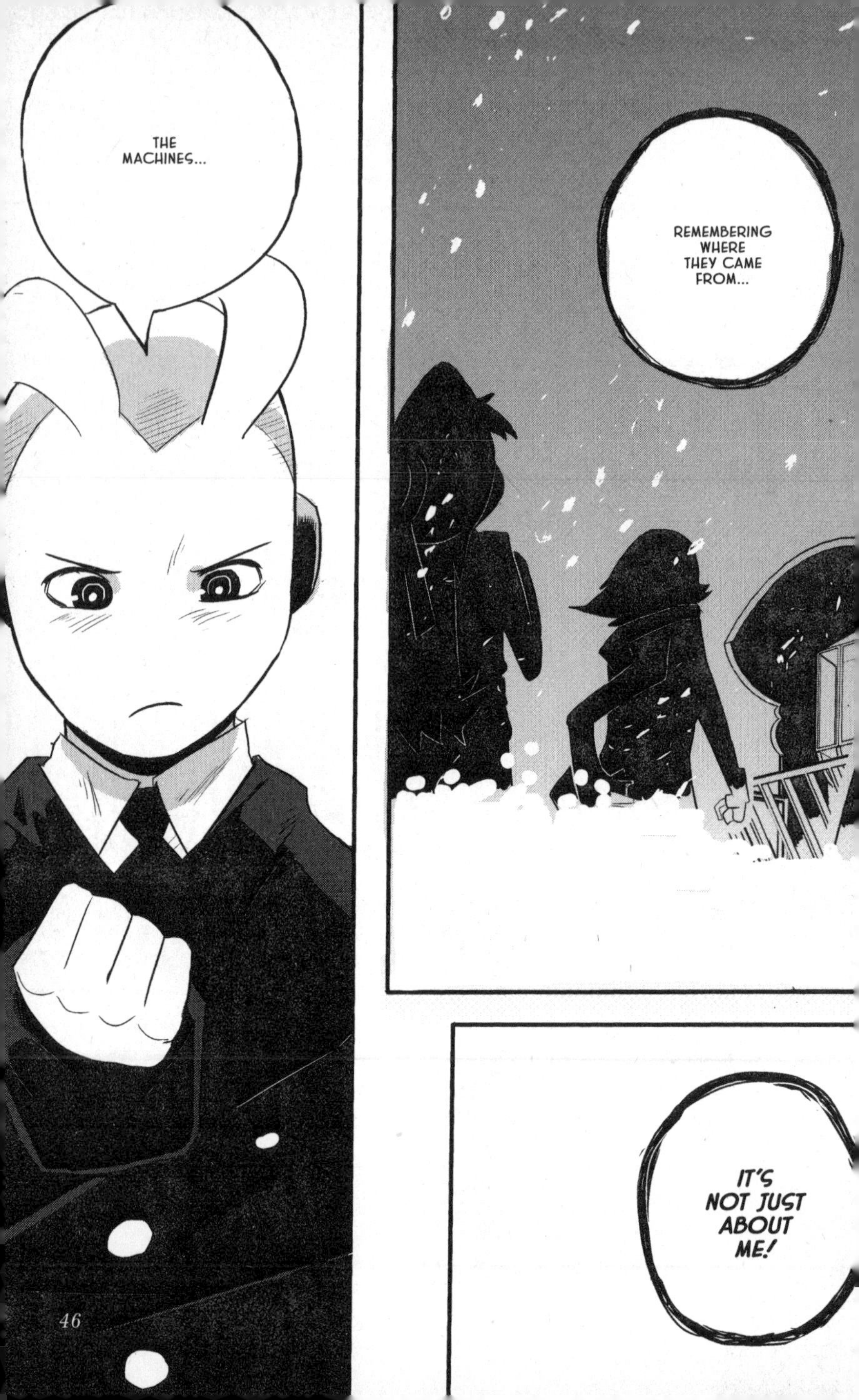
THE MACHINES...
REMEMBERING WHERE THEY CAME FROM...
IT'S NOT JUST ABOUT ME!

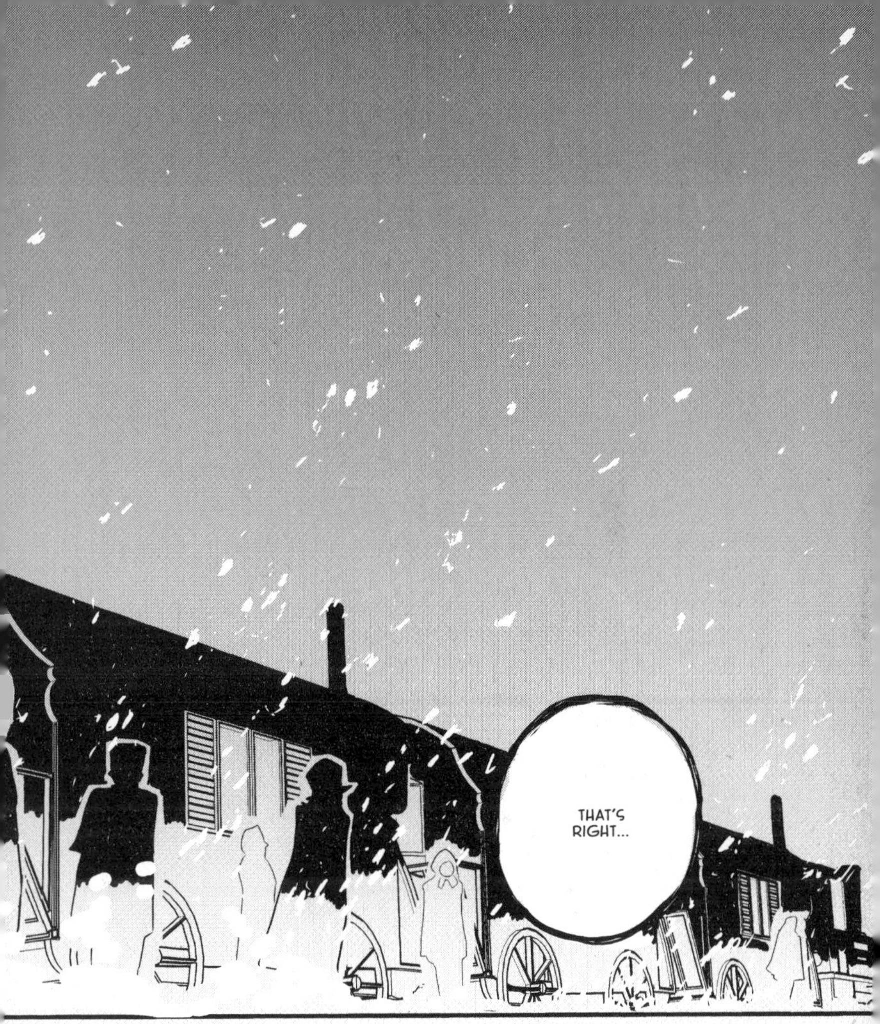
THAT'S
RIGHT...
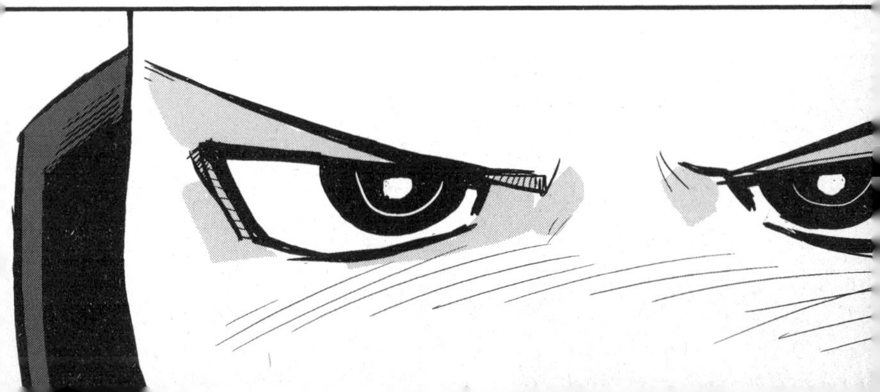

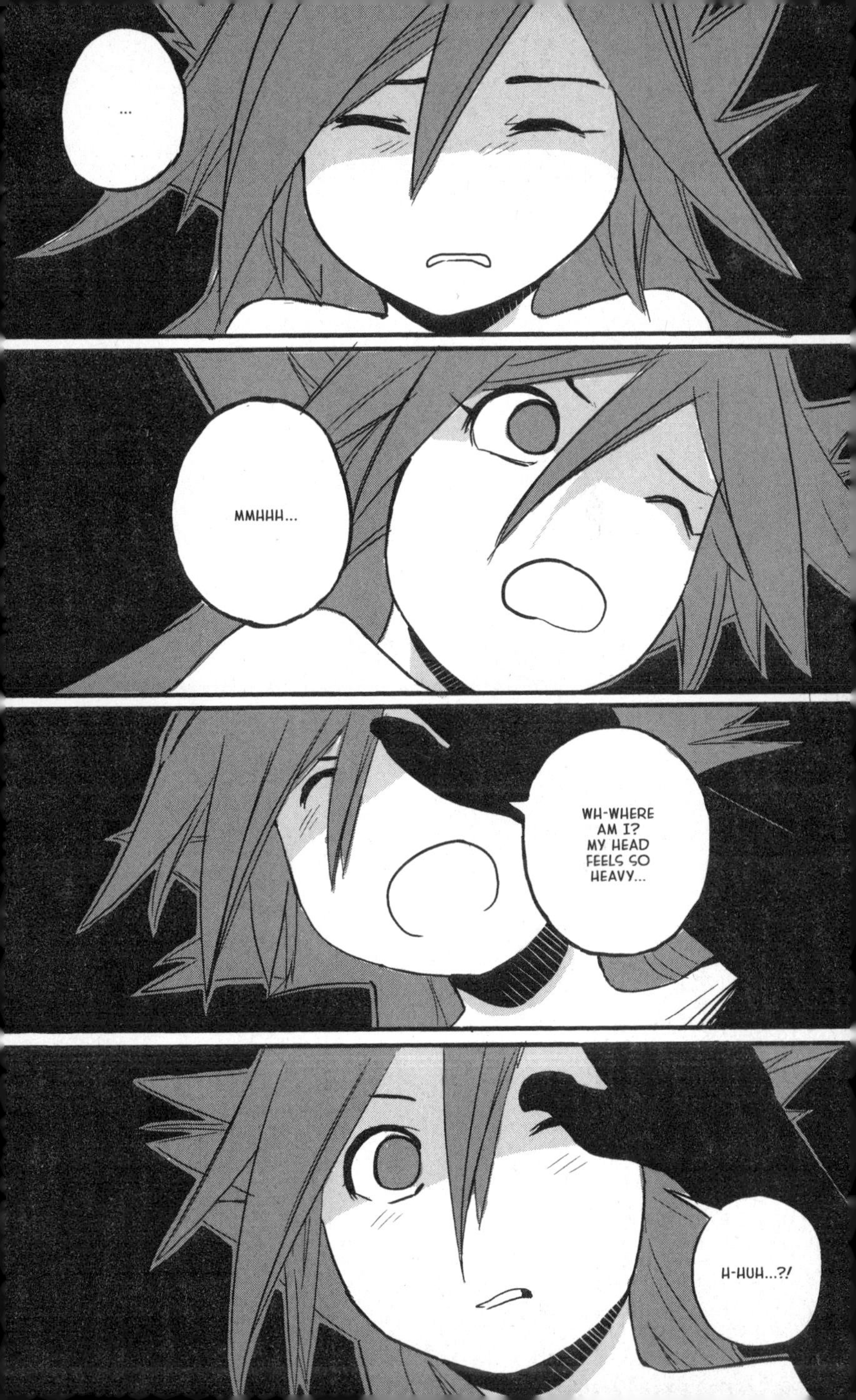
...
MMHHH...
WH-WHERE AM I? MY HEAD FEELS SO HEAVY...
H-HUH...?!

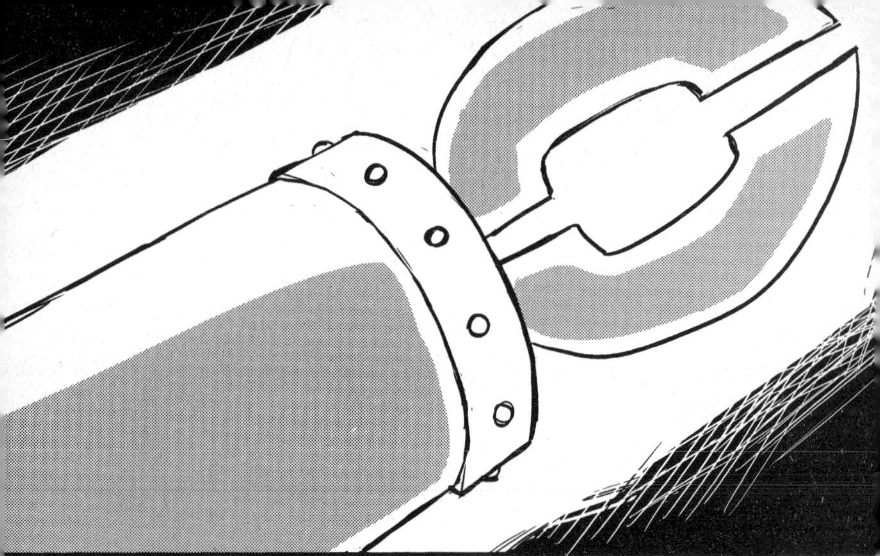

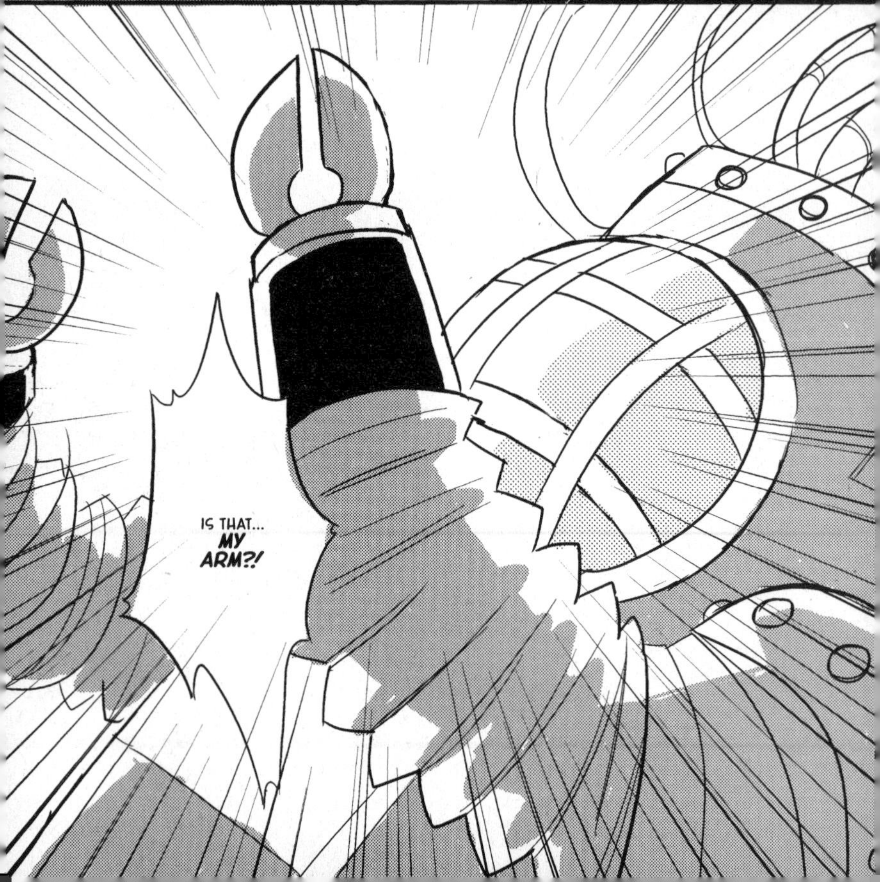
IS THAT... MY ARM?!

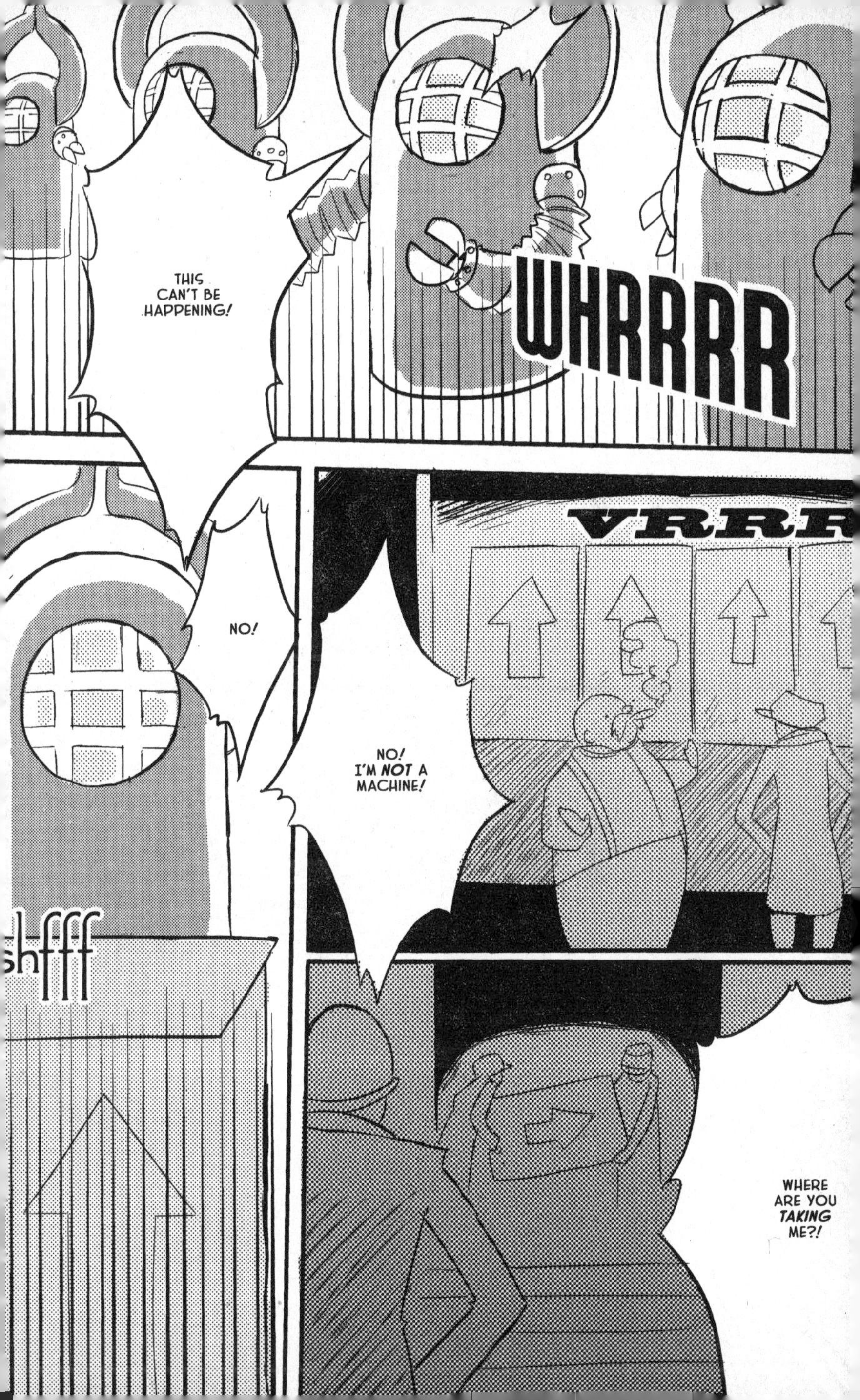
THIS CAN'T BE HAPPENING!
WHRRRR
NO!
VRRR
NO! I'M ***NOT*** A MACHINE!
shfff
WHERE ARE YOU ***TAKING*** ME?!

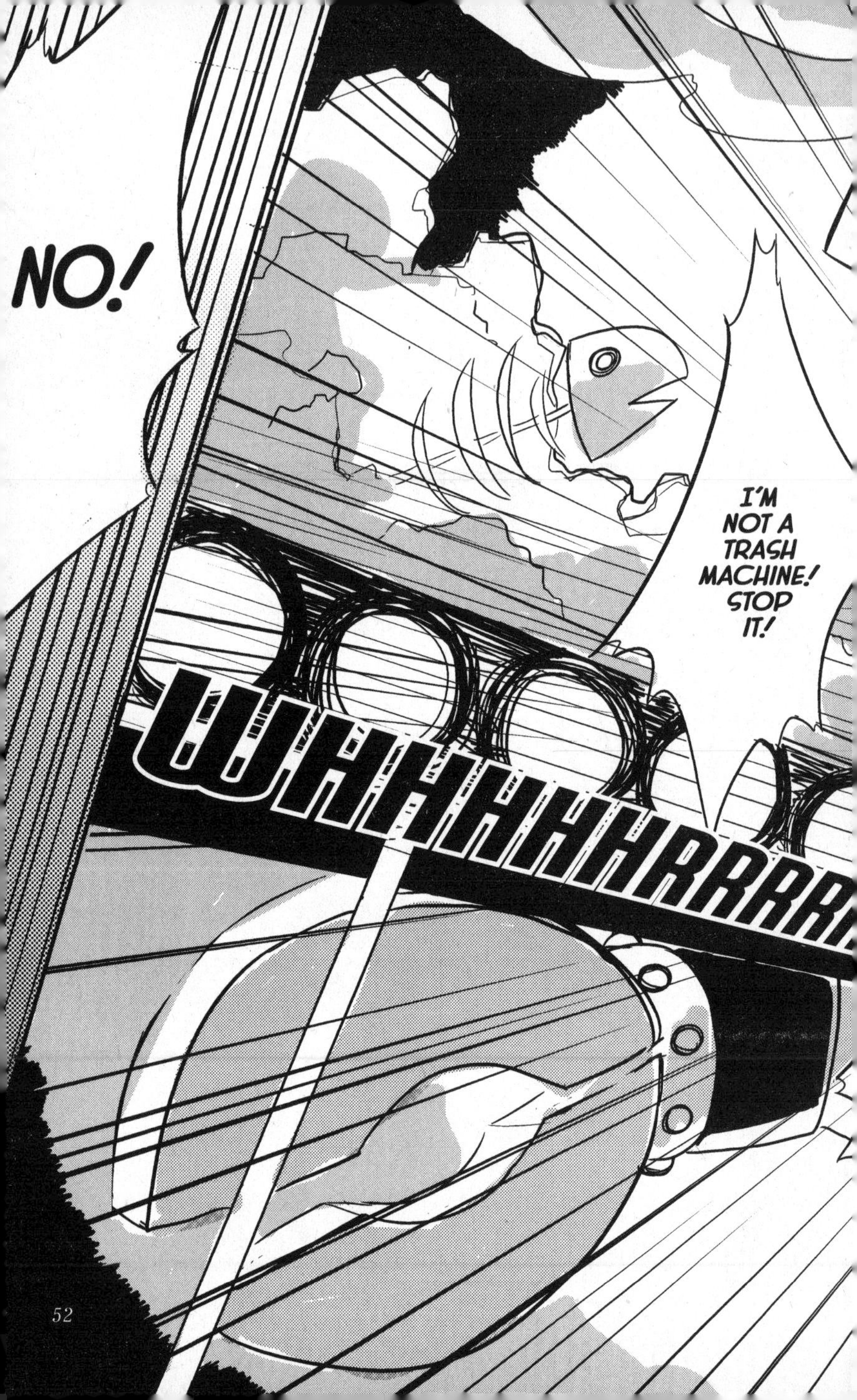
NO!
I'M NOT A TRASH MACHINE! STOP IT!
WHHHHHHRRRRR

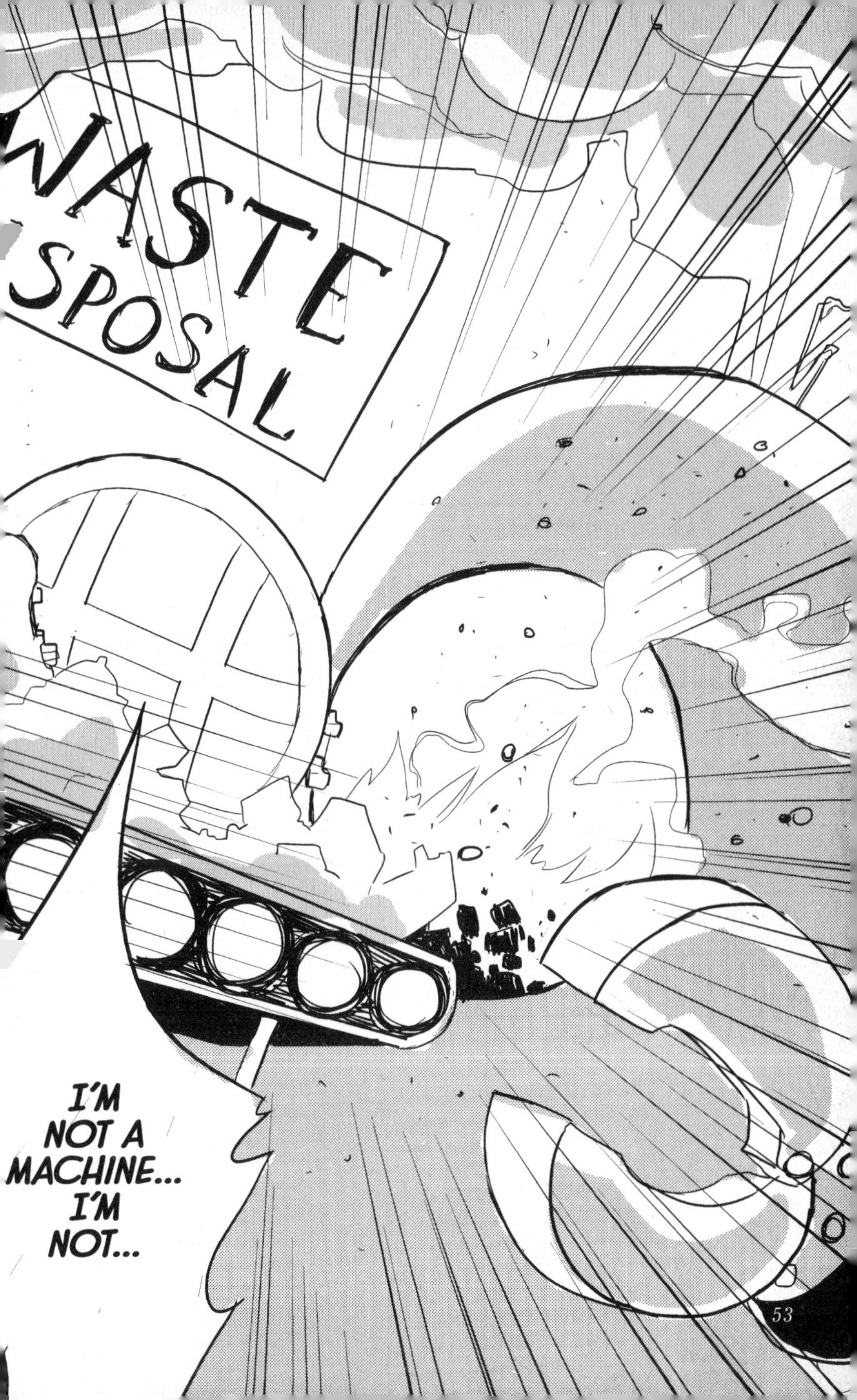
WASTE
SPOSAL
I'M NOT A MACHINE... I'M NOT...

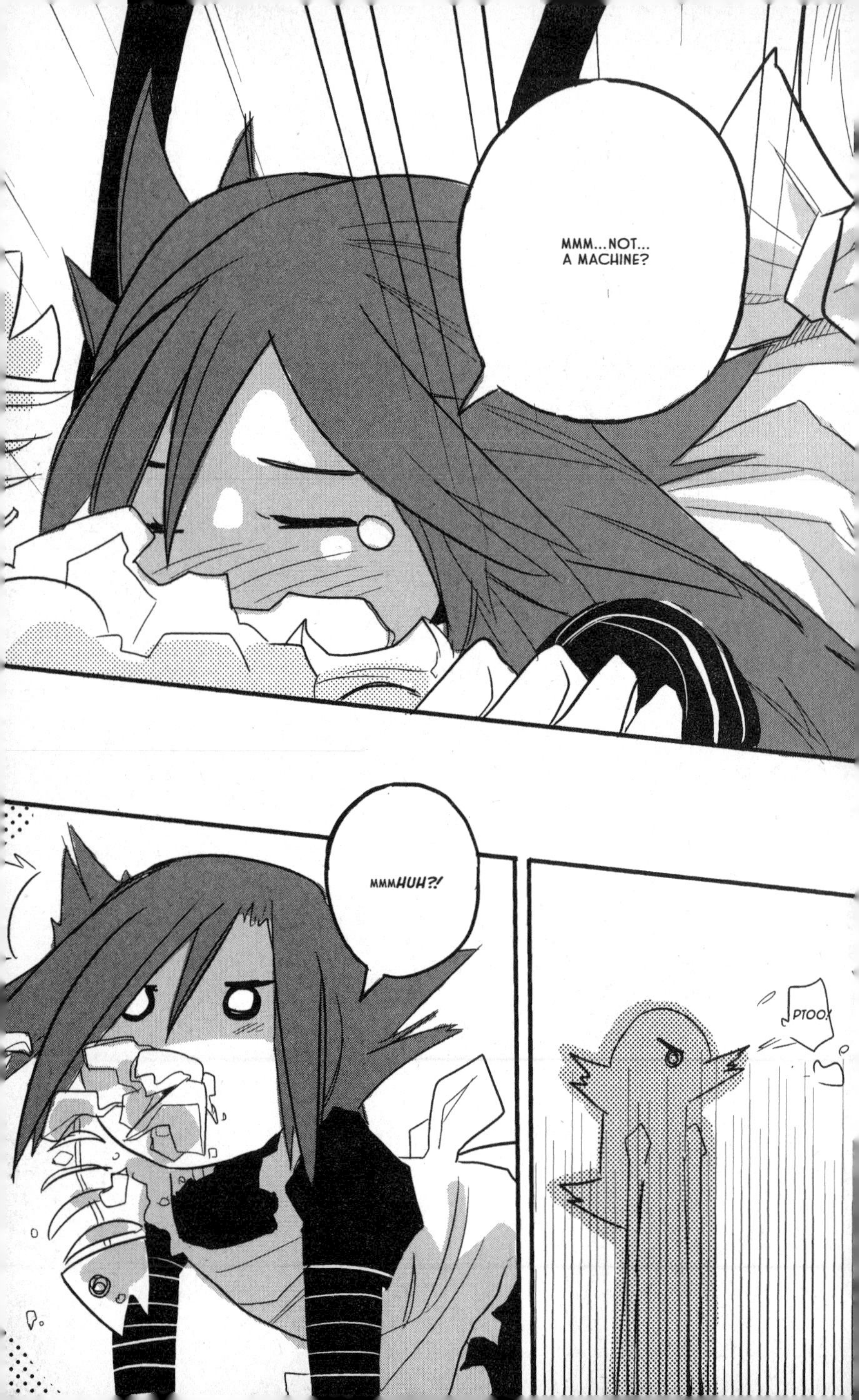
MMM...NOT...
A MACHINE?
MMMHUH?!
PTOO!

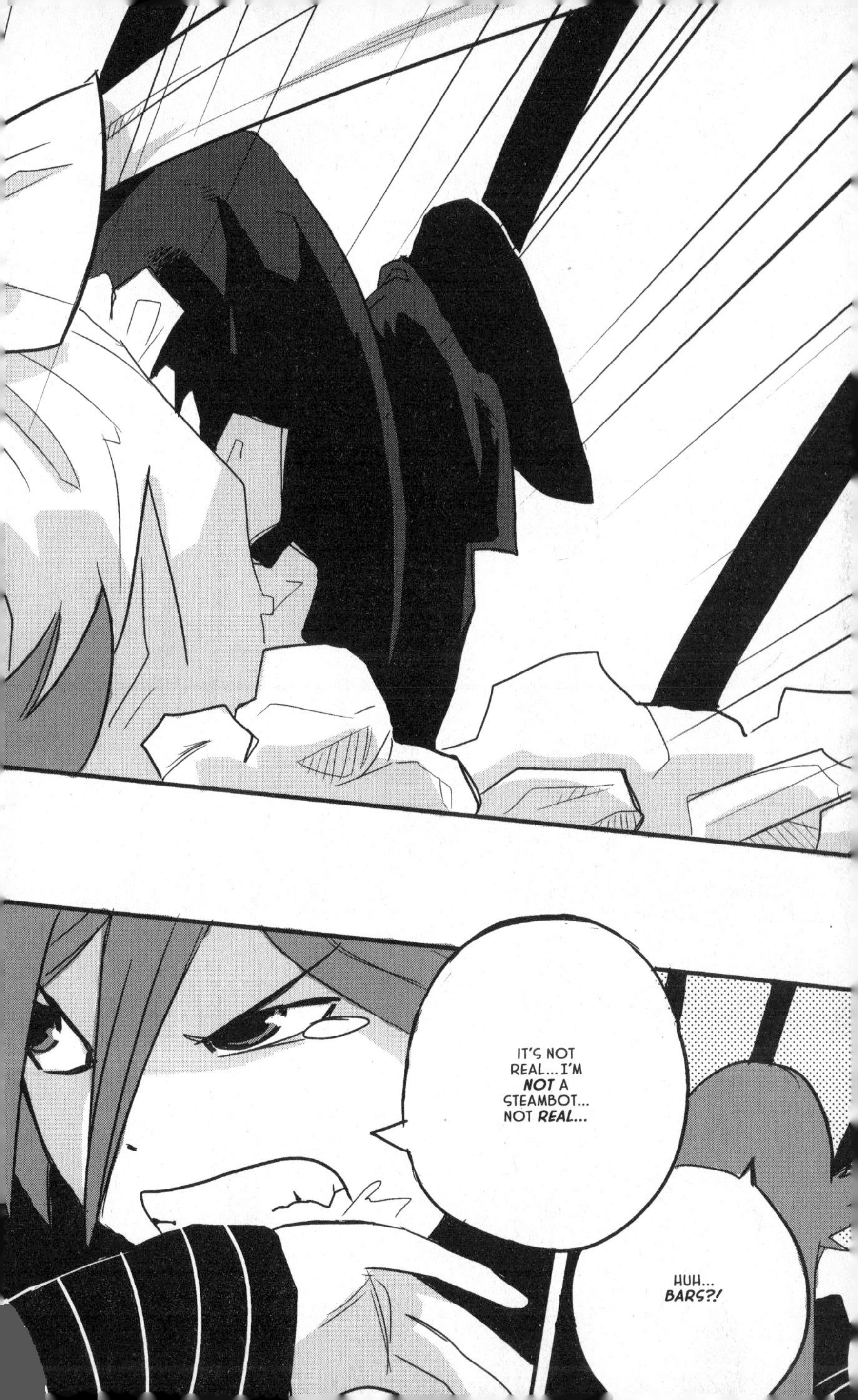
IT'S NOT REAL... I'M **NOT** A STEAMBOT... NOT **REAL**...
HUH... **BARS?!**

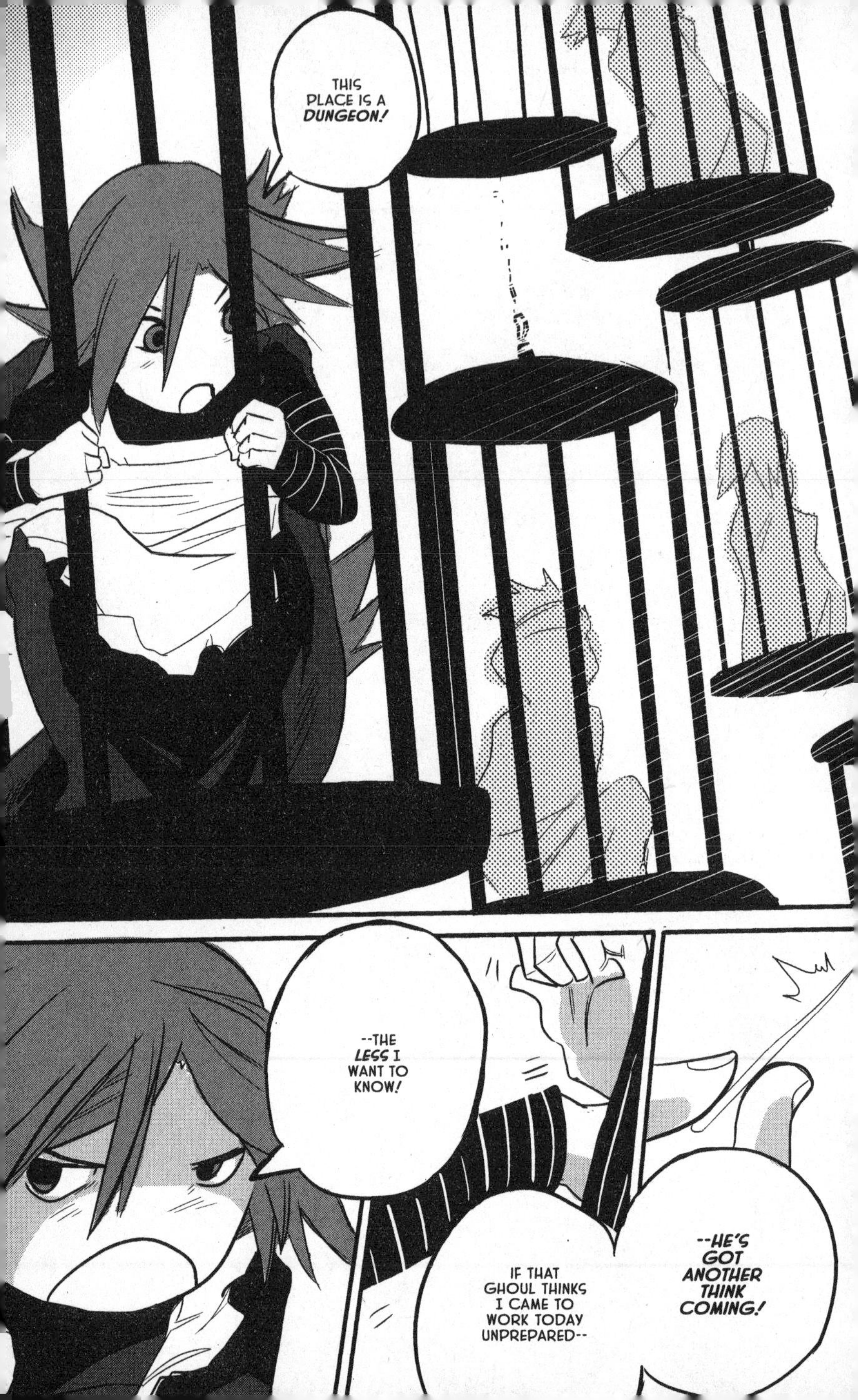
THIS PLACE IS A DUNGEON!
--THE LESS I WANT TO KNOW!
IF THAT GHOUL THINKS I CAME TO WORK TODAY UNPREPARED--
--HE'S GOT ANOTHER THINK COMING!

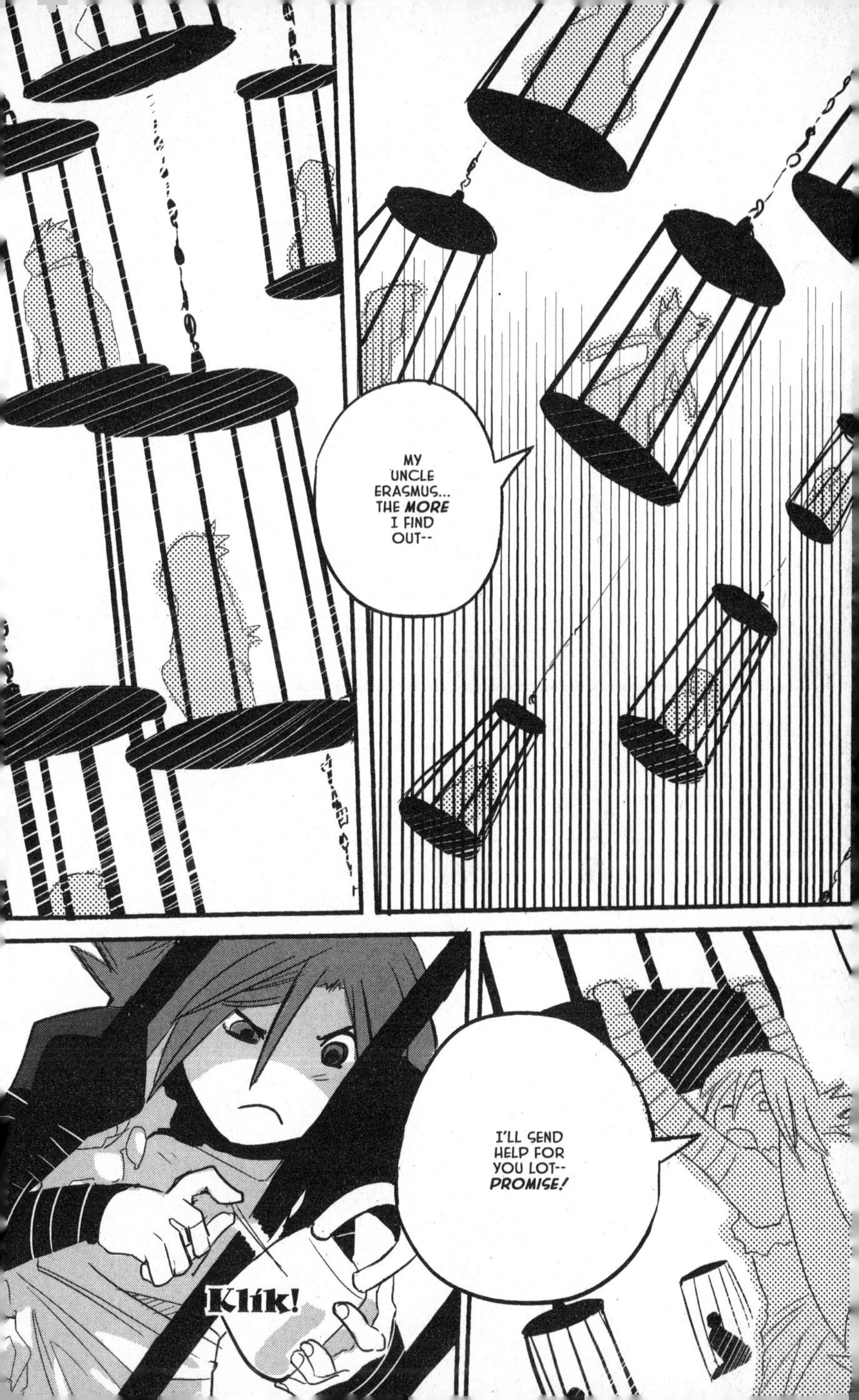
MY UNCLE ERASMUS... THE MORE I FIND OUT--
I'LL SEND HELP FOR YOU LOT-- PROMISE!
Klik!

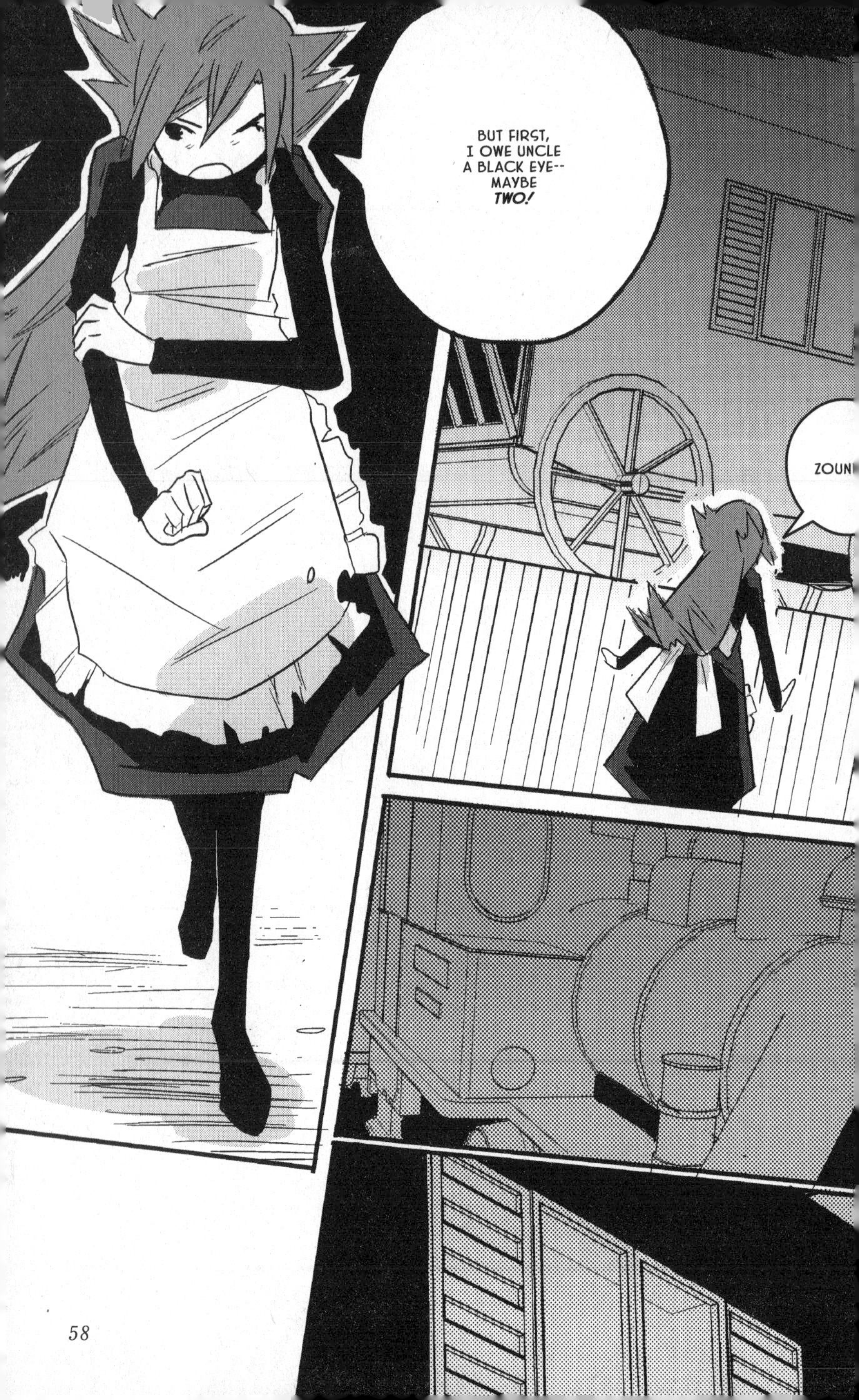
BUT FIRST, I OWE UNCLE A BLACK EYE-- MAYBE ***TWO!***
ZOUN

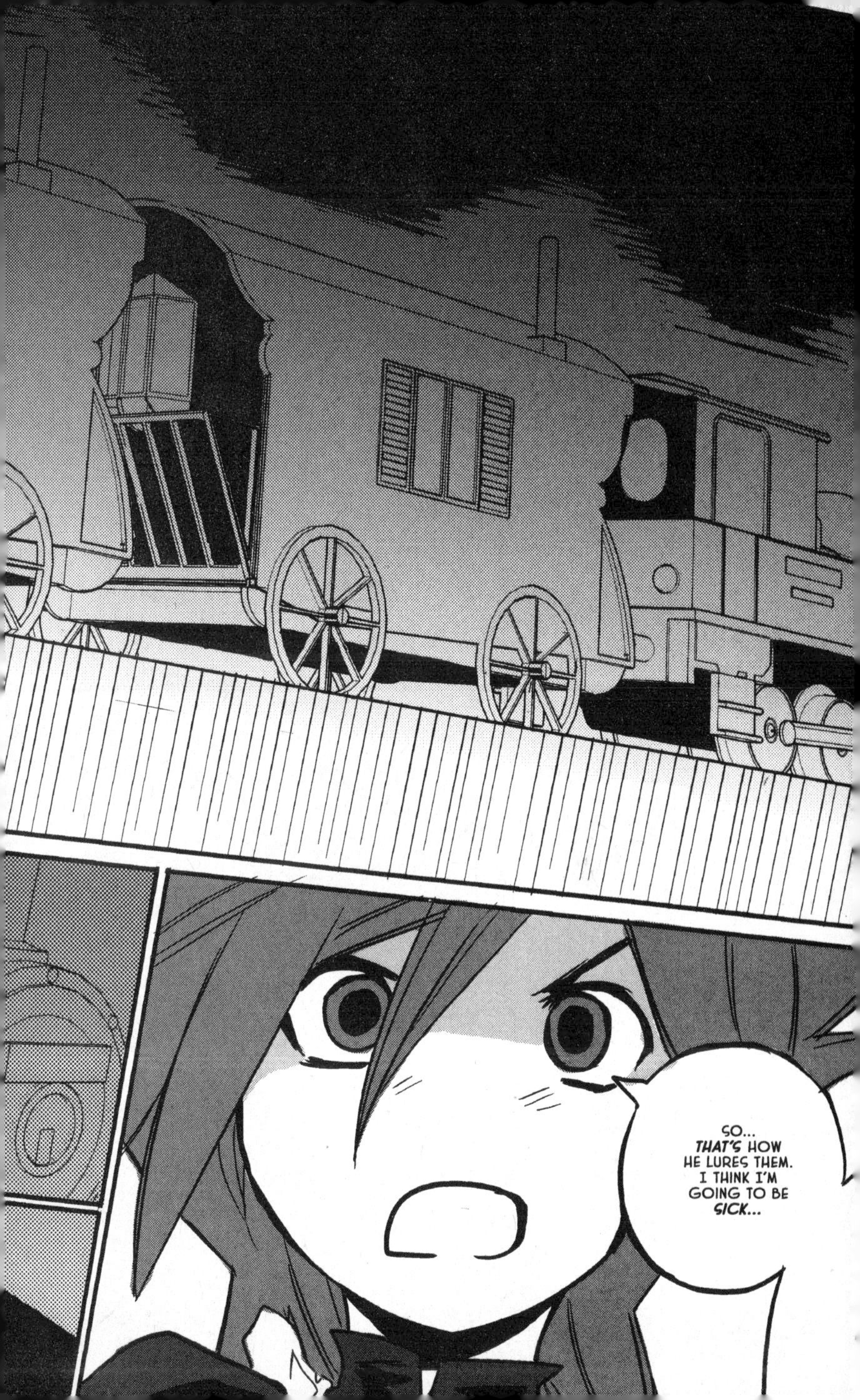
SO... THAT'S HOW HE LURES THEM. I THINK I'M GOING TO BE SICK...

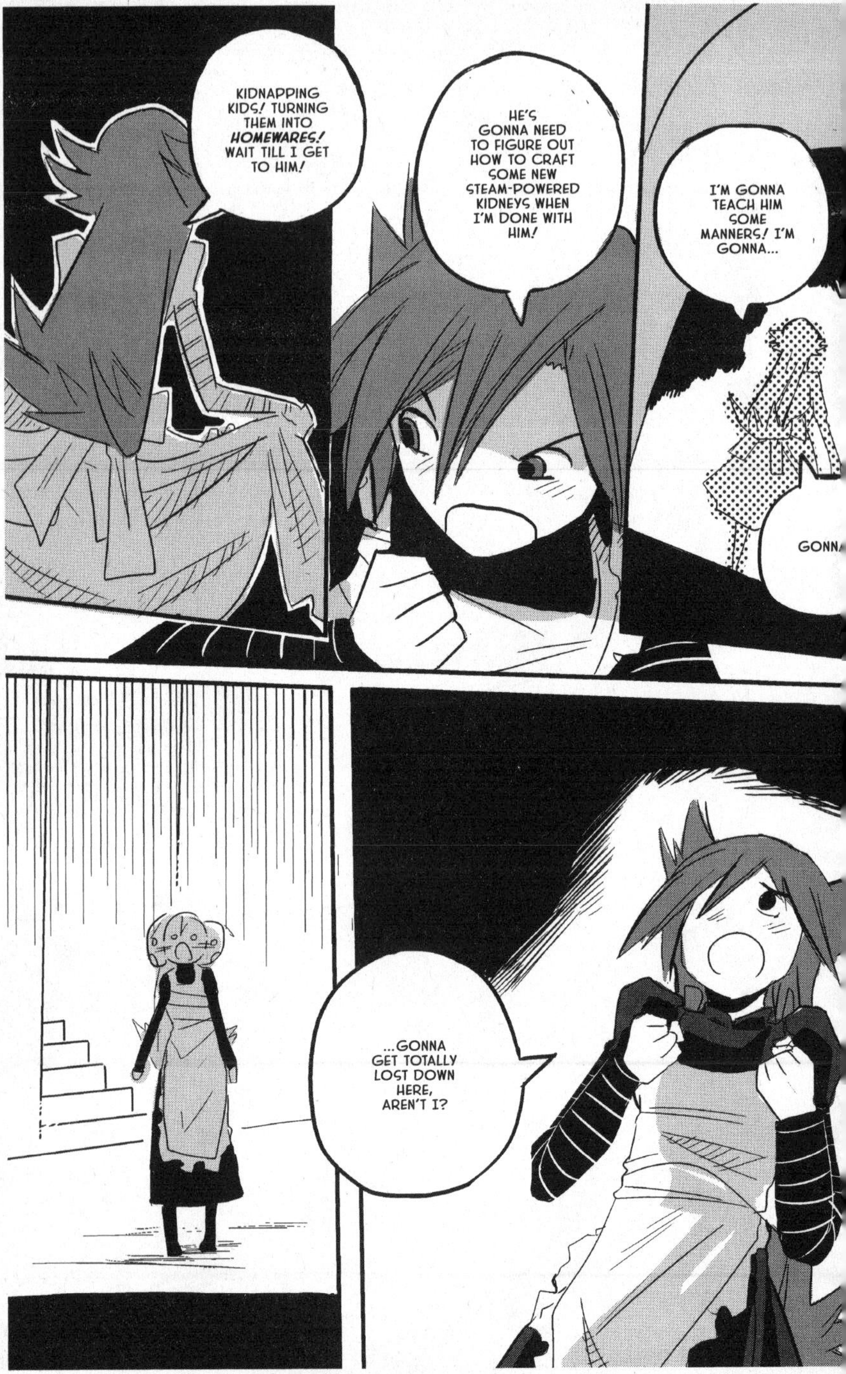
KIDNAPPING KIDS! TURNING THEM INTO **HOMEWARES!** WAIT TILL I GET TO HIM!
HE'S GONNA NEED TO FIGURE OUT HOW TO CRAFT SOME NEW STEAM-POWERED KIDNEYS WHEN I'M DONE WITH HIM!
I'M GONNA TEACH HIM SOME MANNERS! I'M GONNA...
GONNA
...GONNA GET TOTALLY LOST DOWN HERE, AREN'T I?

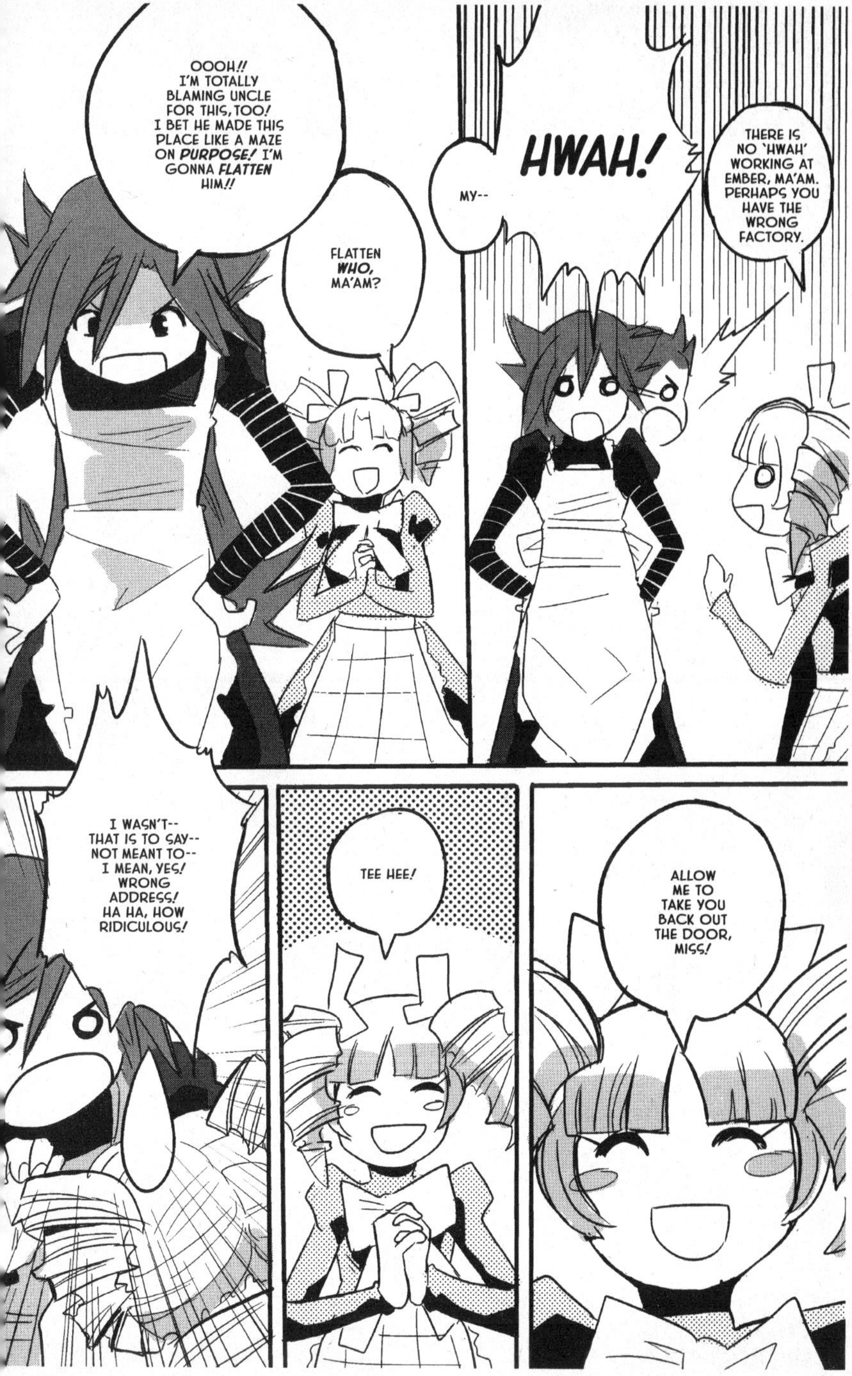
OOOH!! I'M TOTALLY BLAMING UNCLE FOR THIS, TOO! I BET HE MADE THIS PLACE LIKE A MAZE ON *PURPOSE!* I'M GONNA *FLATTEN* HIM!!
FLATTEN *WHO,* MA'AM?
MY--
HWAH!
THERE IS NO 'HWAH' WORKING AT EMBER, MA'AM. PERHAPS YOU HAVE THE WRONG FACTORY.
I WASN'T-- THAT IS TO SAY-- NOT MEANT TO-- I MEAN, YES! WRONG ADDRESS! HA HA, HOW RIDICULOUS!
TEE HEE!
ALLOW ME TO TAKE YOU BACK OUT THE DOOR, MISS!

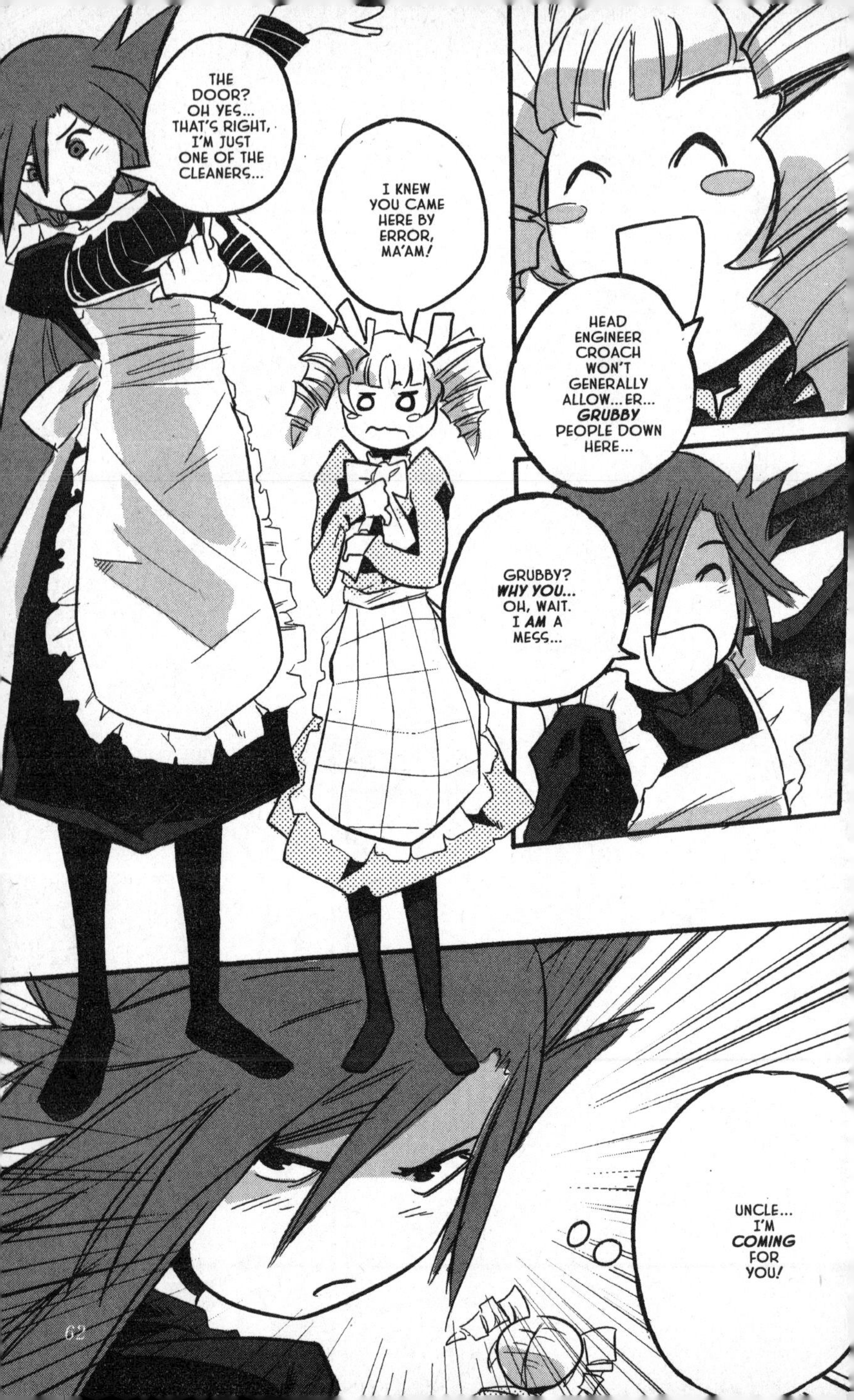
THE DOOR? OH YES... THAT'S RIGHT, I'M JUST ONE OF THE CLEANERS...
I KNEW YOU CAME HERE BY ERROR, MA'AM!
HEAD ENGINEER CROACH WON'T GENERALLY ALLOW... ER... ***GRUBBY*** PEOPLE DOWN HERE...
GRUBBY? ***WHY YOU...*** OH, WAIT. I ***AM*** A MESS...
UNCLE... I'M ***COMING*** FOR YOU!

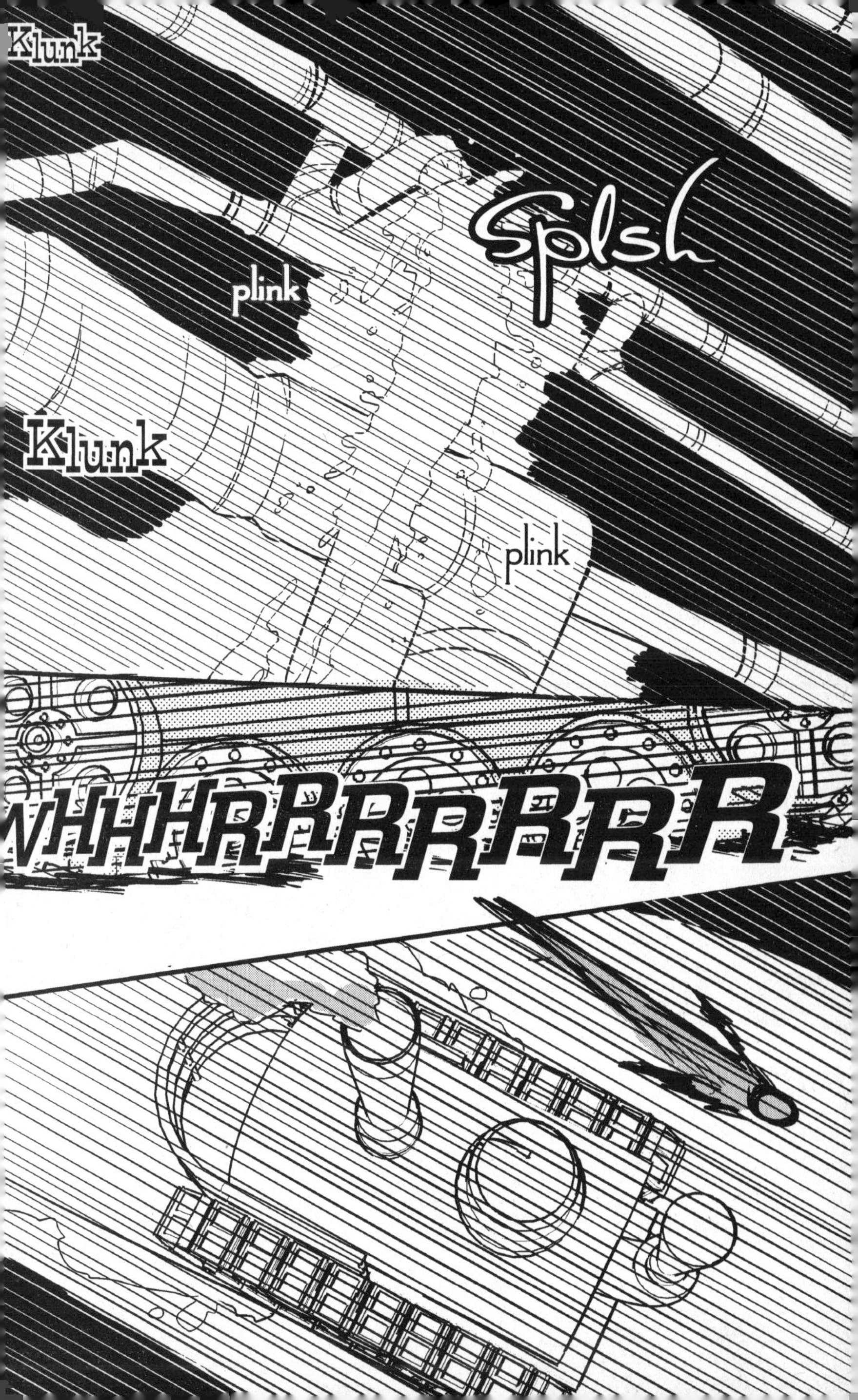
Klunk
Splsh
plink
Klunk
plink
WHHRRRRRRR

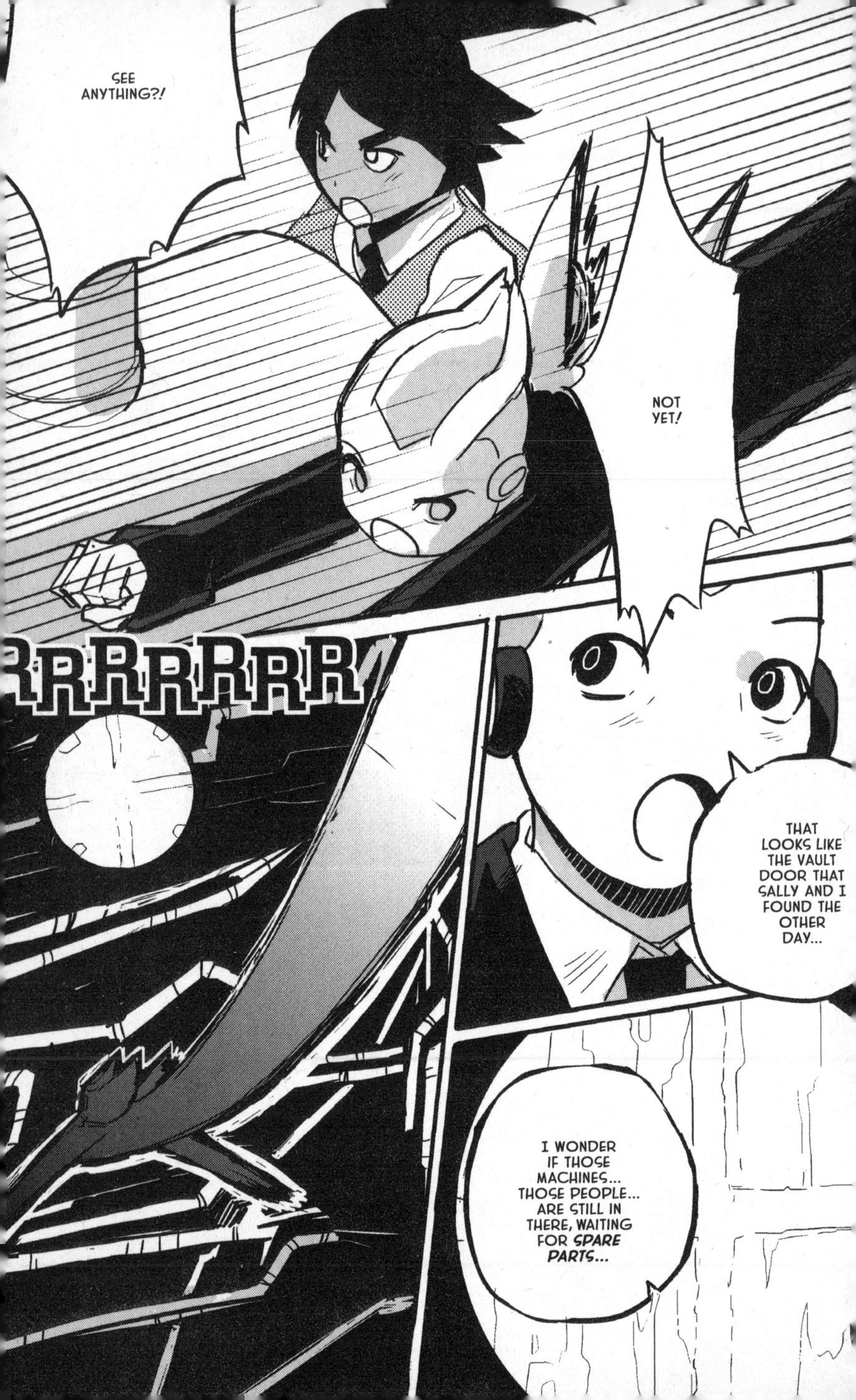
SEE ANYTHING?!
NOT YET!
RRRRRRRR
THAT LOOKS LIKE THE VAULT DOOR THAT SALLY AND I FOUND THE OTHER DAY...
I WONDER IF THOSE MACHINES... THOSE PEOPLE... ARE STILL IN THERE, WAITING FOR *SPARE PARTS*...

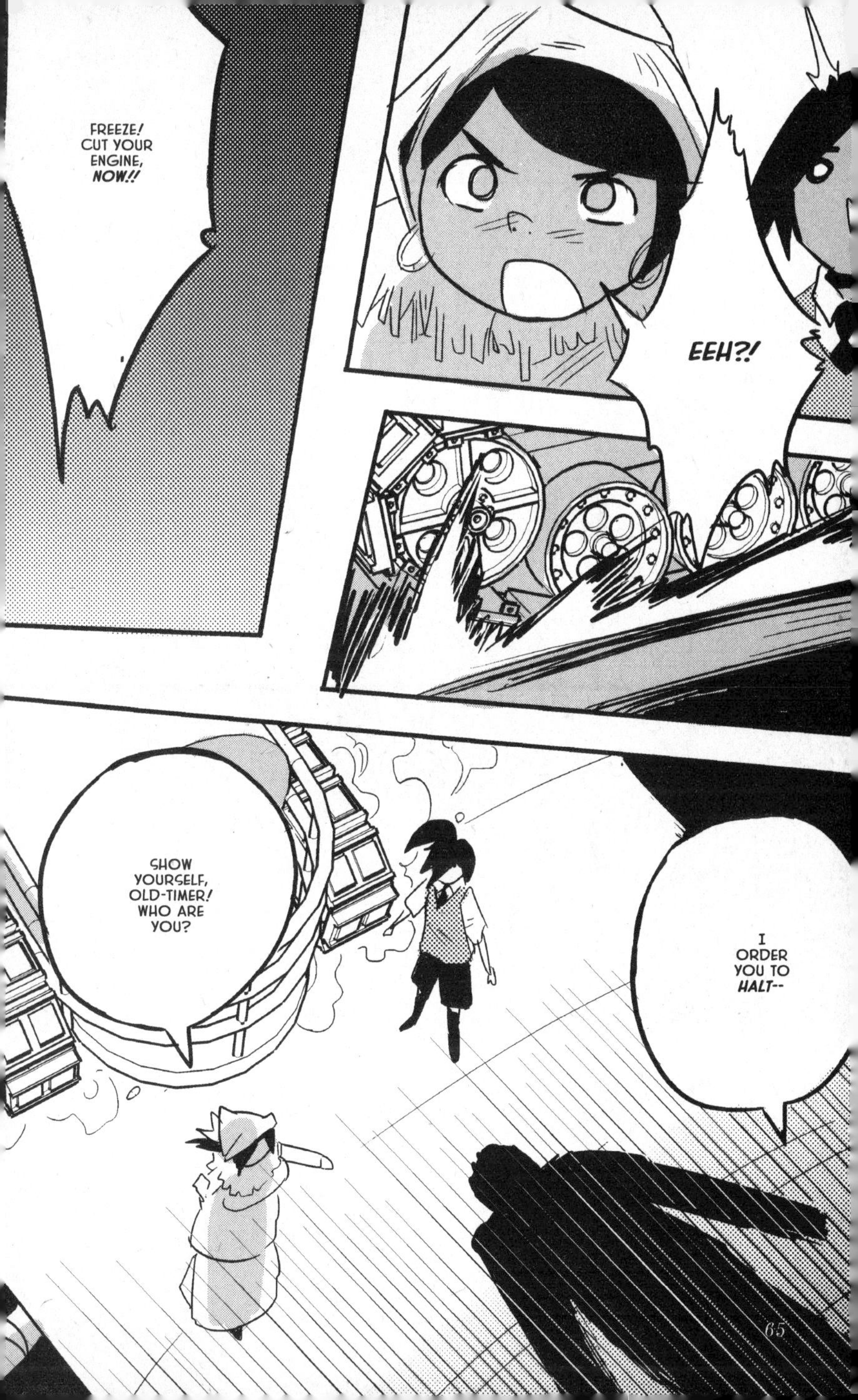

FREEZE! CUT YOUR ENGINE, *NOW!!*
EEH?!
SHOW YOURSELF, OLD-TIMER! WHO ARE YOU?
I ORDER YOU TO *HALT--*

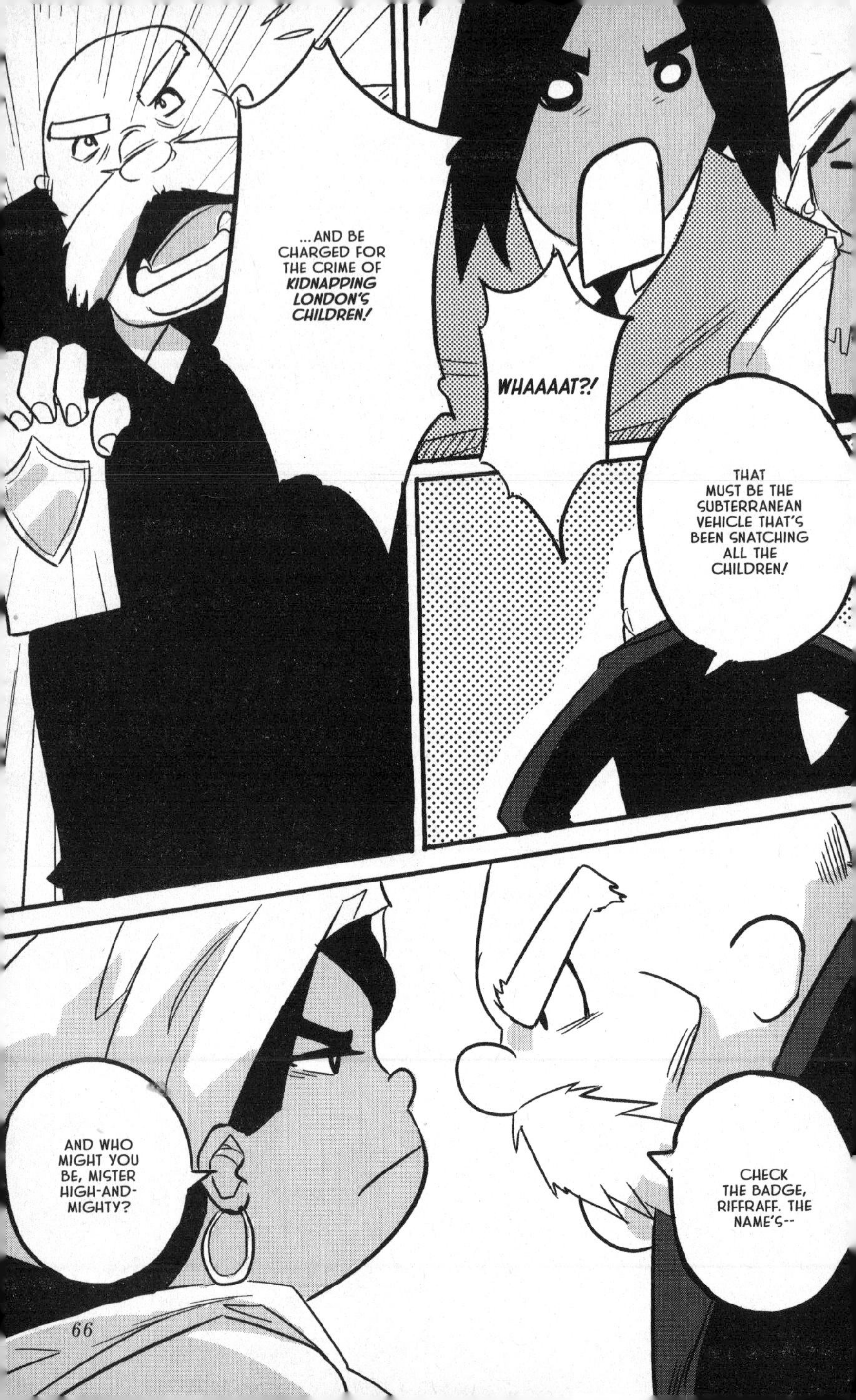
...AND BE CHARGED FOR THE CRIME OF KIDNAPPING LONDON'S CHILDREN!
WHAAAAT?!
THAT MUST BE THE SUBTERRANEAN VEHICLE THAT'S BEEN SNATCHING ALL THE CHILDREN!
AND WHO MIGHT YOU BE, MISTER HIGH-AND-MIGHTY?
CHECK THE BADGE, RIFFRAFF. THE NAME'S--

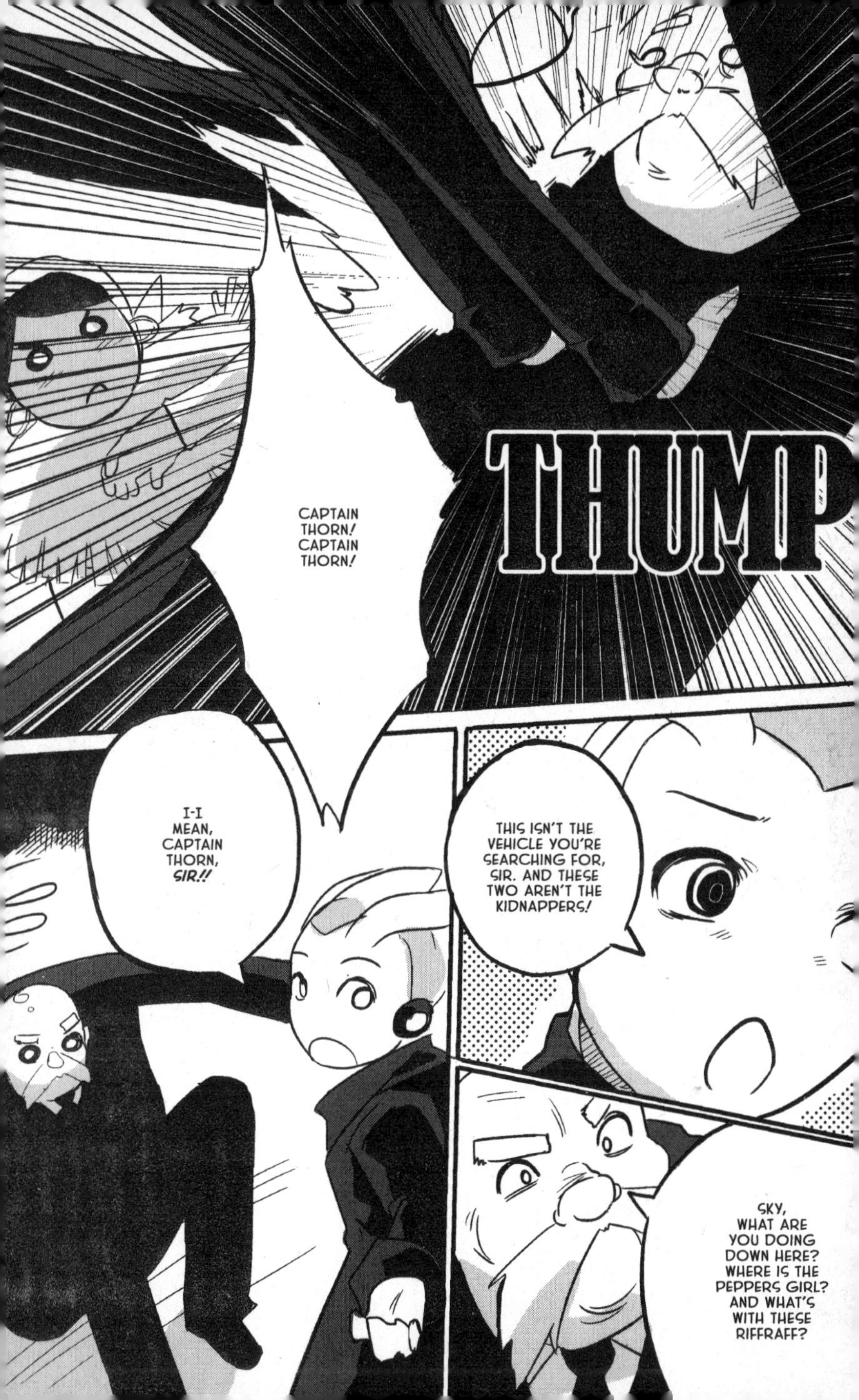
THUMP
CAPTAIN THORN! CAPTAIN THORN!
I-I MEAN, CAPTAIN THORN, *SIR!!*
THIS ISN'T THE VEHICLE YOU'RE SEARCHING FOR, SIR. AND THESE TWO AREN'T THE KIDNAPPERS!
SKY, WHAT ARE YOU DOING DOWN HERE? WHERE IS THE PEPPERS GIRL? AND WHAT'S WITH THESE RIFFRAFF?

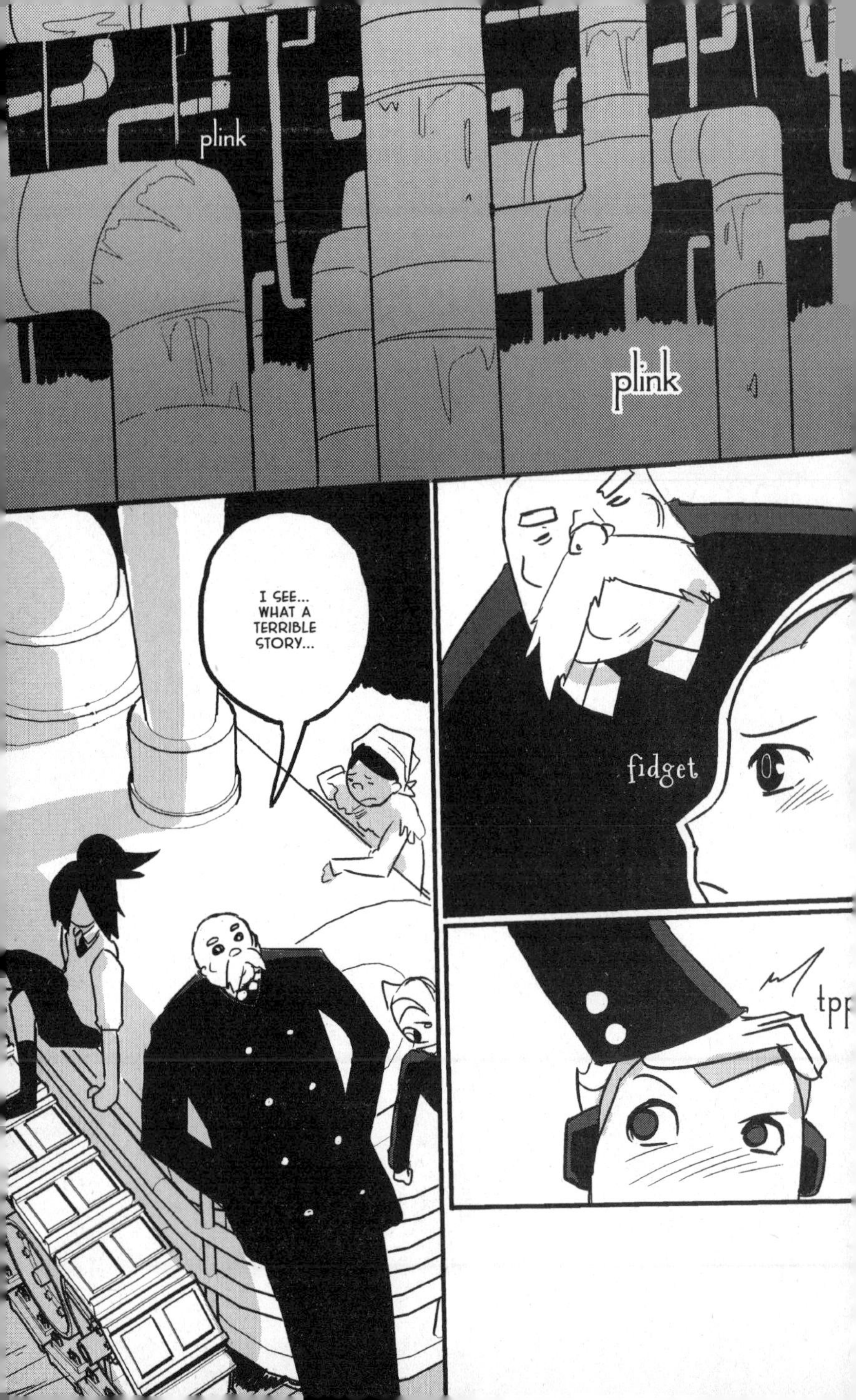
plink
plink
I SEE... WHAT A TERRIBLE STORY...
fidget
tpp

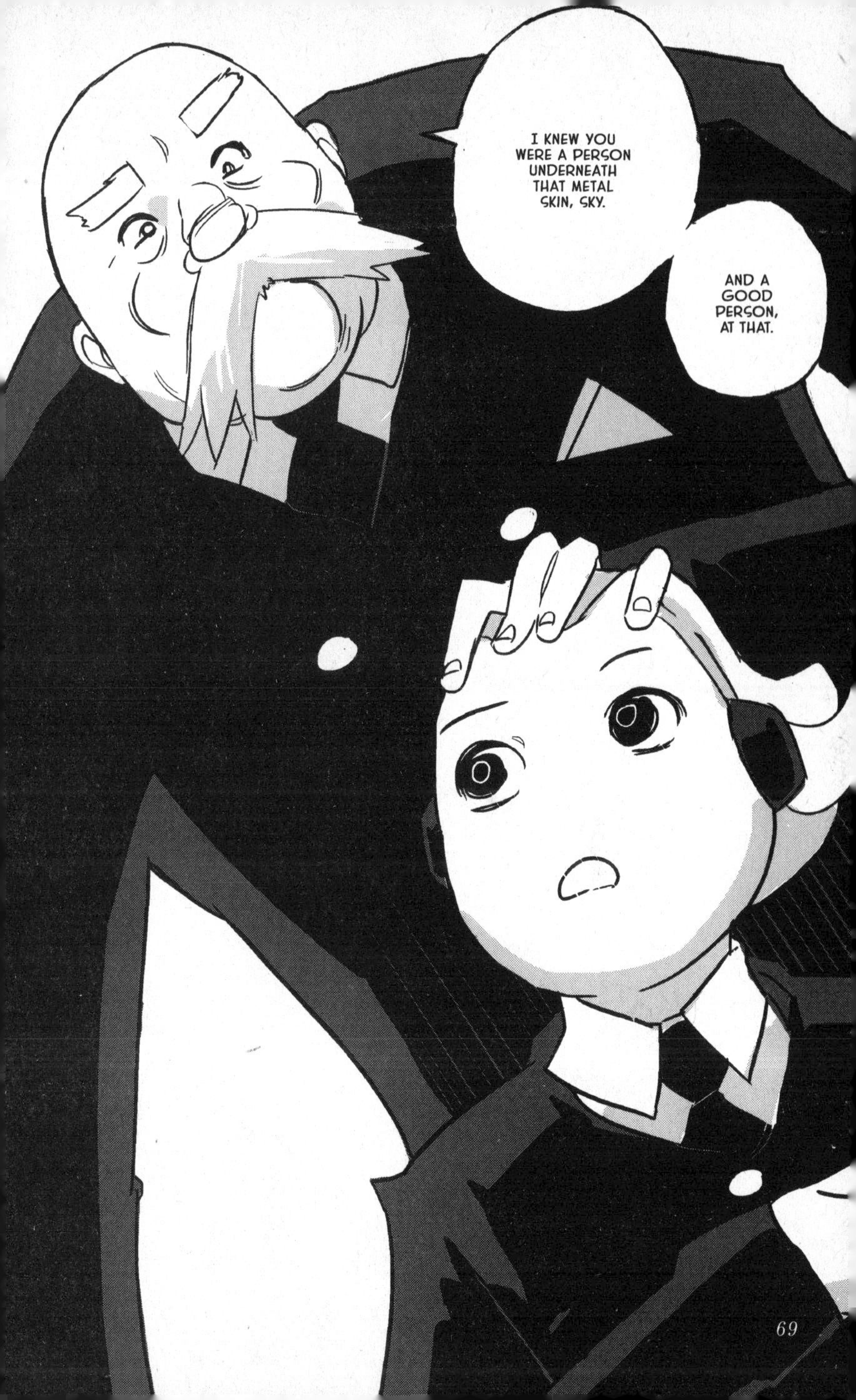
I KNEW YOU WERE A PERSON UNDERNEATH THAT METAL SKIN, SKY.
AND A GOOD PERSON, AT THAT.

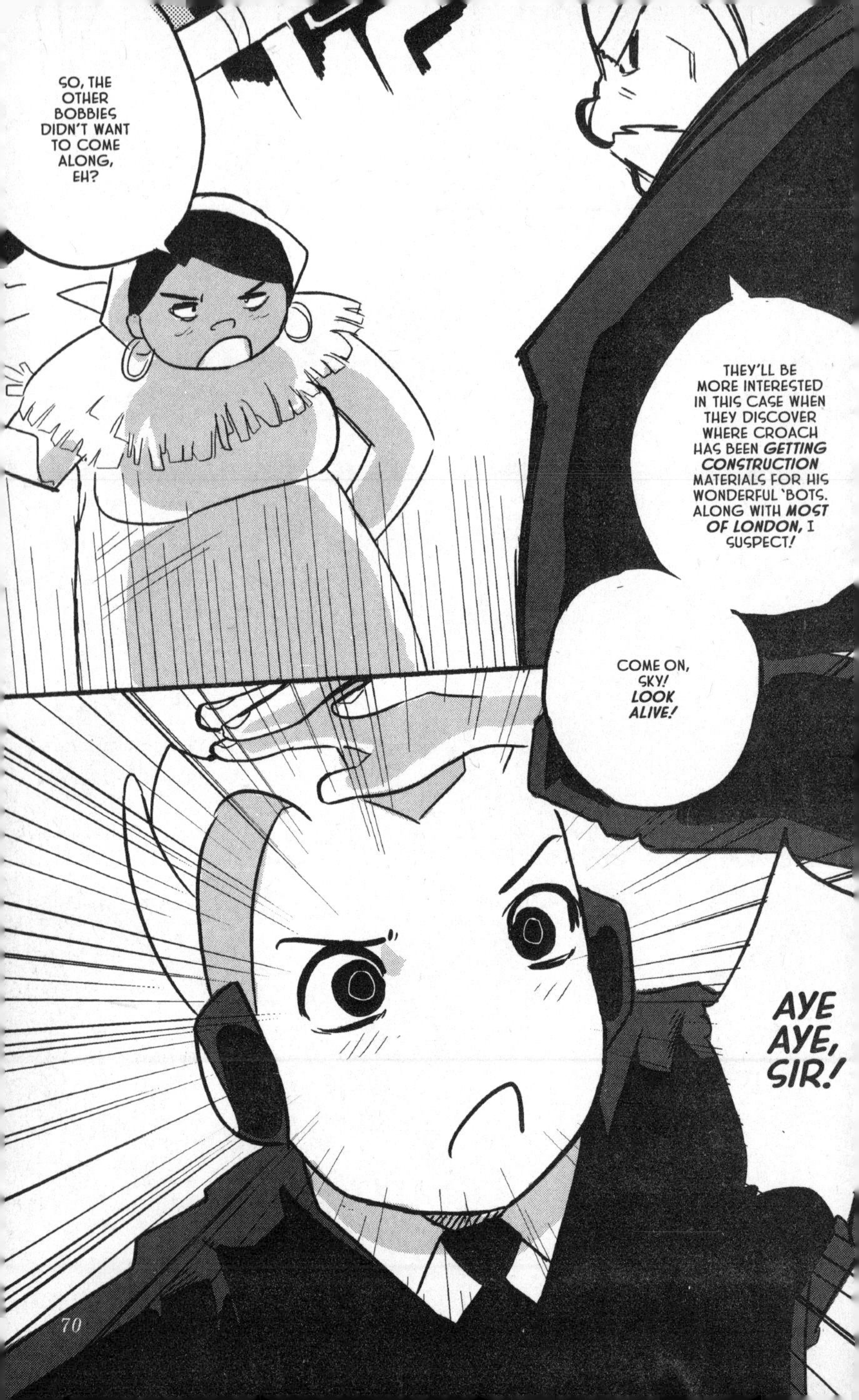
SO, THE OTHER BOBBIES DIDN'T WANT TO COME ALONG, EH?
THEY'LL BE MORE INTERESTED IN THIS CASE WHEN THEY DISCOVER WHERE CROACH HAS BEEN *GETTING CONSTRUCTION* MATERIALS FOR HIS WONDERFUL 'BOTS. ALONG WITH *MOST OF LONDON*, I SUSPECT!
COME ON, SKY! *LOOK ALIVE!*
AYE AYE, SIR!

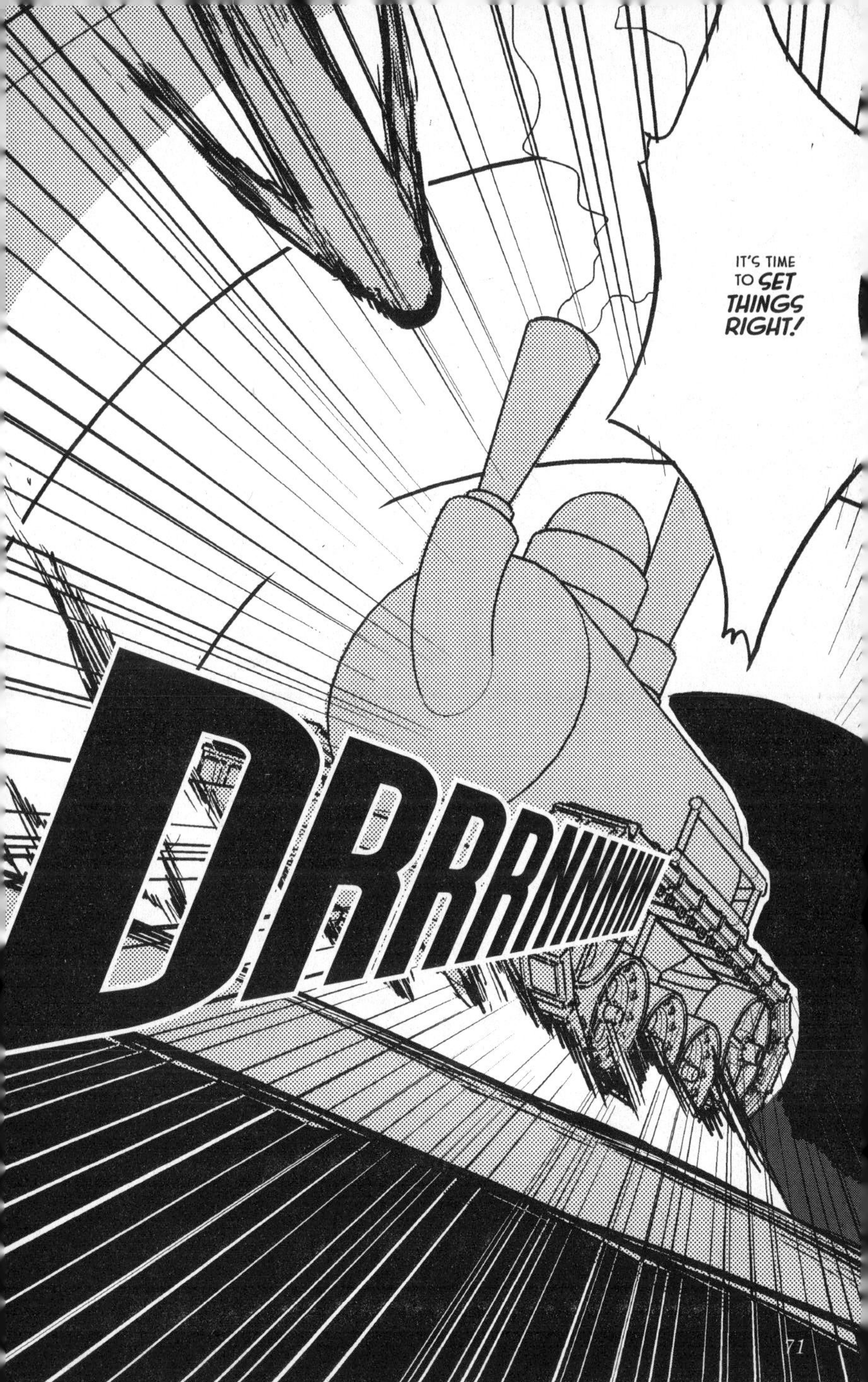
IT'S TIME TO SET THINGS RIGHT!
DRRRNNNNN

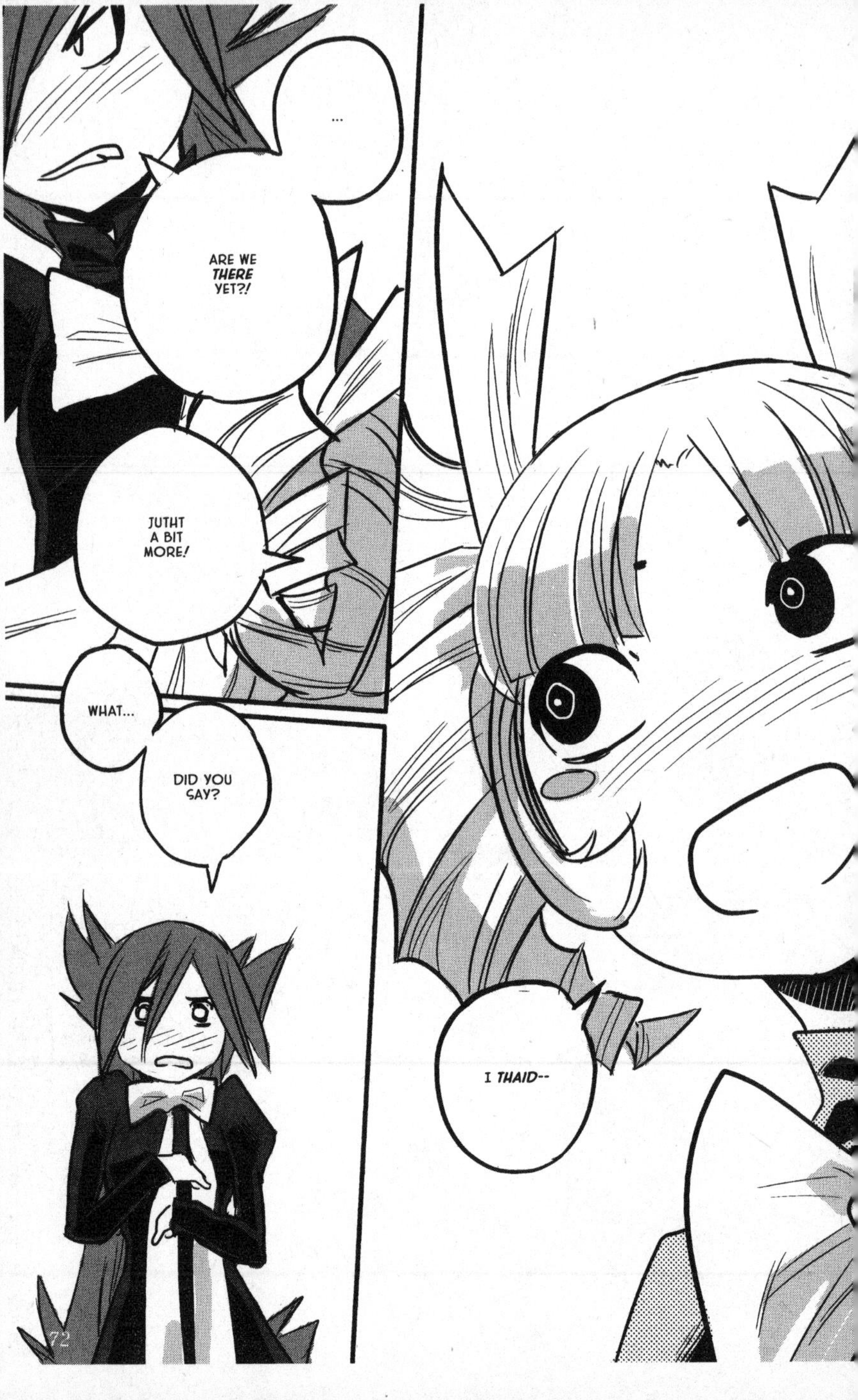
...
ARE WE *THERE* YET?!
JUTHT A BIT MORE!
WHAT...
DID YOU SAY?
I *THAID*--

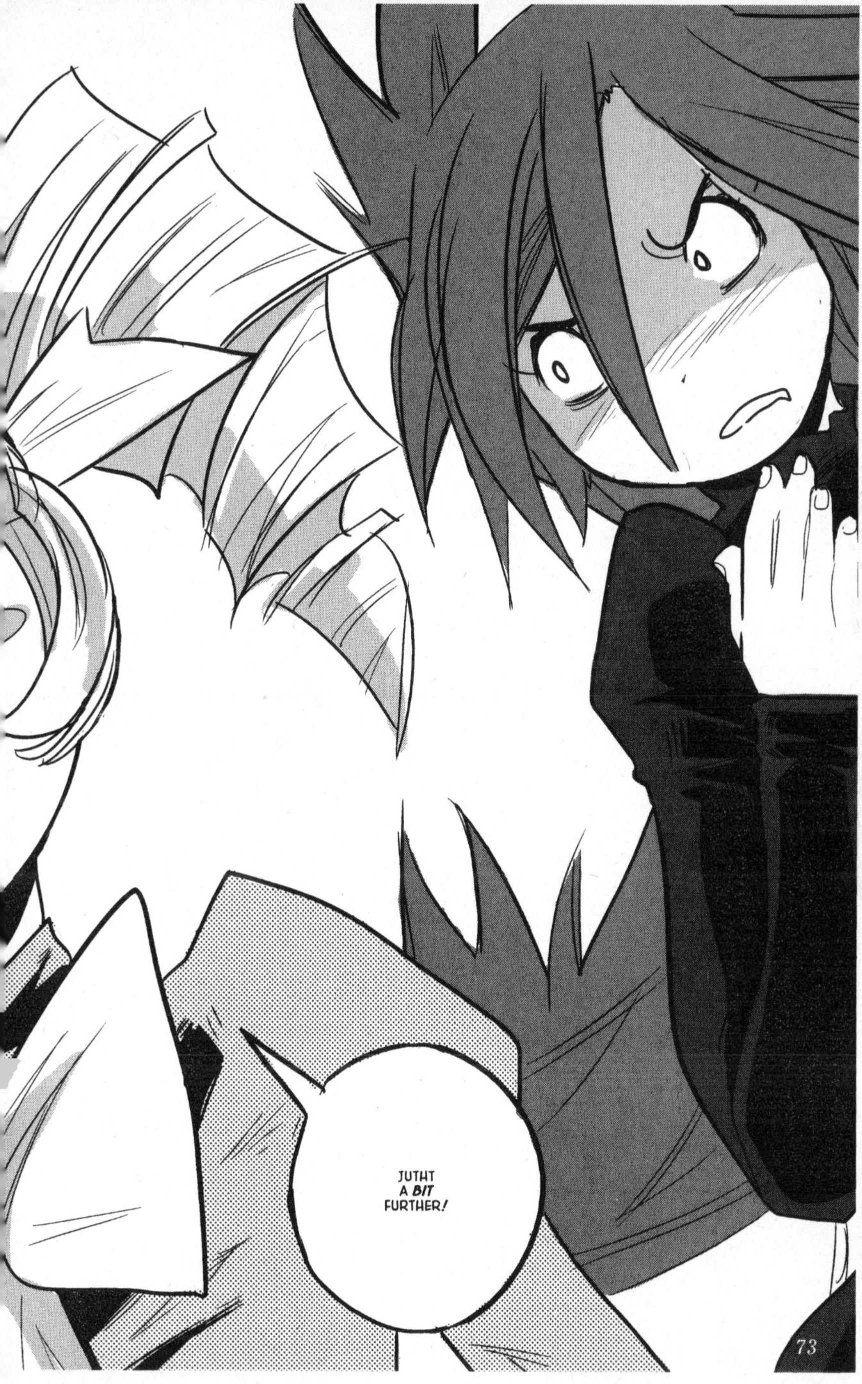
JUTHT A *BIT* FURTHER!

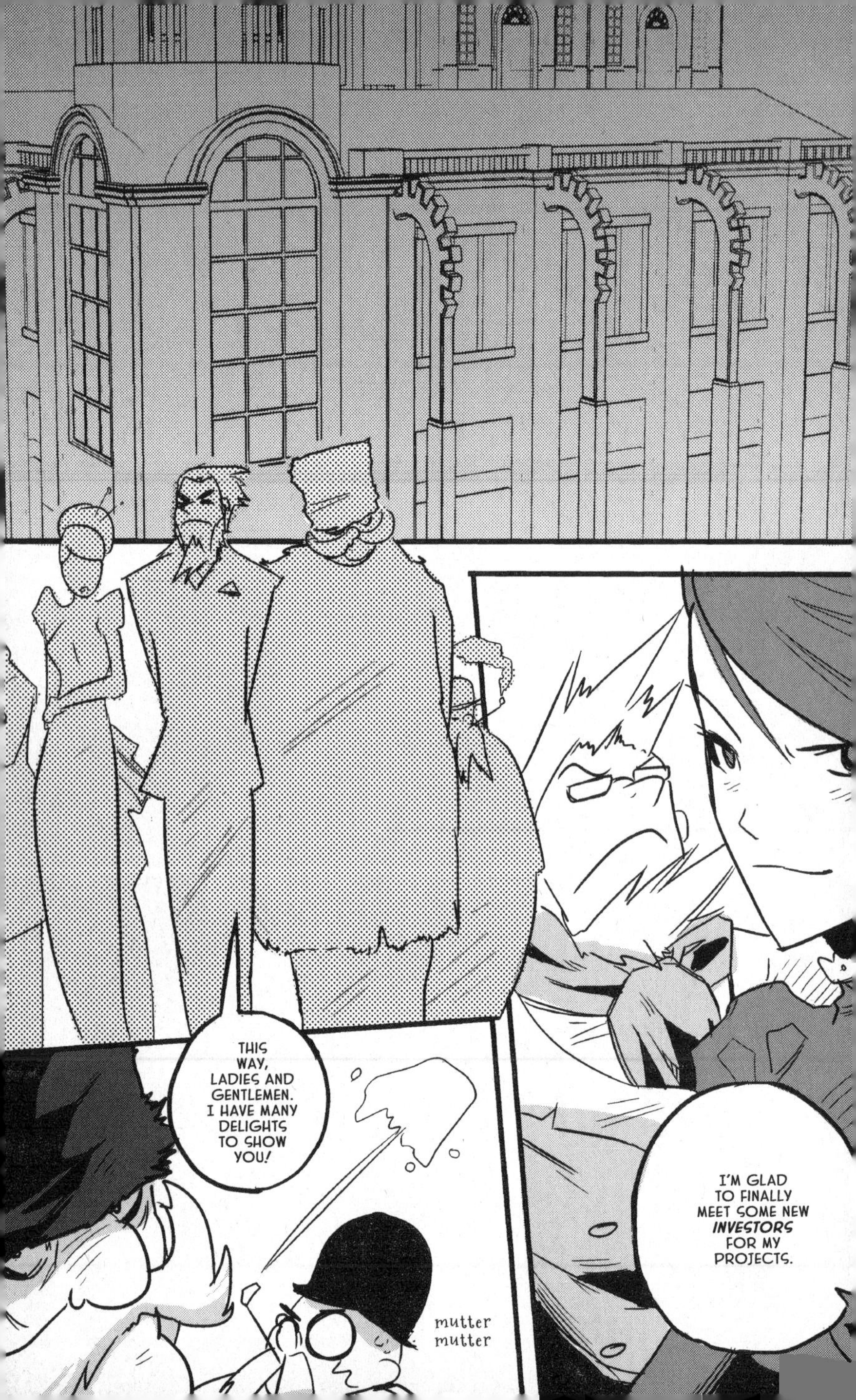
THIS WAY, LADIES AND GENTLEMEN. I HAVE MANY DELIGHTS TO SHOW YOU!
mutter mutter
I'M GLAD TO FINALLY MEET SOME NEW *INVESTORS* FOR MY PROJECTS.

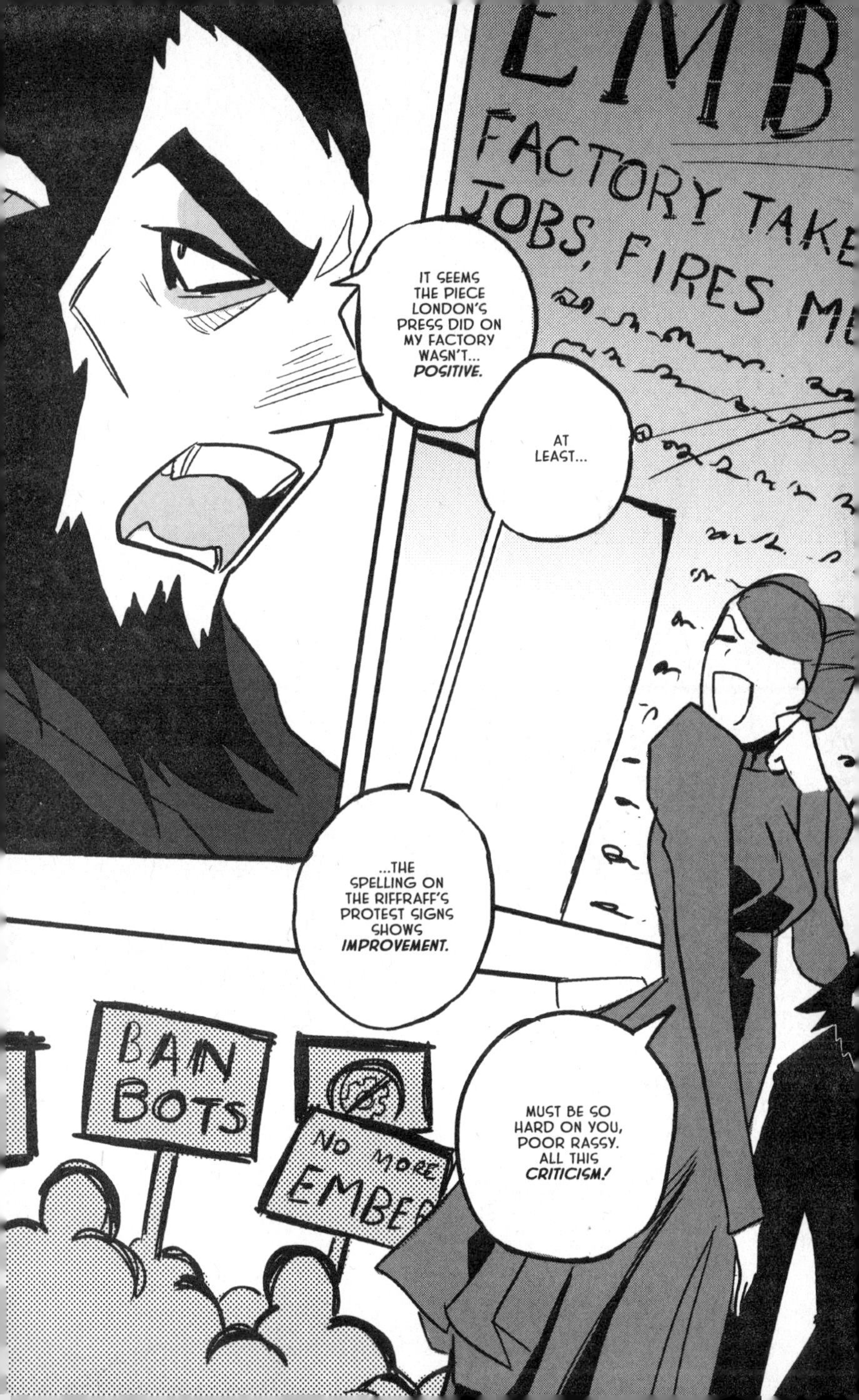
EMB
FACTORY TAKE
JOBS, FIRES ME
IT SEEMS THE PIECE LONDON'S PRESS DID ON MY FACTORY WASN'T... *POSITIVE.*
AT LEAST...
...THE SPELLING ON THE RIFFRAFF'S PROTEST SIGNS SHOWS *IMPROVEMENT.*
BAN BOTS
NO MORE EMBE
MUST BE SO HARD ON YOU, POOR RASSY. ALL THIS *CRITICISM!*

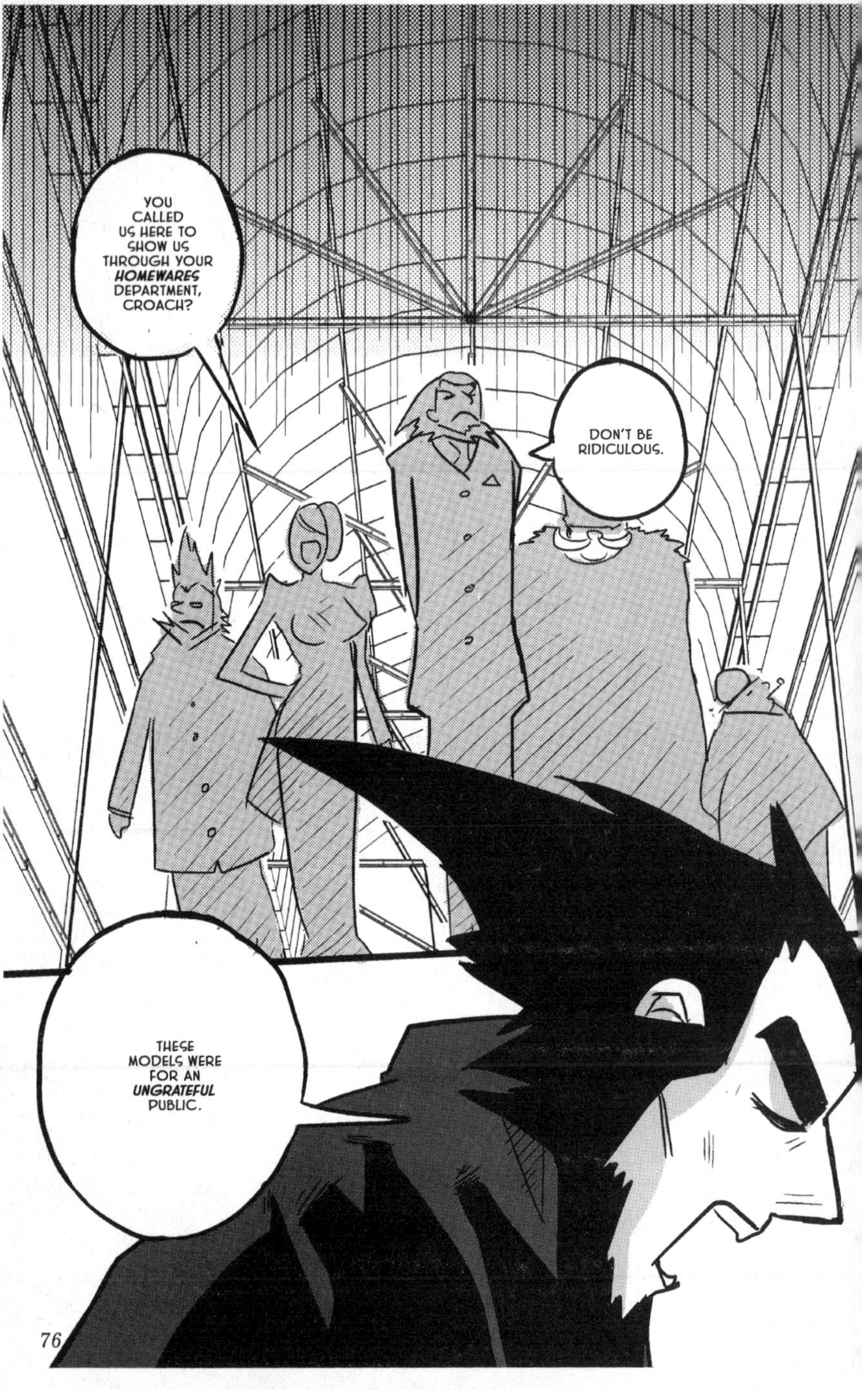
YOU CALLED US HERE TO SHOW US THROUGH YOUR ***HOMEWARES*** DEPARTMENT, CROACH?
DON'T BE RIDICULOUS.
THESE MODELS WERE FOR AN ***UNGRATEFUL*** PUBLIC.

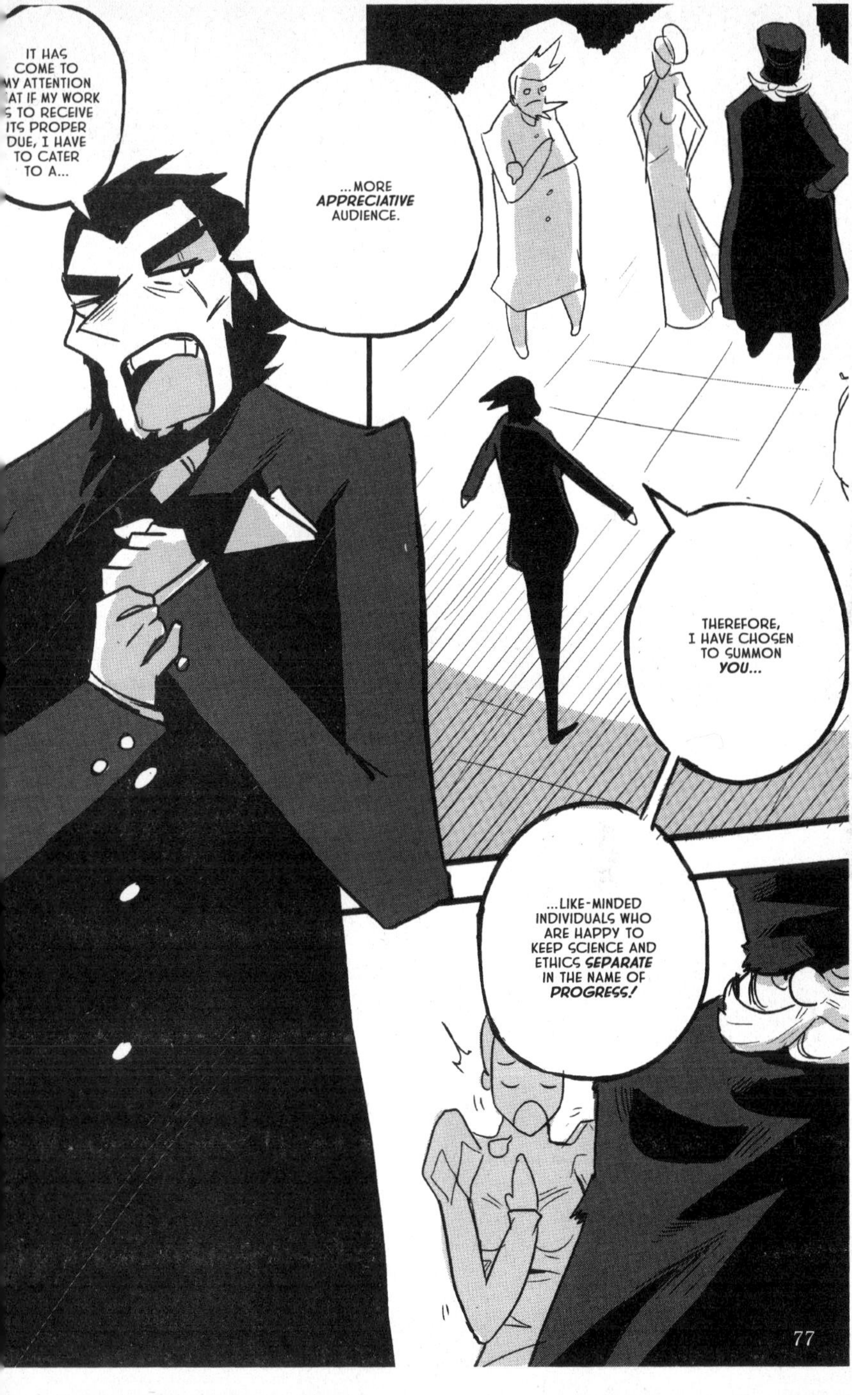
IT HAS COME TO MY ATTENTION THAT IF MY WORK IS TO RECEIVE ITS PROPER DUE, I HAVE TO CATER TO A...
...MORE *APPRECIATIVE* AUDIENCE.
THEREFORE, I HAVE CHOSEN TO SUMMON *YOU...*
...LIKE-MINDED INDIVIDUALS WHO ARE HAPPY TO KEEP SCIENCE AND ETHICS *SEPARATE* IN THE NAME OF *PROGRESS!*

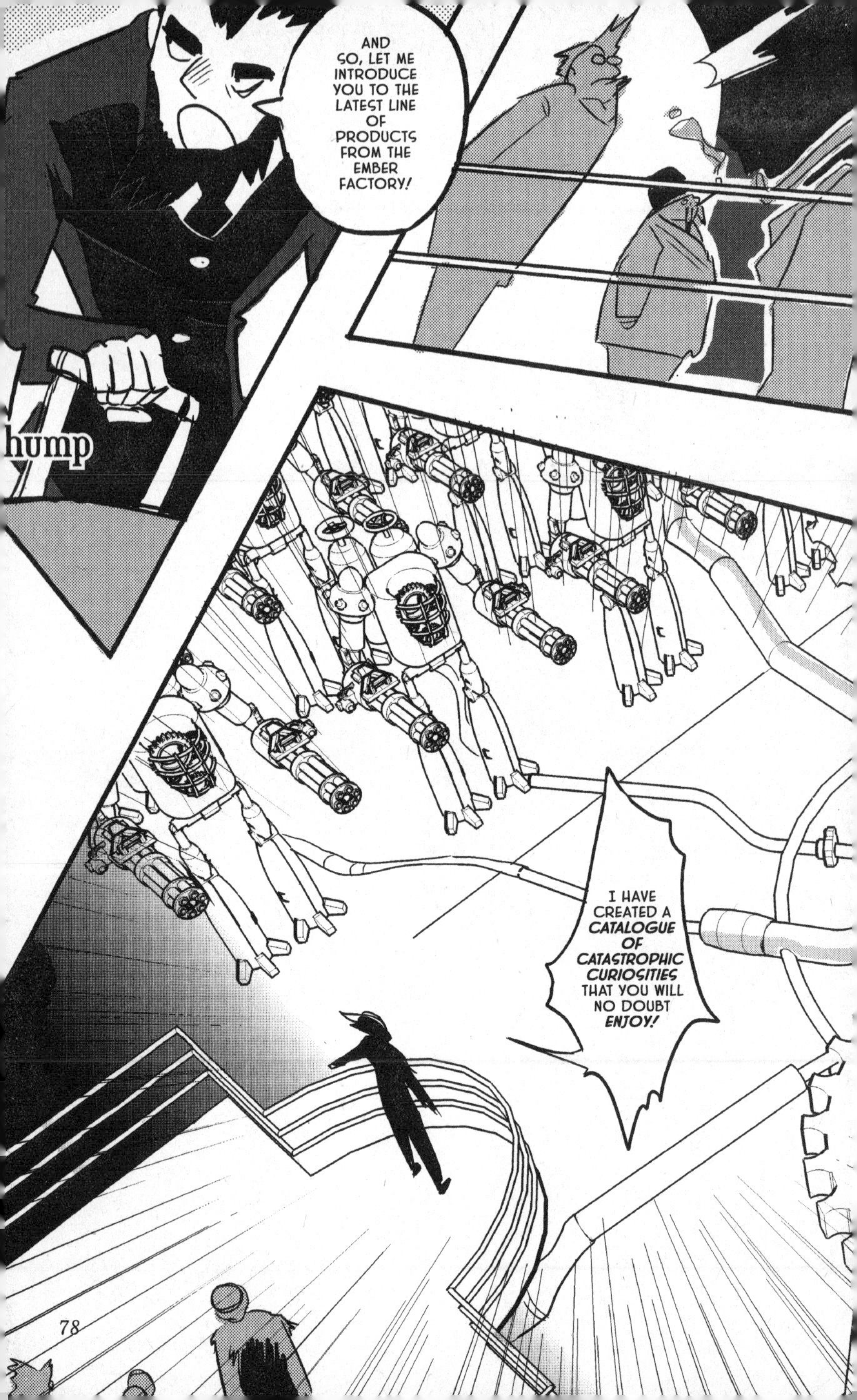
AND SO, LET ME INTRODUCE YOU TO THE LATEST LINE OF PRODUCTS FROM THE EMBER FACTORY!
hump
I HAVE CREATED A ***CATALOGUE OF CATASTROPHIC CURIOSITIES*** THAT YOU WILL NO DOUBT ***ENJOY!***

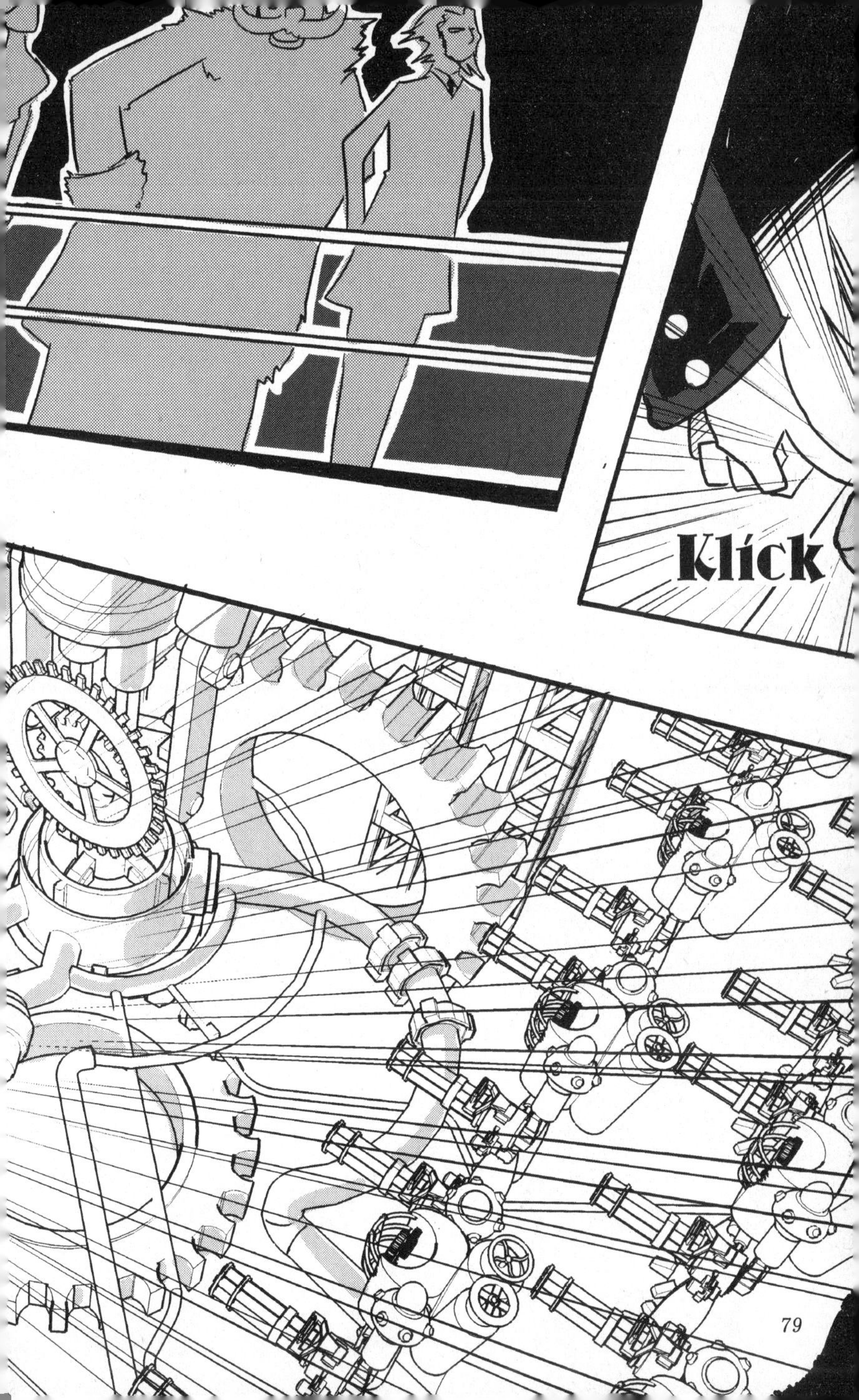
Klick

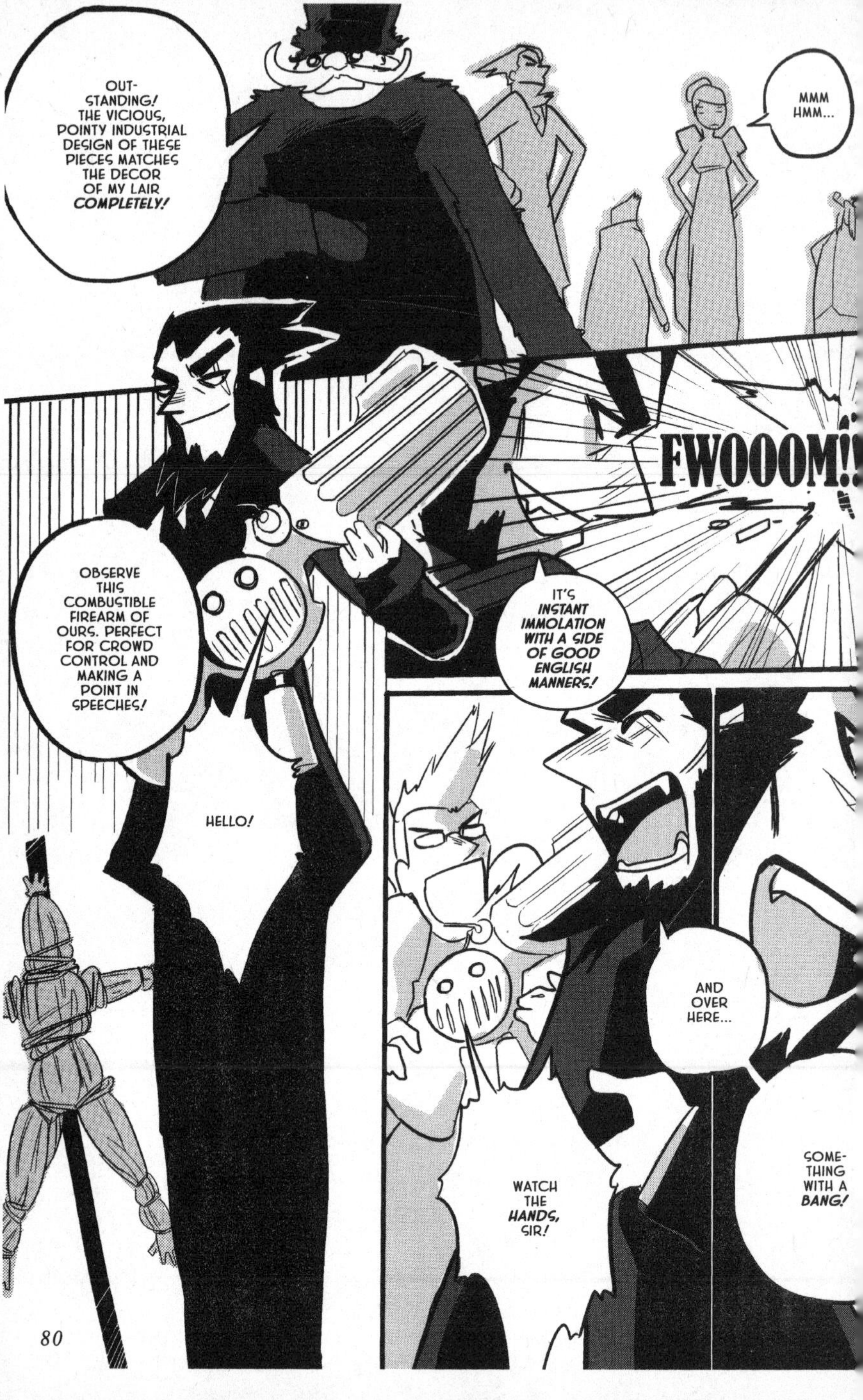
OUT-STANDING! THE VICIOUS, POINTY INDUSTRIAL DESIGN OF THESE PIECES MATCHES THE DECOR OF MY LAIR *COMPLETELY!*
MMM HMM...
FWOOOM!!
OBSERVE THIS COMBUSTIBLE FIREARM OF OURS. PERFECT FOR CROWD CONTROL AND MAKING A POINT IN SPEECHES!
IT'S *INSTANT IMMOLATION WITH A SIDE OF GOOD ENGLISH MANNERS!*
HELLO!
AND OVER HERE...
WATCH THE *HANDS,* SIR!
SOME-THING WITH A *BANG!*

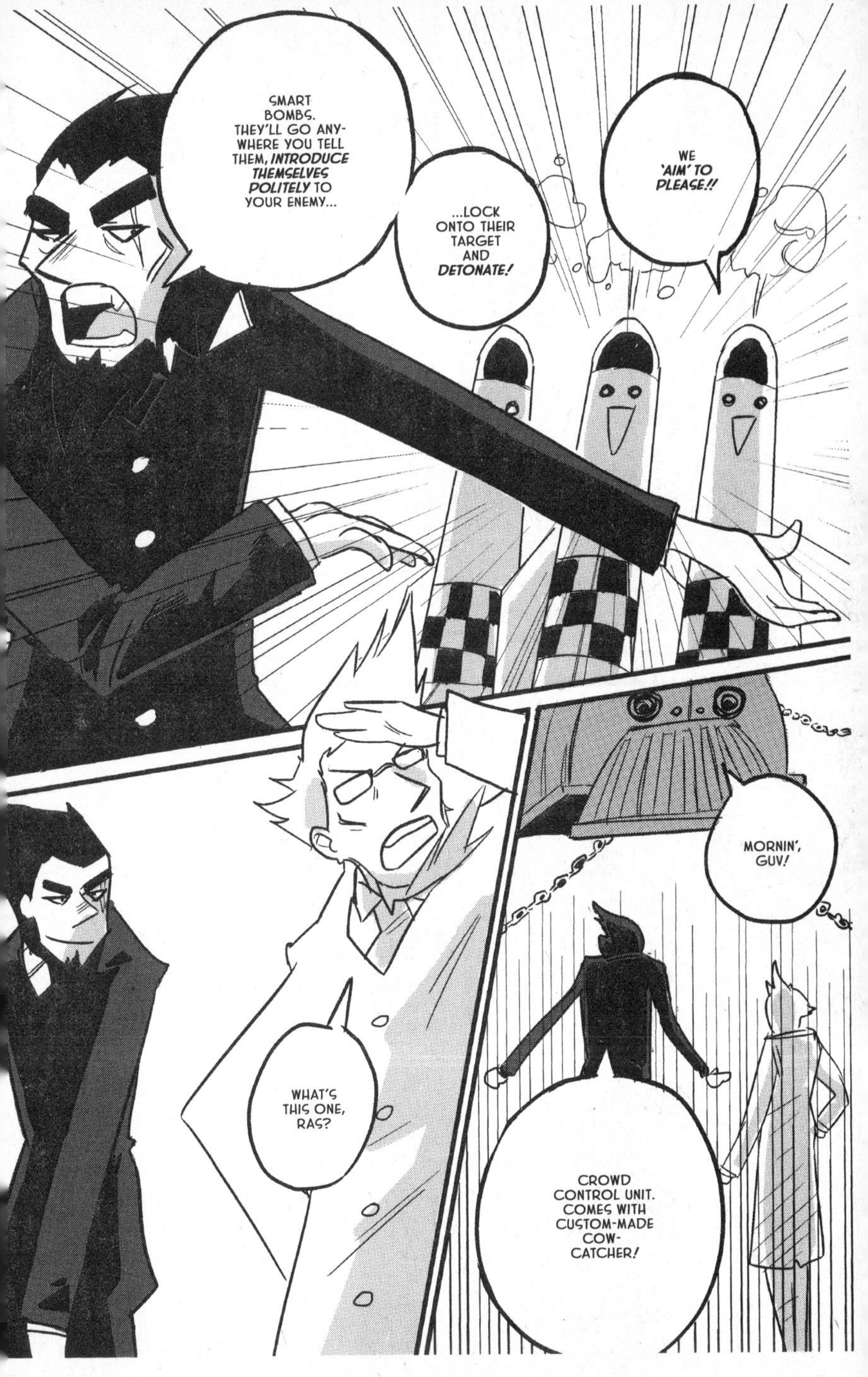
SMART BOMBS. THEY'LL GO ANYWHERE YOU TELL THEM, *INTRODUCE THEMSELVES POLITELY* TO YOUR ENEMY...
...LOCK ONTO THEIR TARGET AND *DETONATE!*
WE *'AIM' TO PLEASE!!*
WHAT'S THIS ONE, RAS?
MORNIN', GUV!
CROWD CONTROL UNIT. COMES WITH CUSTOM-MADE COW-CATCHER!

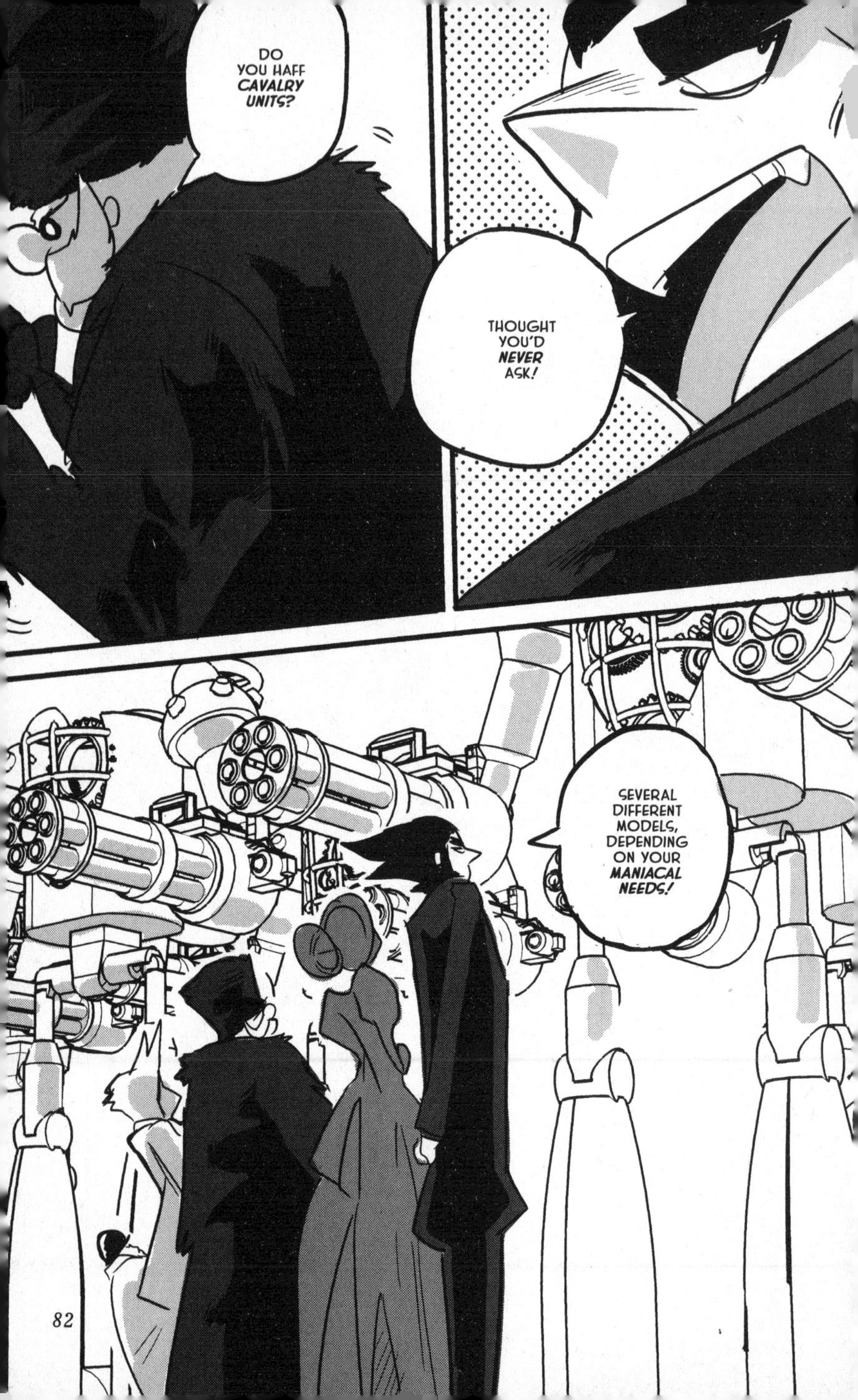

DO YOU HAFF *CAVALRY UNITS?*
THOUGHT YOU'D *NEVER* ASK!
SEVERAL DIFFERENT MODELS, DEPENDING ON YOUR *MANIACAL NEEDS!*

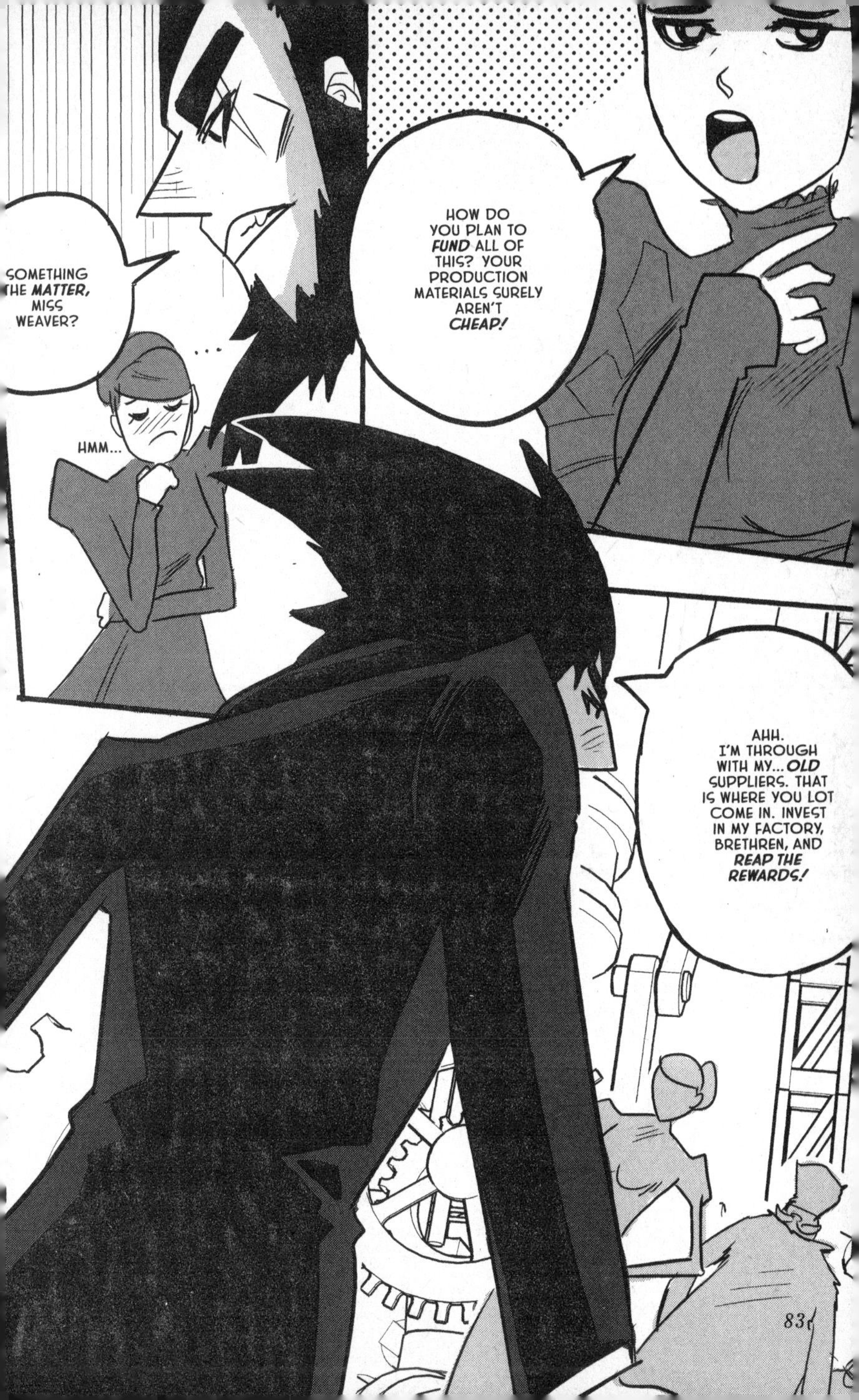
SOMETHING THE MATTER, MISS WEAVER?
...
HMM...
HOW DO YOU PLAN TO FUND ALL OF THIS? YOUR PRODUCTION MATERIALS SURELY AREN'T CHEAP!
AHH. I'M THROUGH WITH MY... OLD SUPPLIERS. THAT IS WHERE YOU LOT COME IN. INVEST IN MY FACTORY, BRETHREN, AND REAP THE REWARDS!

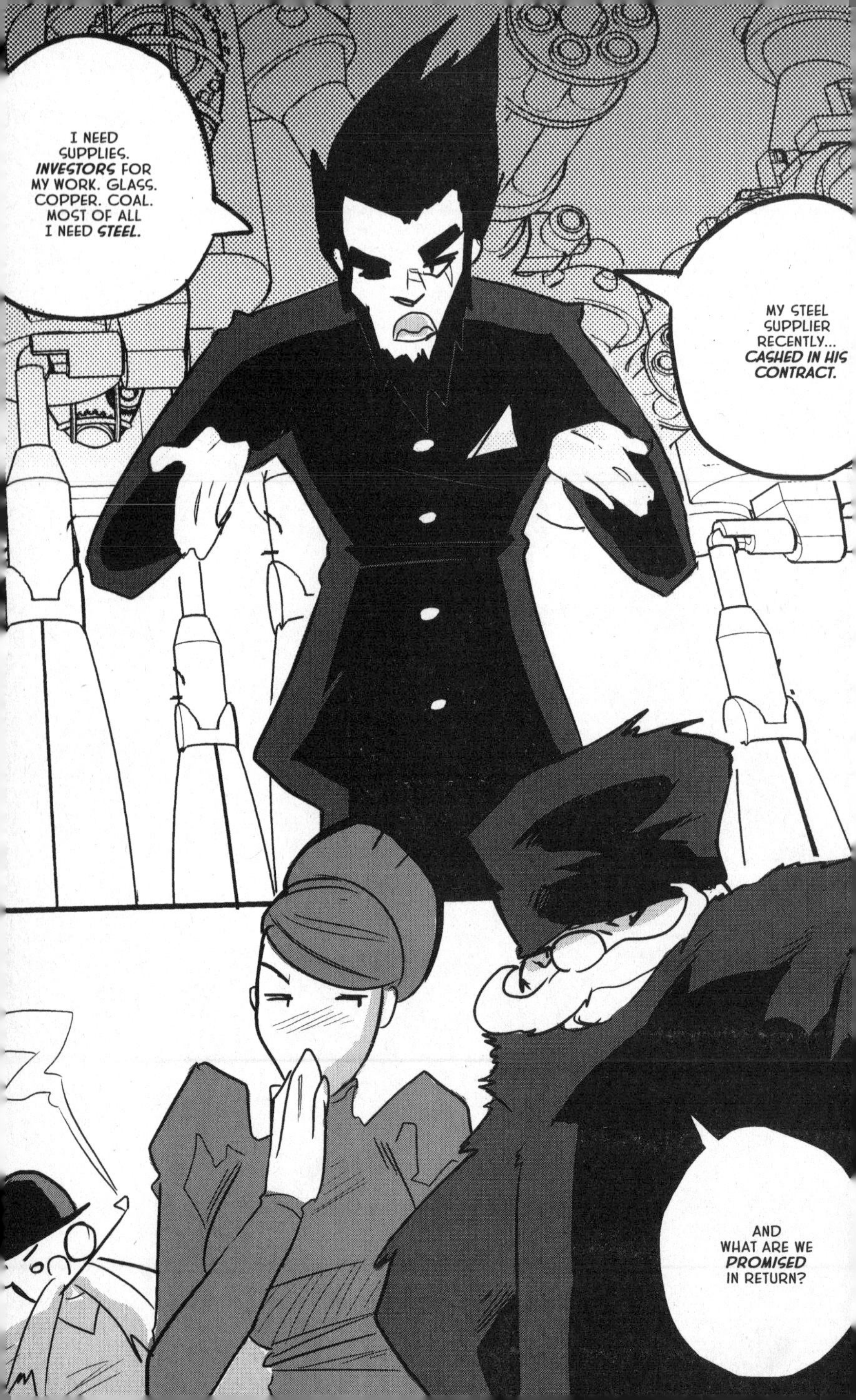
I NEED SUPPLIES. INVESTORS FOR MY WORK. GLASS. COPPER. COAL. MOST OF ALL I NEED STEEL.
MY STEEL SUPPLIER RECENTLY... CASHED IN HIS CONTRACT.
AND WHAT ARE WE PROMISED IN RETURN?

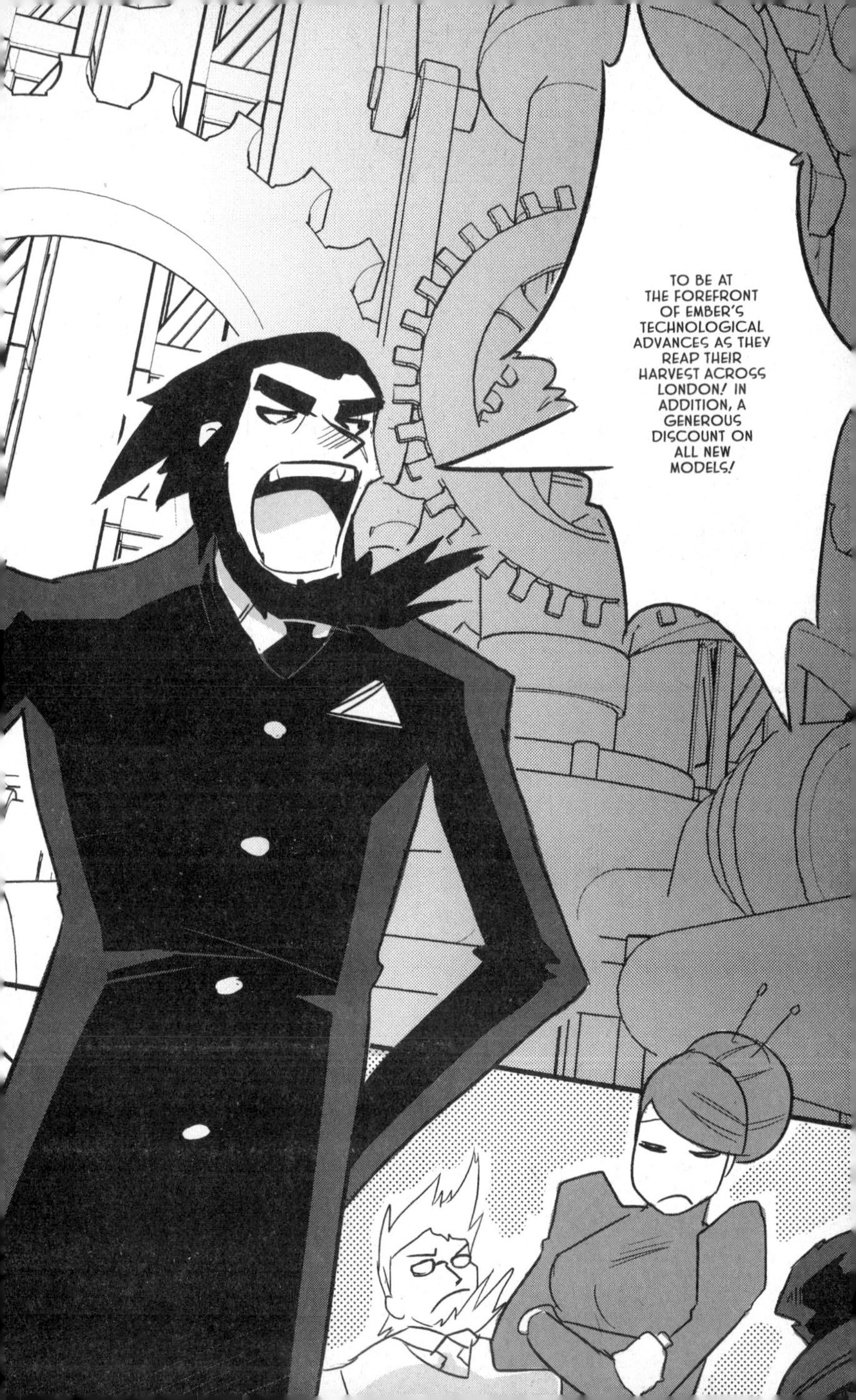
TO BE AT THE FOREFRONT OF EMBER'S TECHNOLOGICAL ADVANCES AS THEY REAP THEIR HARVEST ACROSS LONDON! IN ADDITION, A GENEROUS DISCOUNT ON ALL NEW MODELS!

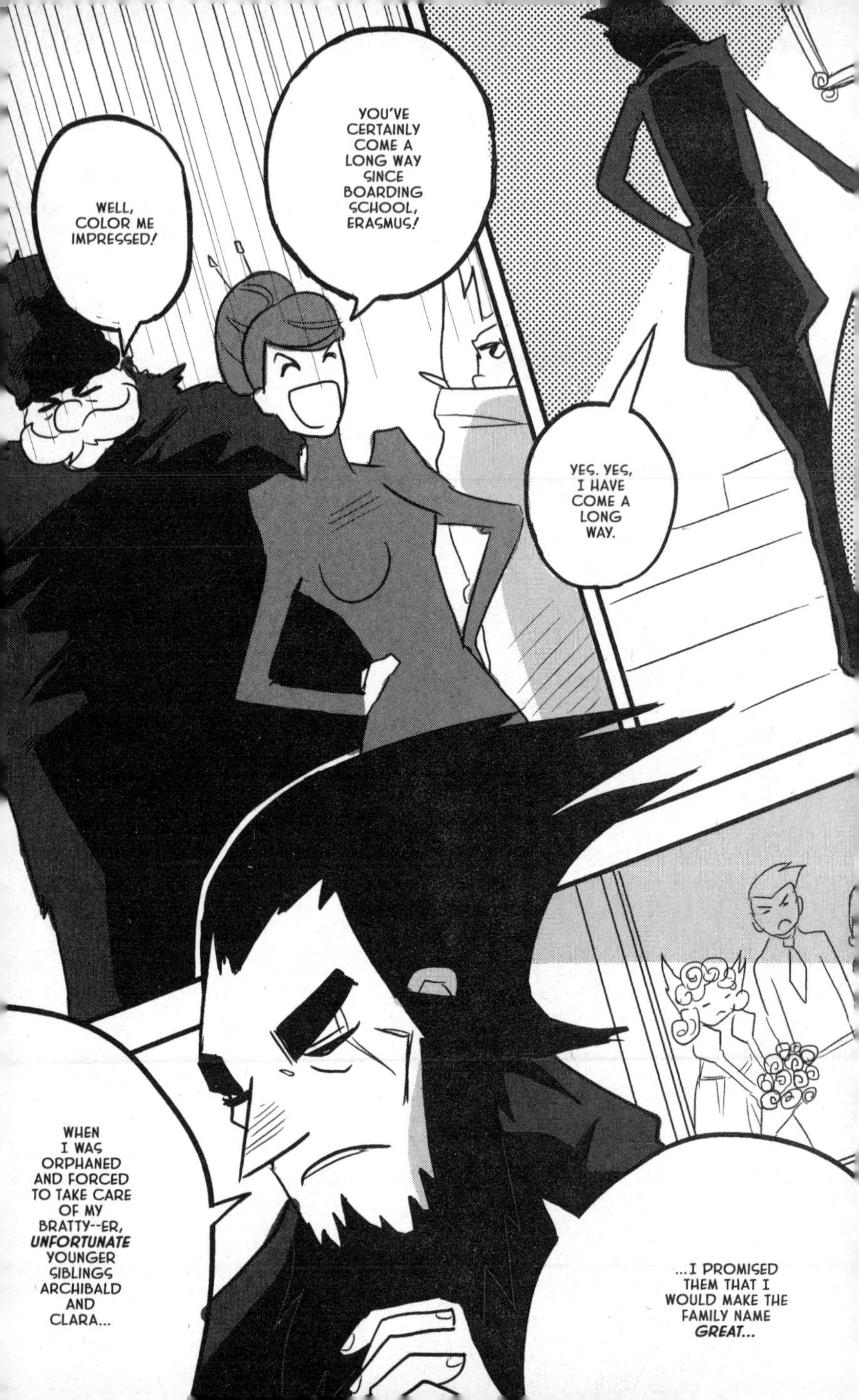
WELL, COLOR ME IMPRESSED!
YOU'VE CERTAINLY COME A LONG WAY SINCE BOARDING SCHOOL, ERASMUS!
YES. YES, I HAVE COME A LONG WAY.
WHEN I WAS ORPHANED AND FORCED TO TAKE CARE OF MY BRATTY--ER, ***UNFORTUNATE*** YOUNGER SIBLINGS ARCHIBALD AND CLARA...
...I PROMISED THEM THAT I WOULD MAKE THE FAMILY NAME ***GREAT...***

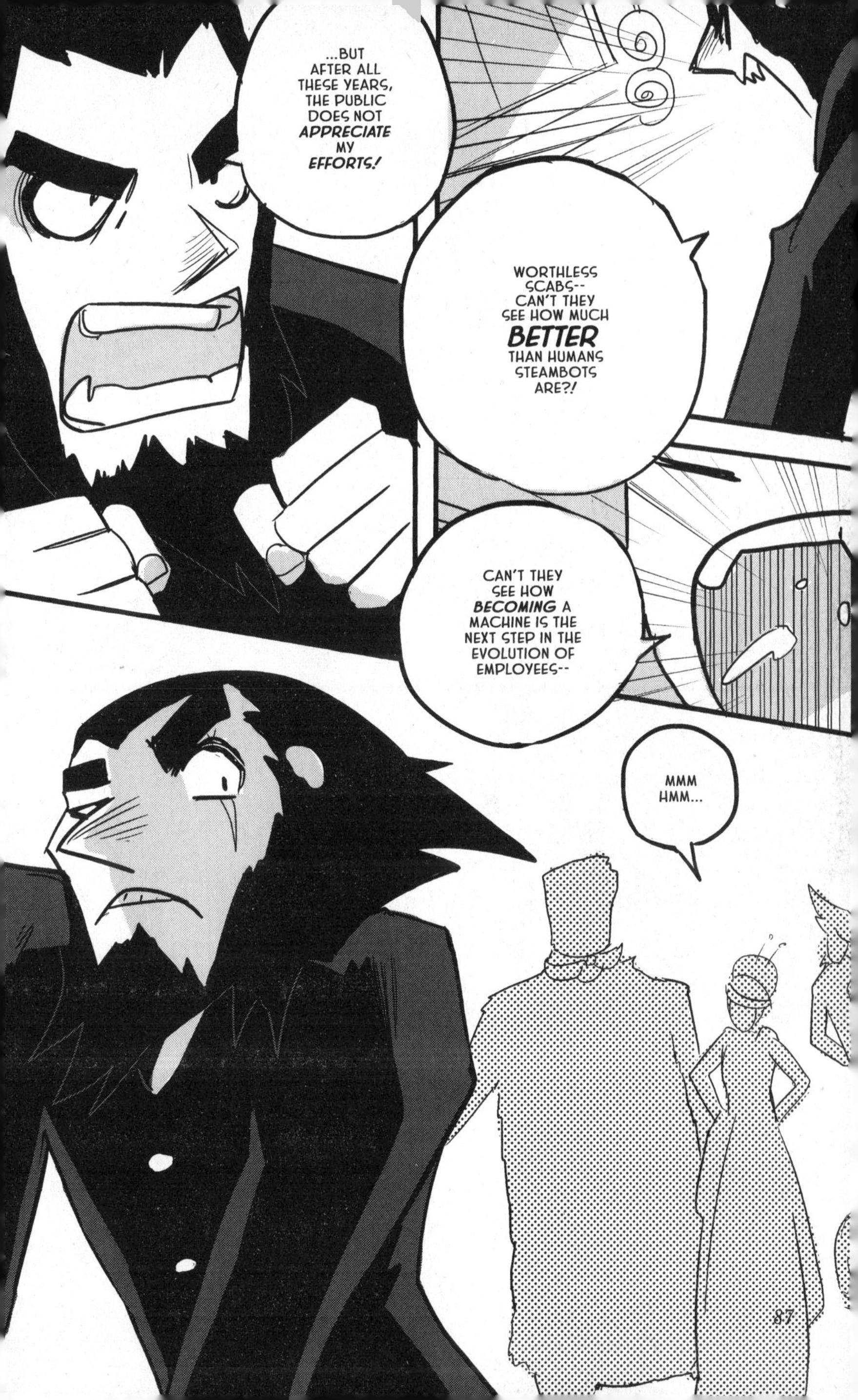
...BUT AFTER ALL THESE YEARS, THE PUBLIC DOES NOT APPRECIATE MY EFFORTS!
WORTHLESS SCABS-- CAN'T THEY SEE HOW MUCH BETTER THAN HUMANS STEAMBOTS ARE?!
CAN'T THEY SEE HOW BECOMING A MACHINE IS THE NEXT STEP IN THE EVOLUTION OF EMPLOYEES--
MMM HMM...

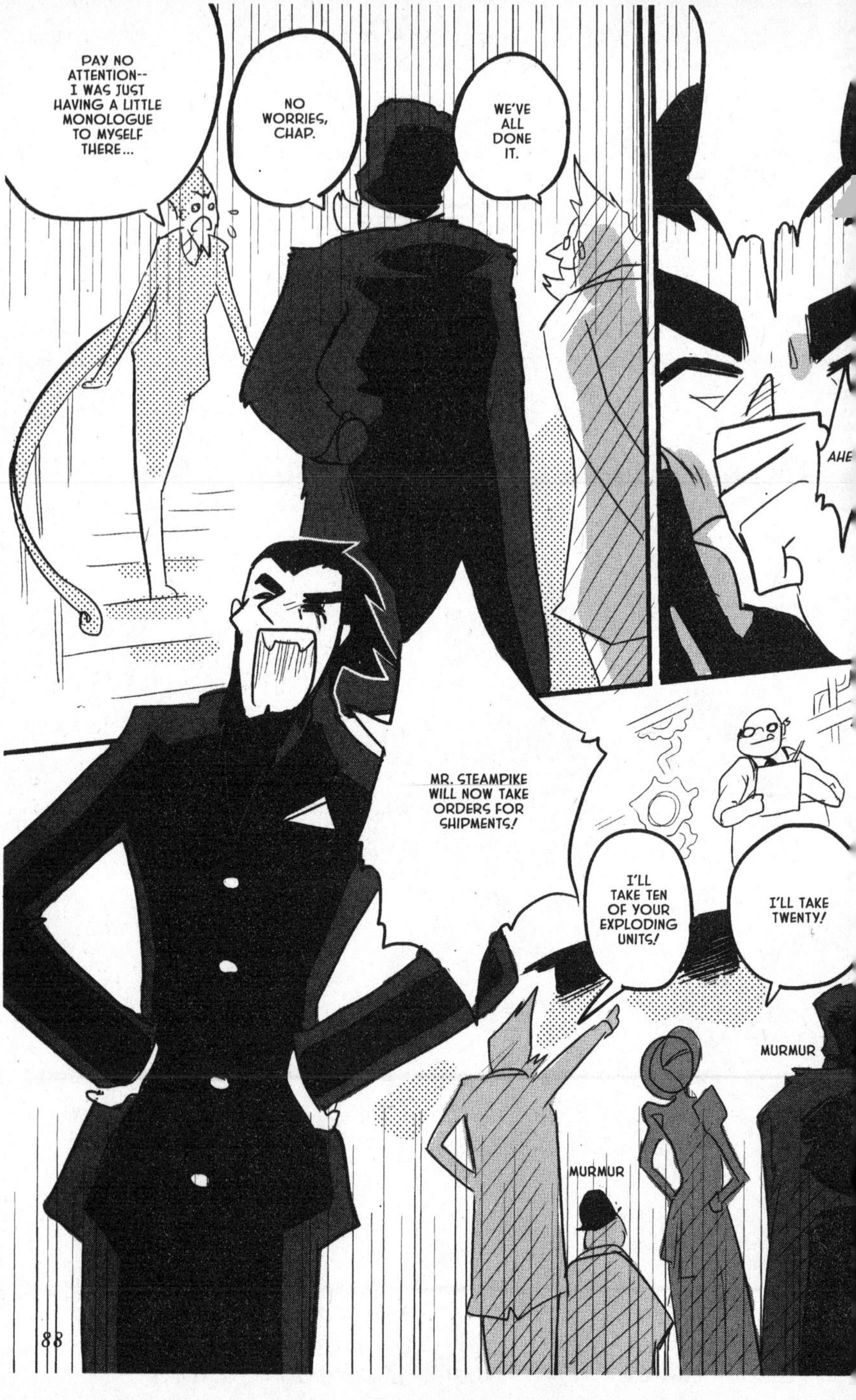
PAY NO ATTENTION-- I WAS JUST HAVING A LITTLE MONOLOGUE TO MYSELF THERE...
NO WORRIES, CHAP.
WE'VE ALL DONE IT.
AHE
MR. STEAMPIKE WILL NOW TAKE ORDERS FOR SHIPMENTS!
I'LL TAKE TEN OF YOUR EXPLODING UNITS!
I'LL TAKE TWENTY!
MURMUR
MURMUR

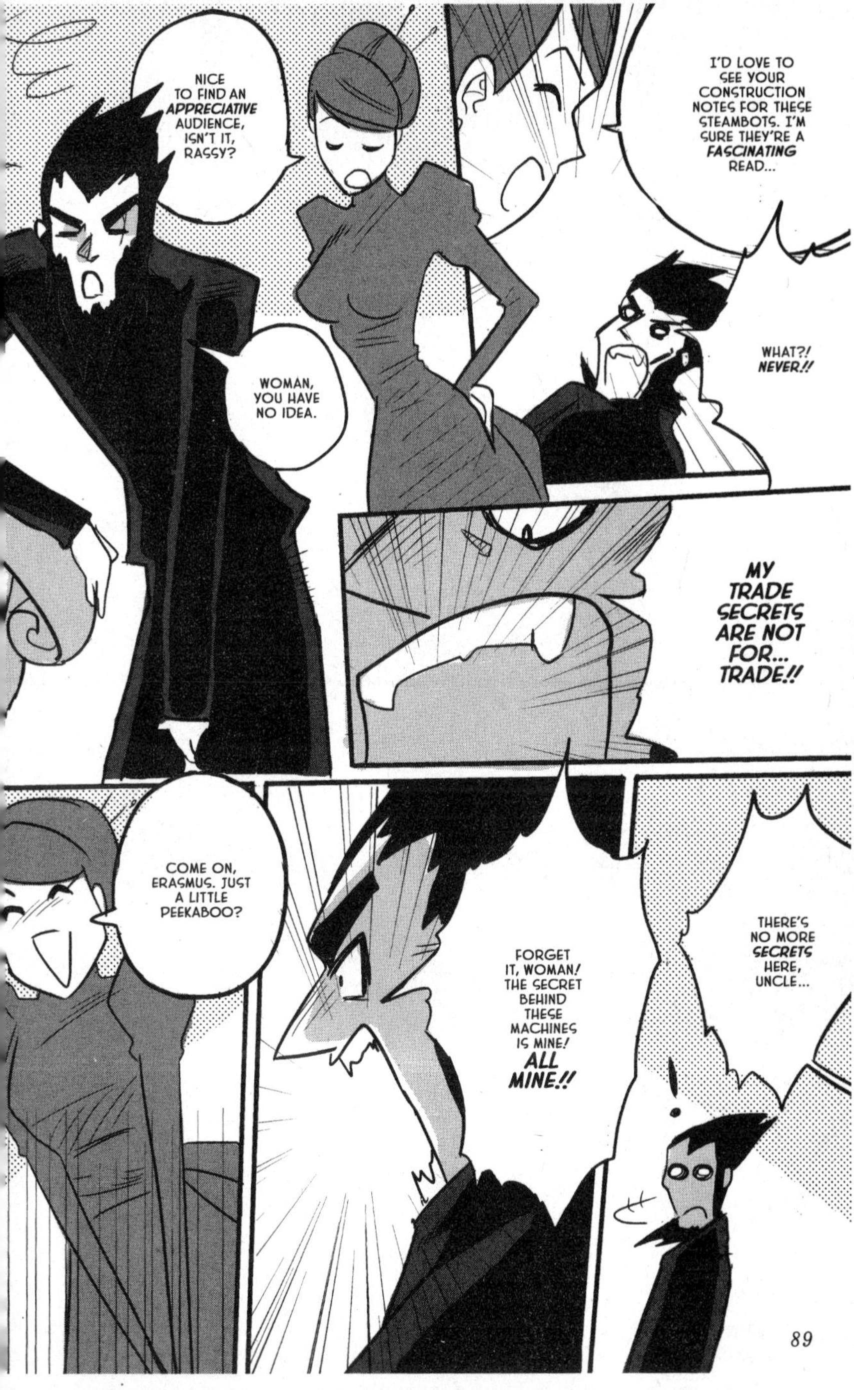
NICE TO FIND AN *APPRECIATIVE* AUDIENCE, ISN'T IT, RASSY?
WOMAN, YOU HAVE NO IDEA.
I'D LOVE TO SEE YOUR CONSTRUCTION NOTES FOR THESE STEAMBOTS. I'M SURE THEY'RE A *FASCINATING* READ...
WHAT?! *NEVER!!*
MY TRADE SECRETS ARE NOT FOR... TRADE!!
COME ON, ERASMUS. JUST A LITTLE PEEKABOO?
FORGET IT, WOMAN! THE SECRET BEHIND THESE MACHINES IS MINE! *ALL MINE!!*
THERE'S NO MORE *SECRETS* HERE, UNCLE...

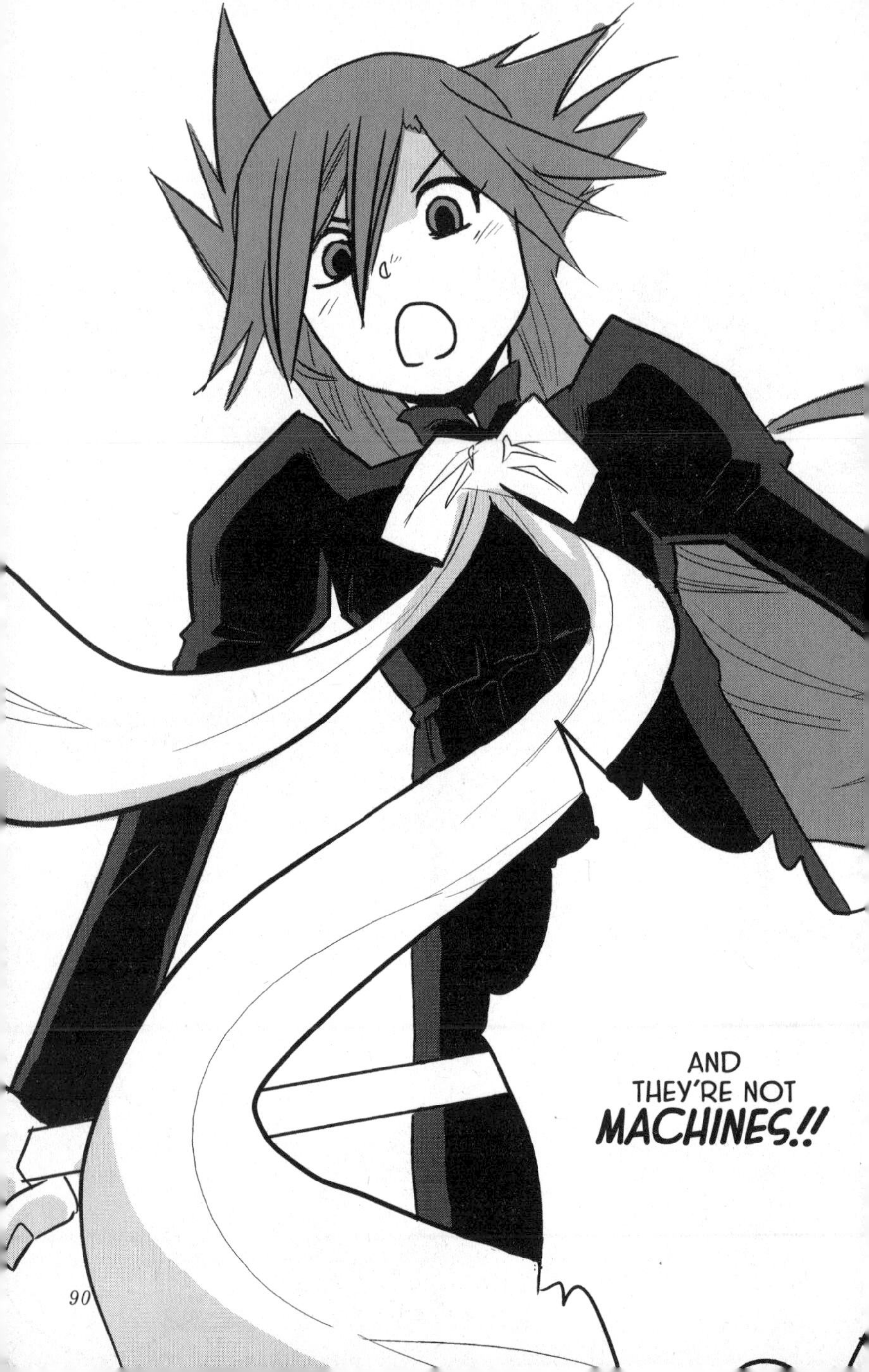
AND THEY'RE NOT MACHINES!!

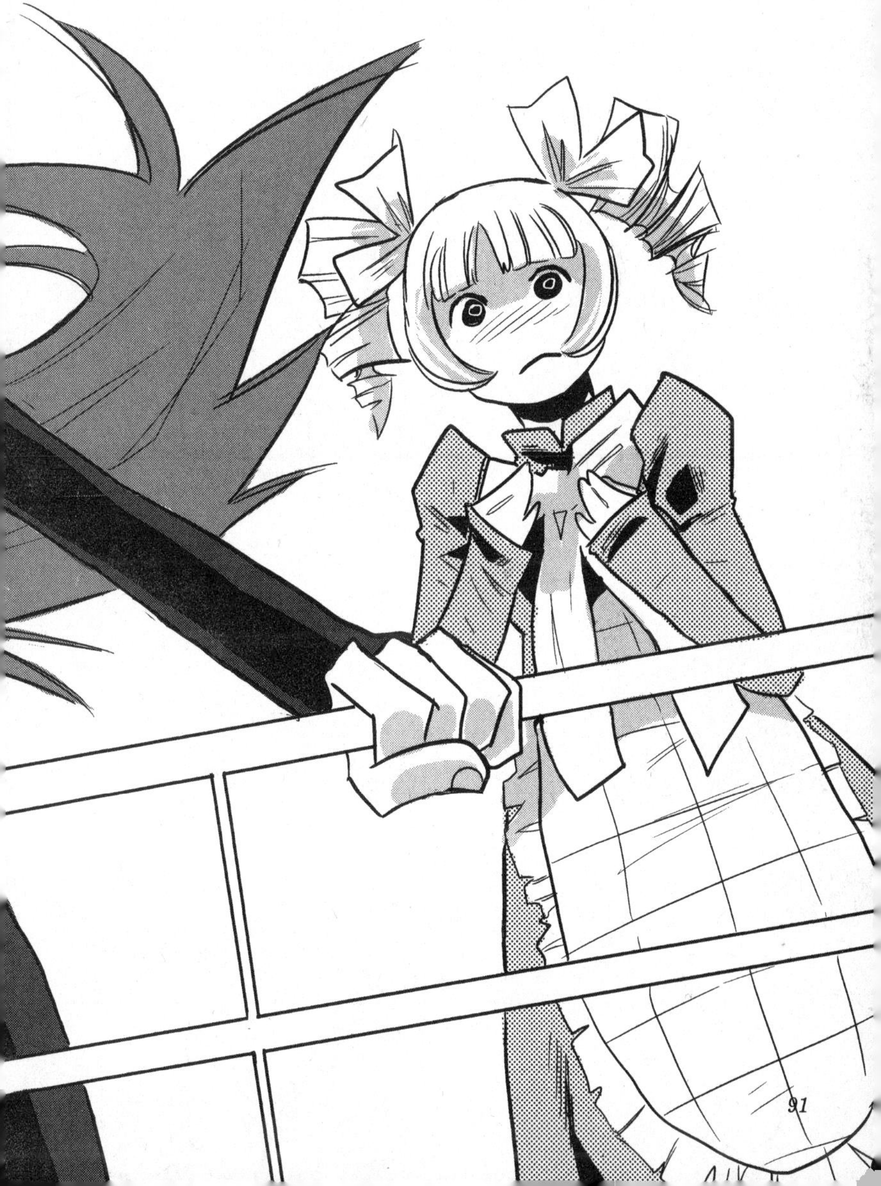

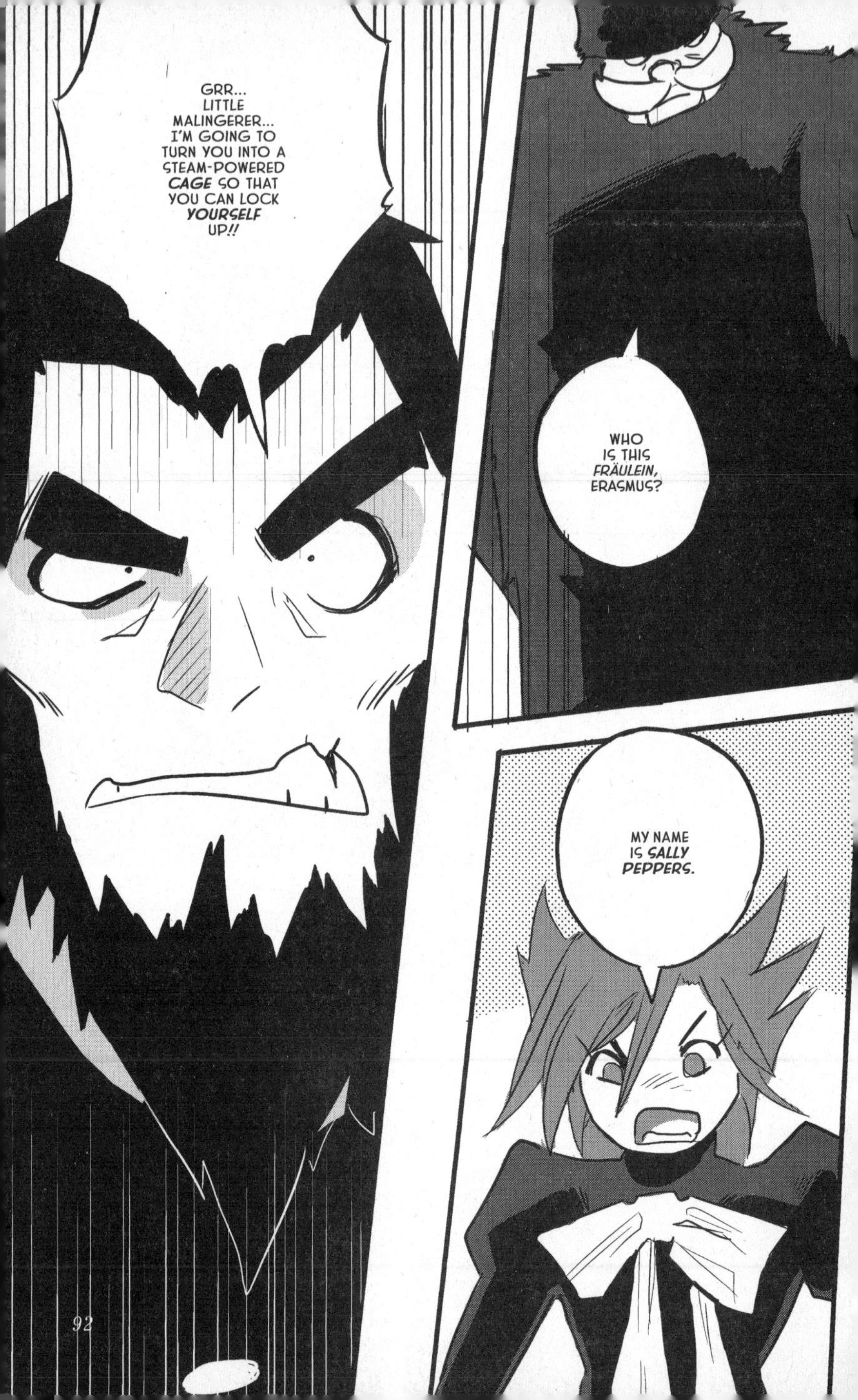
GRR... LITTLE MALINGERER... I'M GOING TO TURN YOU INTO A STEAM-POWERED *CAGE* SO THAT YOU CAN LOCK *YOURSELF* UP!!
WHO IS THIS *FRÄULEIN*, ERASMUS?
MY NAME IS *SALLY PEPPERS*.

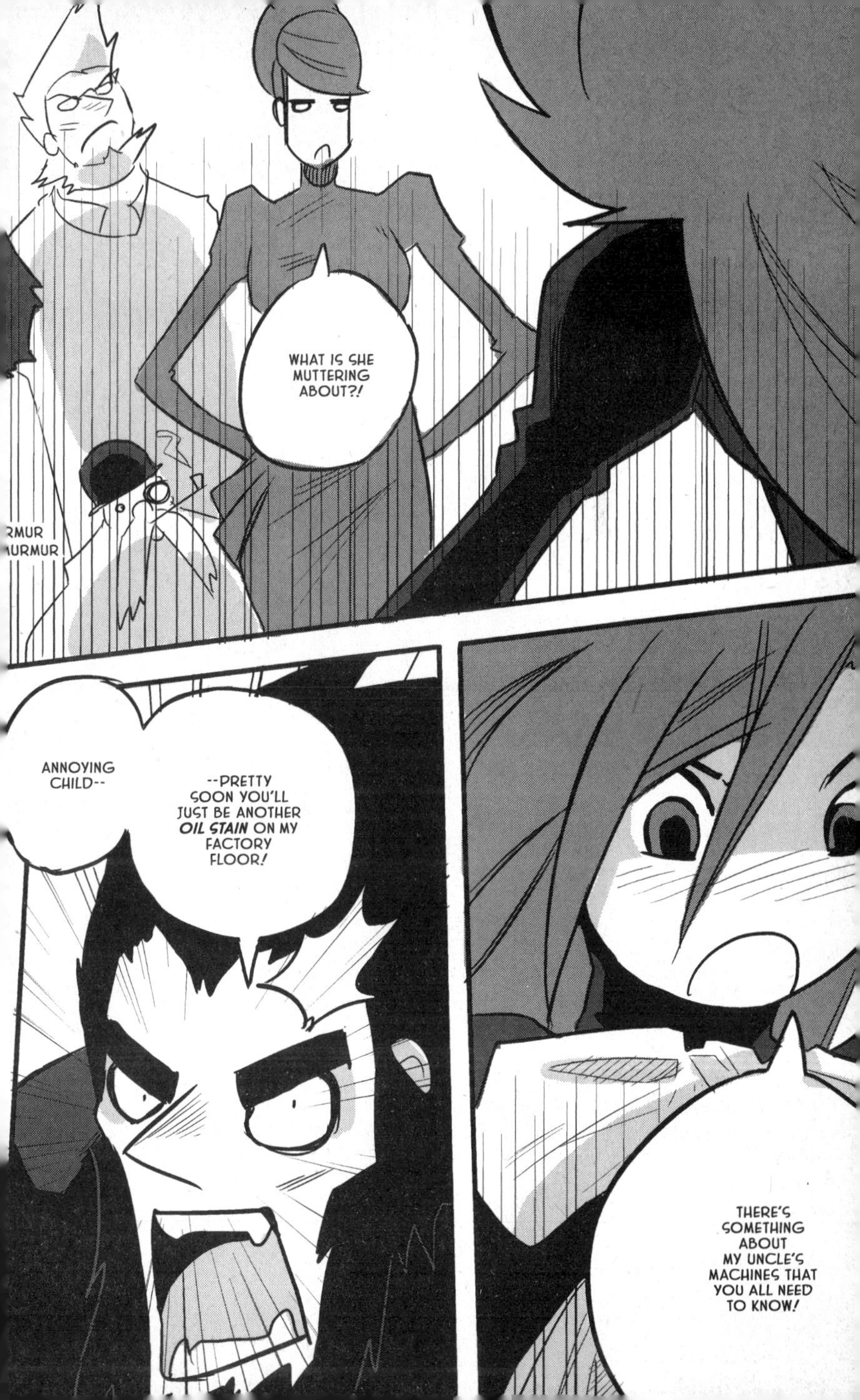
WHAT IS SHE MUTTERING ABOUT?!
RMUR
URMUR
ANNOYING CHILD--
--PRETTY SOON YOU'LL JUST BE ANOTHER **OIL STAIN** ON MY FACTORY FLOOR!
THERE'S SOMETHING ABOUT MY UNCLE'S MACHINES THAT YOU ALL NEED TO KNOW!

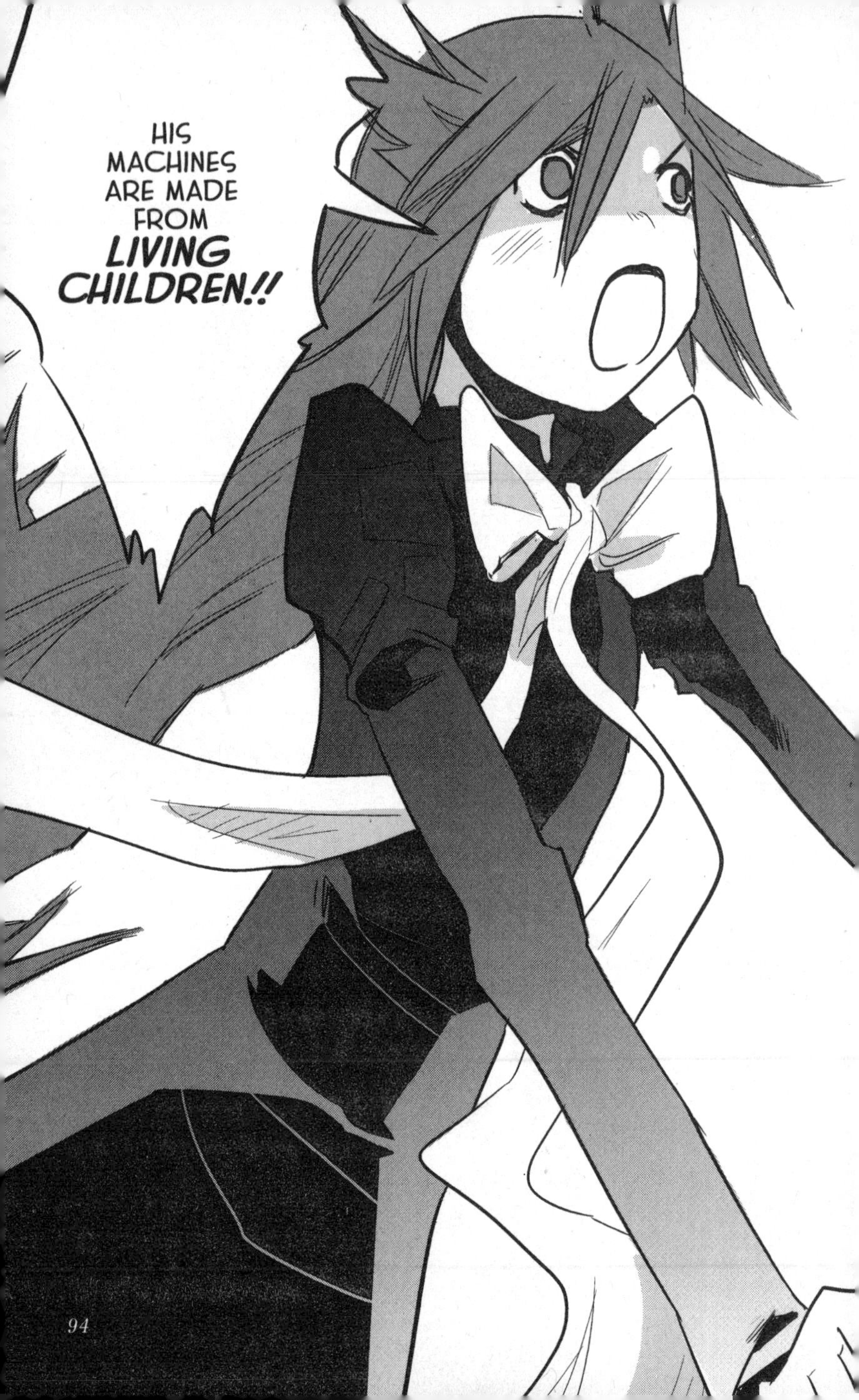
HIS MACHINES ARE MADE FROM LIVING CHILDREN.!!

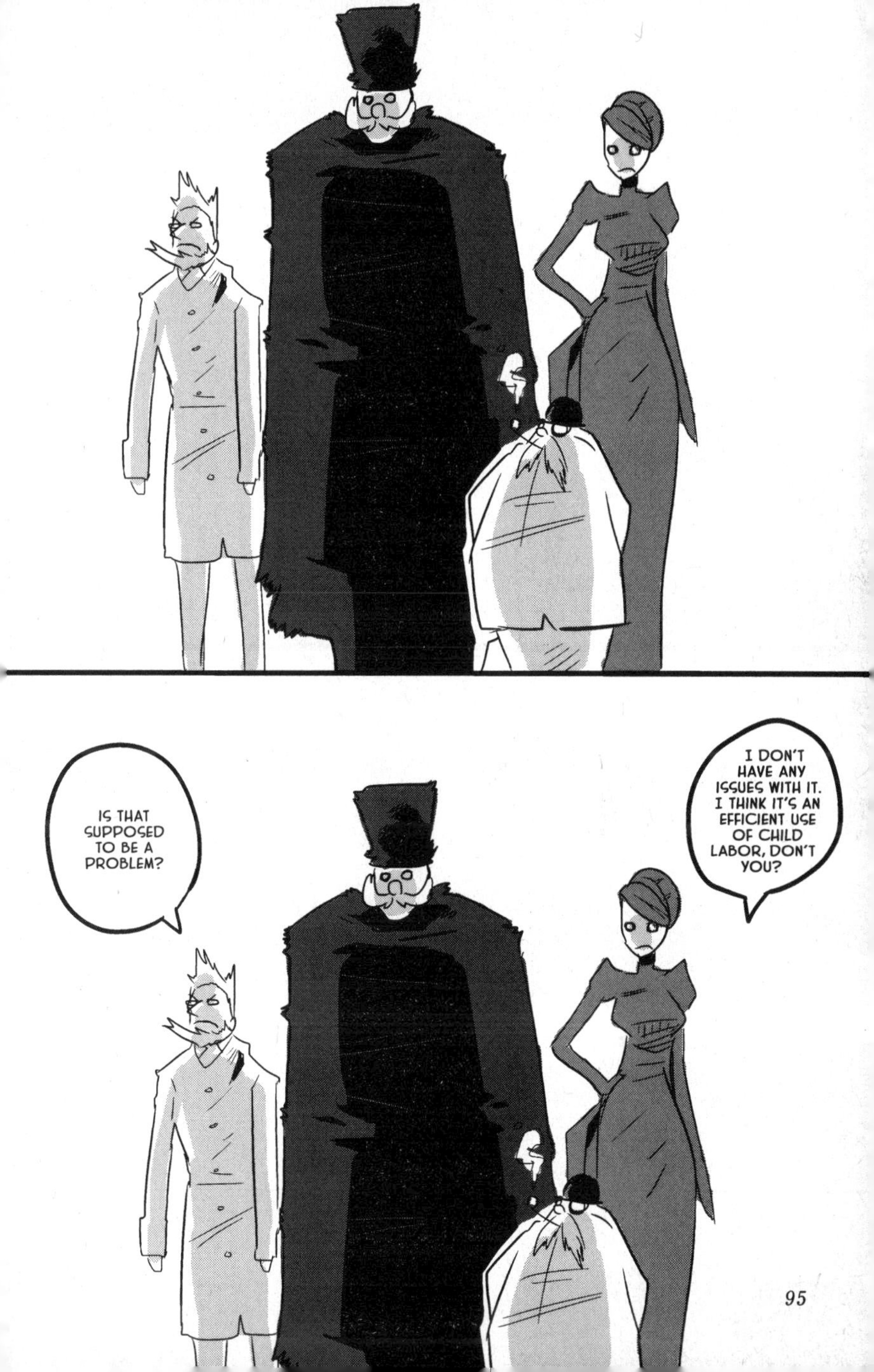
IS THAT SUPPOSED TO BE A PROBLEM?
I DON'T HAVE ANY ISSUES WITH IT. I THINK IT'S AN EFFICIENT USE OF CHILD LABOR, DON'T YOU?

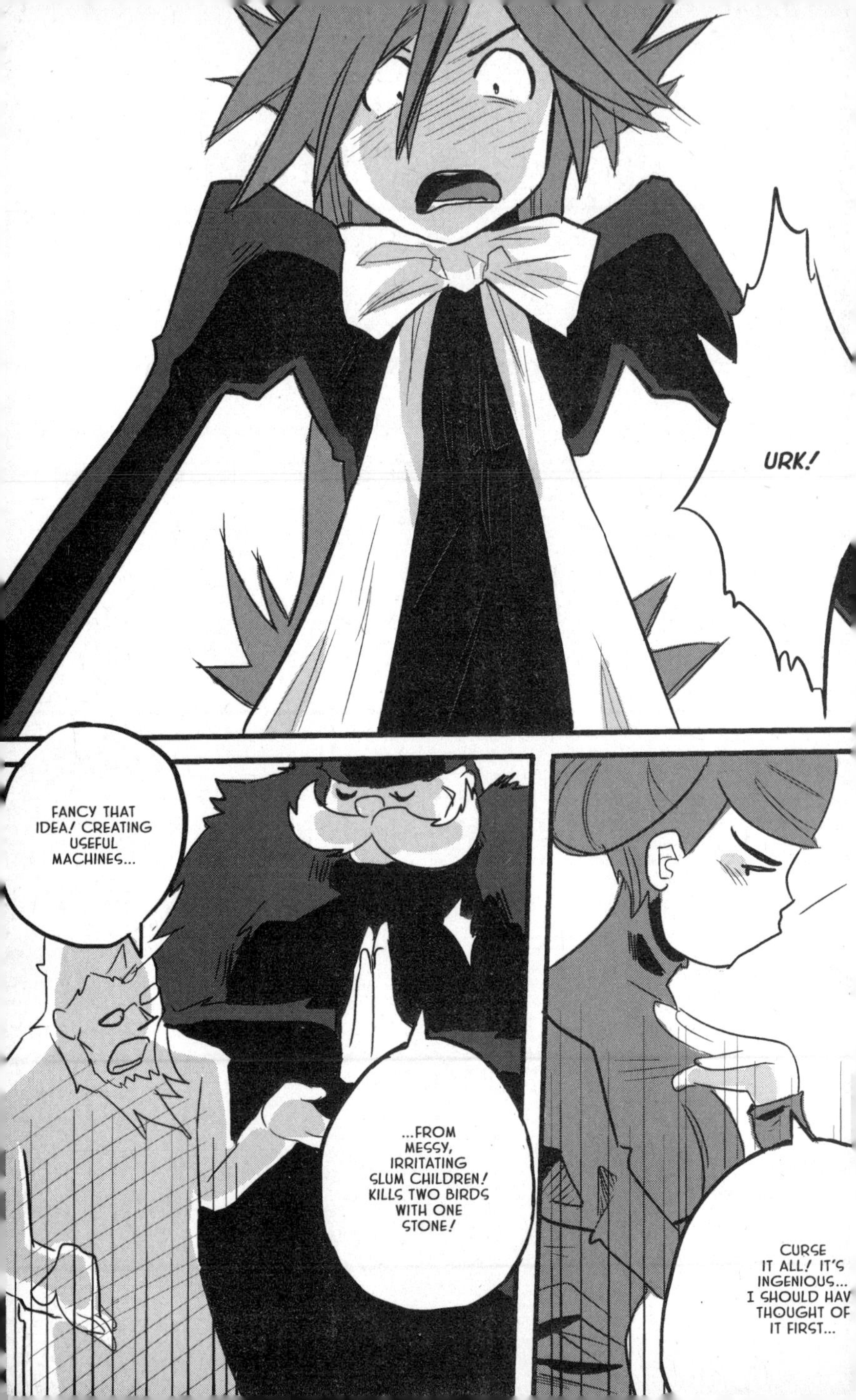
URK!
FANCY THAT IDEA! CREATING USEFUL MACHINES...
...FROM MESSY, IRRITATING SLUM CHILDREN! KILLS TWO BIRDS WITH ONE STONE!
CURSE IT ALL! IT'S INGENIOUS... I SHOULD HAV THOUGHT OF IT FIRST...

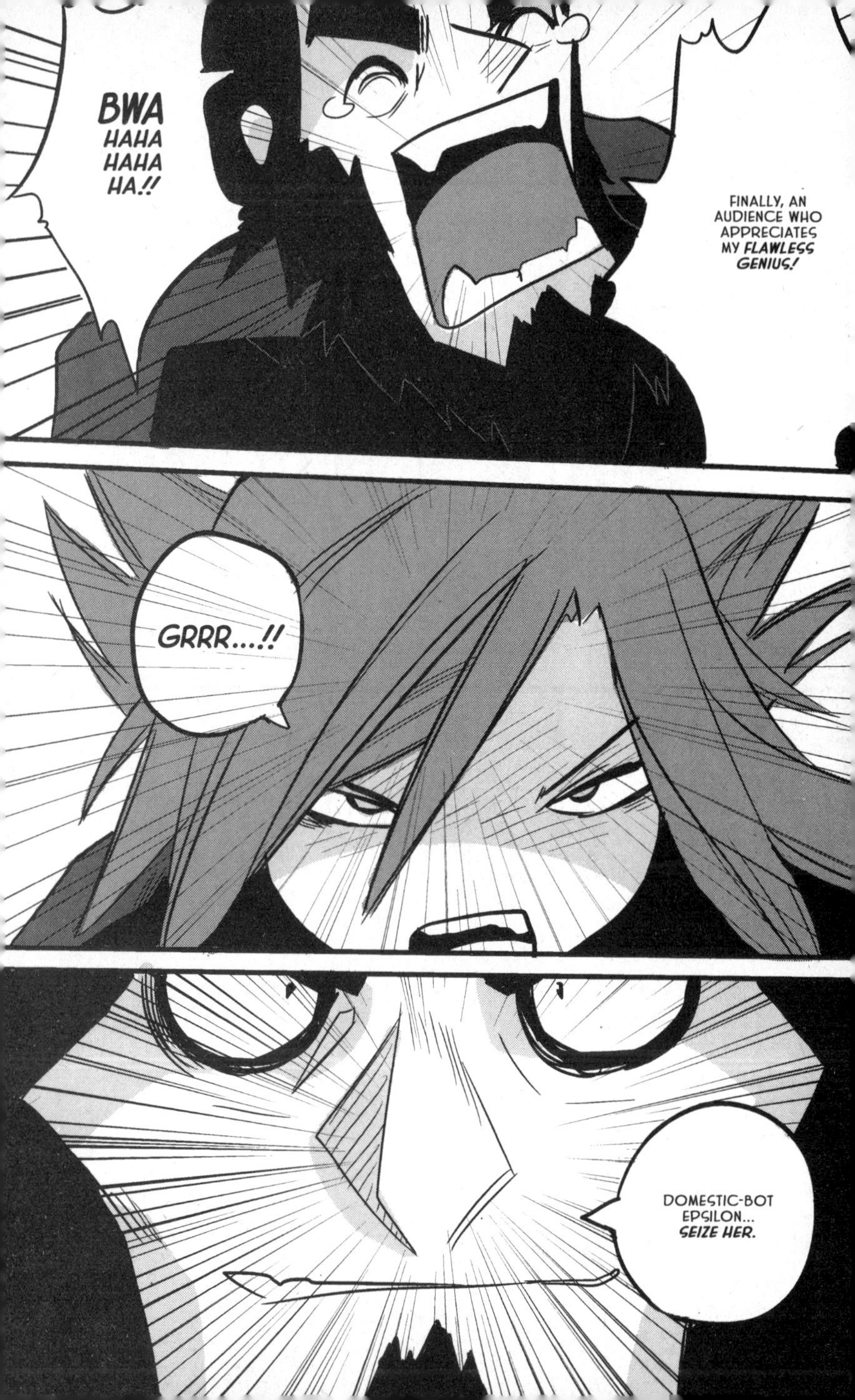
BWA HAHA HAHA HA.!!
FINALLY, AN AUDIENCE WHO APPRECIATES MY *FLAWLESS GENIUS!*
GRRR....!!
DOMESTIC-BOT EPSILON... ***SEIZE HER.***

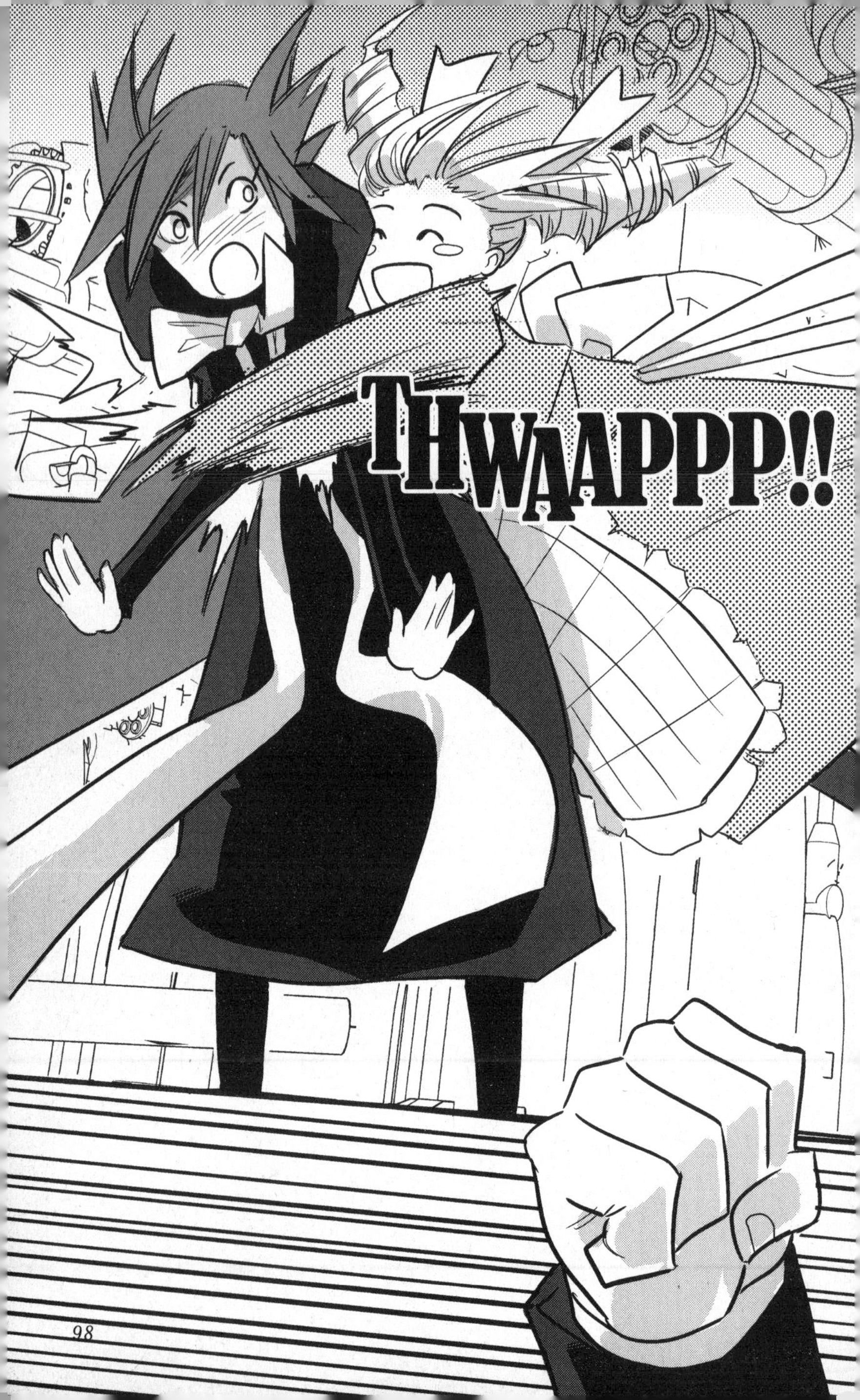
THWAAPPP!!

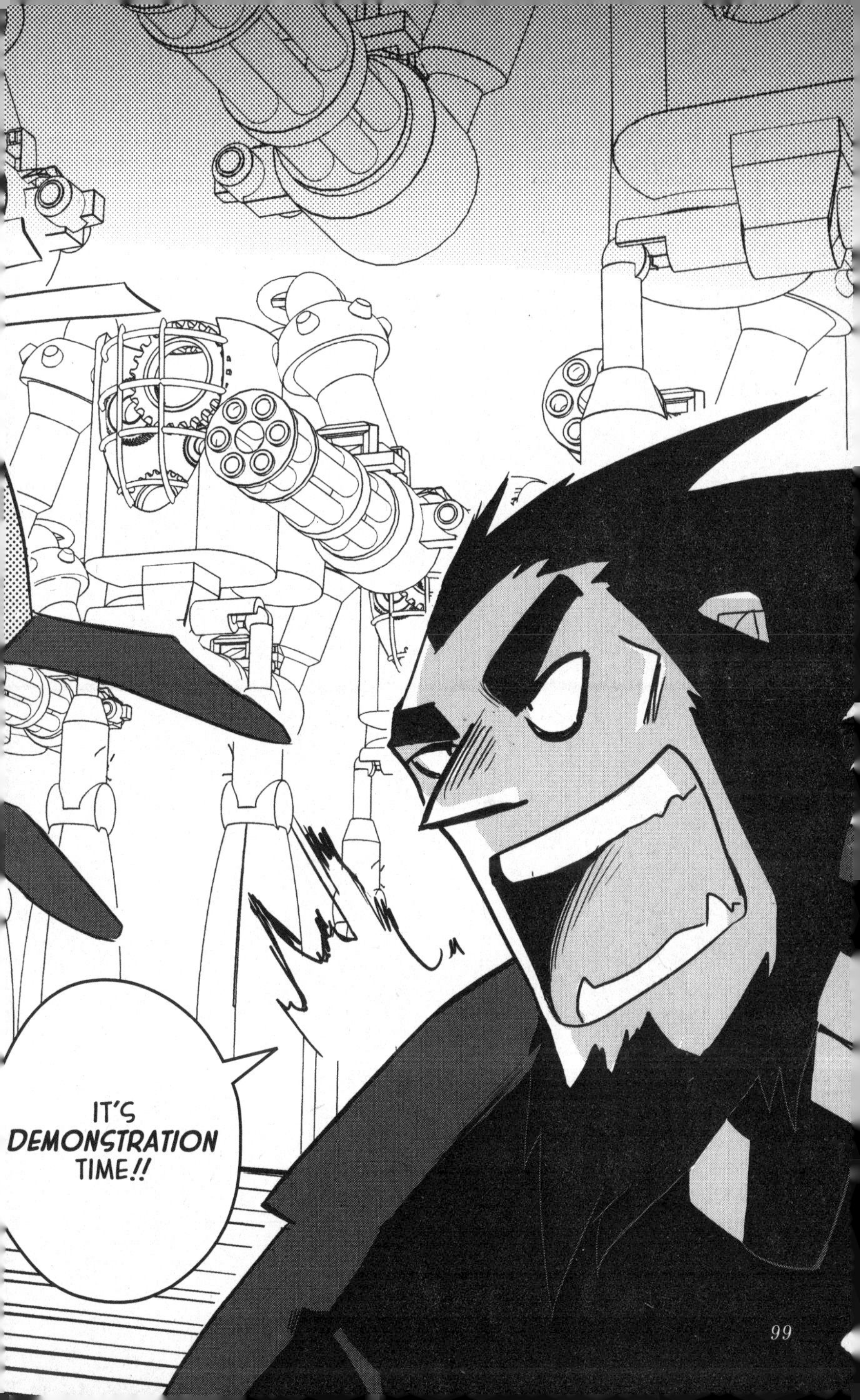
IT'S DEMONSTRATION TIME!!

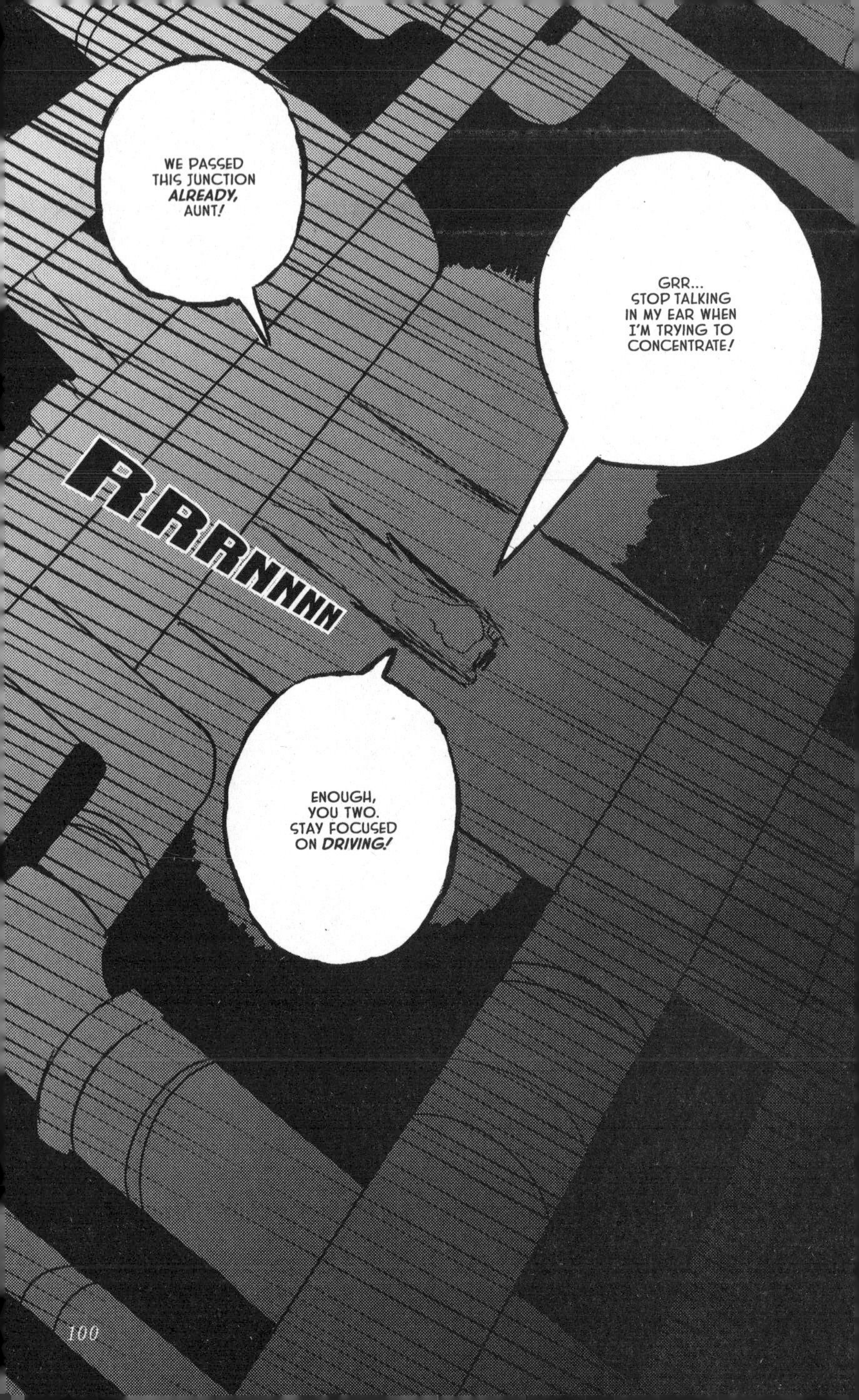
WE PASSED THIS JUNCTION ALREADY, AUNT!
GRR... STOP TALKING IN MY EAR WHEN I'M TRYING TO CONCENTRATE!
RRRNNNNN
ENOUGH, YOU TWO. STAY FOCUSED ON DRIVING!

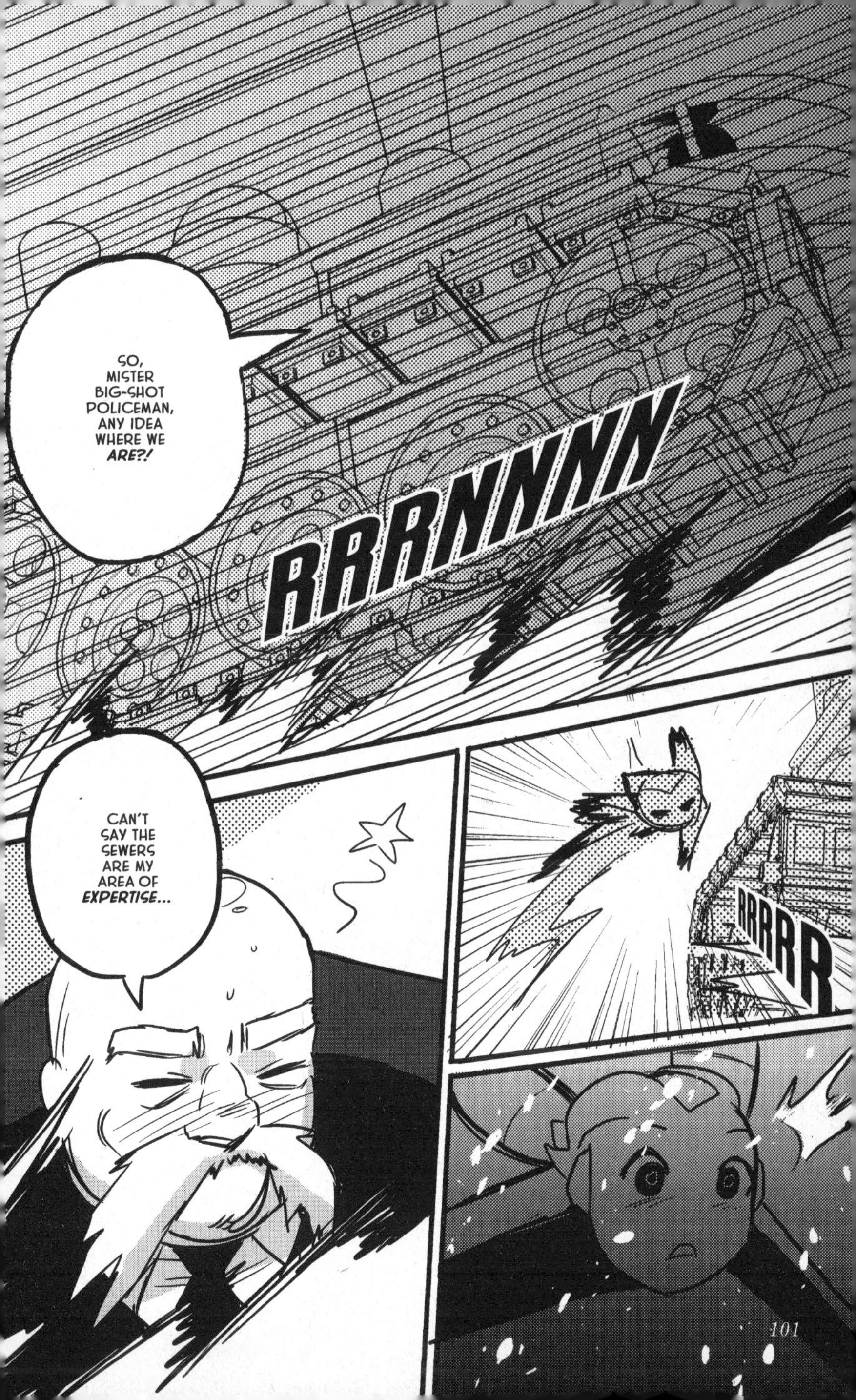
SO, MISTER BIG-SHOT POLICEMAN, ANY IDEA WHERE WE *ARE?!*
RRRNNNNN
CAN'T SAY THE SEWERS ARE MY AREA OF *EXPERTISE...*
RRRRR

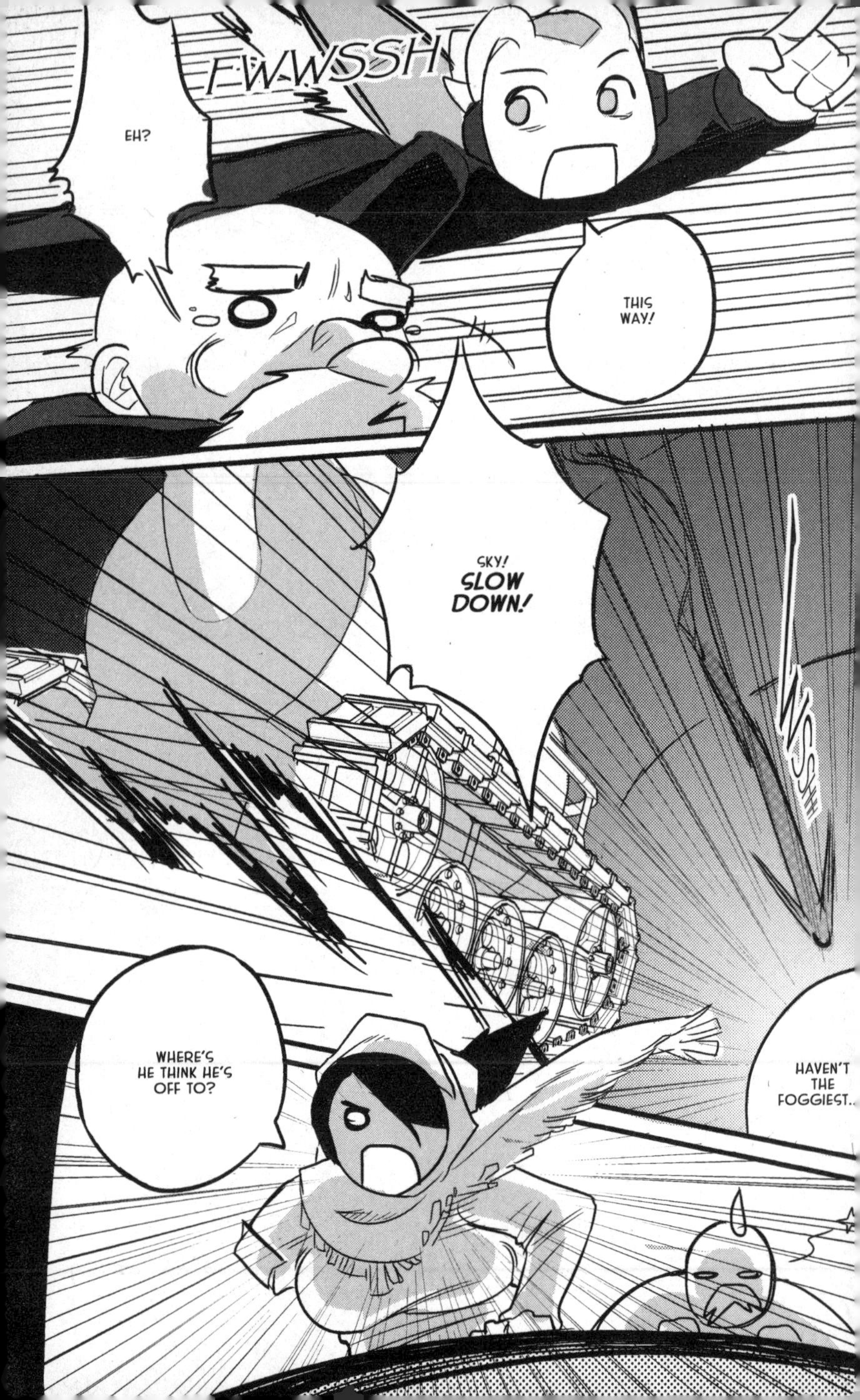
FWWSSH
EH?
THIS WAY!
SKY! SLOW DOWN!
WSSH
WHERE'S HE THINK HE'S OFF TO?
HAVEN'T THE FOGGIEST...

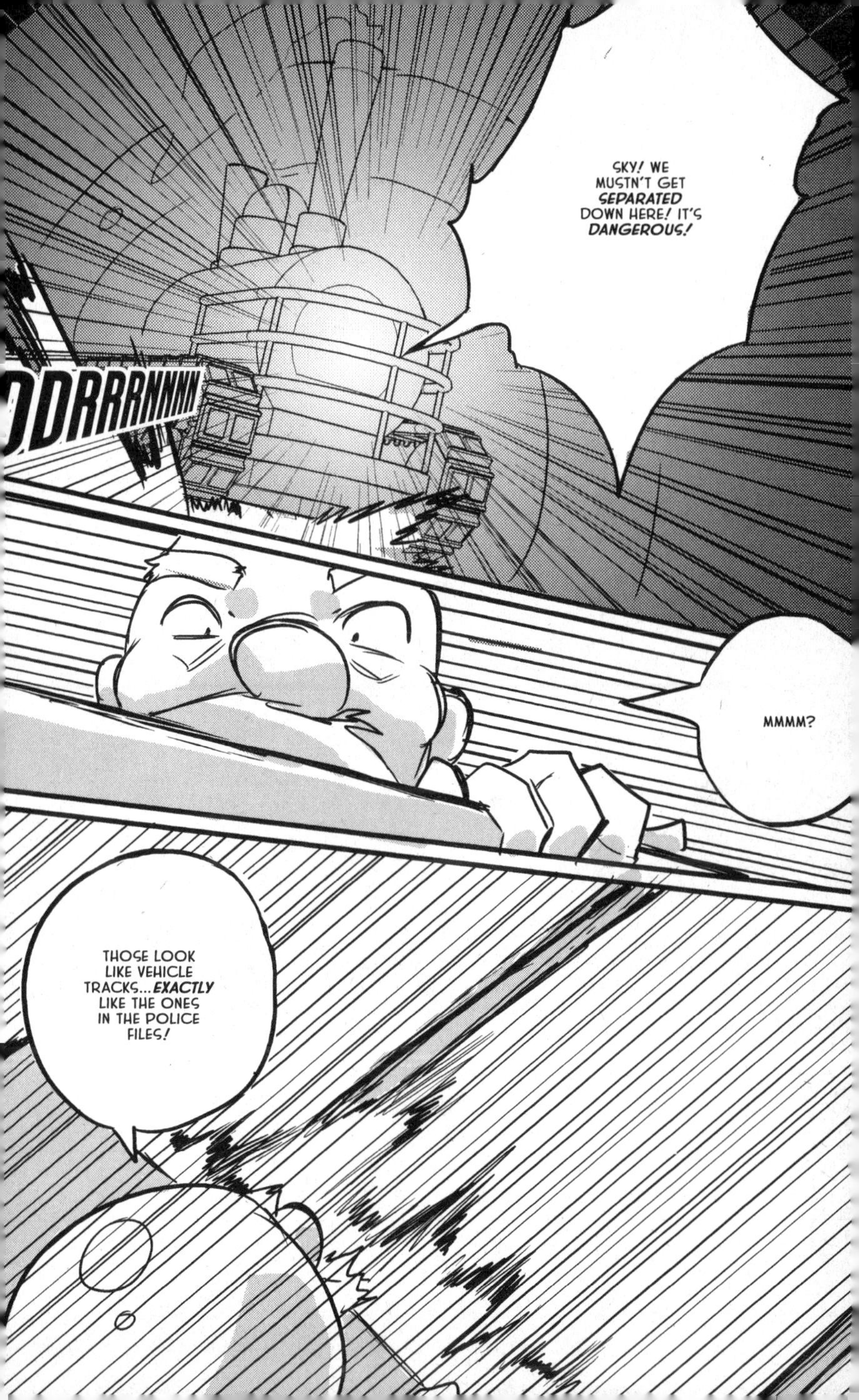
DDRRRNNNN
SKY! WE MUSTN'T GET SEPARATED DOWN HERE! IT'S DANGEROUS!
MMMM?
THOSE LOOK LIKE VEHICLE TRACKS...EXACTLY LIKE THE ONES IN THE POLICE FILES!

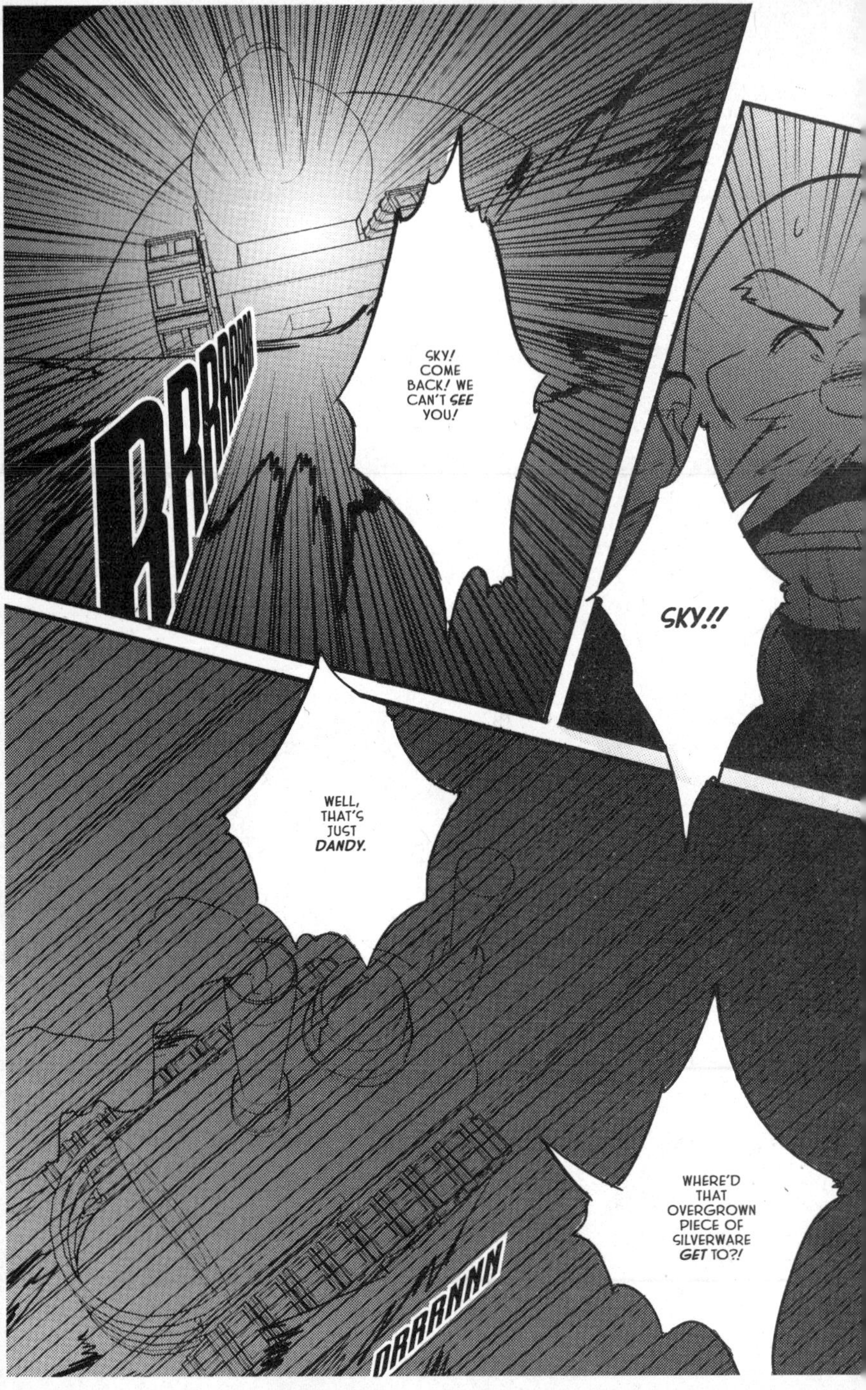
RRRRRRR
SKY! COME BACK! WE CAN'T *SEE* YOU!
SKY!!
WELL, THAT'S JUST ***DANDY.***
WHERE'D THAT OVERGROWN PIECE OF SILVERWARE ***GET*** TO?!
DRRRNNN

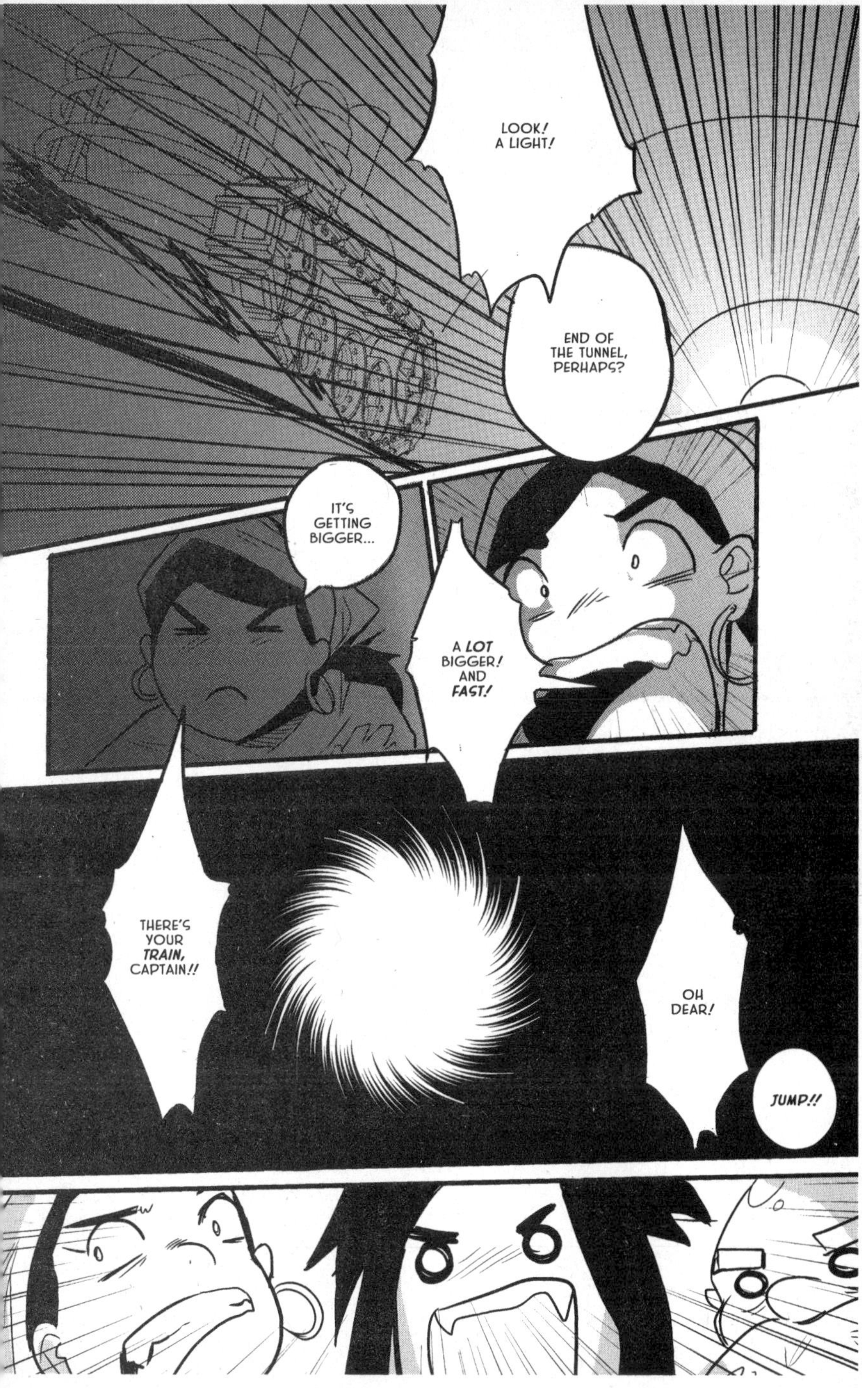
LOOK! A LIGHT!
END OF THE TUNNEL, PERHAPS?
IT'S GETTING BIGGER...
A ***LOT*** BIGGER! AND ***FAST!***
THERE'S YOUR ***TRAIN,*** CAPTAIN!!
OH DEAR!
JUMP!!

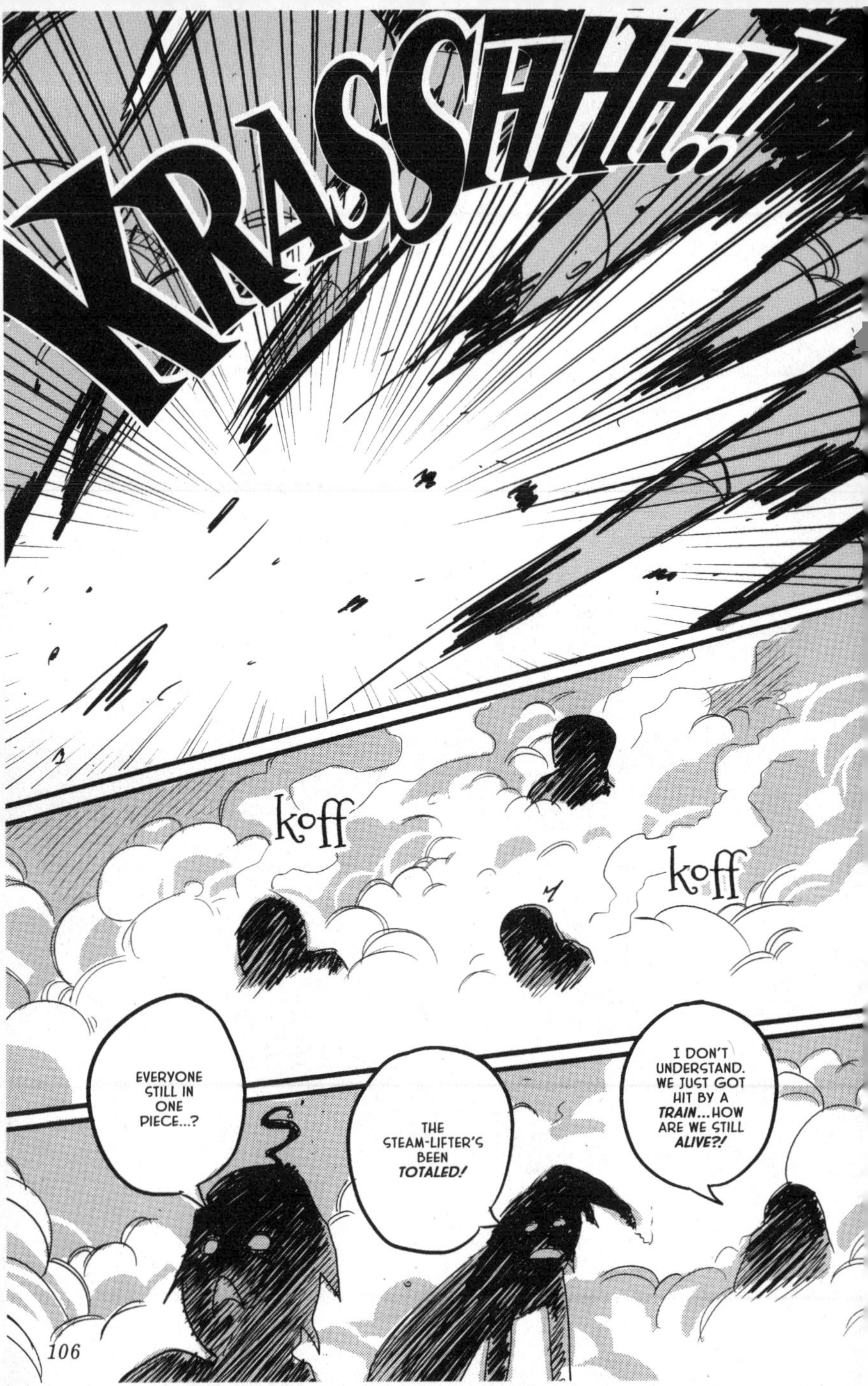
KRASSHH!!
koff
koff
EVERYONE STILL IN ONE PIECE...?
THE STEAM-LIFTER'S BEEN *TOTALED!*
I DON'T UNDERSTAND. WE JUST GOT HIT BY A *TRAIN*...HOW ARE WE STILL *ALIVE?!*

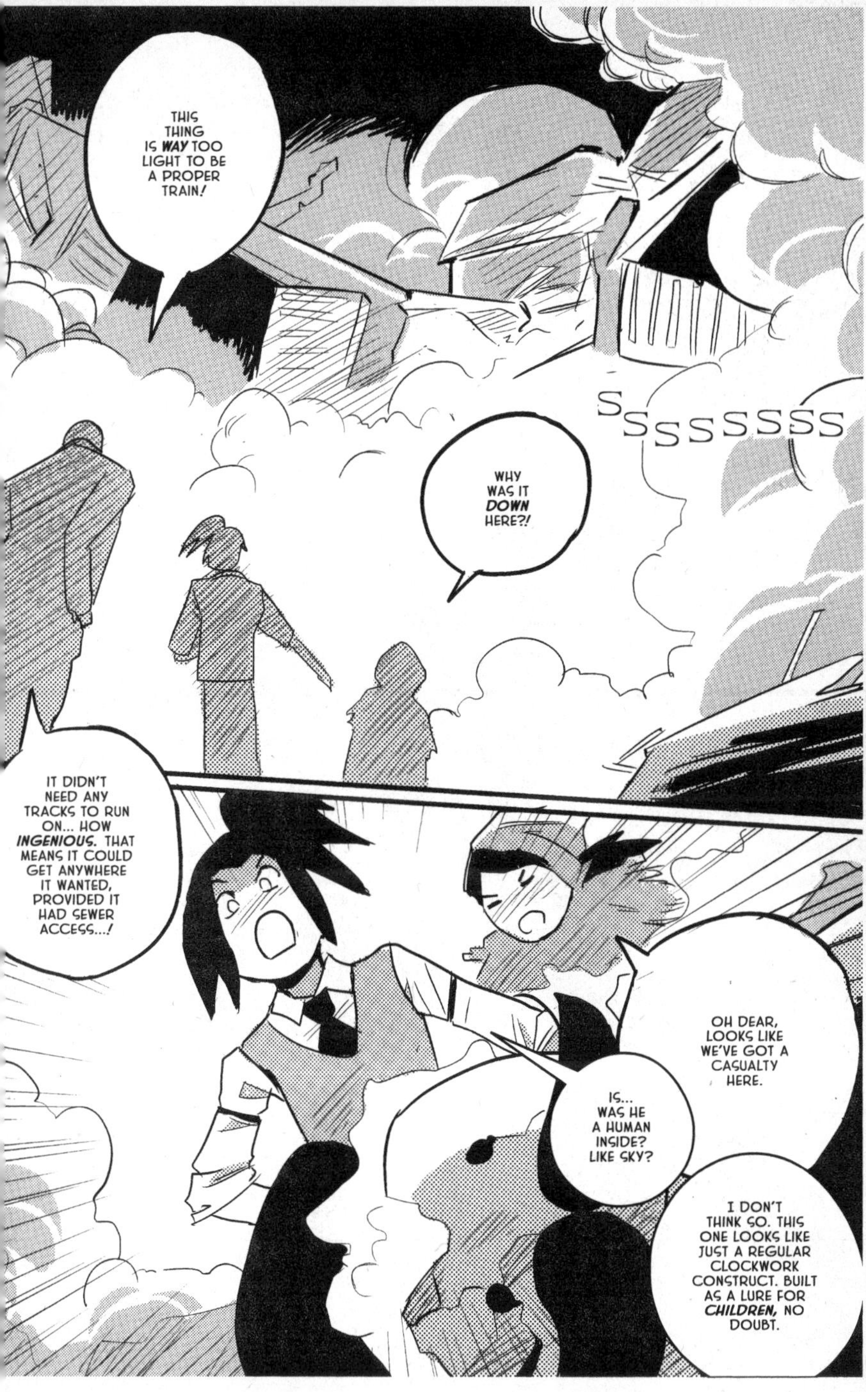
THIS THING IS **WAY** TOO LIGHT TO BE A PROPER TRAIN!
SSSSSSSSS
WHY WAS IT **DOWN** HERE?!
IT DIDN'T NEED ANY TRACKS TO RUN ON... HOW **INGENIOUS.** THAT MEANS IT COULD GET ANYWHERE IT WANTED, PROVIDED IT HAD SEWER ACCESS...!
OH DEAR, LOOKS LIKE WE'VE GOT A CASUALTY HERE.
IS... WAS HE A HUMAN INSIDE? LIKE SKY?
I DON'T THINK SO. THIS ONE LOOKS LIKE JUST A REGULAR CLOCKWORK CONSTRUCT. BUILT AS A LURE FOR **CHILDREN,** NO DOUBT.

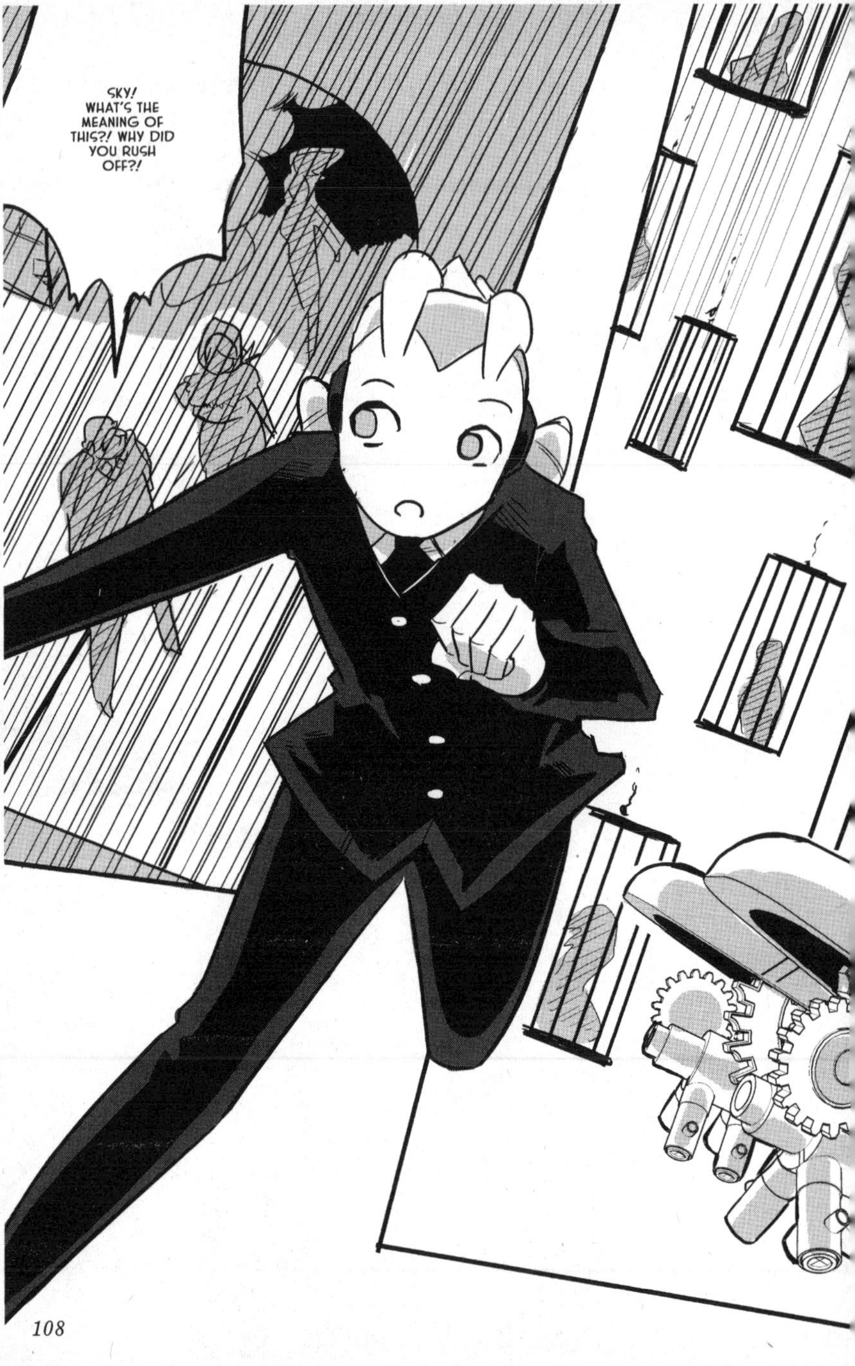
SKY! WHAT'S THE MEANING OF THIS?! WHY DID YOU RUSH OFF?!

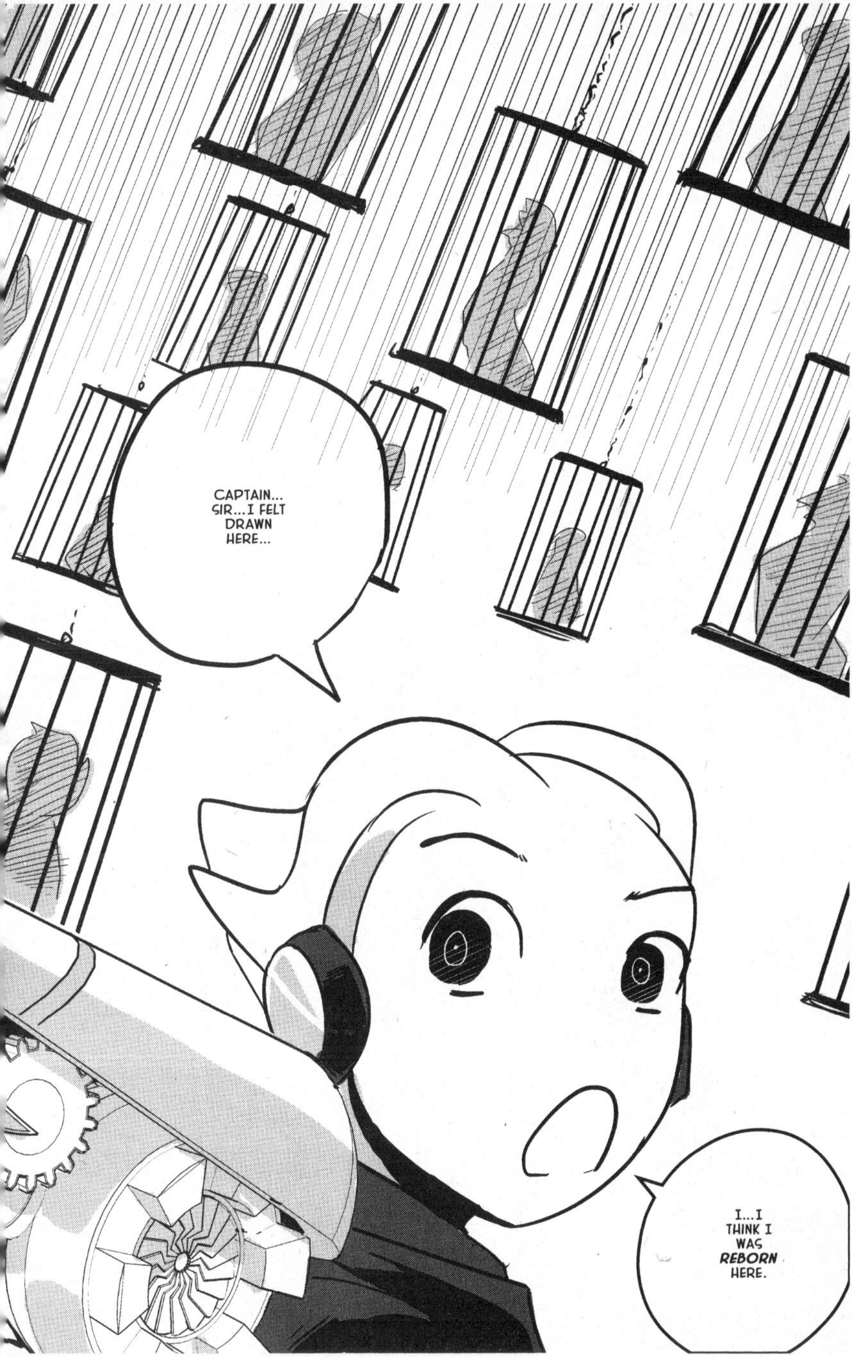
CAPTAIN... SIR...I FELT DRAWN HERE...
I...I THINK I WAS ***REBORN*** HERE.

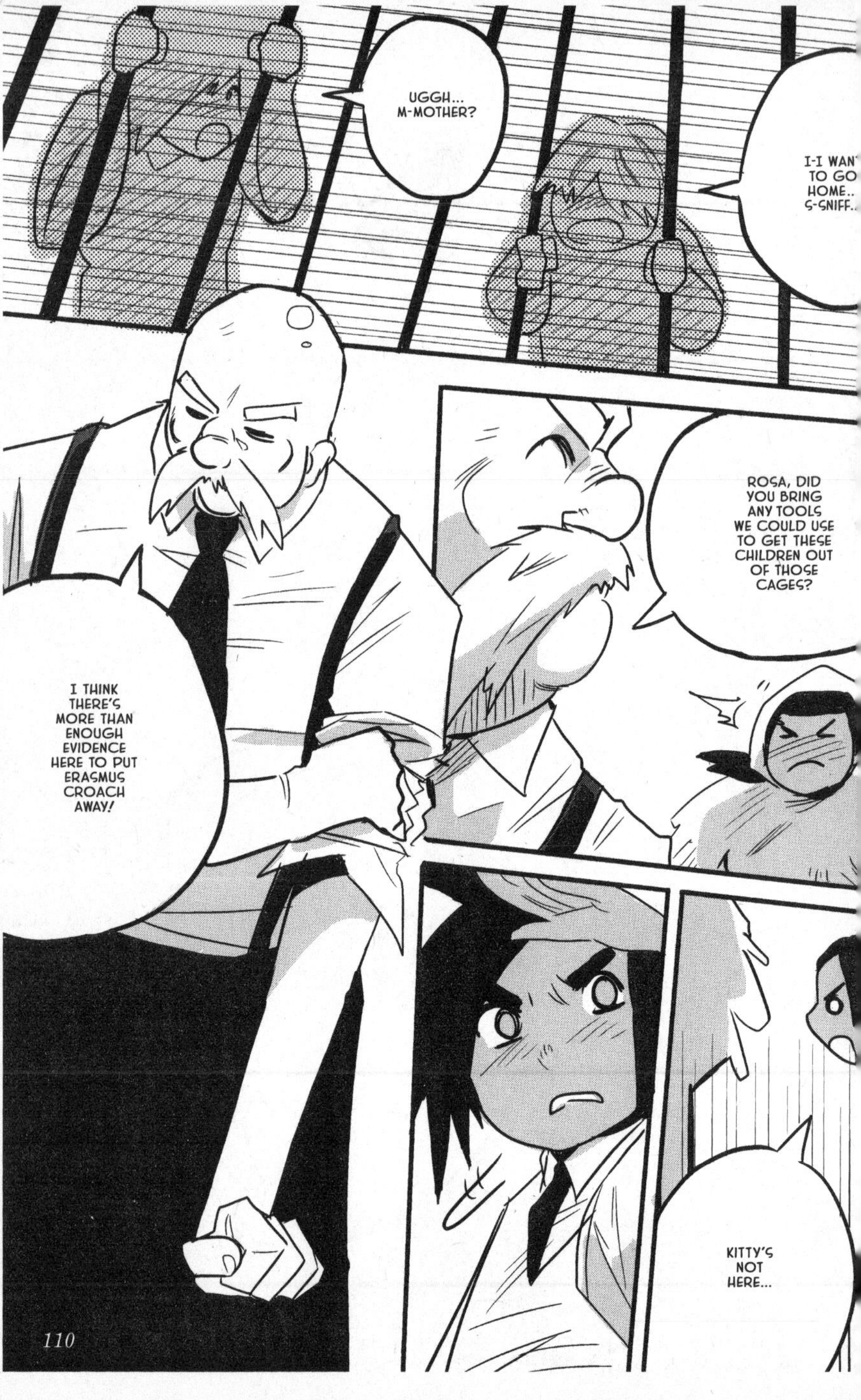
UGGH... M-MOTHER?
I-I WAN' TO GO HOME.. S-SNIFF..
ROSA, DID YOU BRING ANY TOOLS WE COULD USE TO GET THESE CHILDREN OUT OF THOSE CAGES?
I THINK THERE'S MORE THAN ENOUGH EVIDENCE HERE TO PUT ERASMUS CROACH AWAY!
KITTY'S NOT HERE...

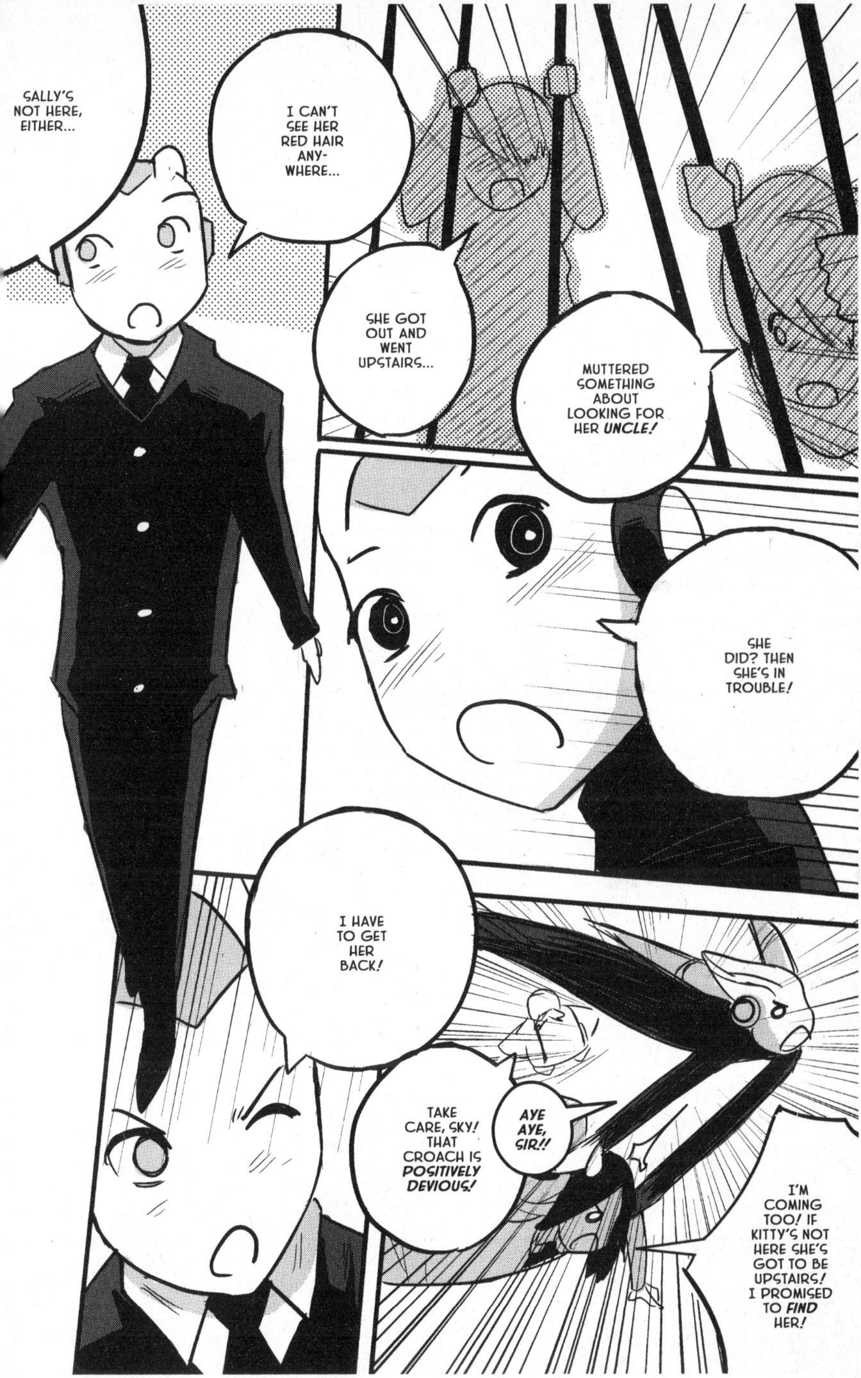
SALLY'S NOT HERE, EITHER...
I CAN'T SEE HER RED HAIR ANY-WHERE...
SHE GOT OUT AND WENT UPSTAIRS...
MUTTERED SOMETHING ABOUT LOOKING FOR HER *UNCLE!*
SHE DID? THEN SHE'S IN TROUBLE!
I HAVE TO GET HER BACK!
TAKE CARE, SKY! THAT CROACH IS ***POSITIVELY DEVIOUS!***
AYE AYE, SIR!!
I'M COMING TOO! IF KITTY'S NOT HERE SHE'S GOT TO BE UPSTAIRS! I PROMISED TO *FIND* HER!

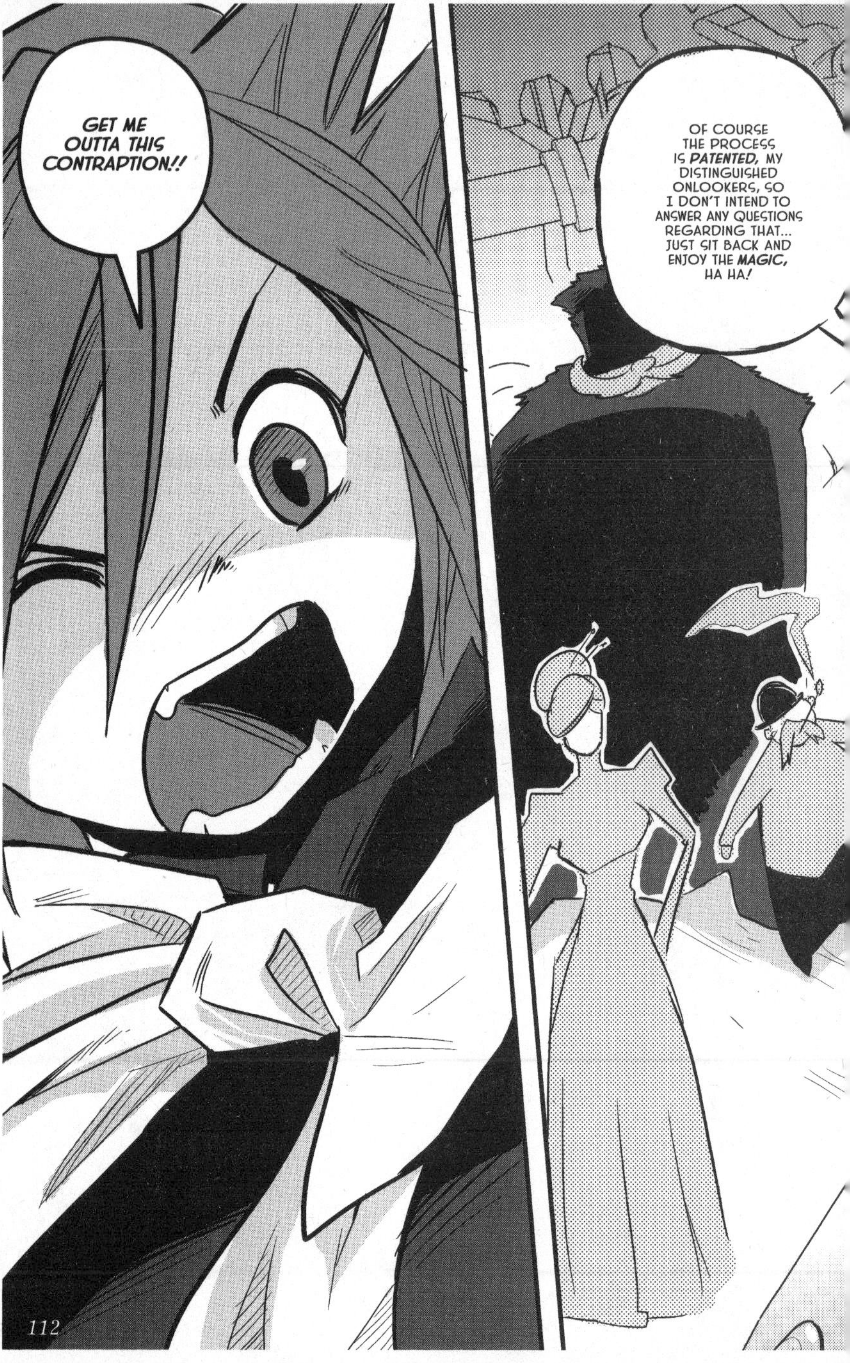
GET ME OUTTA THIS CONTRAPTION!!
OF COURSE THE PROCESS IS PATENTED, MY DISTINGUISHED ONLOOKERS, SO I DON'T INTEND TO ANSWER ANY QUESTIONS REGARDING THAT... JUST SIT BACK AND ENJOY THE MAGIC, HA HA!

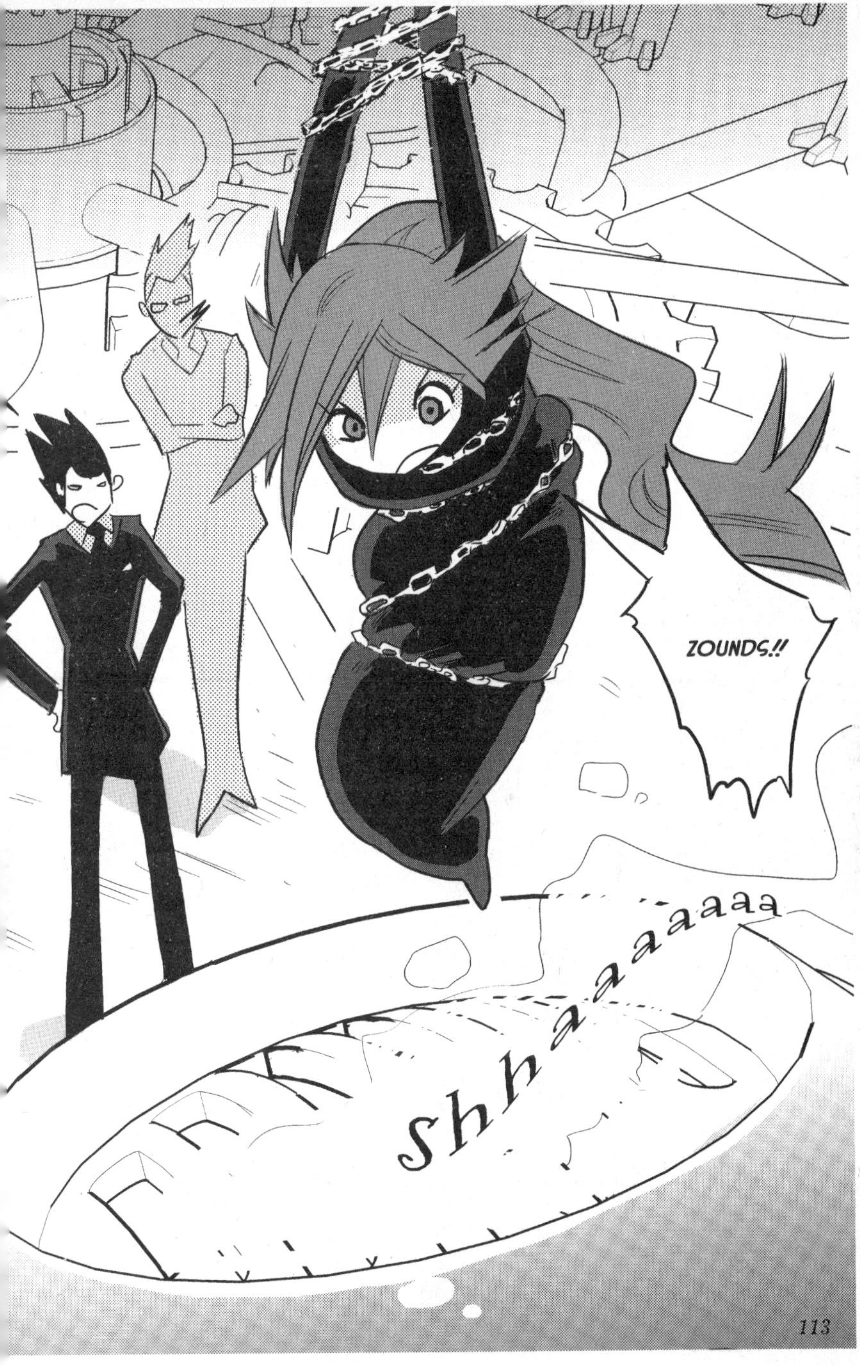
ZOUNDS!!
Shhaaaaaaaaa

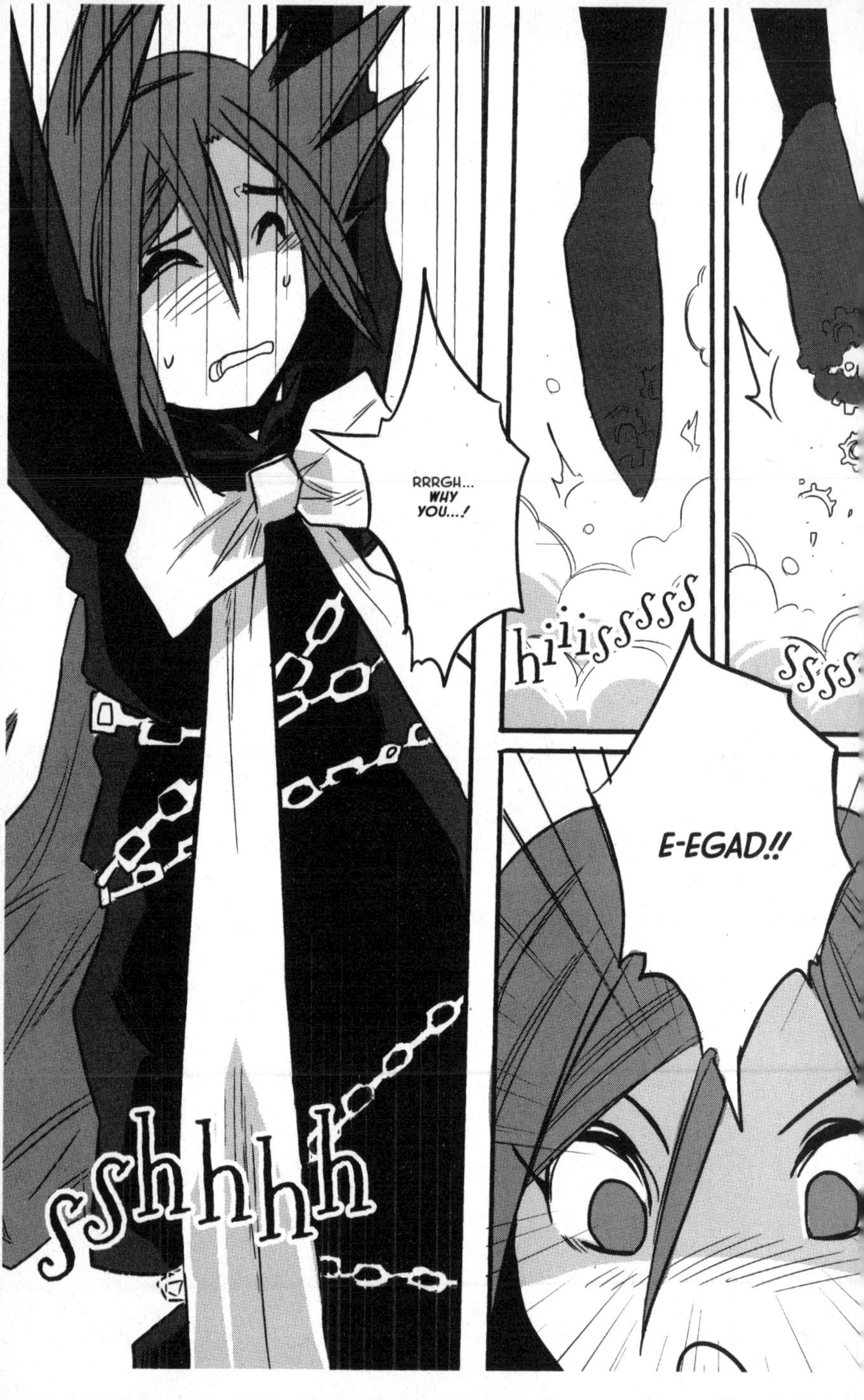
RRRGH... WHY YOU...!
sshhhh
hiiisssss
ssss
E-EGAD!!

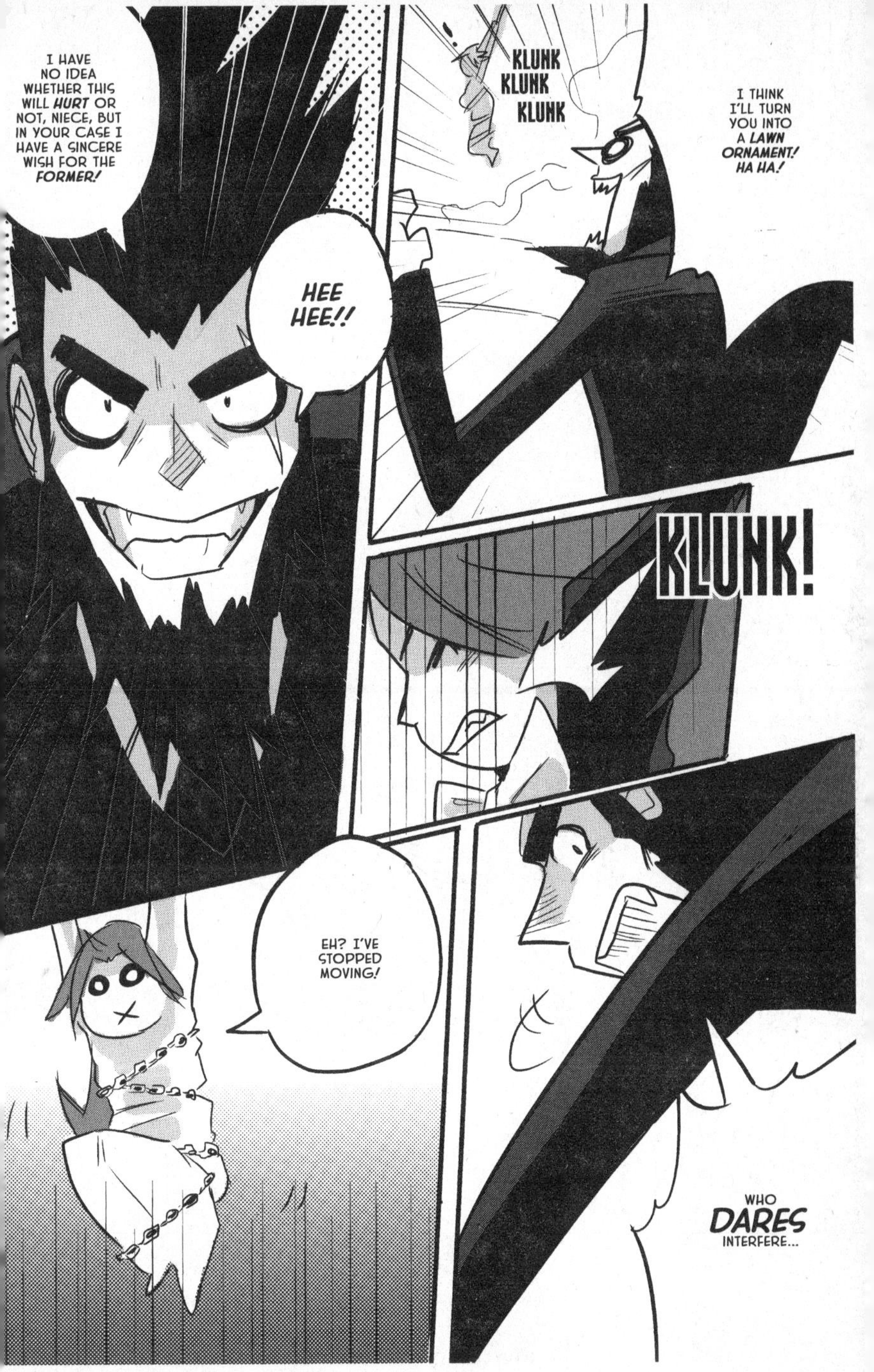
I HAVE NO IDEA WHETHER THIS WILL HURT OR NOT, NIECE, BUT IN YOUR CASE I HAVE A SINCERE WISH FOR THE FORMER!
HEE HEE!!
KLUNK KLUNK KLUNK
I THINK I'LL TURN YOU INTO A LAWN ORNAMENT! HA HA!
KLUNK!
EH? I'VE STOPPED MOVING!
WHO DARES INTERFERE...

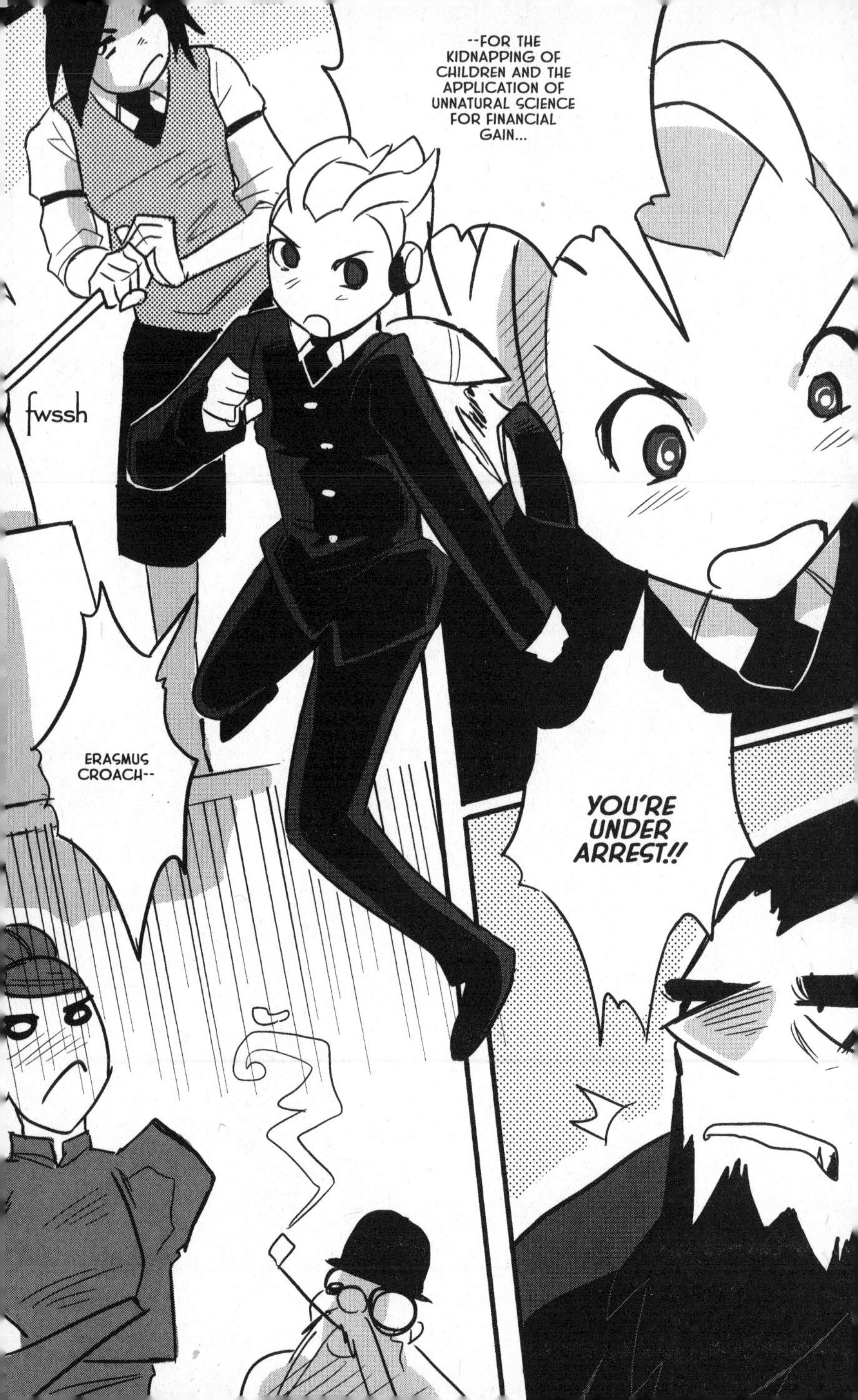
--FOR THE KIDNAPPING OF CHILDREN AND THE APPLICATION OF UNNATURAL SCIENCE FOR FINANCIAL GAIN...
fwssh
ERASMUS CROACH--
YOU'RE UNDER ARREST!!

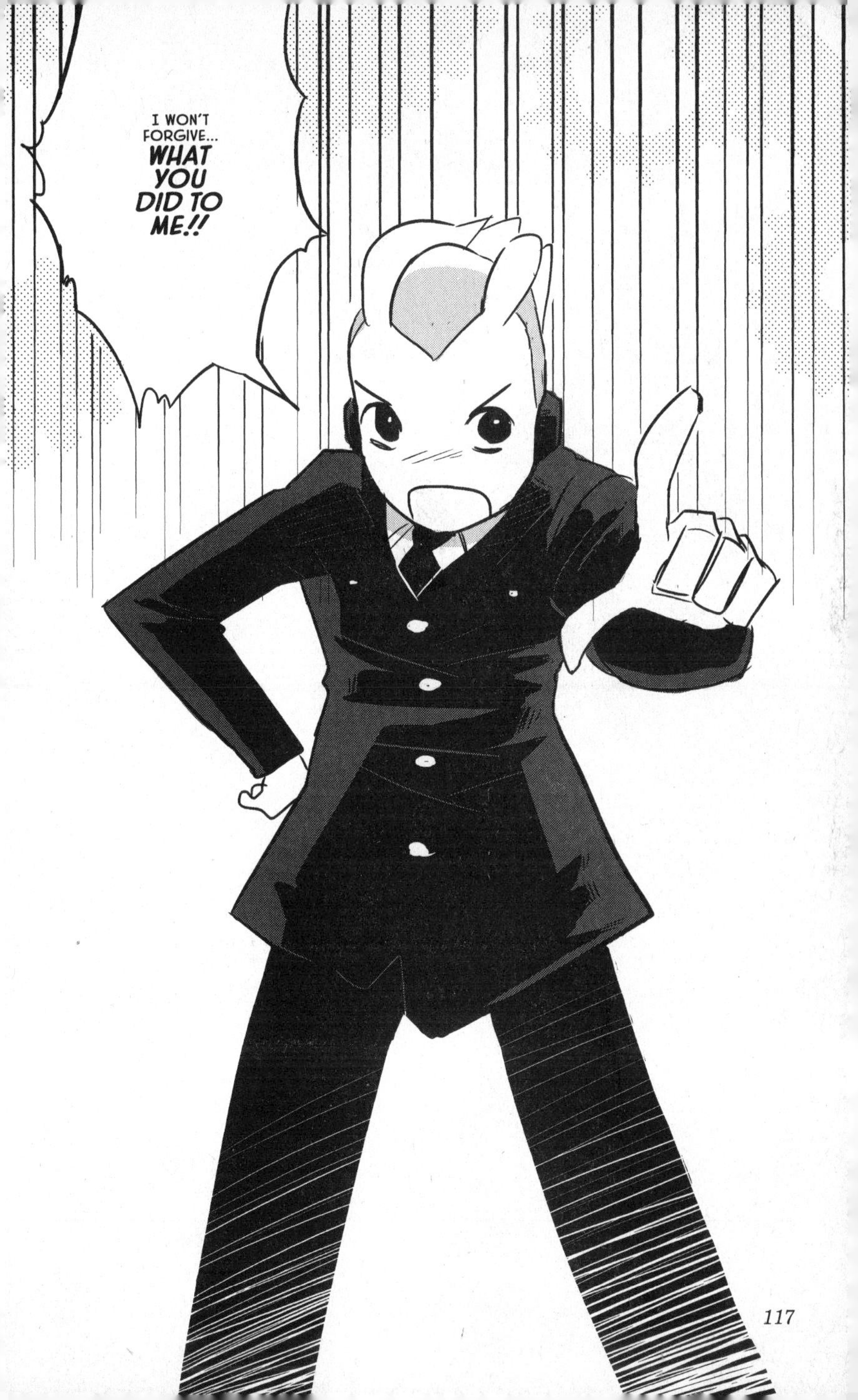
I WON'T FORGIVE... WHAT YOU DID TO ME!!

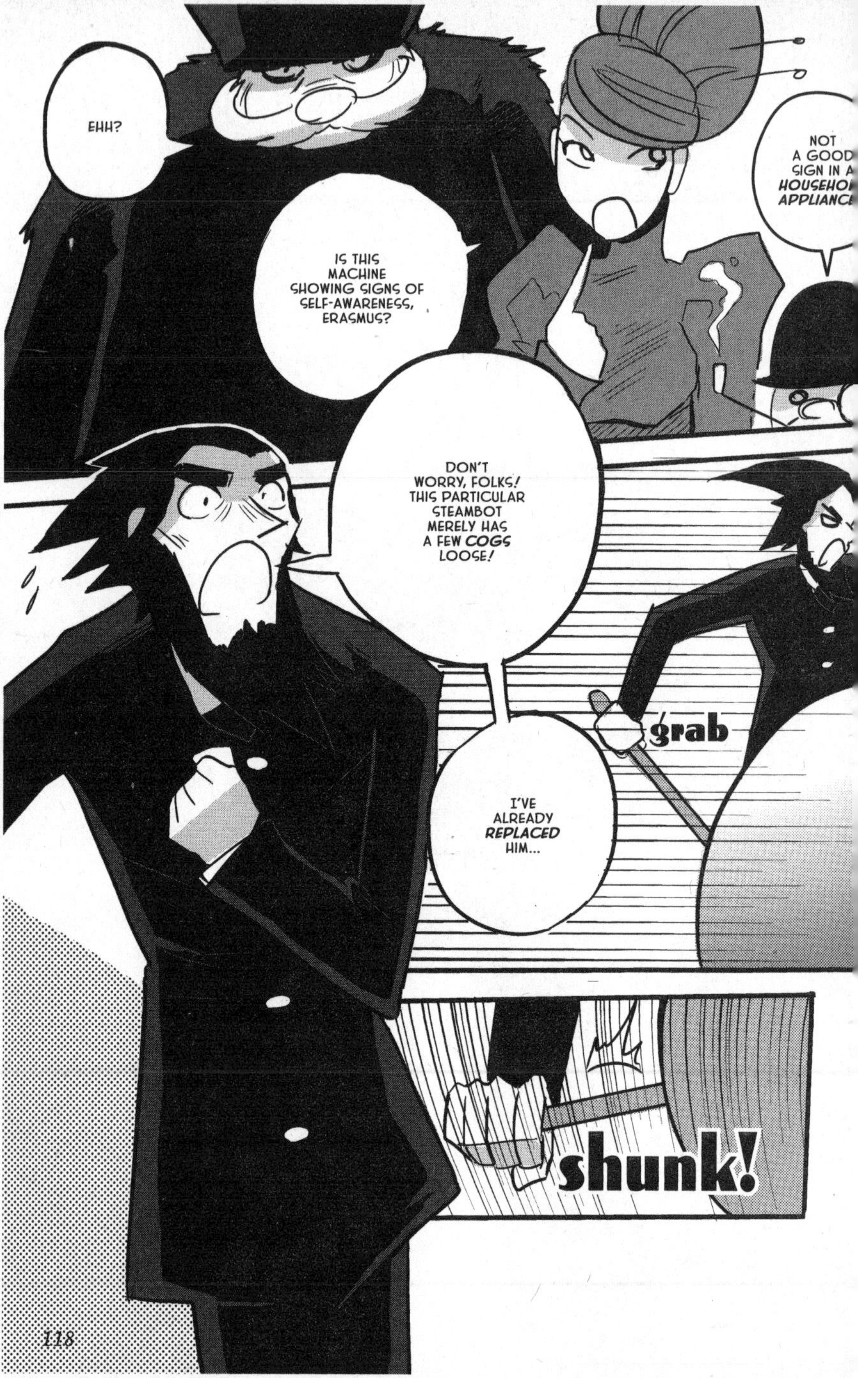

EHH?
IS THIS MACHINE SHOWING SIGNS OF SELF-AWARENESS, ERASMUS?
NOT A GOOD SIGN IN A HOUSEHO APPLIANCE
DON'T WORRY, FOLKS! THIS PARTICULAR STEAMBOT MERELY HAS A FEW COGS LOOSE!
I'VE ALREADY REPLACED HIM...
grab
shunk!

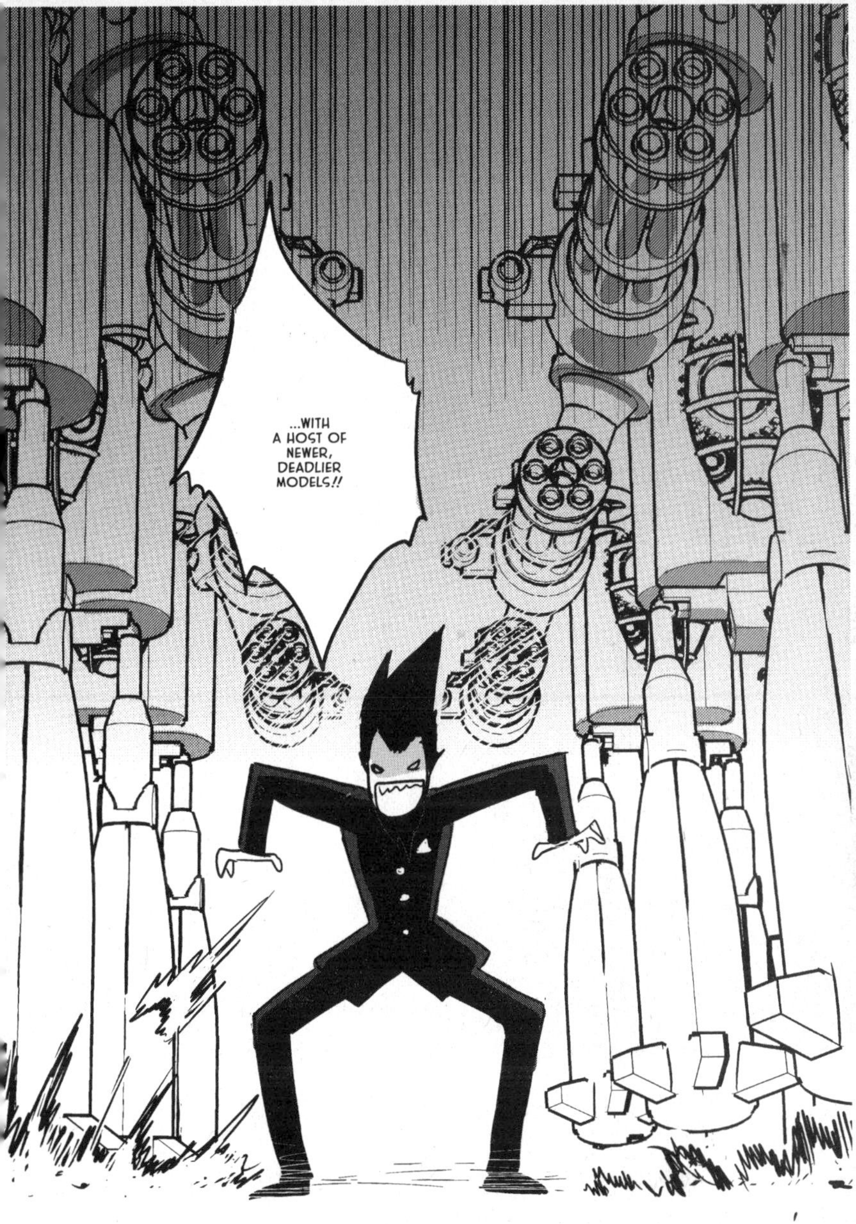
...WITH A HOST OF NEWER, DEADLIER MODELS!!

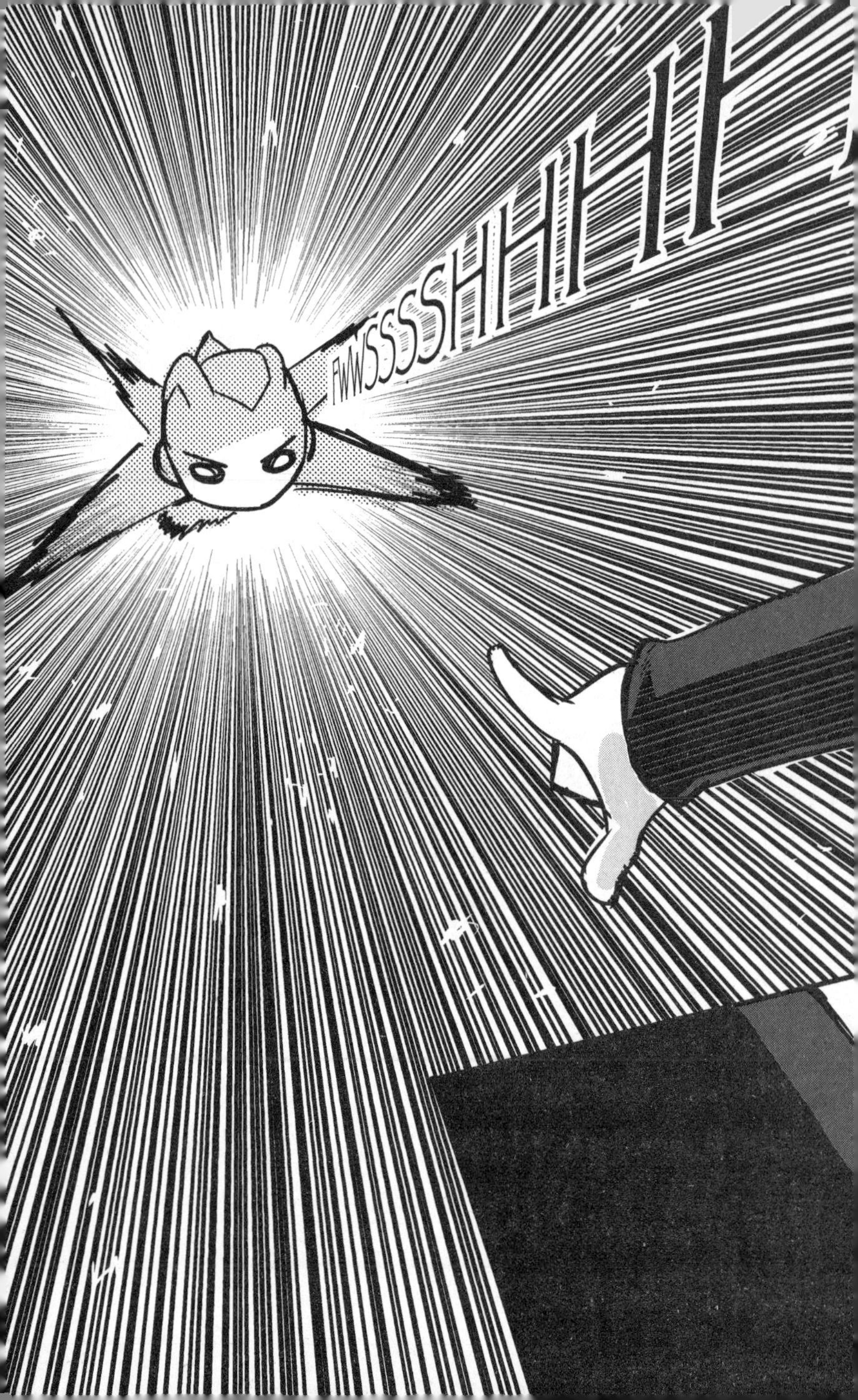
FWWSSSSHHHH!!

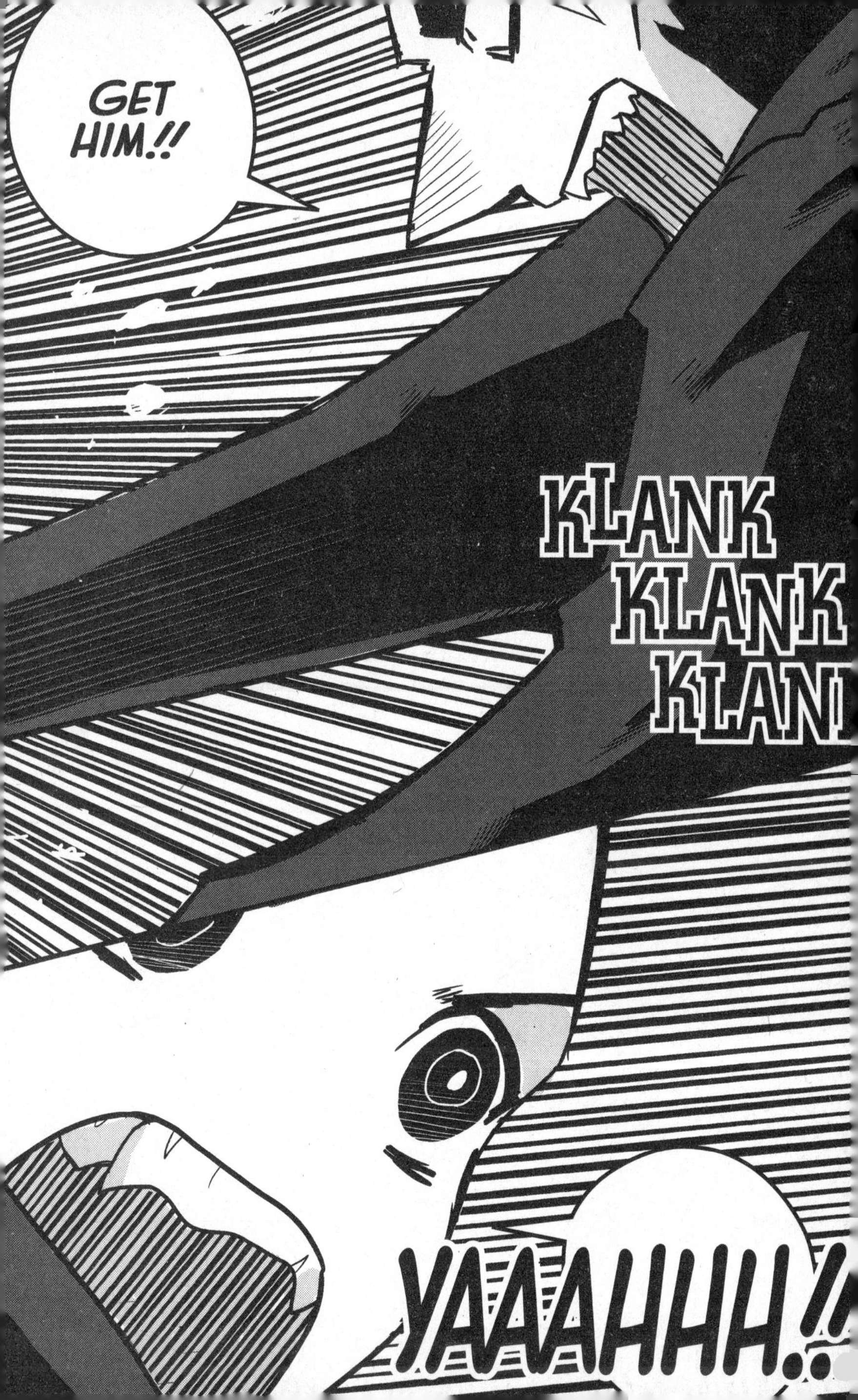
GET HIM.!!
KLANK
KLANK
KLAN
YAAAHHH.!!

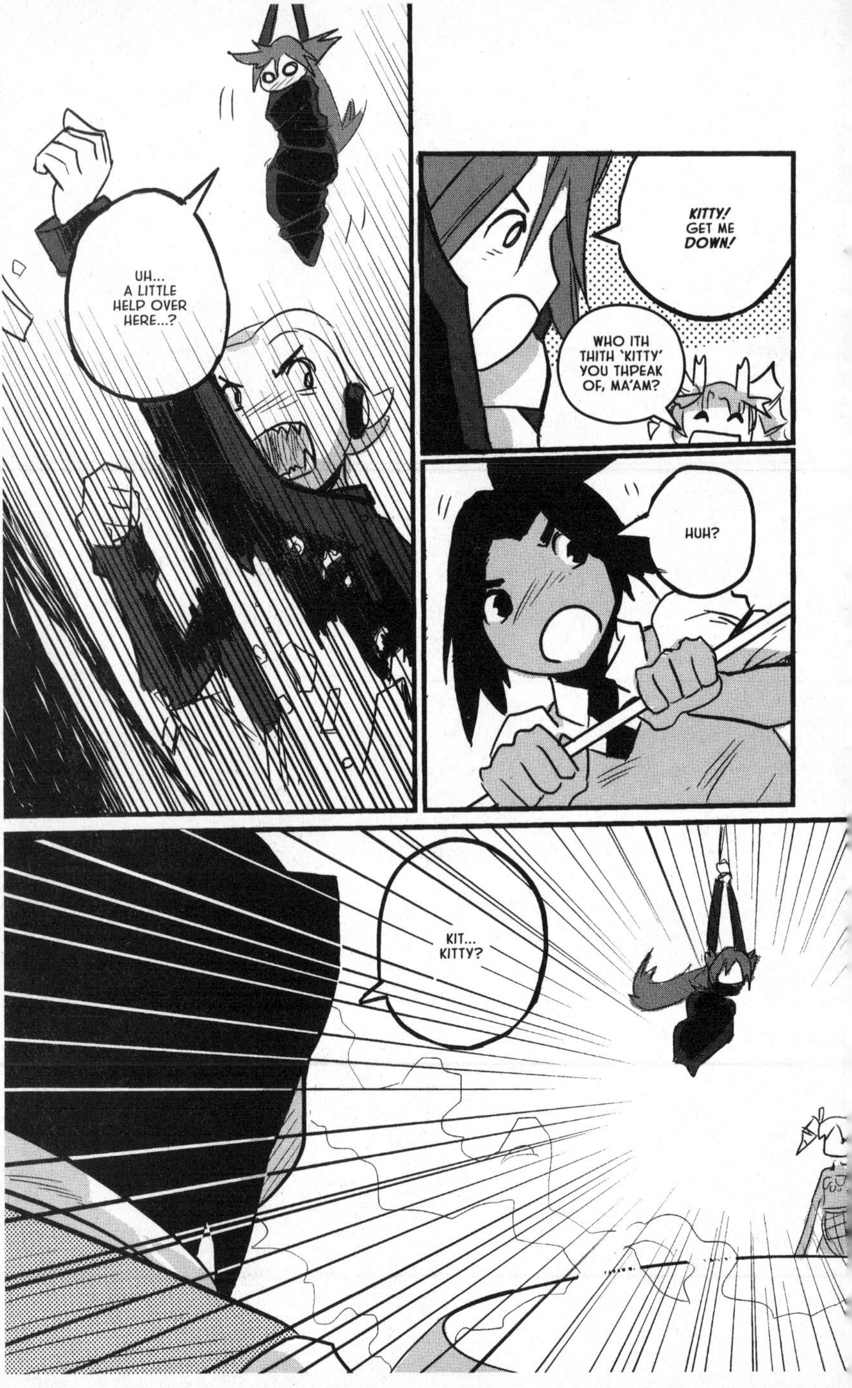
UH... A LITTLE HELP OVER HERE...?
KITTY! GET ME DOWN!
WHO ITH THITH 'KITTY' YOU THPEAK OF, MA'AM?
HUH?
KIT... KITTY?

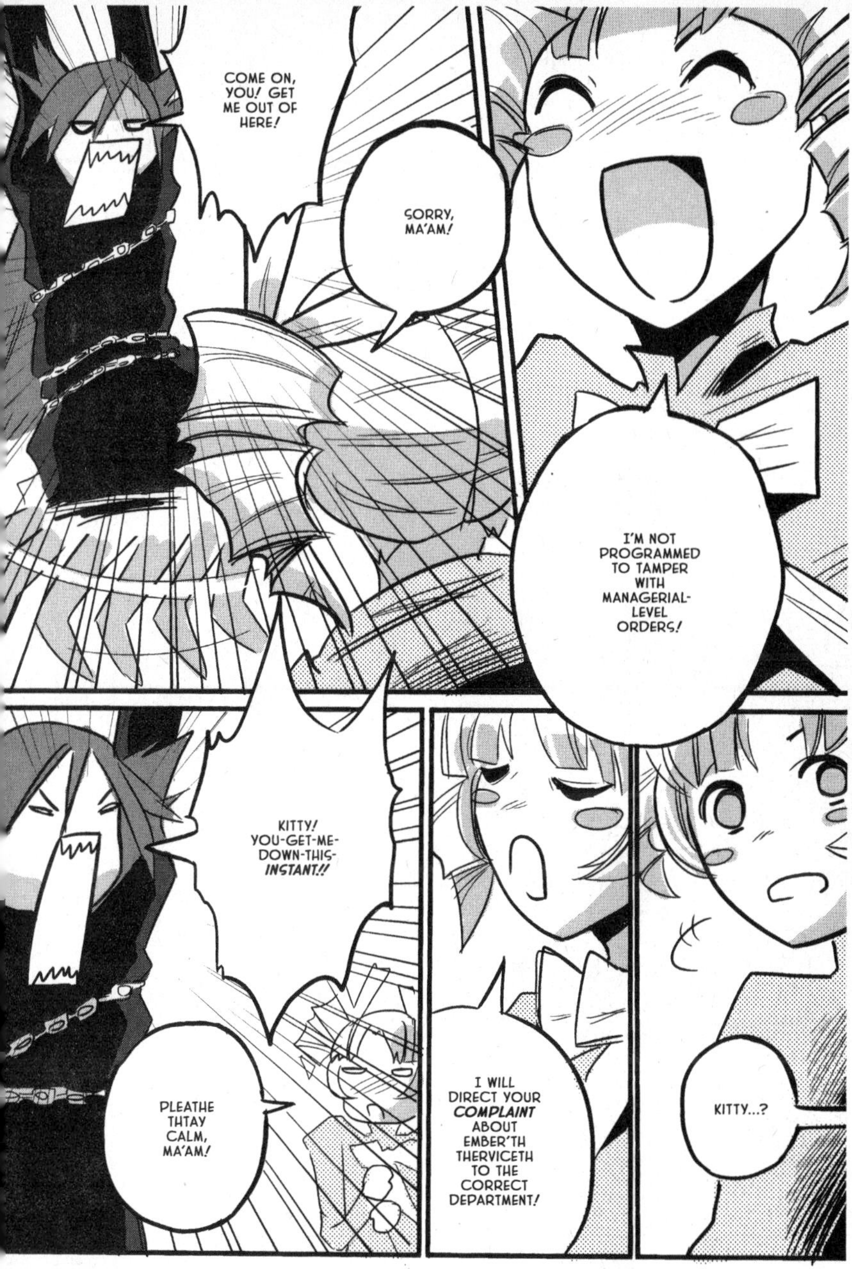
COME ON, YOU! GET ME OUT OF HERE!
SORRY, MA'AM!
I'M NOT PROGRAMMED TO TAMPER WITH MANAGERIAL-LEVEL ORDERS!
KITTY! YOU-GET-ME-DOWN-THIS-*INSTANT!!*
PLEATHE THTAY CALM, MA'AM!
I WILL DIRECT YOUR ***COMPLAINT*** ABOUT EMBER'TH THERVICETH TO THE CORRECT DEPARTMENT!
KITTY...?

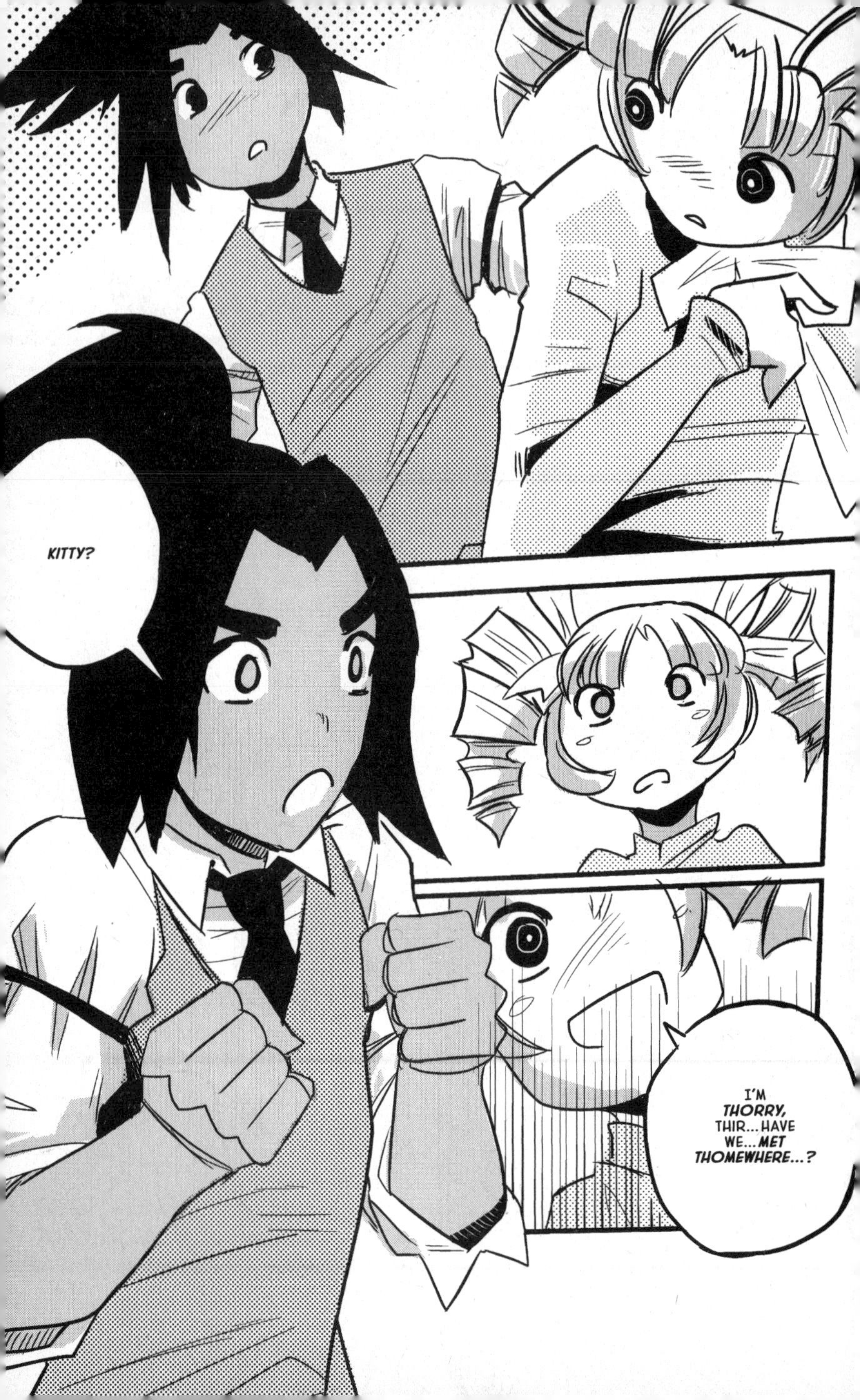
KITTY?
I'M THORRY, THIR... HAVE WE... MET THOMEWHERE...?

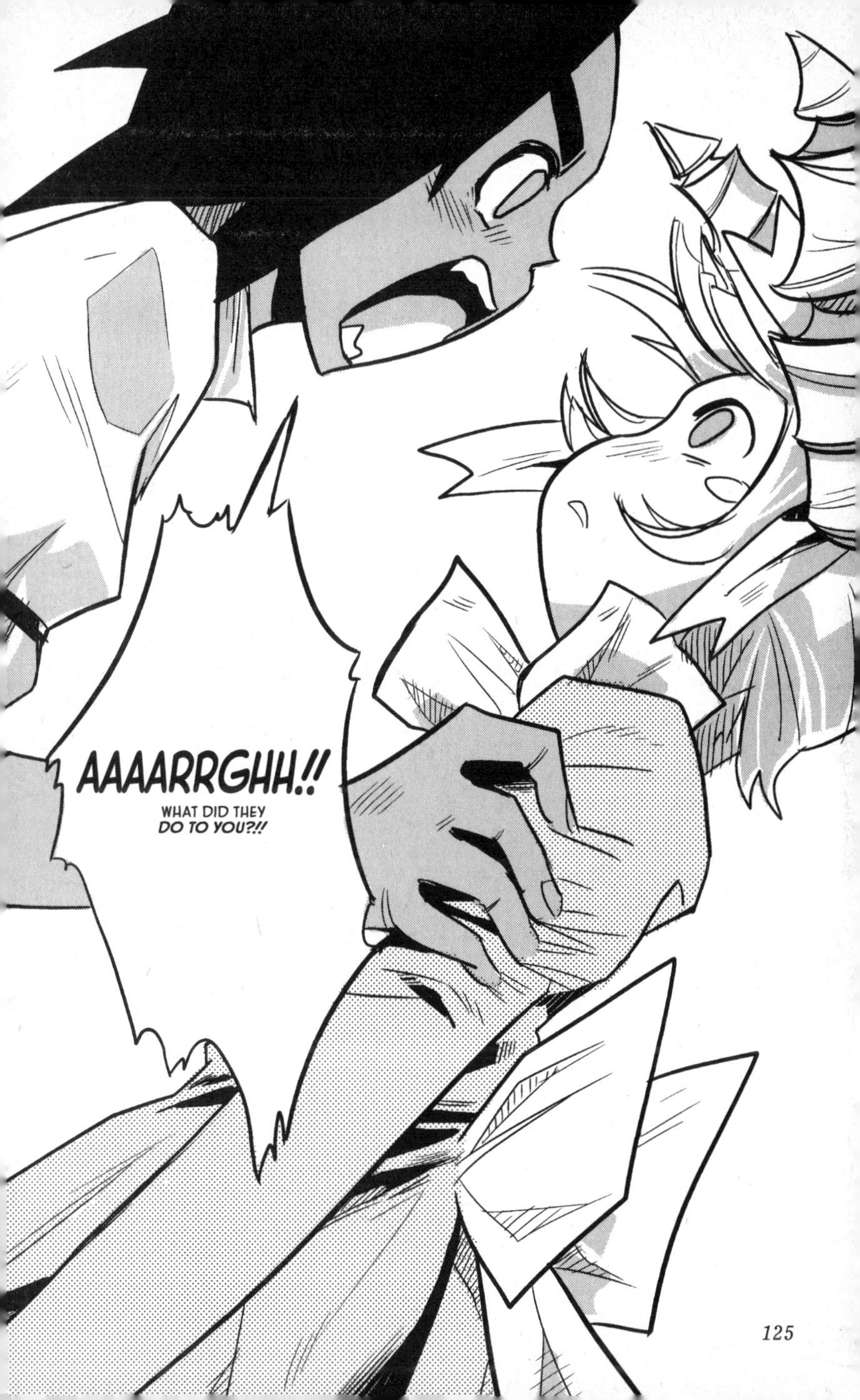
AAAARRGHH!!
WHAT DID THEY DO TO YOU?!!

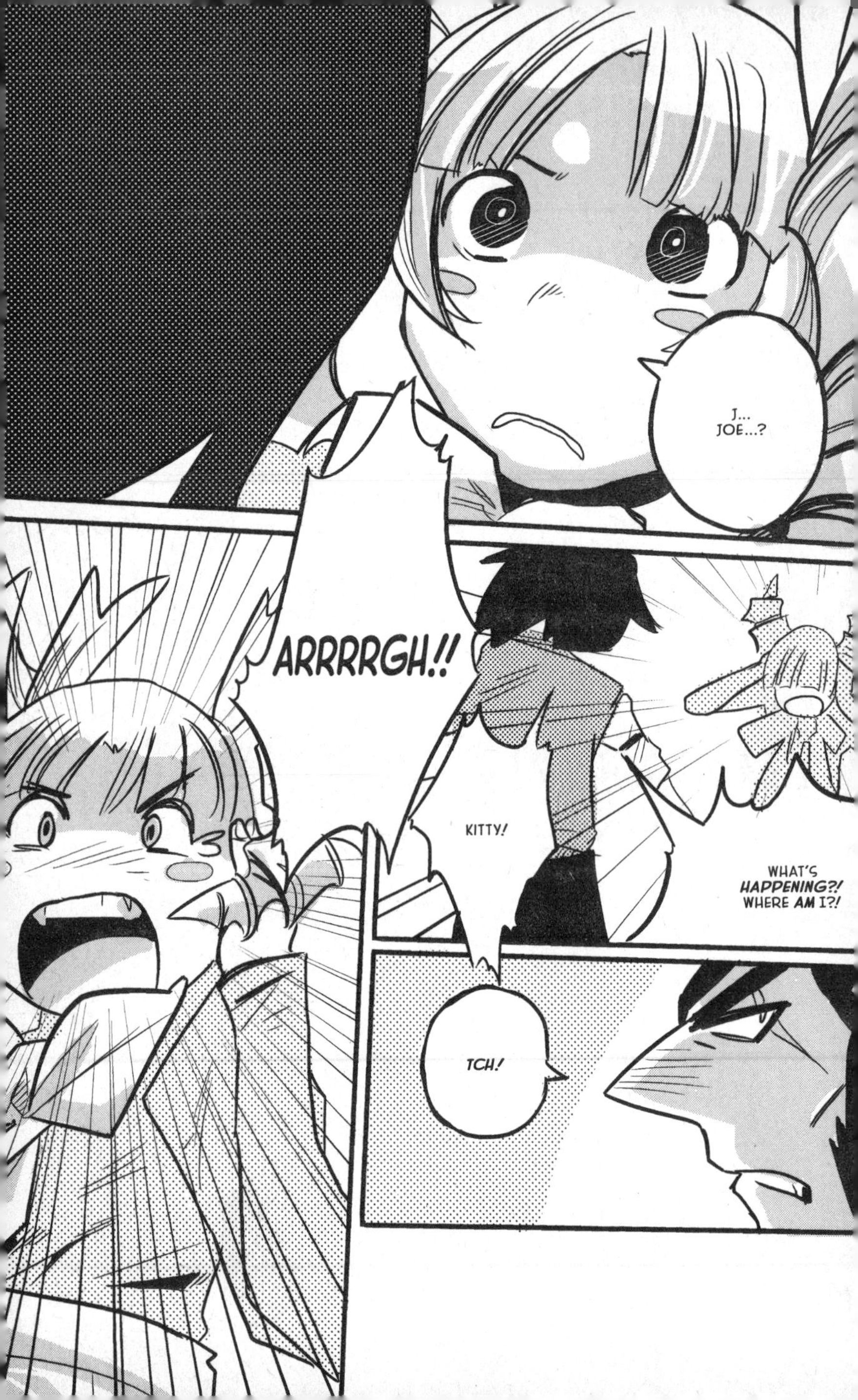
J... JOE...?
ARRRRGH.!!
KITTY!
WHAT'S HAPPENING?! WHERE AM I?!
TCH!

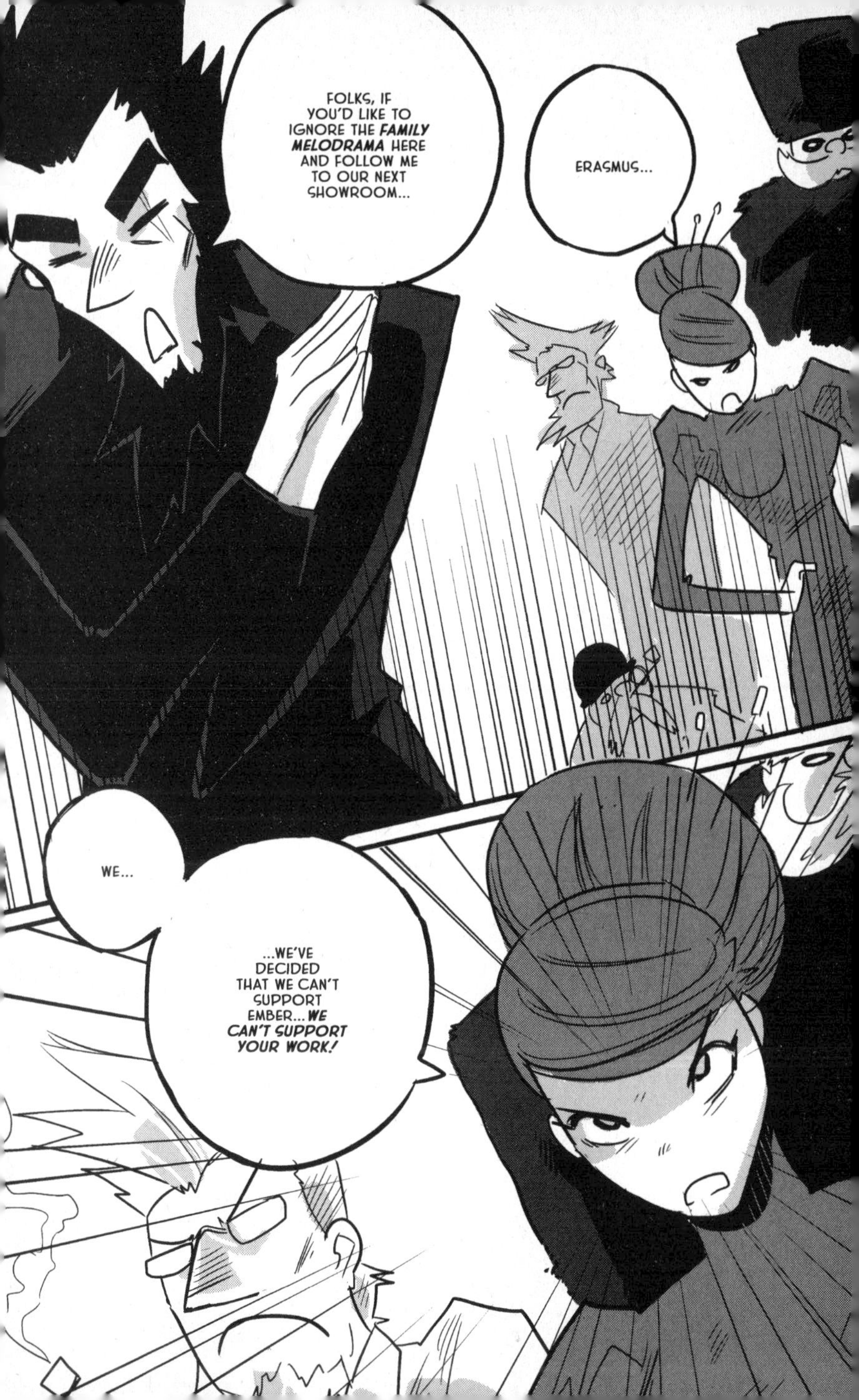
FOLKS, IF YOU'D LIKE TO IGNORE THE *FAMILY MELODRAMA* HERE AND FOLLOW ME TO OUR NEXT SHOWROOM...
ERASMUS...
WE...
...WE'VE DECIDED THAT WE CAN'T SUPPORT EMBER... *WE CAN'T SUPPORT YOUR WORK!*

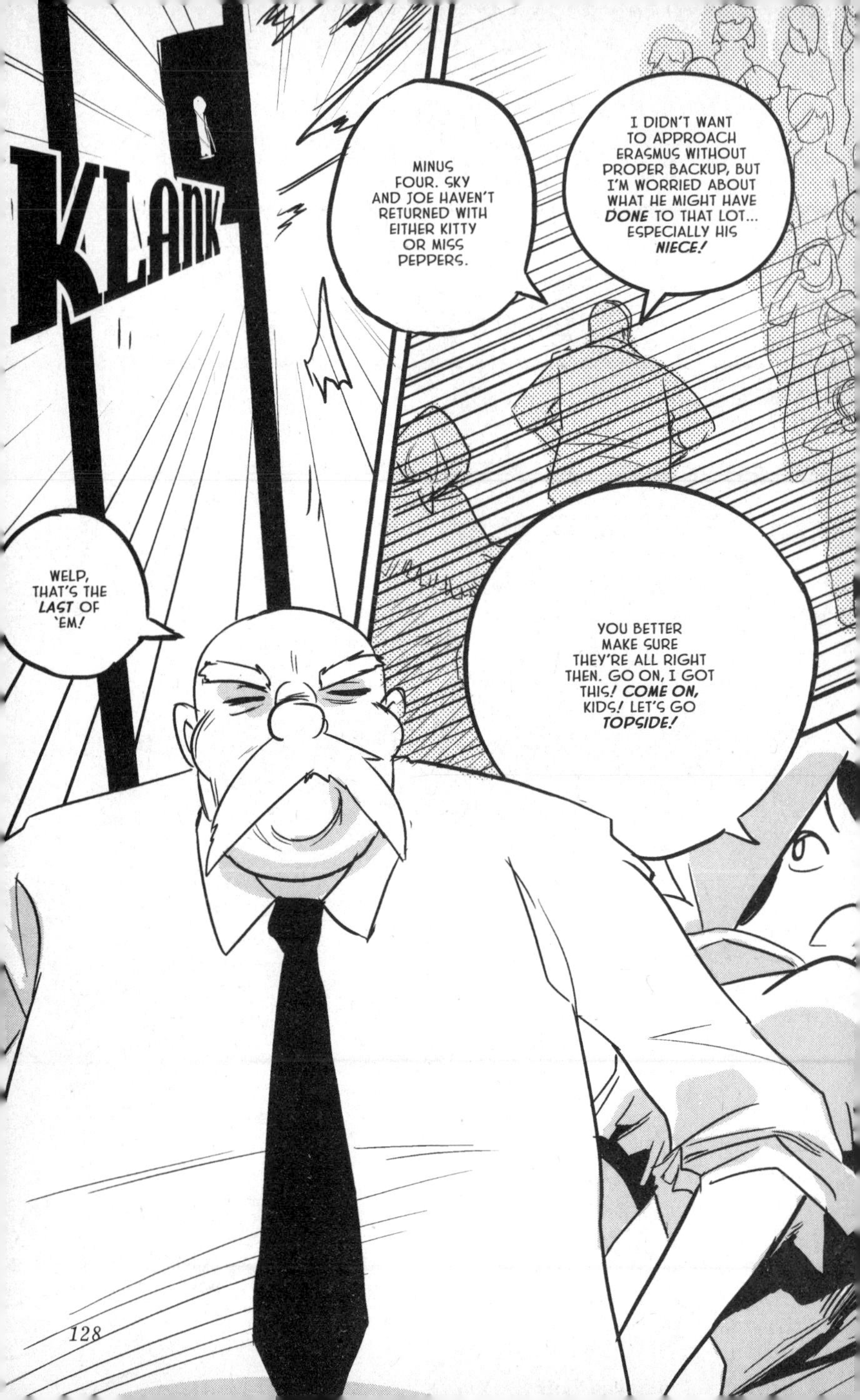
KLANK
WELP, THAT'S THE *LAST* OF 'EM!
MINUS FOUR. SKY AND JOE HAVEN'T RETURNED WITH EITHER KITTY OR MISS PEPPERS.
I DIDN'T WANT TO APPROACH ERASMUS WITHOUT PROPER BACKUP, BUT I'M WORRIED ABOUT WHAT HE MIGHT HAVE ***DONE*** TO THAT LOT... ESPECIALLY HIS ***NIECE!***
YOU BETTER MAKE SURE THEY'RE ALL RIGHT THEN. GO ON, I GOT THIS! ***COME ON,*** KIDS! LET'S GO ***TOPSIDE!***

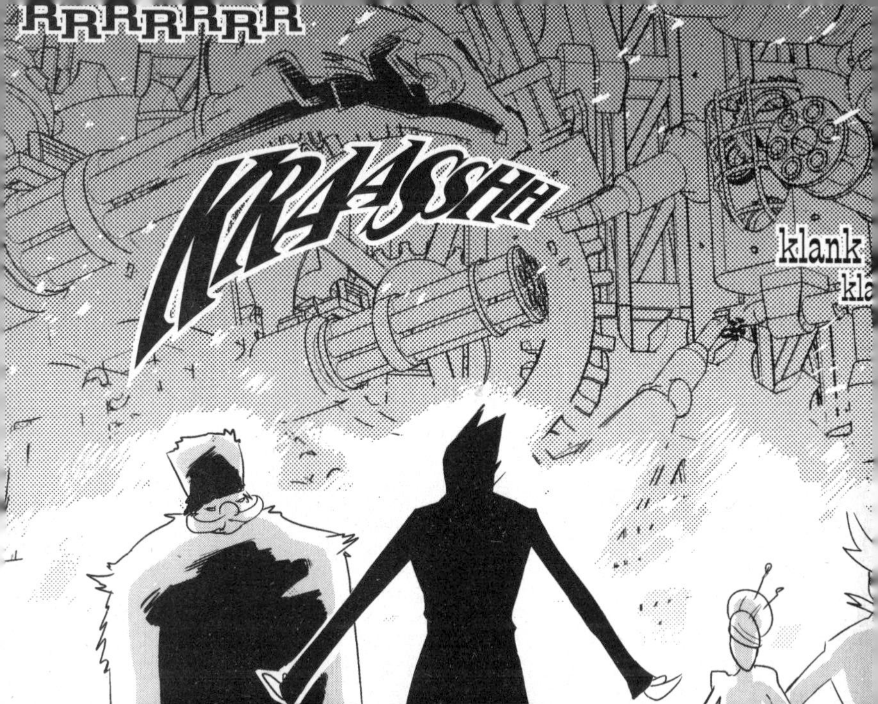
RRRRRRRR
KRAASSHH
klank
kla
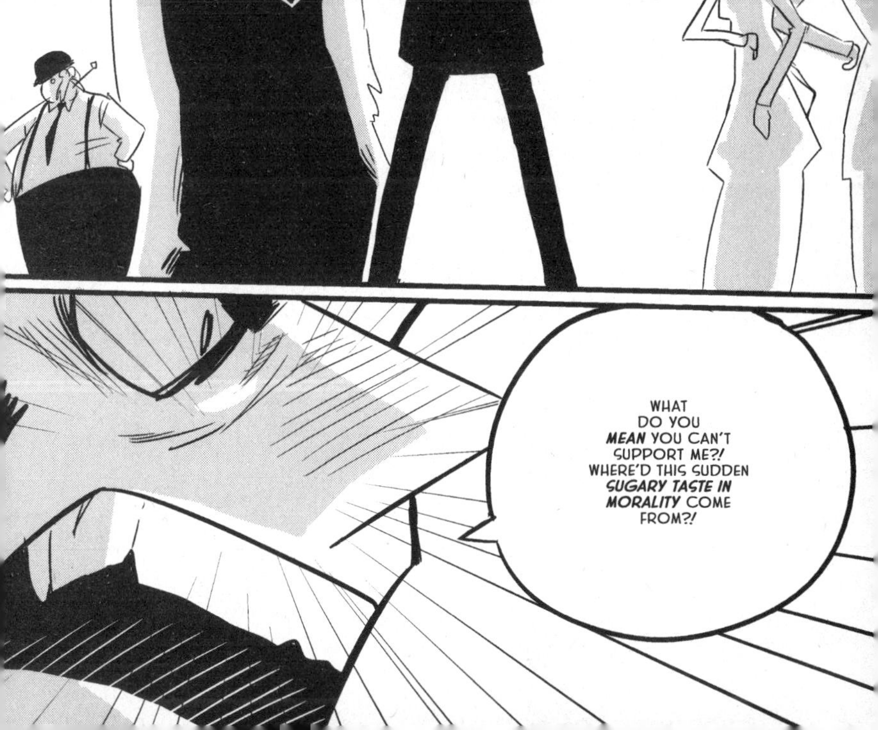
WHAT DO YOU MEAN YOU CAN'T SUPPORT ME?! WHERE'D THIS SUDDEN SUGARY TASTE IN MORALITY COME FROM?!

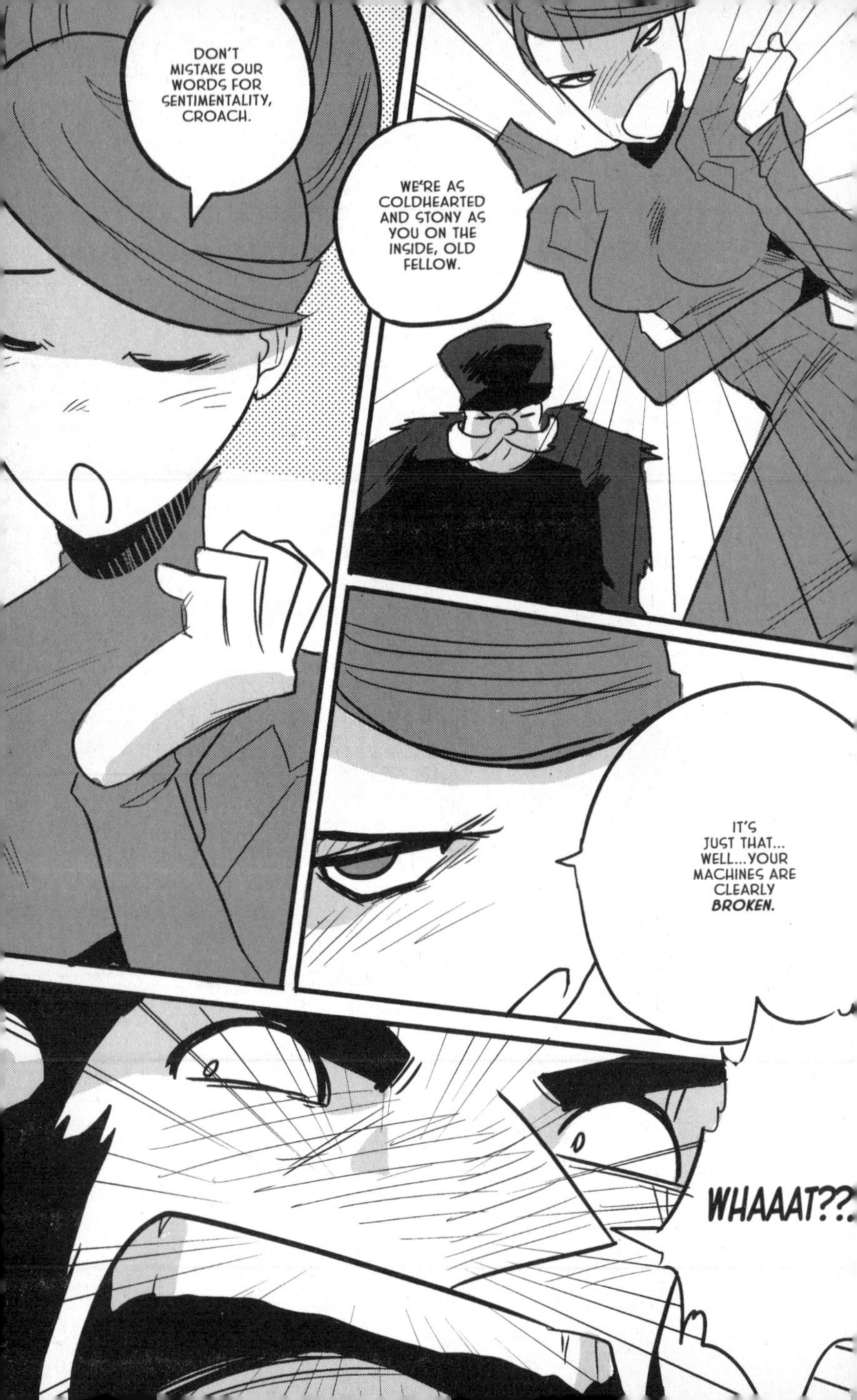
DON'T MISTAKE OUR WORDS FOR SENTIMENTALITY, CROACH.
WE'RE AS COLDHEARTED AND STONY AS YOU ON THE INSIDE, OLD FELLOW.
IT'S JUST THAT... WELL...YOUR MACHINES ARE CLEARLY **BROKEN.**
WHAAAT??!

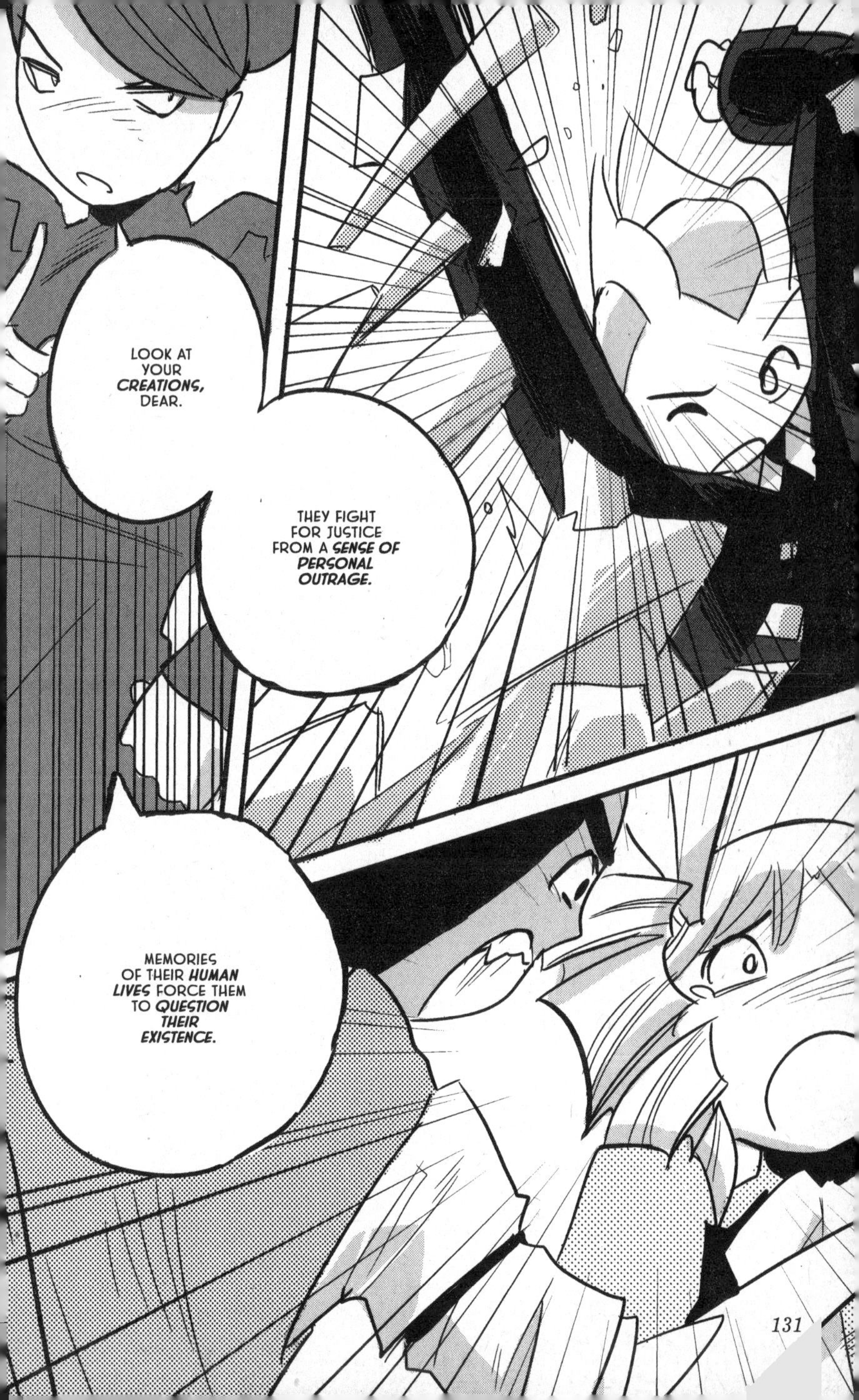
LOOK AT YOUR *CREATIONS,* DEAR.
THEY FIGHT FOR JUSTICE FROM A *SENSE OF PERSONAL OUTRAGE.*
MEMORIES OF THEIR *HUMAN LIVES* FORCE THEM TO *QUESTION THEIR EXISTENCE.*

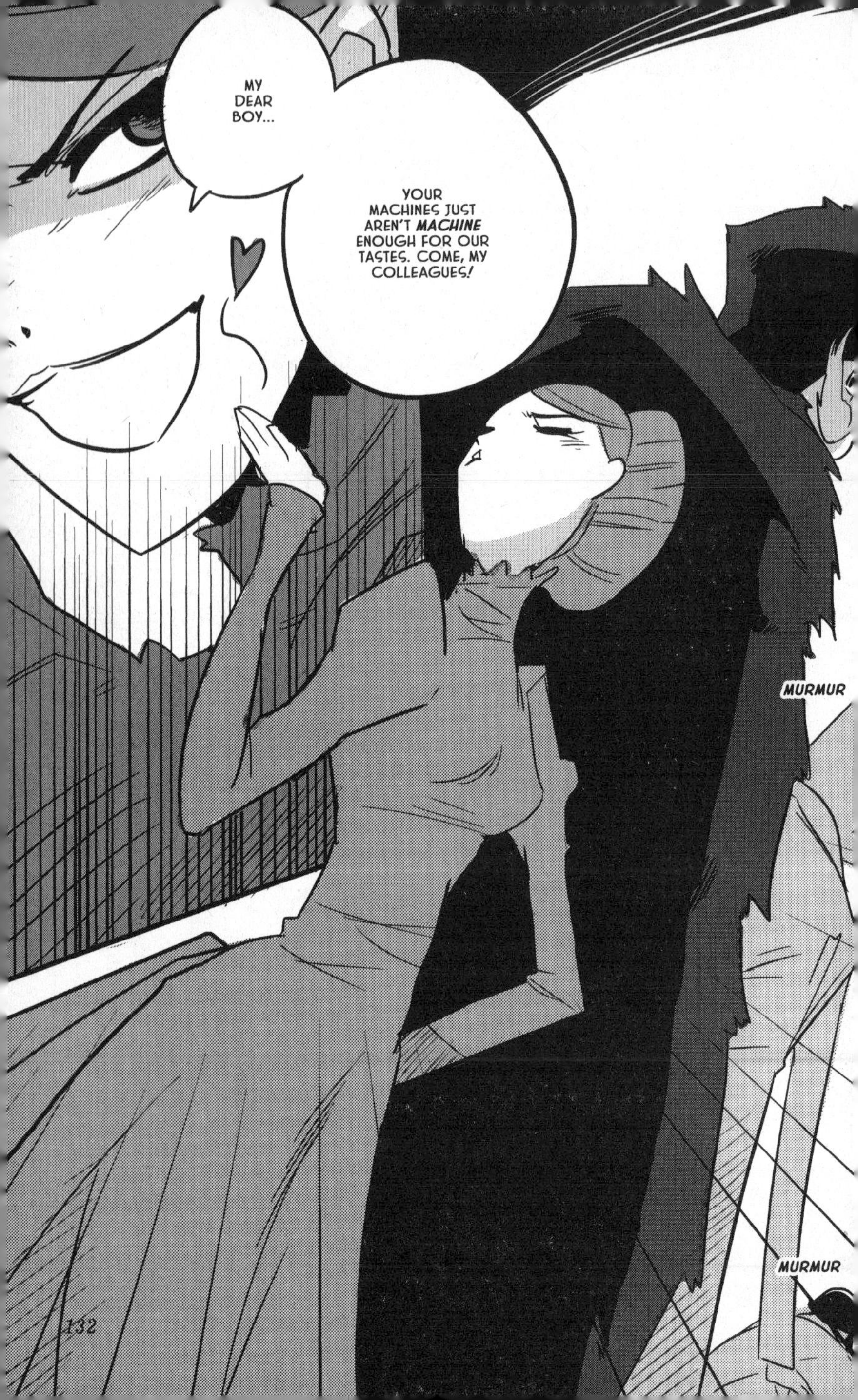
MY DEAR BOY...
YOUR MACHINES JUST AREN'T MACHINE ENOUGH FOR OUR TASTES. COME, MY COLLEAGUES!
MURMUR
MURMUR

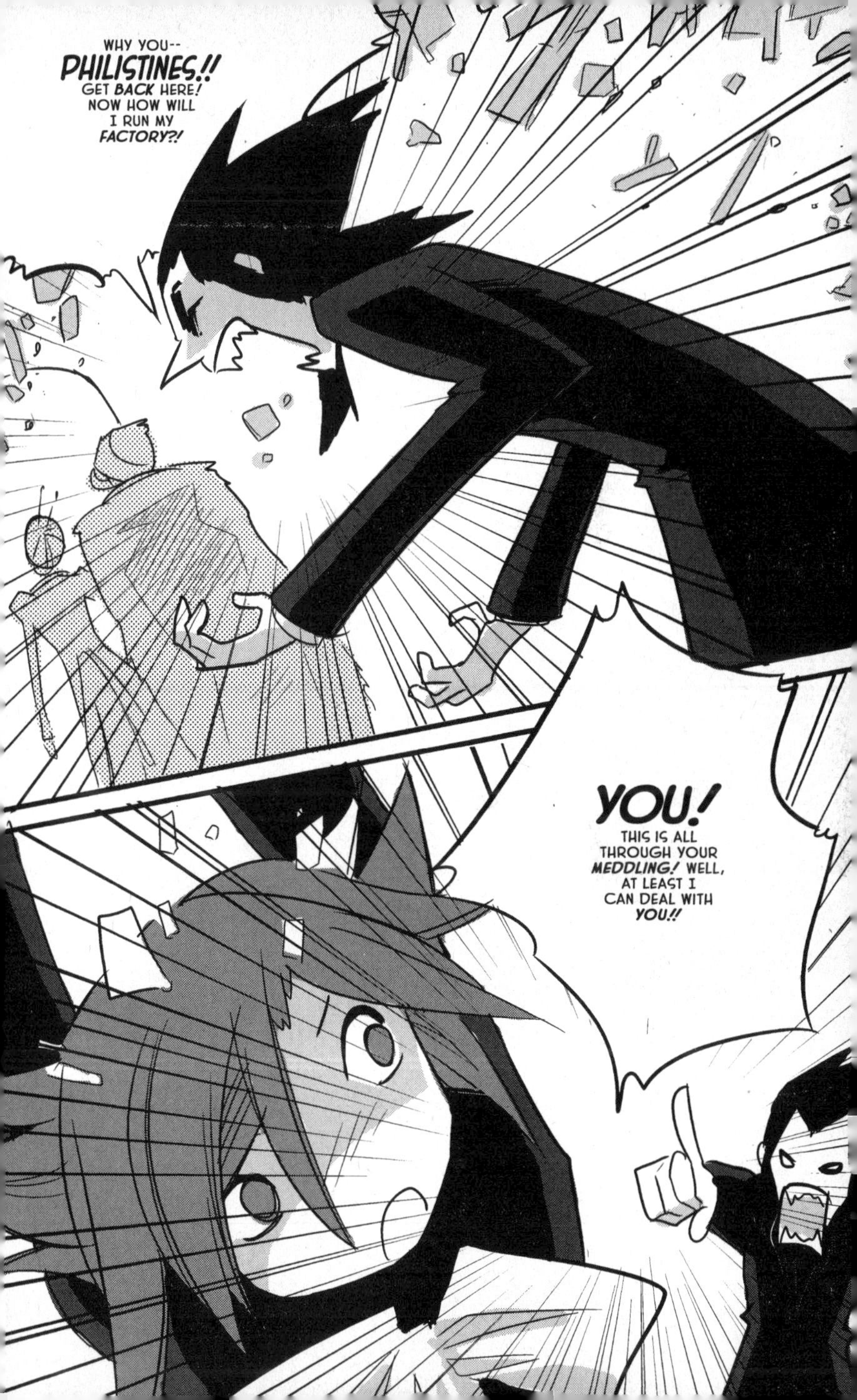
WHY YOU--
PHILISTINES!!
GET BACK HERE! NOW HOW WILL I RUN MY FACTORY?!
YOU!
THIS IS ALL THROUGH YOUR MEDDLING! WELL, AT LEAST I CAN DEAL WITH YOU!!

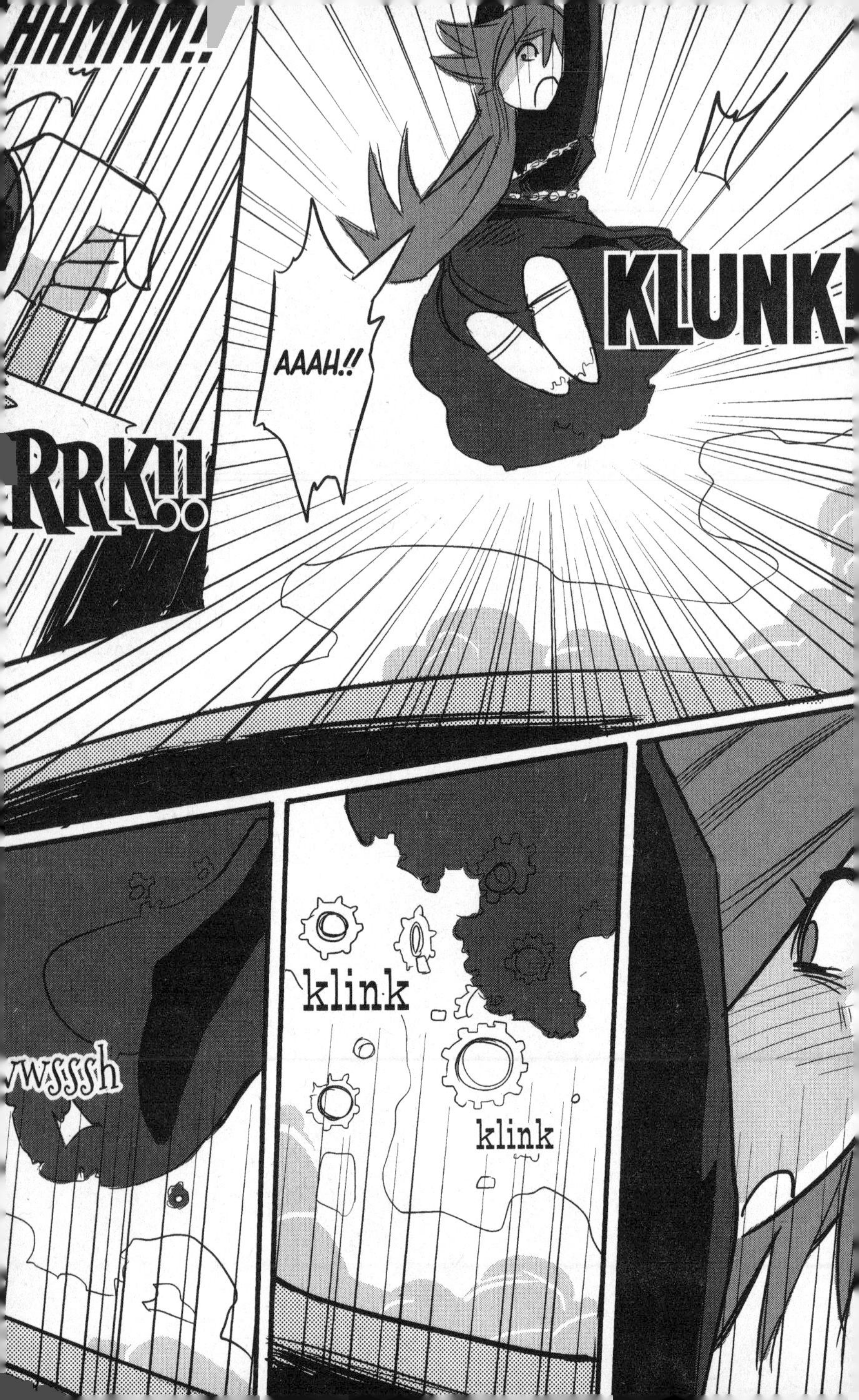
HHMMM!!
KLUNK!
AAAH!!
RRK!!
wsssh
klink
klink

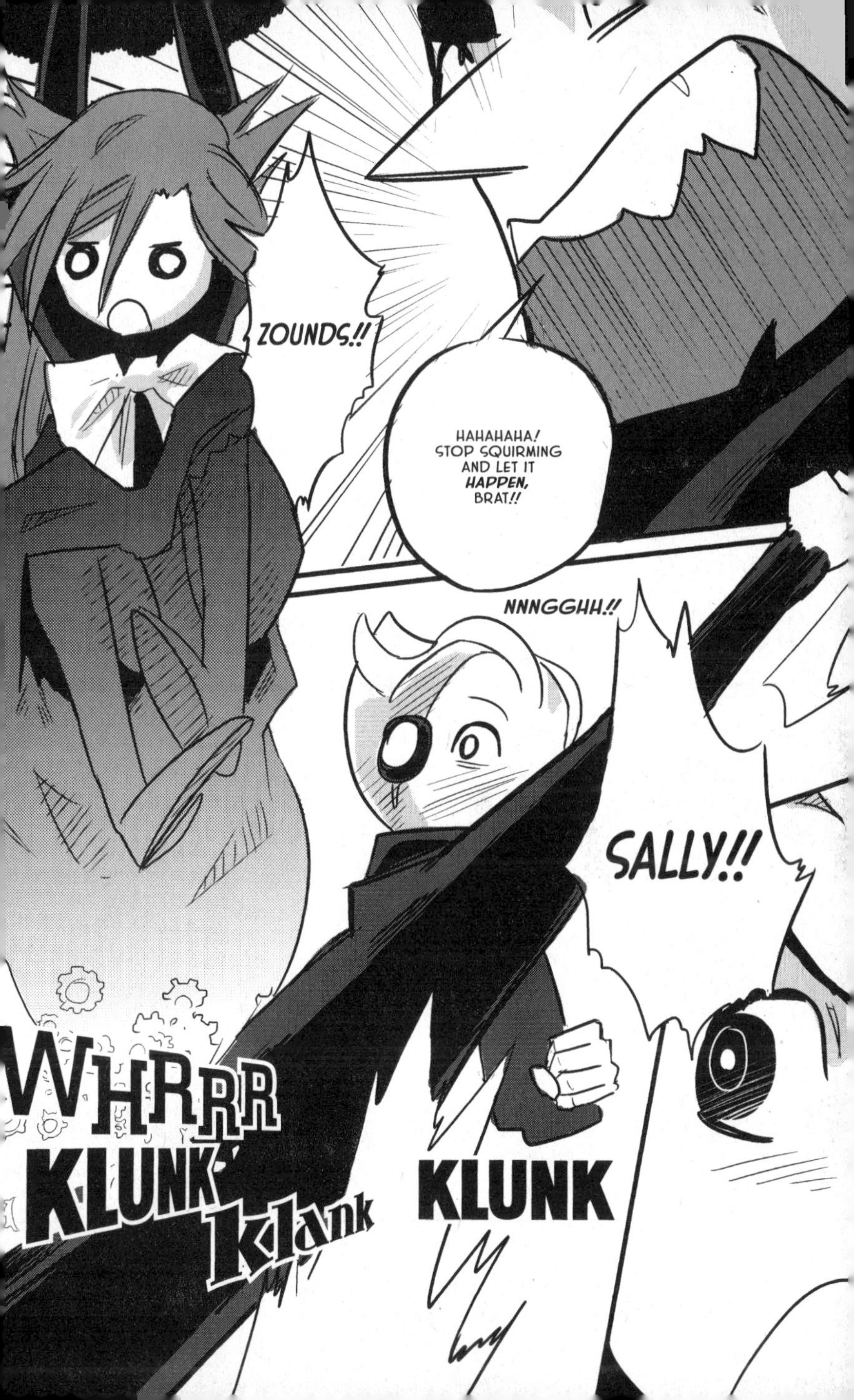
ZOUNDS!!
HAHAHAHA! STOP SQUIRMING AND LET IT HAPPEN, BRAT!!
NNNGGHH!!
SALLY!!
WHRRR
KLUNK
Klank
KLUNK

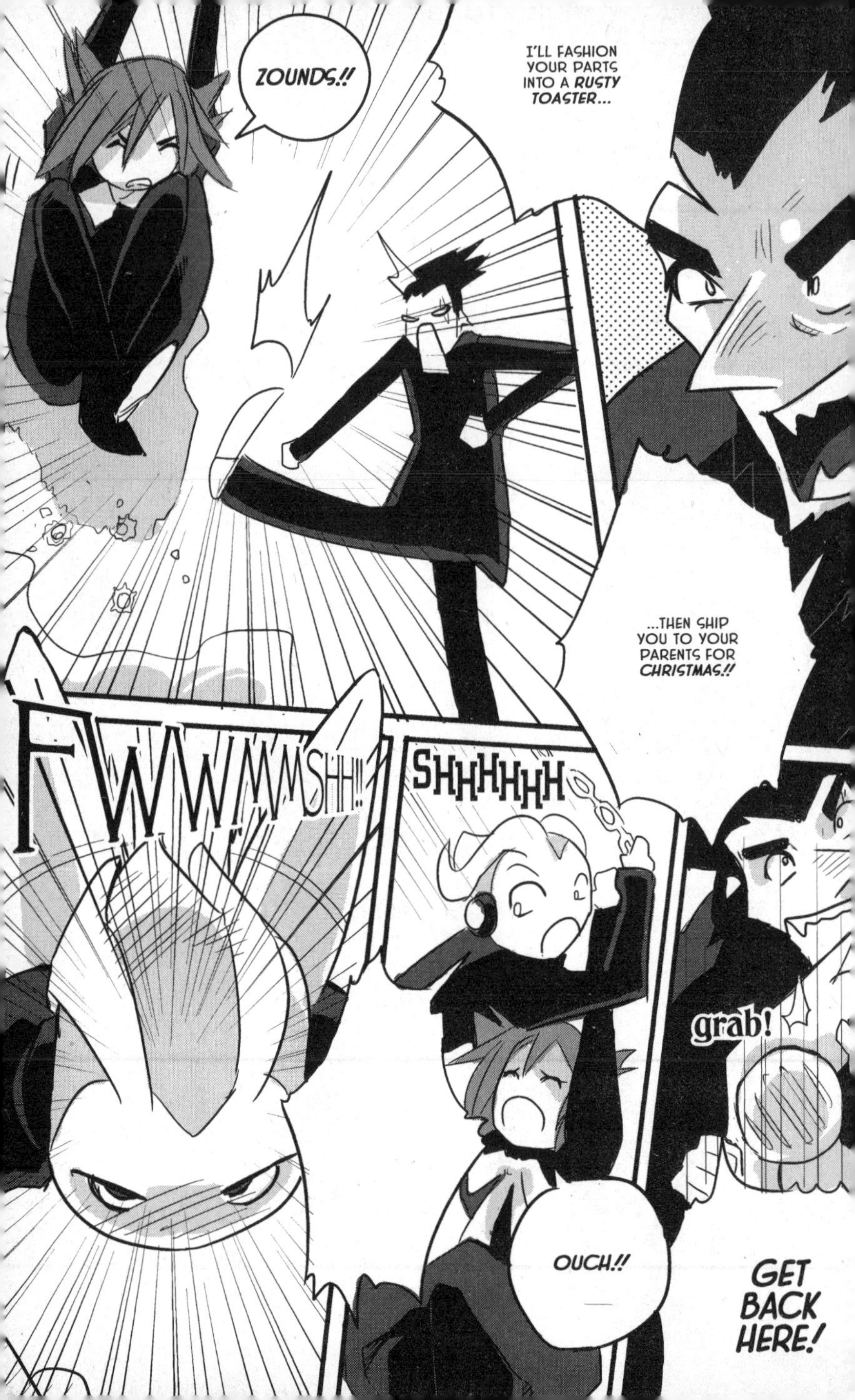
ZOUNDS!!
I'LL FASHION YOUR PARTS INTO A *RUSTY TOASTER*...
...THEN SHIP YOU TO YOUR PARENTS FOR *CHRISTMAS!!*
FWWMMSHH!!
SHHHHHH
grab!
OUCH!!
GET BACK HERE!

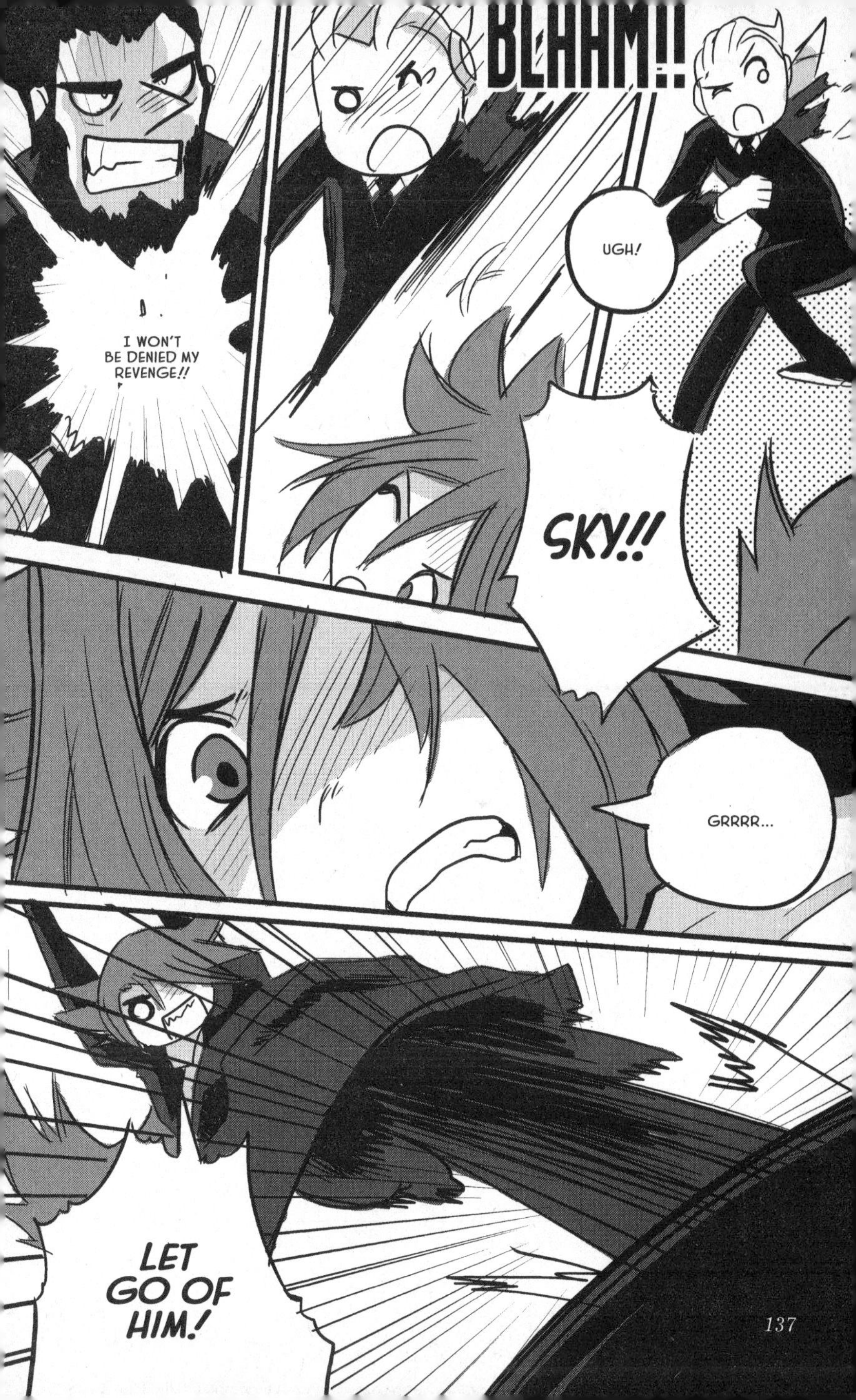
I WON'T BE DENIED MY REVENGE!!
BLAAM!!
UGH!
SKY!!
GRRRR...
LET GO OF HIM!

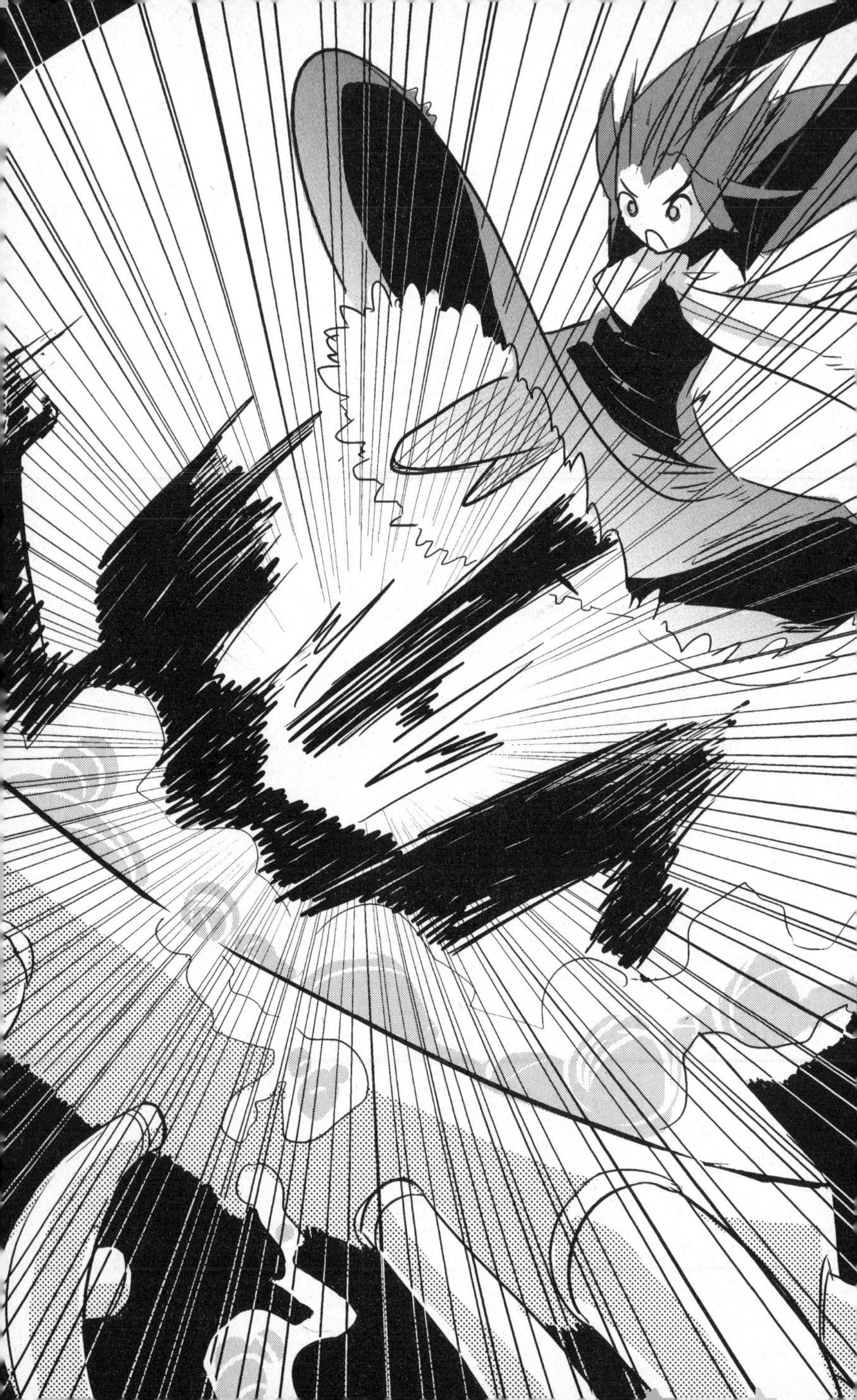

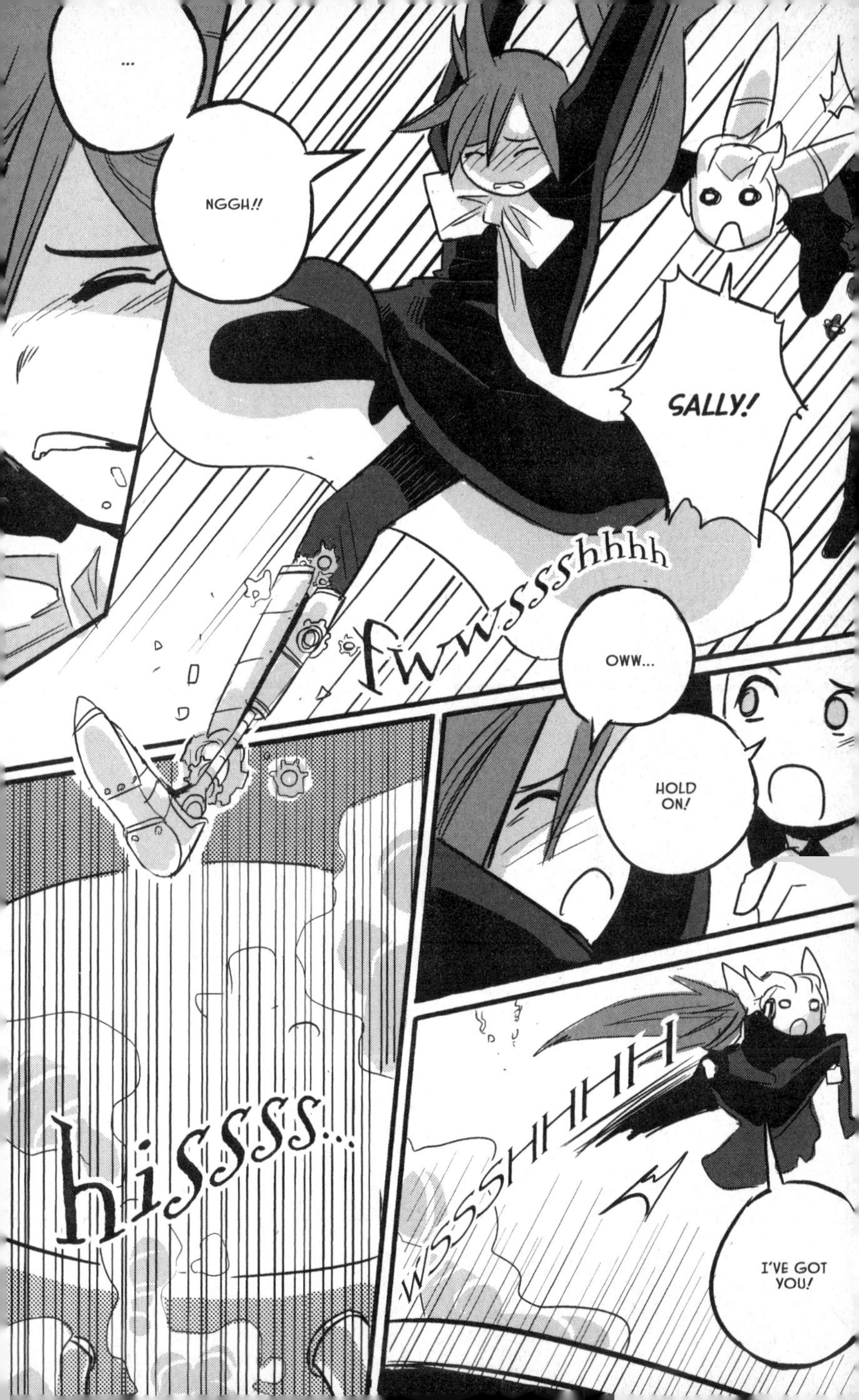
...
NGGH!!
SALLY!
fwwsssshhhh
hissss...
OWW...
HOLD ON!
WSSSHHHHH
I'VE GOT YOU!

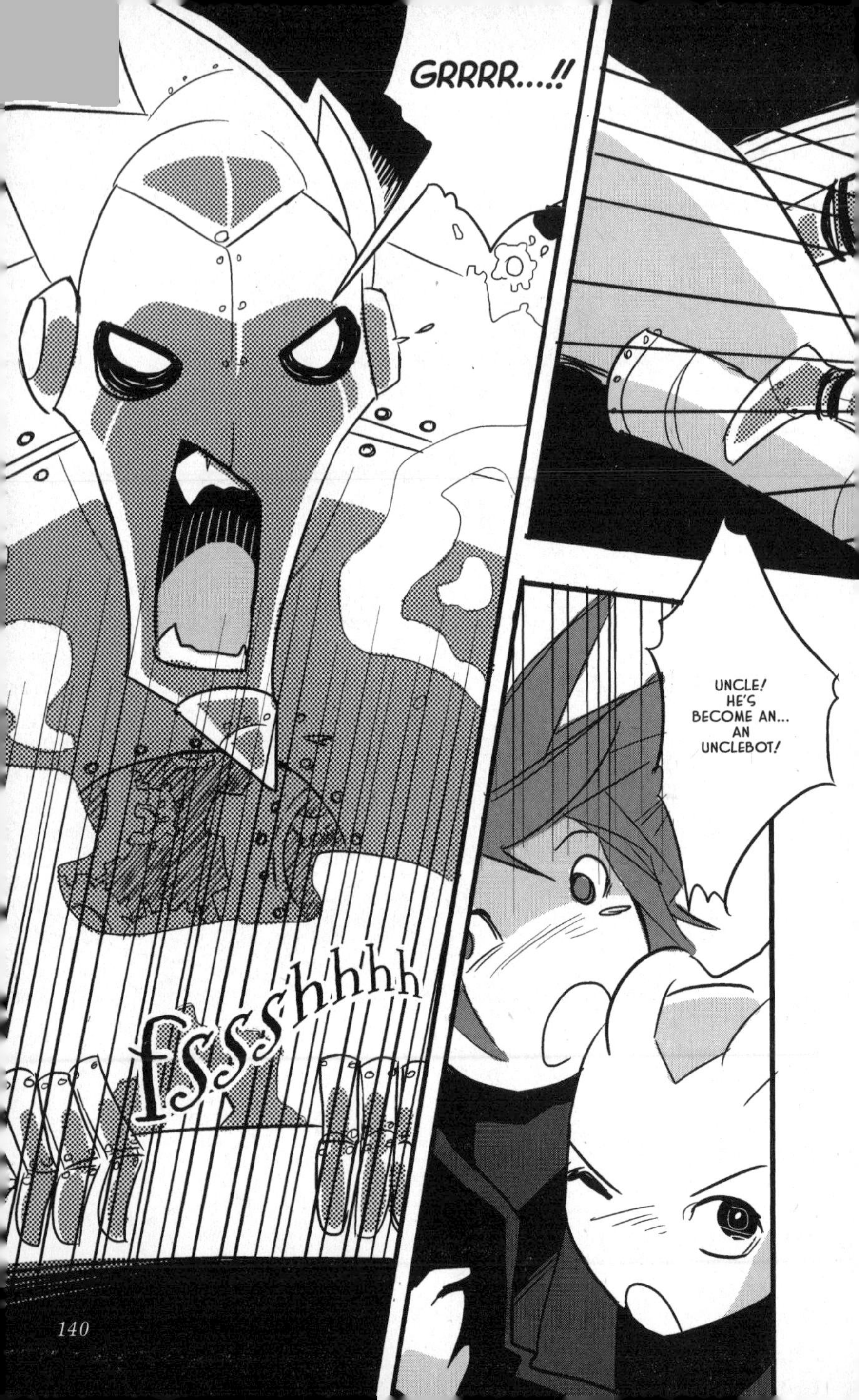
GRRRR...!!
fsssshhhh
UNCLE! HE'S BECOME AN... AN UNCLEBOT!

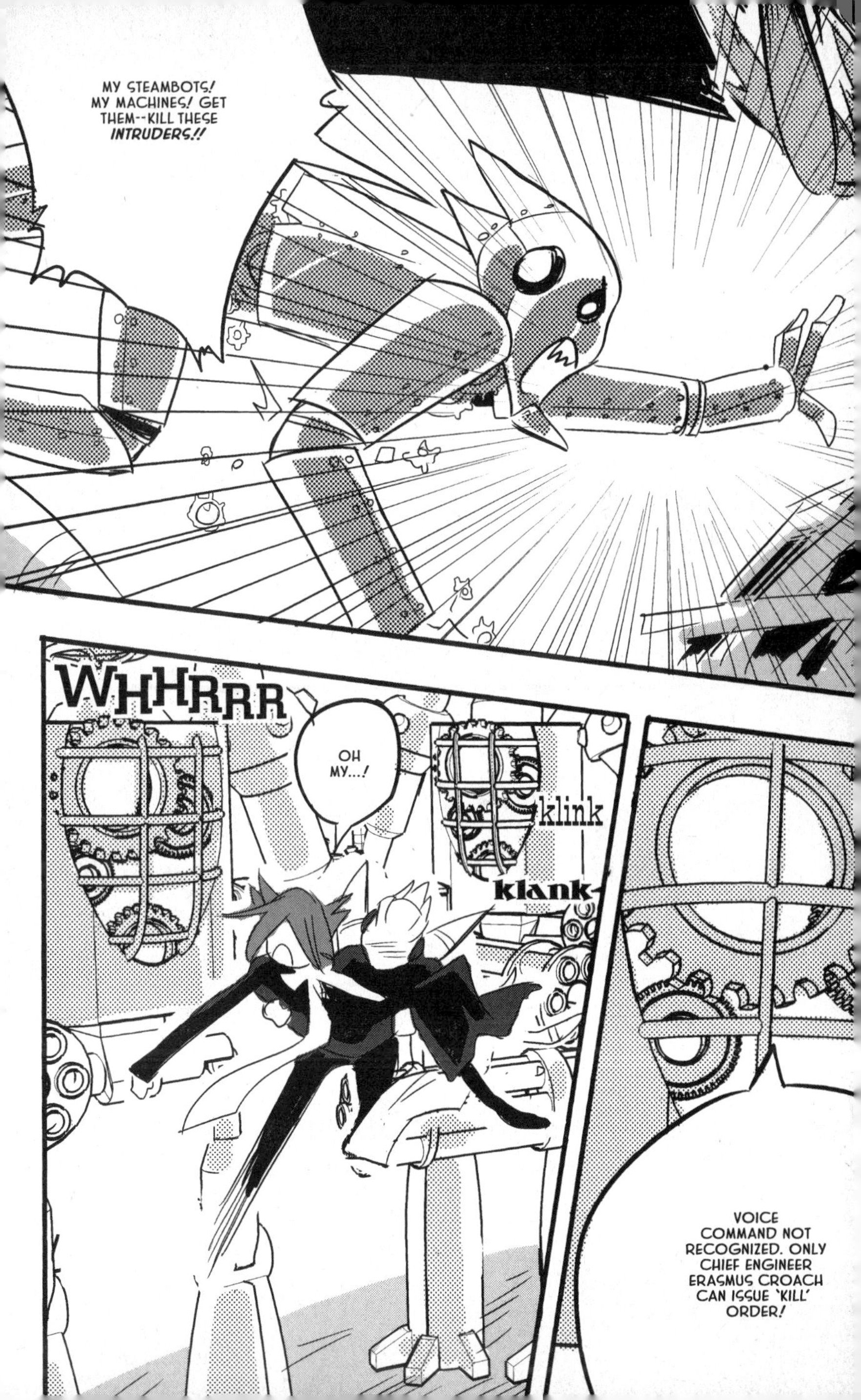
MY STEAMBOTS! MY MACHINES! GET THEM--KILL THESE *INTRUDERS!!*
WHHRRR
OH MY...!
klink
klank
VOICE COMMAND NOT RECOGNIZED. ONLY CHIEF ENGINEER ERASMUS CROACH CAN ISSUE 'KILL' ORDER!

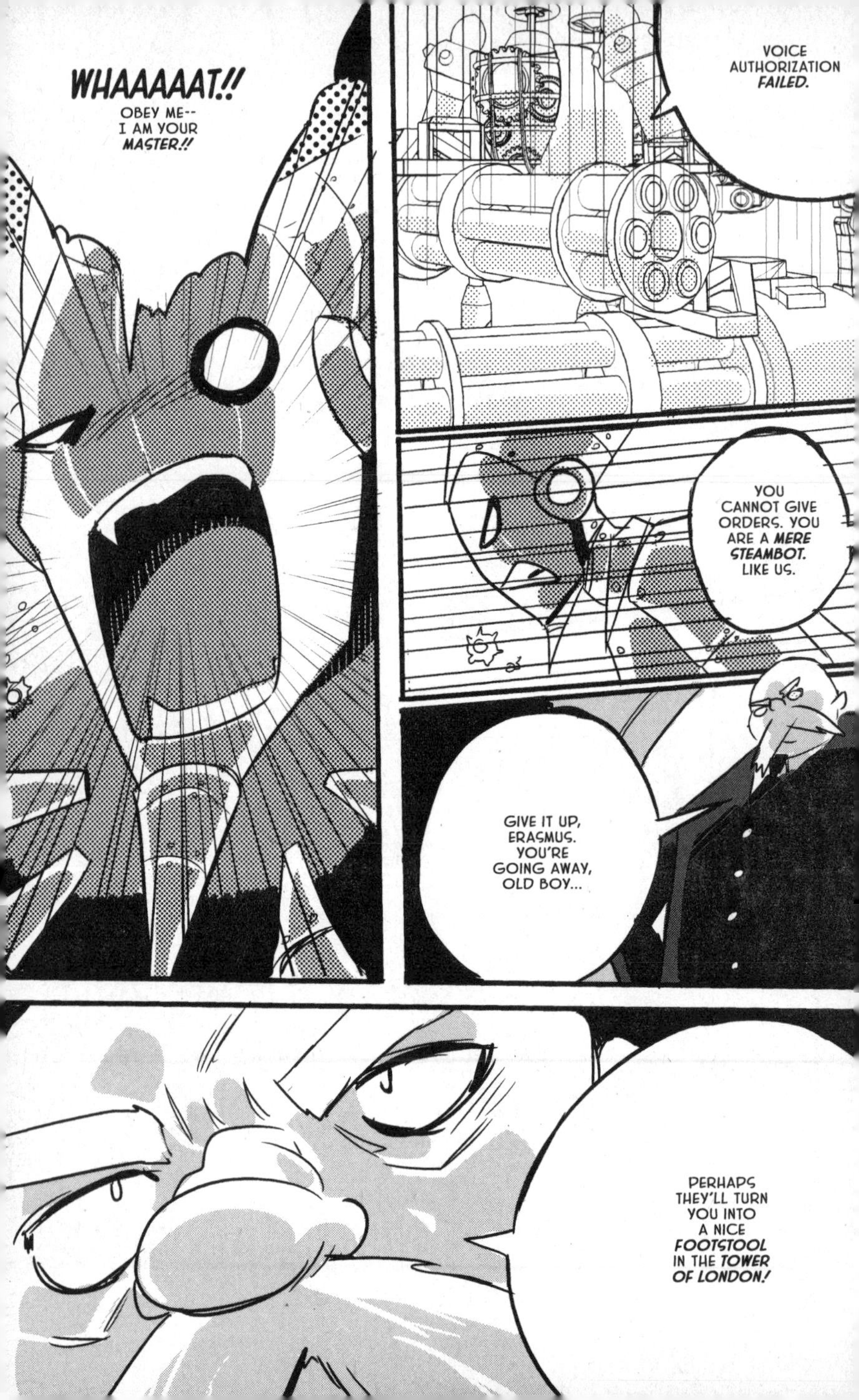
WHAAAAAT!!
OBEY ME-- I AM YOUR MASTER!!
VOICE AUTHORIZATION FAILED.
YOU CANNOT GIVE ORDERS. YOU ARE A MERE STEAMBOT. LIKE US.
GIVE IT UP, ERASMUS. YOU'RE GOING AWAY, OLD BOY...
PERHAPS THEY'LL TURN YOU INTO A NICE FOOTSTOOL IN THE TOWER OF LONDON!

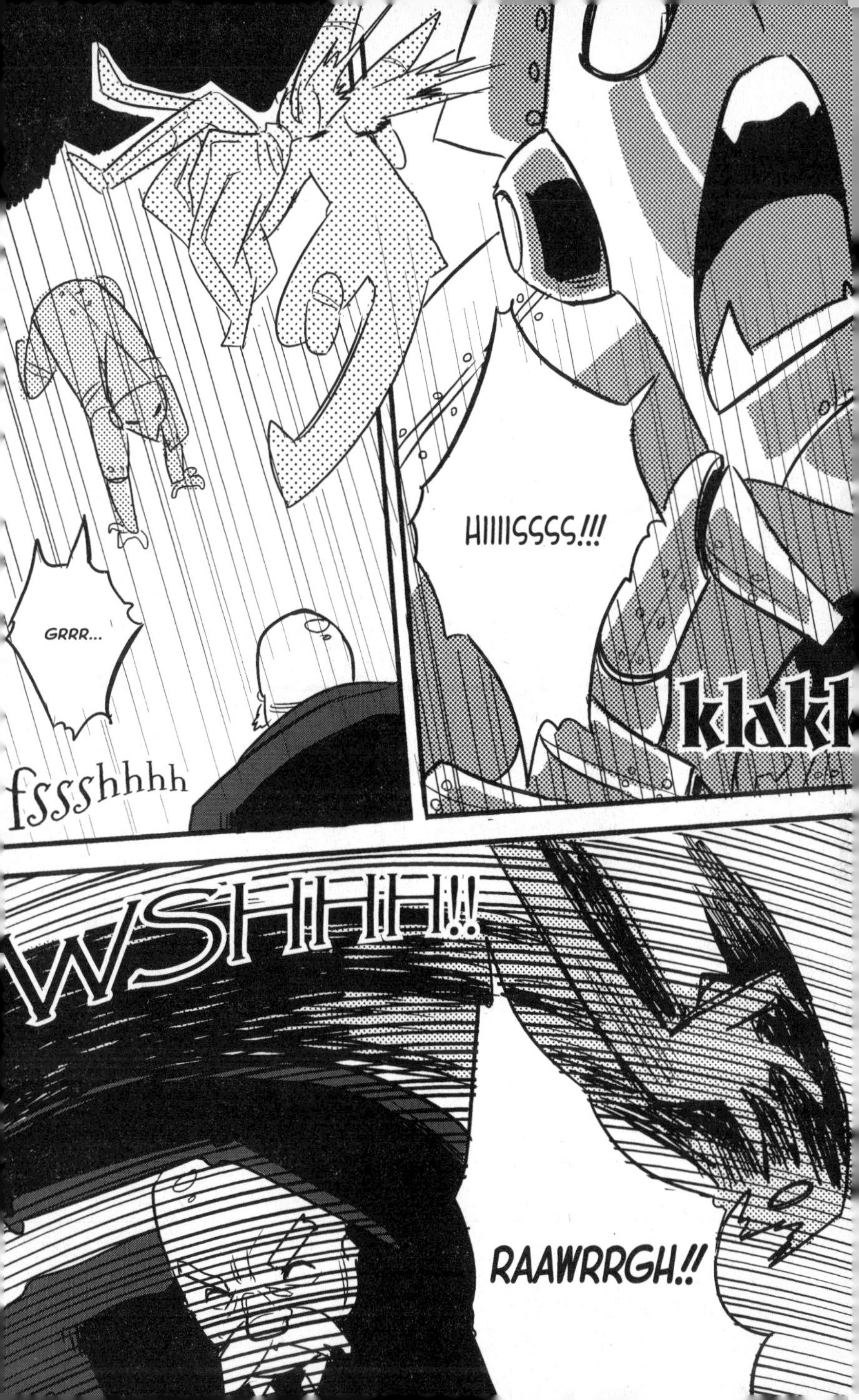
GRRR...
fssshhhh
HIIIISSSS!!!
klakk
WSHIHH!!
RAAWRRGH!!

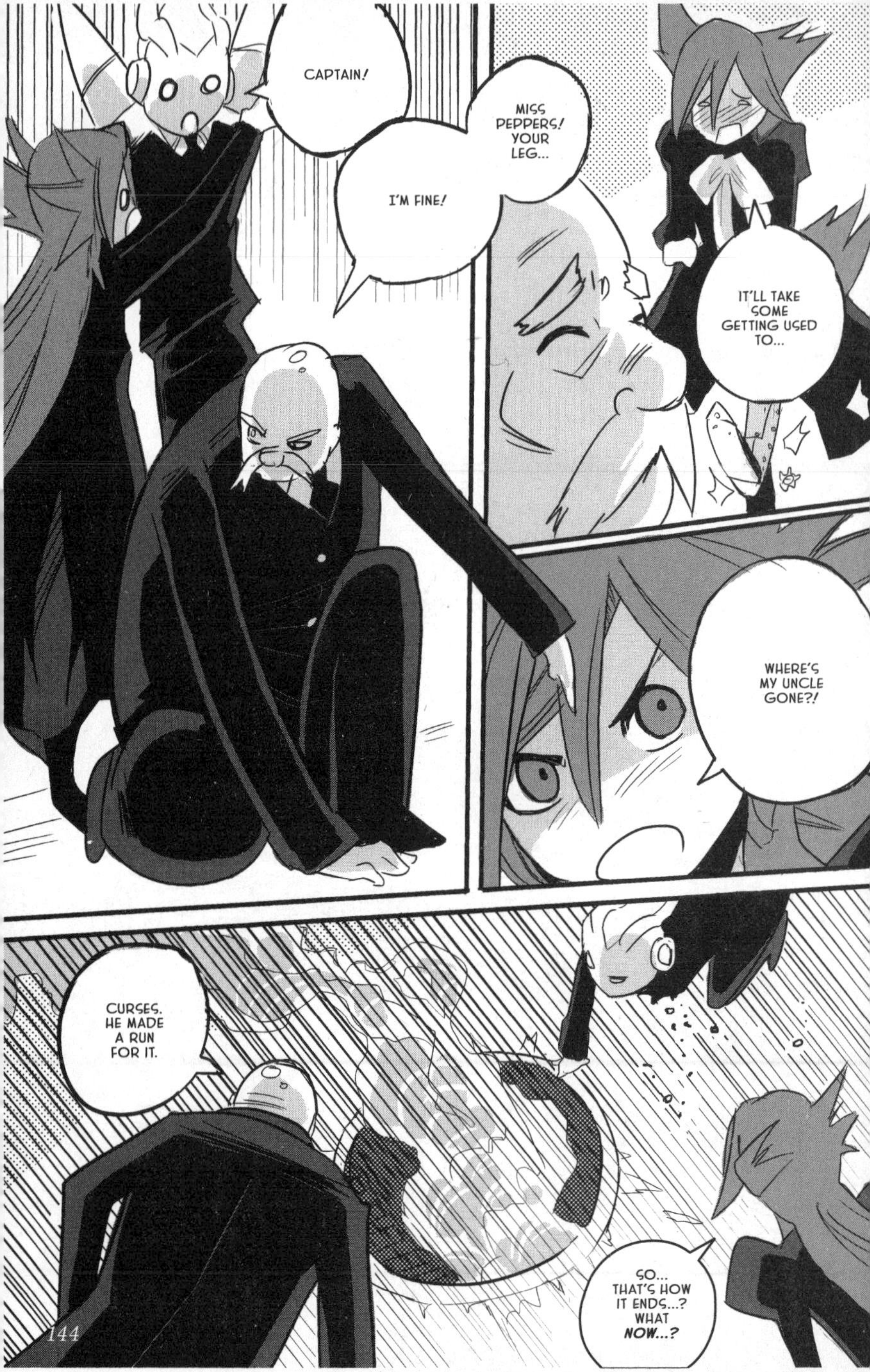
CAPTAIN!
MISS PEPPERS! YOUR LEG...
I'M FINE!
IT'LL TAKE SOME GETTING USED TO...
WHERE'S MY UNCLE GONE?!
CURSES. HE MADE A RUN FOR IT.
SO... THAT'S HOW IT ENDS...? WHAT **NOW...?**

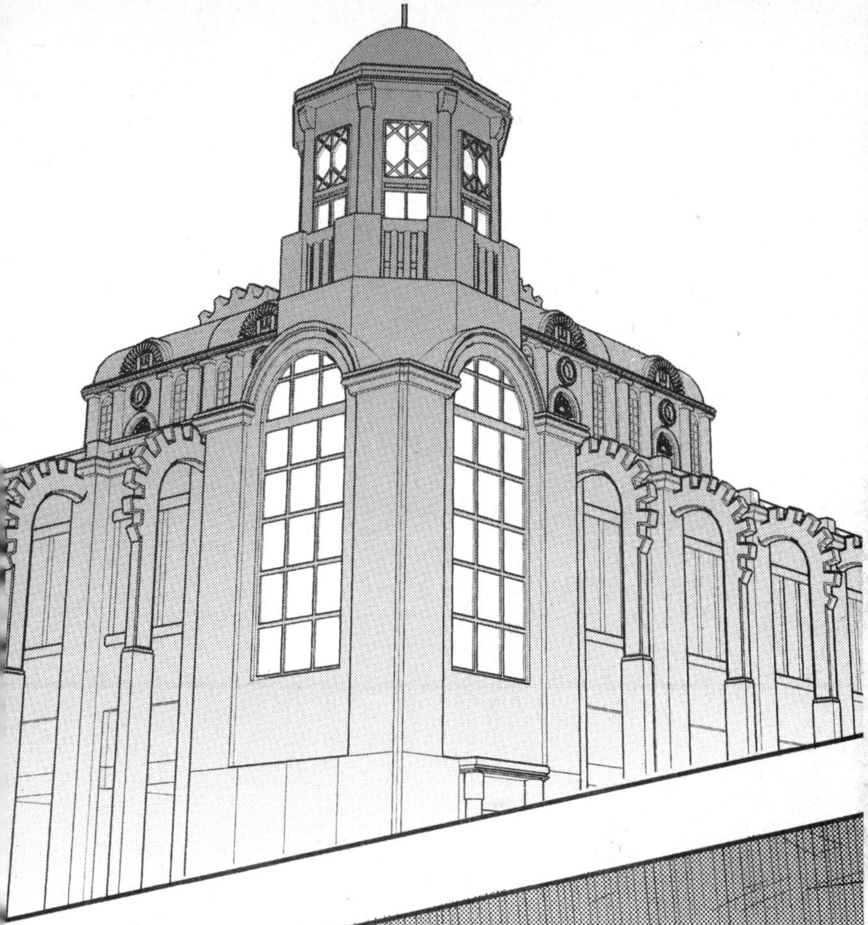

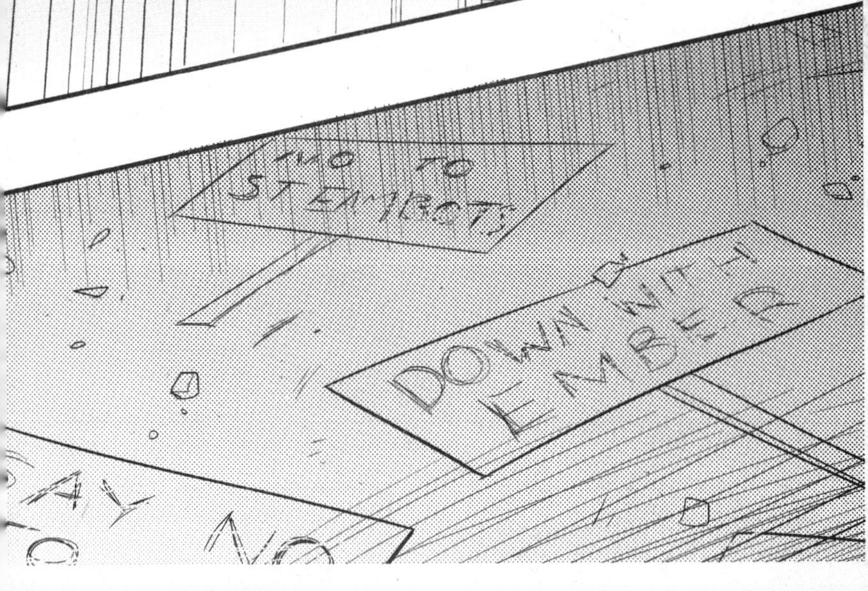
NO TO STEAMBOTS
DOWN WITH EMBER!

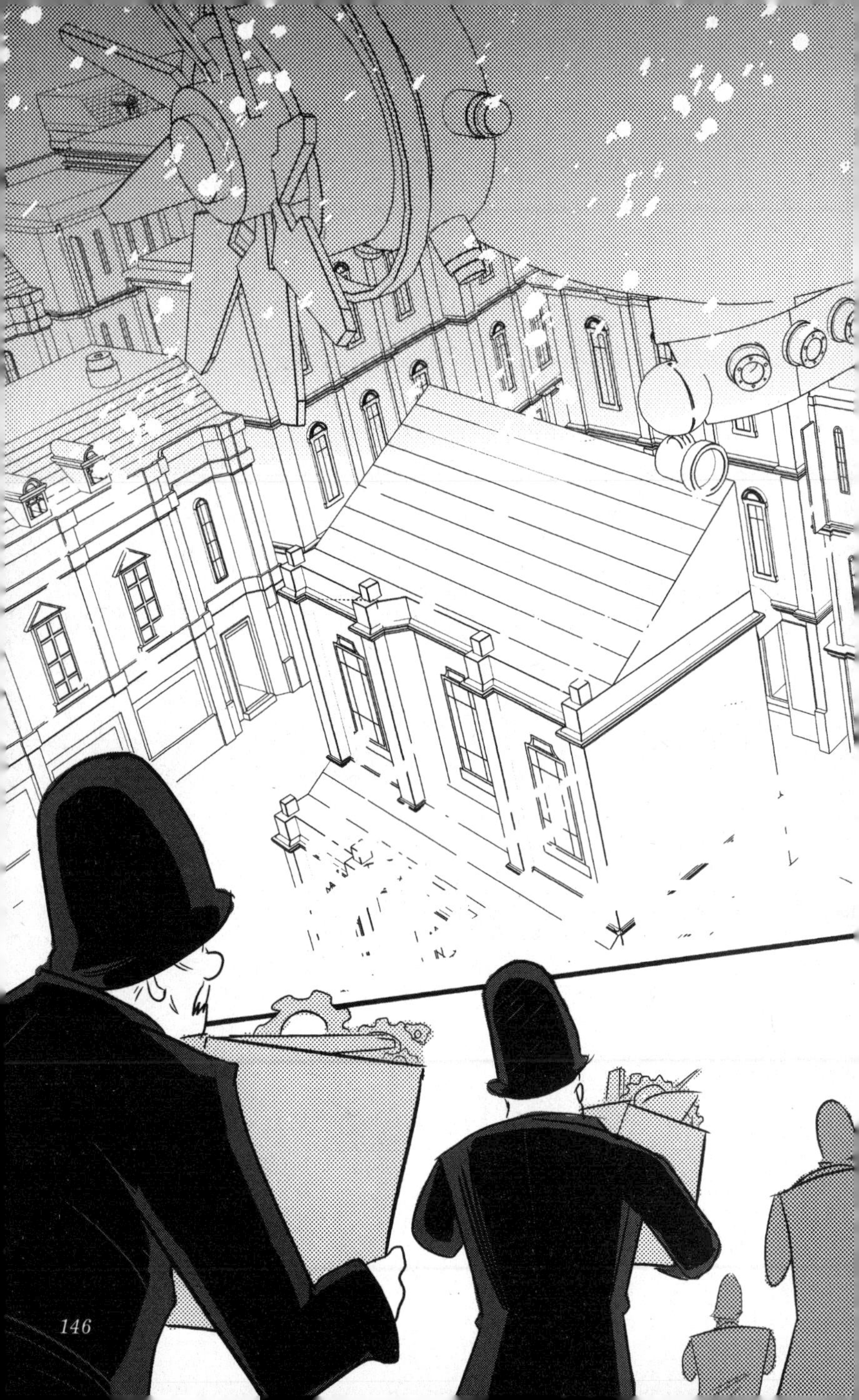

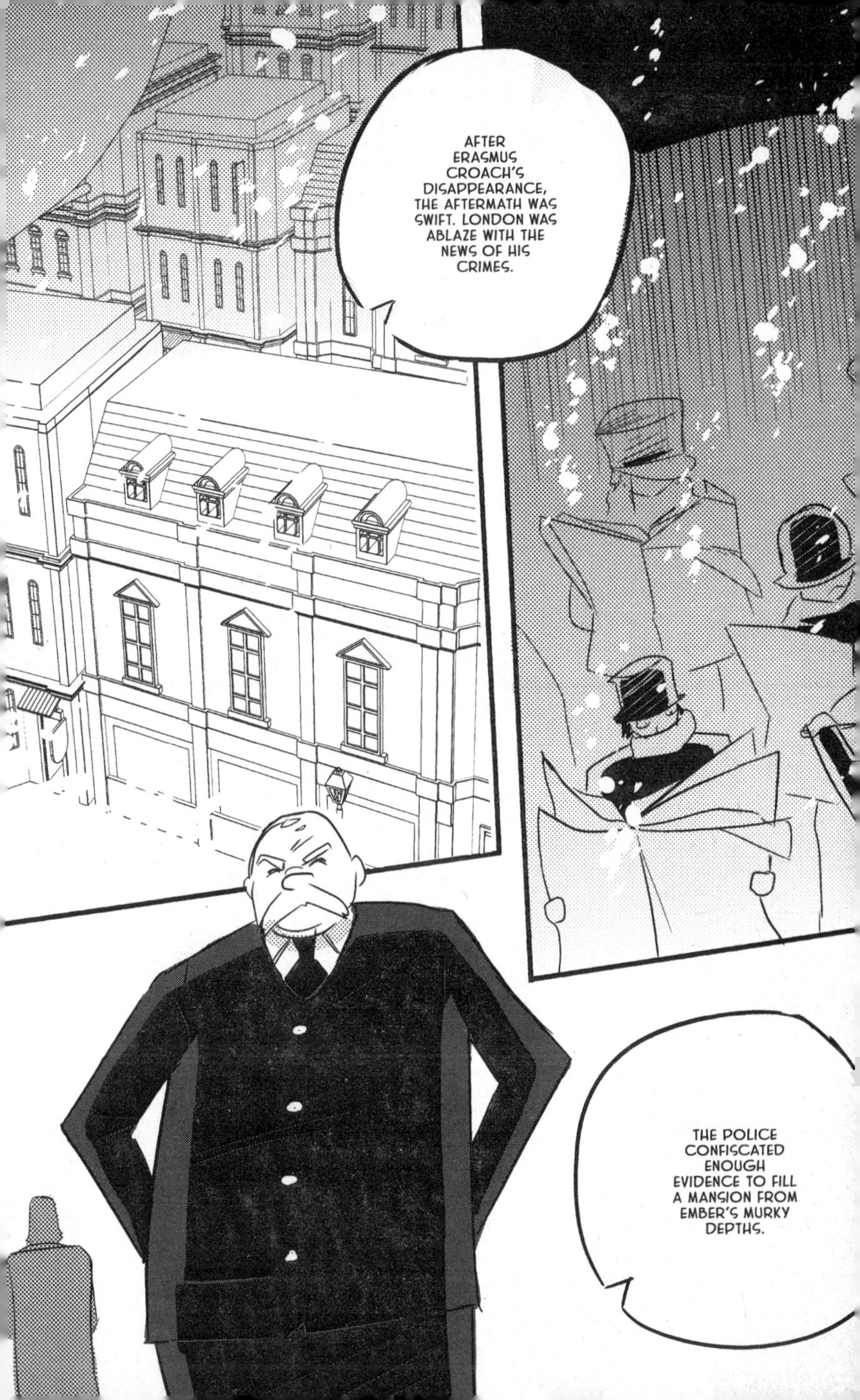

AFTER ERASMUS CROACH'S DISAPPEARANCE, THE AFTERMATH WAS SWIFT. LONDON WAS ABLAZE WITH THE NEWS OF HIS CRIMES.
THE POLICE CONFISCATED ENOUGH EVIDENCE TO FILL A MANSION FROM EMBER'S MURKY DEPTHS.

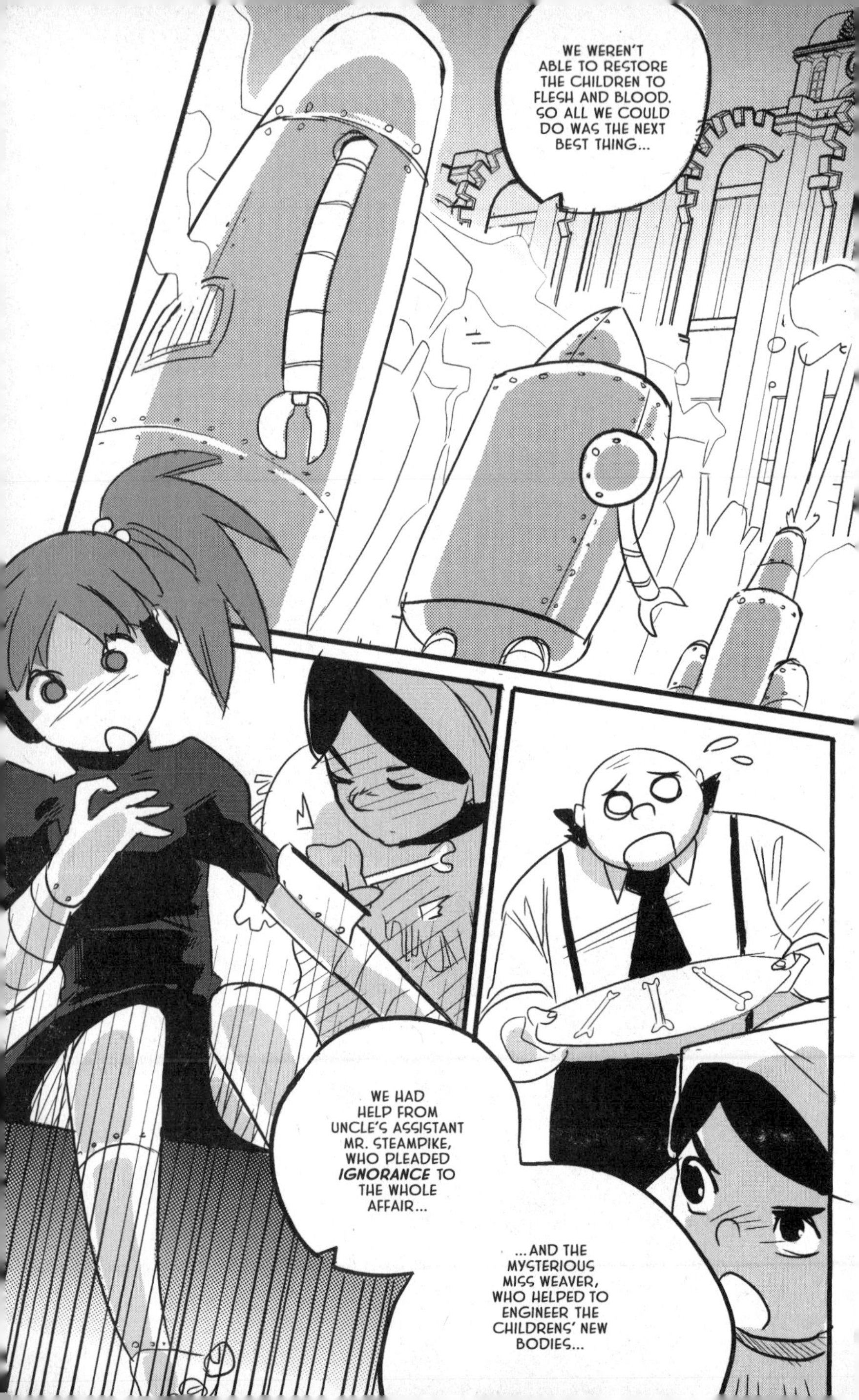
WE WEREN'T ABLE TO RESTORE THE CHILDREN TO FLESH AND BLOOD. SO ALL WE COULD DO WAS THE NEXT BEST THING...
WE HAD HELP FROM UNCLE'S ASSISTANT MR. STEAMPIKE, WHO PLEADED *IGNORANCE* TO THE WHOLE AFFAIR...
...AND THE MYSTERIOUS MISS WEAVER, WHO HELPED TO ENGINEER THE CHILDRENS' NEW BODIES...

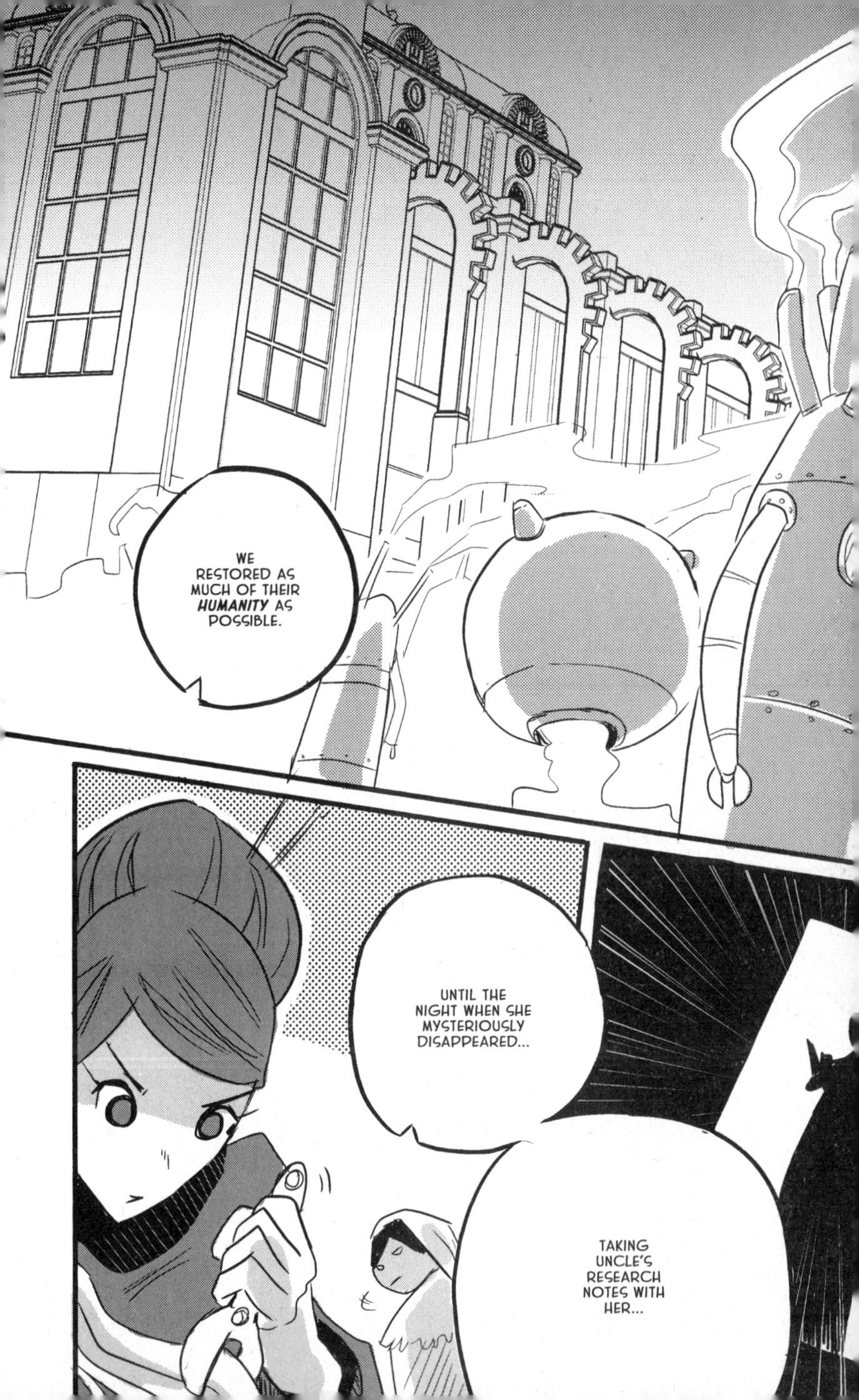
WE RESTORED AS MUCH OF THEIR *HUMANITY* AS POSSIBLE.
UNTIL THE NIGHT WHEN SHE MYSTERIOUSLY DISAPPEARED...
TAKING UNCLE'S RESEARCH NOTES WITH HER...

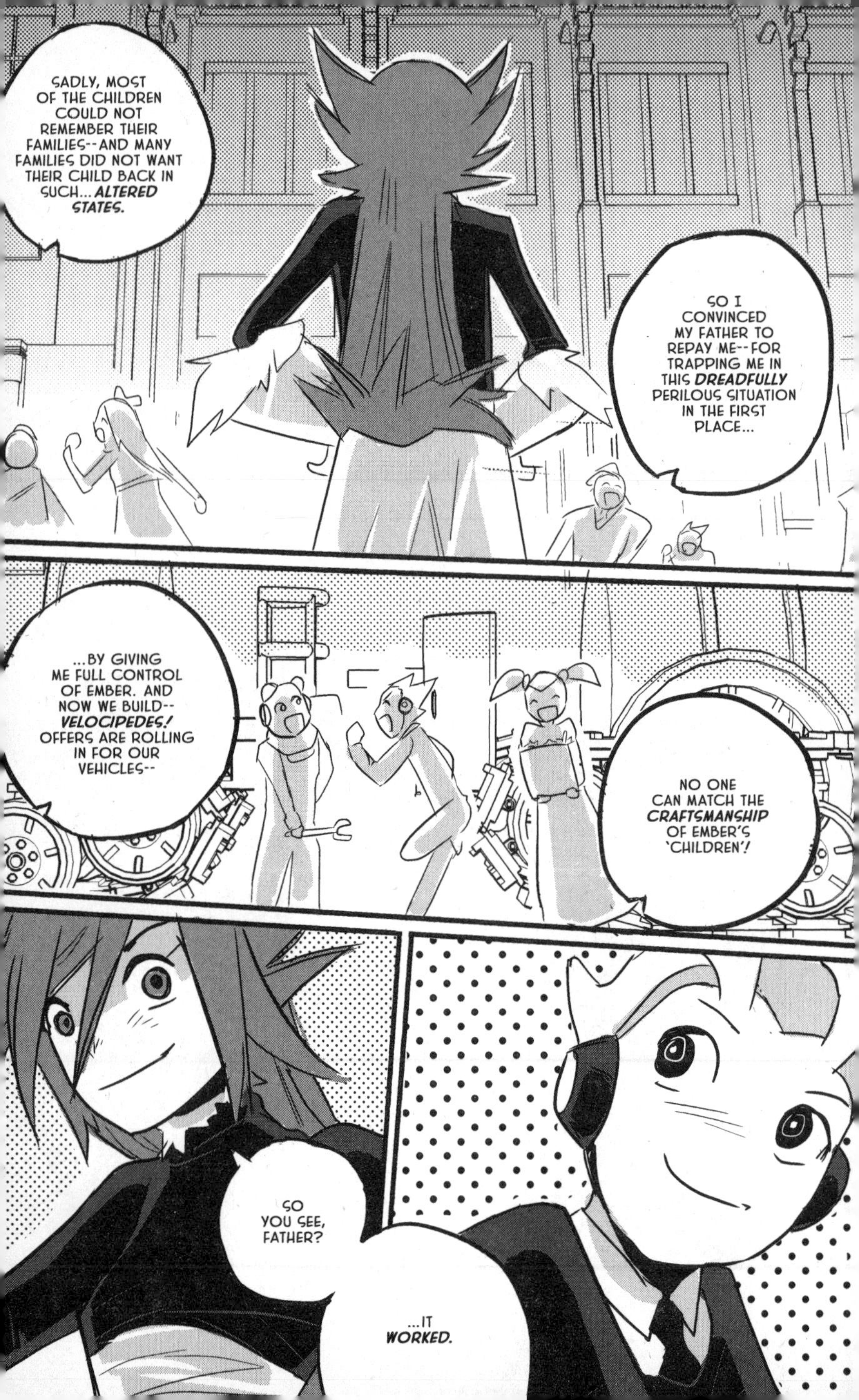
SADLY, MOST OF THE CHILDREN COULD NOT REMEMBER THEIR FAMILIES--AND MANY FAMILIES DID NOT WANT THEIR CHILD BACK IN SUCH... ***ALTERED STATES.***
SO I CONVINCED MY FATHER TO REPAY ME--FOR TRAPPING ME IN THIS ***DREADFULLY*** PERILOUS SITUATION IN THE FIRST PLACE...
...BY GIVING ME FULL CONTROL OF EMBER. AND NOW WE BUILD-- ***VELOCIPEDES!*** OFFERS ARE ROLLING IN FOR OUR VEHICLES--
NO ONE CAN MATCH THE ***CRAFTSMANSHIP*** OF EMBER'S 'CHILDREN'!
SO YOU SEE, FATHER?
...IT ***WORKED.***

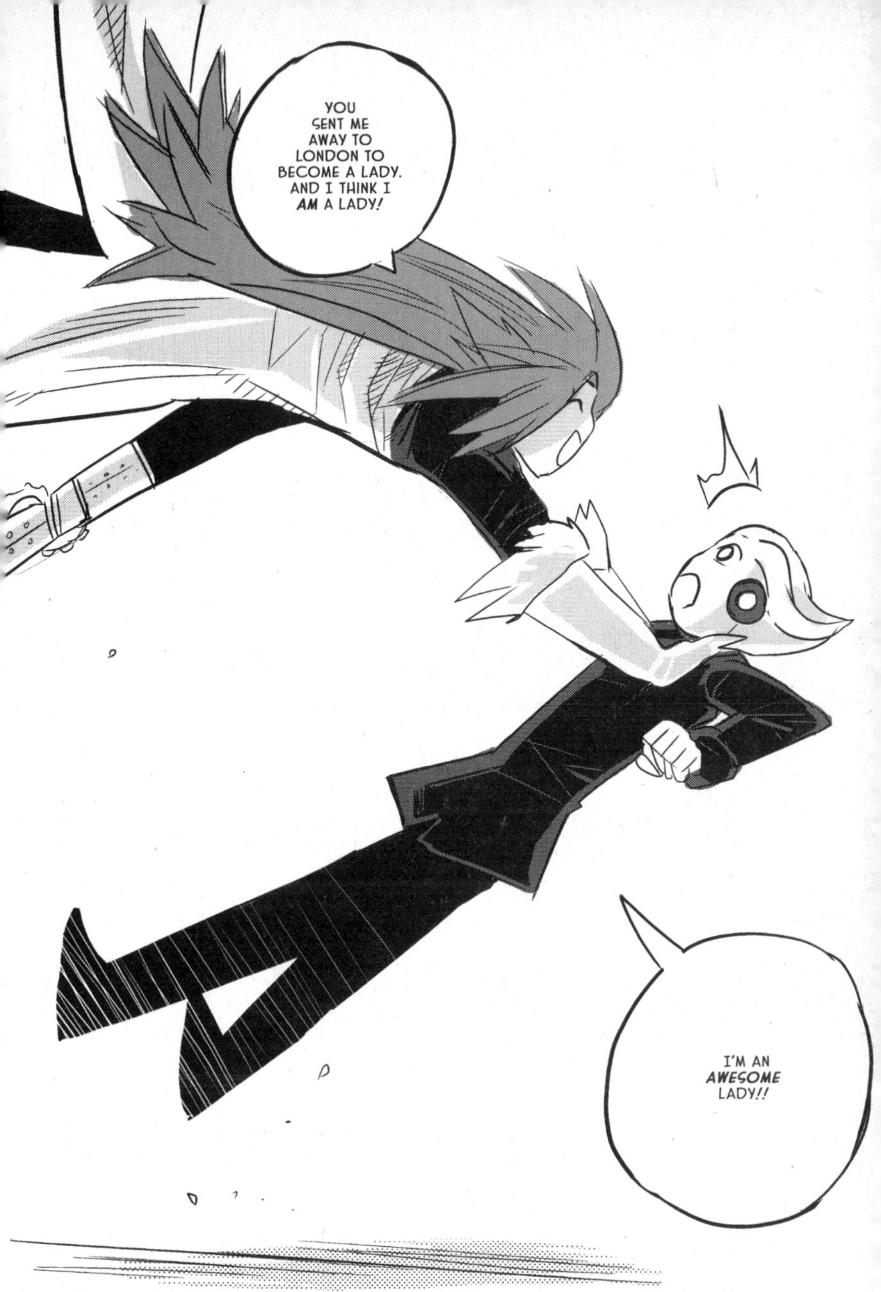
YOU SENT ME AWAY TO LONDON TO BECOME A LADY. AND I THINK I *AM* A LADY!
I'M AN ***AWESOME*** LADY!!

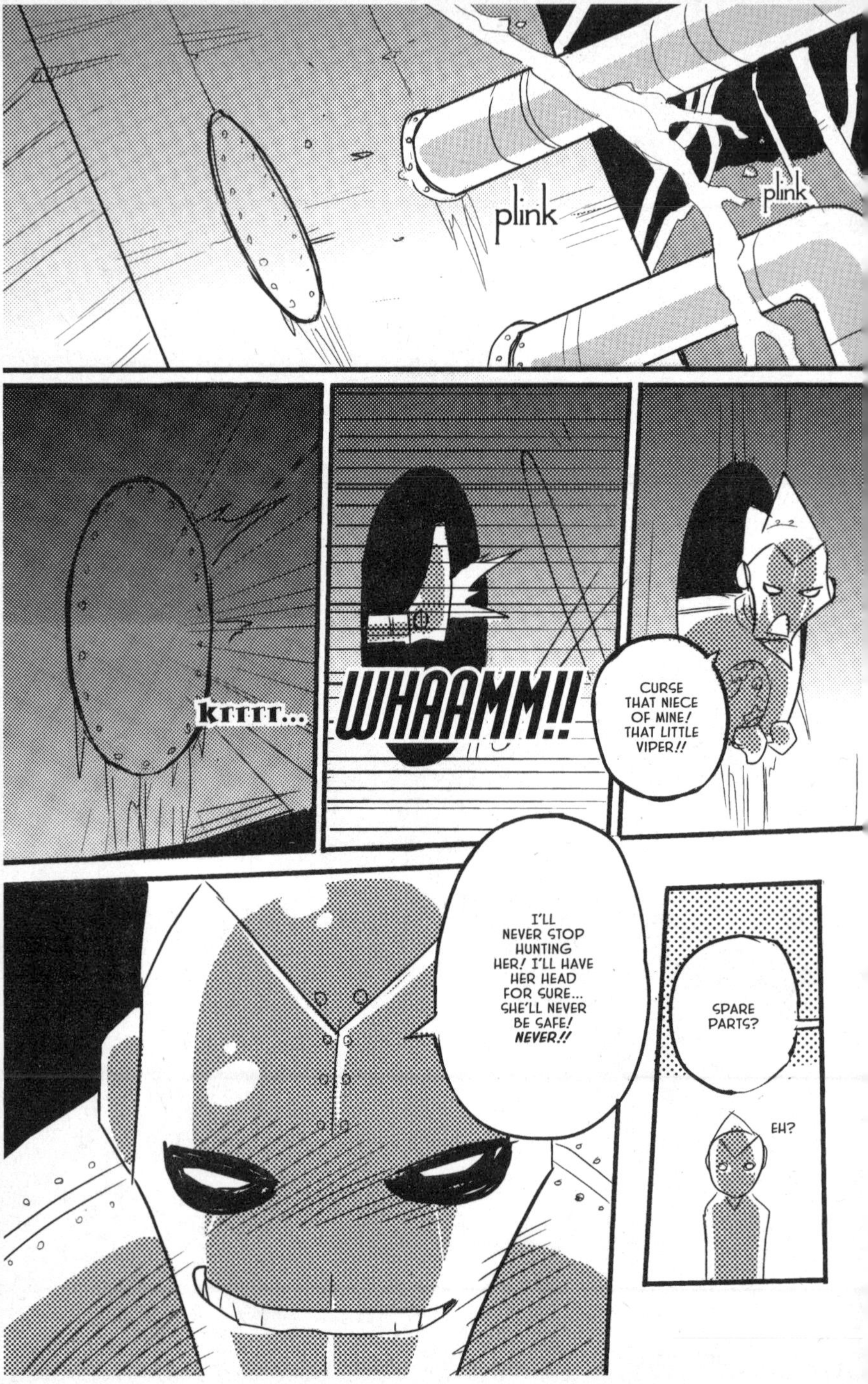
plink
plink
krrrr...
WHAAMM!!
CURSE THAT NIECE OF MINE! THAT LITTLE VIPER!!
I'LL NEVER STOP HUNTING HER! I'LL HAVE HER HEAD FOR SURE... SHE'LL NEVER BE SAFE! ***NEVER!!***
SPARE PARTS?
EH?

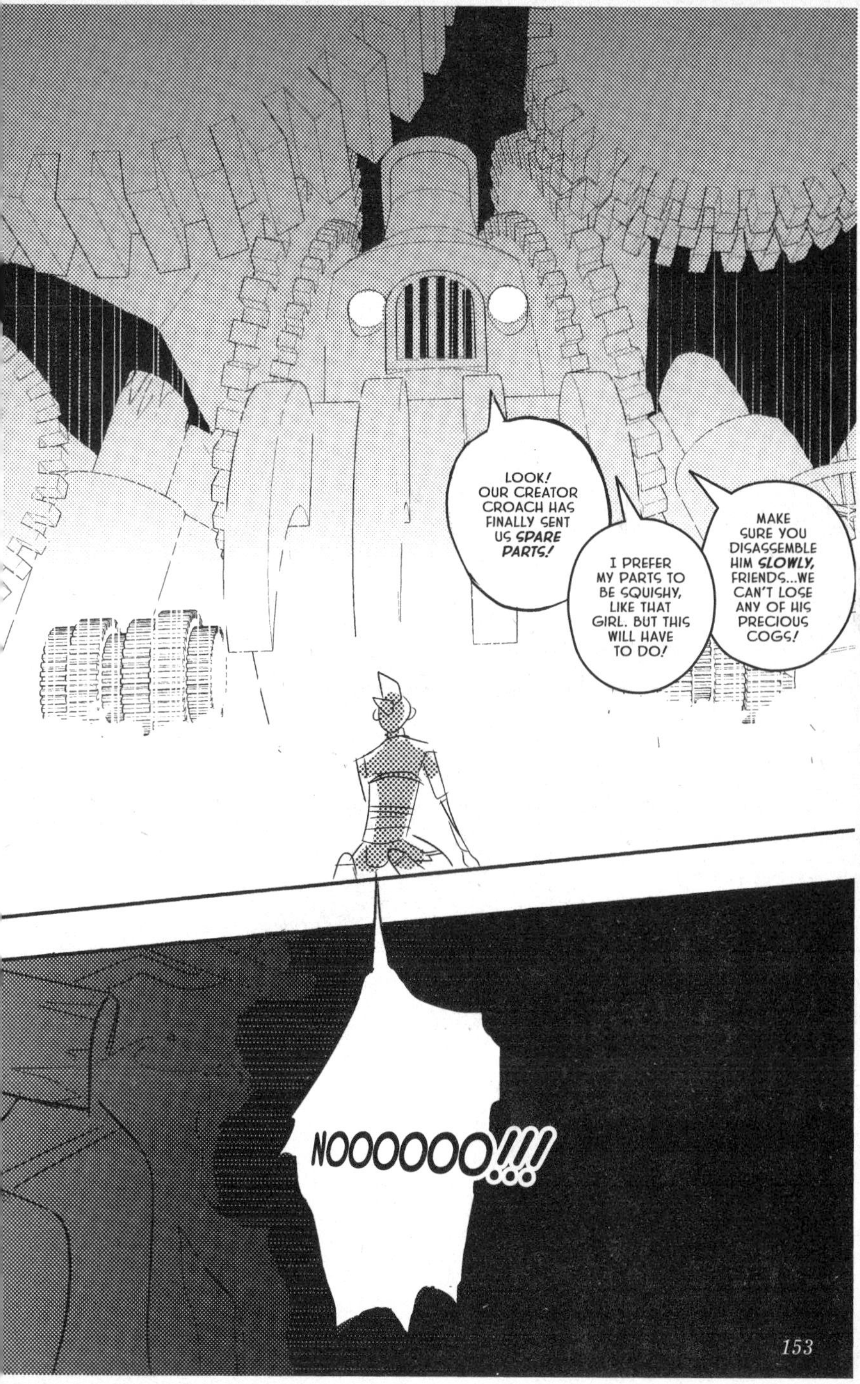
LOOK! OUR CREATOR CROACH HAS FINALLY SENT US SPARE PARTS!
I PREFER MY PARTS TO BE SQUISHY, LIKE THAT GIRL. BUT THIS WILL HAVE TO DO!
MAKE SURE YOU DISASSEMBLE HIM SLOWLY, FRIENDS...WE CAN'T LOSE ANY OF HIS PRECIOUS COGS!
NOOOOOO!!!

The
END.

ABOUT THE AUTHOR

Madeleine Rosca debuted as a manga creator in 2007 with her three-volume series Hollow Fields, which won an encouragement award from Japan's foreign ministry for best international manga and also won for Best New Original English Language (OEL) Manga from About.com. Her series was nominated for best graphic novel in the Aurealis Awards for Australian science fiction and fantasy. Rosca was nominated for a best new talent award by Friends of Lulu. She lives and works in Hobart, Tasmania, with her husband and cat.

www.clockworkhands.com
Twitter: @MadeleineRosca

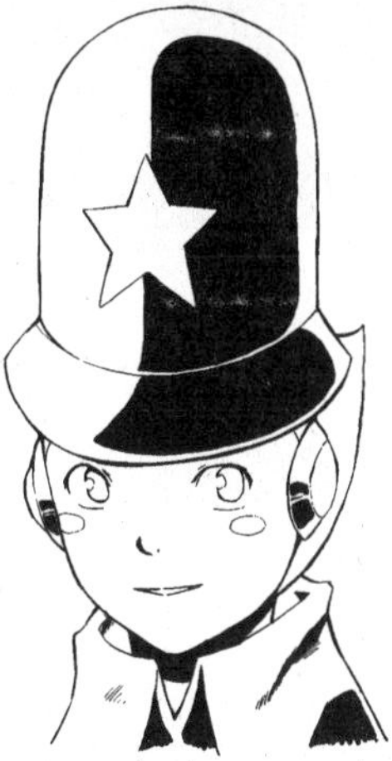

Sky

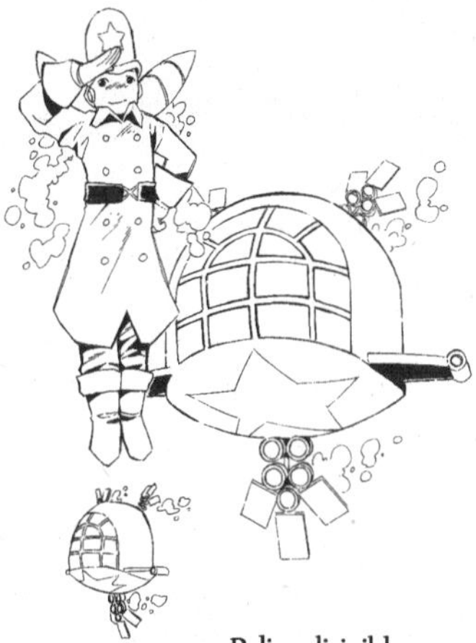

Police dirigibles

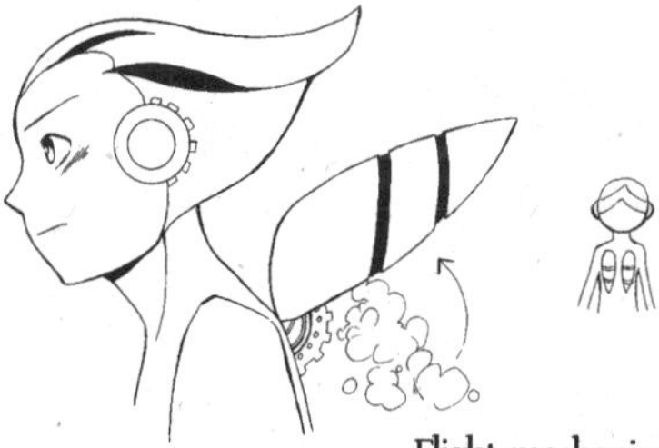

Flight mechanism

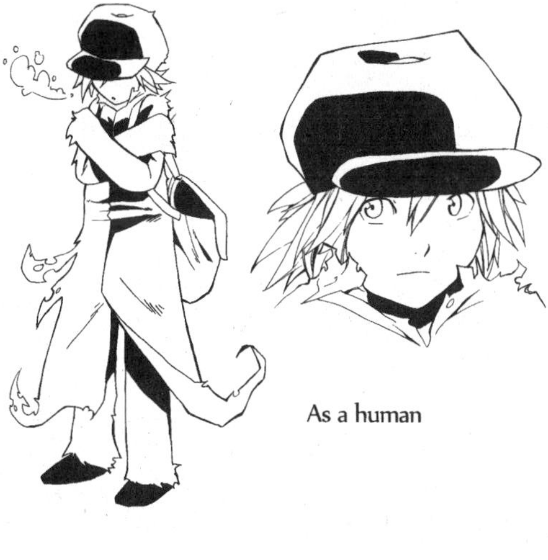

As a human

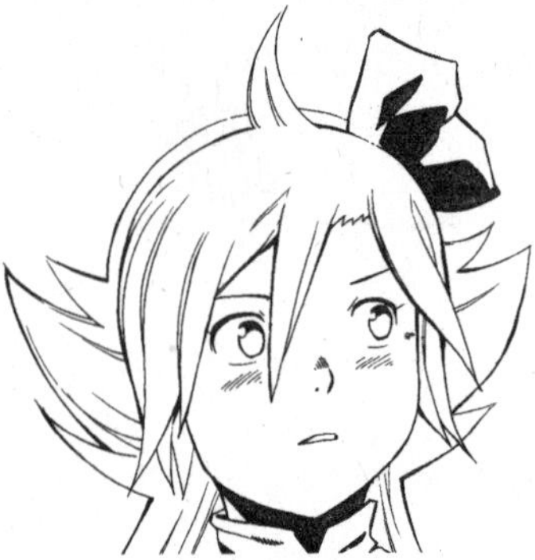

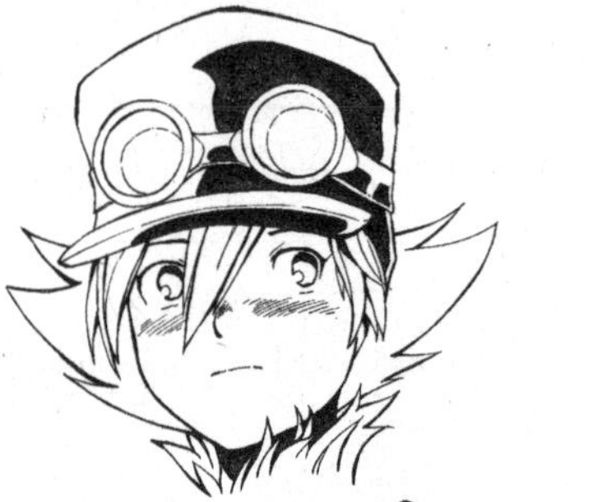

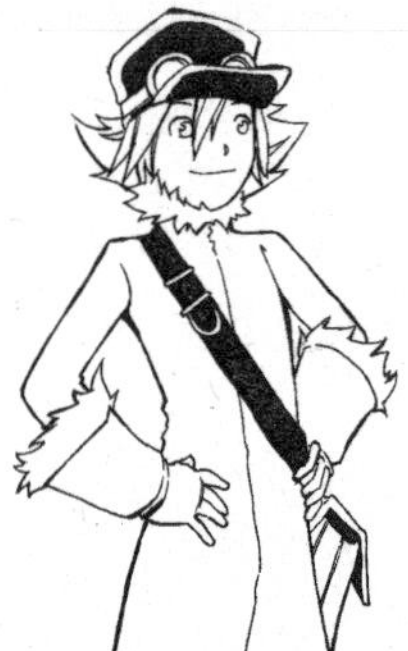

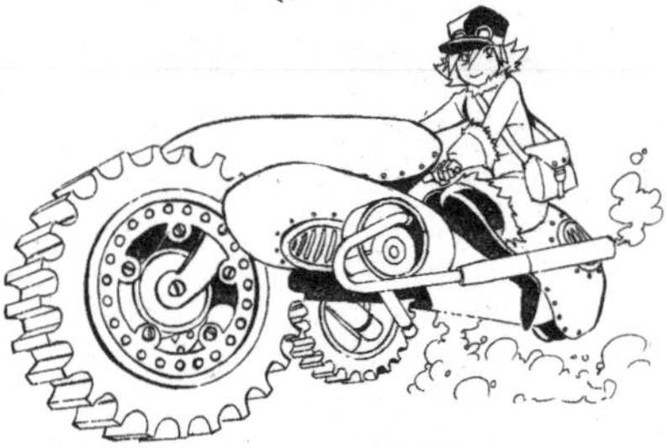

Velocipede

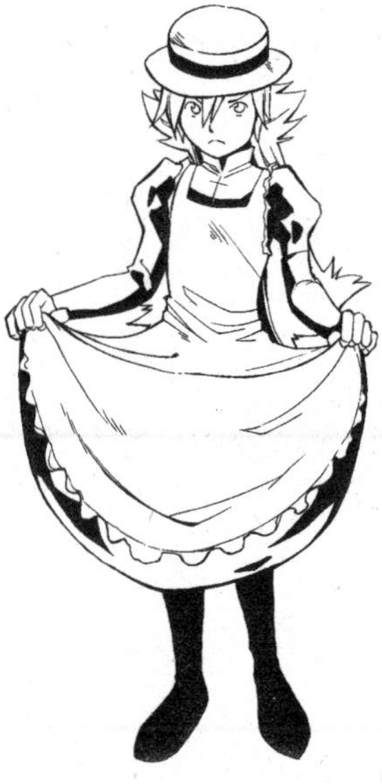

Sally Peppers

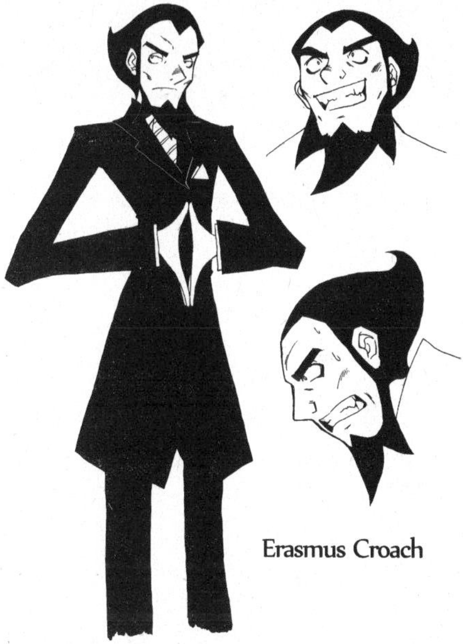

Erasmus Croach

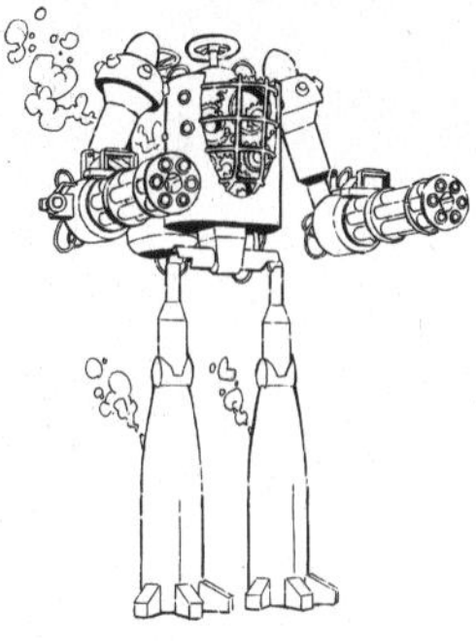

Superbot

Ember's Security Bots

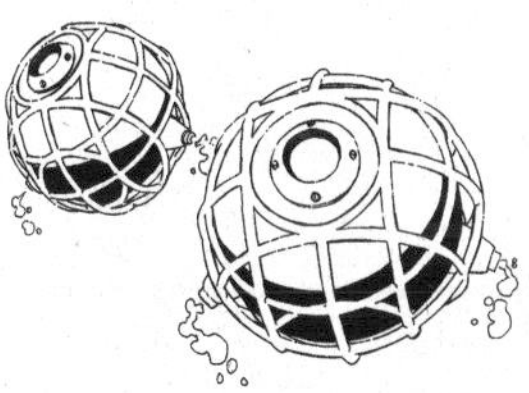

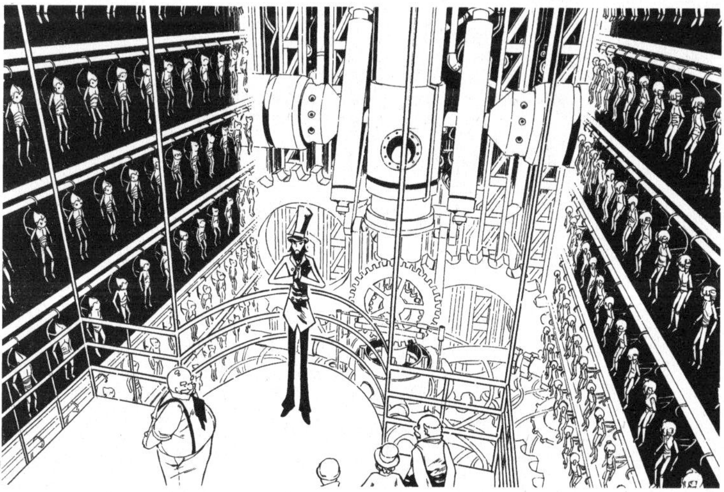

Ember's Factory Floor

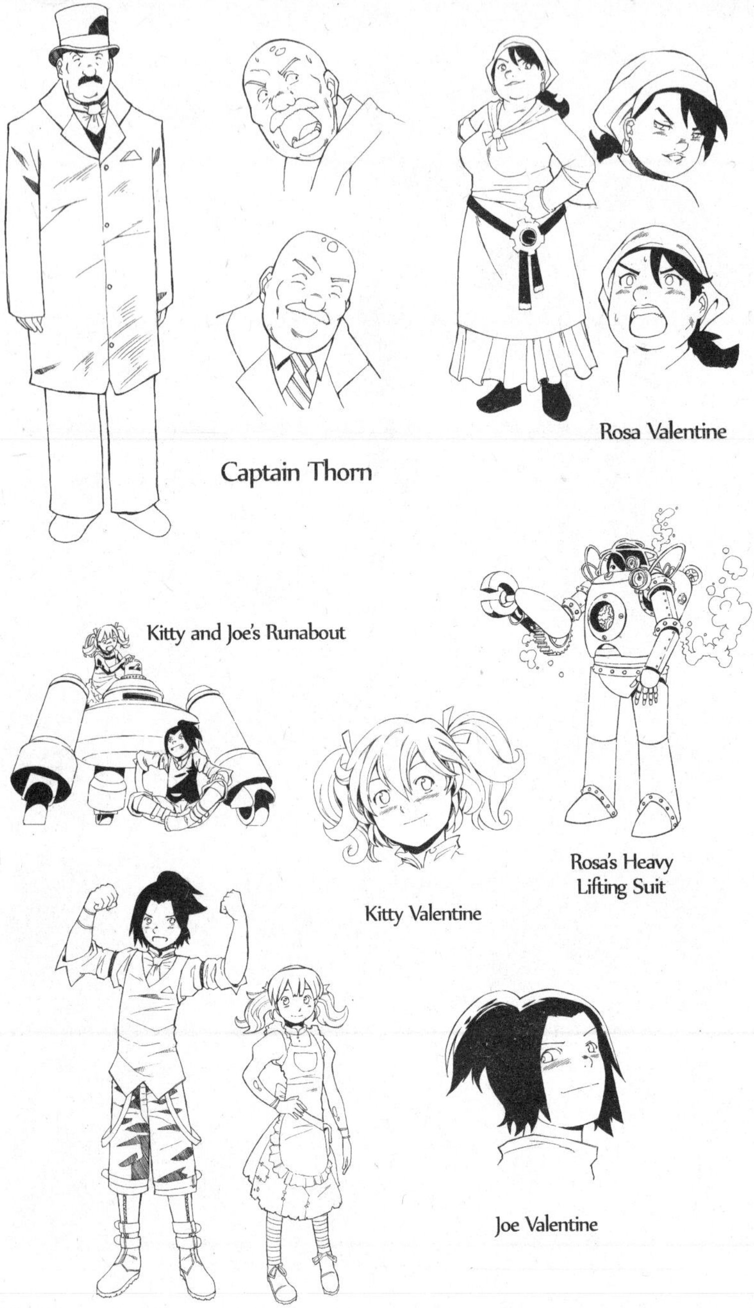
Rosa Valentine
Captain Thorn
Kitty and Joe's Runabout
Rosa's Heavy Lifting Suit
Kitty Valentine
Joe Valentine